THE BOOKMAN'S PROMISE

A CLIFF JANEWAY NOVEL

JOHN DUNNING

SCRIBNER

New York London Toronto Sydney

SCRIBNER
1230 Avenue of the Americas
New York, NY 10020

Copyright © 2004 by John Dunning

SCRIBNER and design are trademarks of Macmillan Library Reference USA, Inc., used under license by Simon & Schuster, the publisher of this work.

Manufactured in the United States of America

ISBN 0-7432-4992-5

To Pat McGuire,
for long friendship, timely brainstorming,
and other mysterious reasons

THE BOOKMAN'S PROMISE

The man said, "Welcome to Book Beat, Mr. Janeway" and this was how it began.

We were sitting in a Boston studio before the entire invisible listening audience of National Public Radio. I was here against my better judgment, and my first words into the microphone, "Just don't call me an expert on anything," staked out the conditions under which I had become such an unlikely guest. Saying it now into the microphone had a calming effect, but the man's polite laugh again left me exposed on both flanks. Not only was I an expert, his laugh implied, I was a modest one. His opening remarks deepened my discomfort.

"Tonight we are departing from our usual talk about current books. As many of you know, our guest was to have been Allen Gleason, author of the surprising literary bestseller, Roses for Adessa. Unfortunately, Mr. Gleason suffered a heart attack last week in New York, and I know all of you join me in wishing him a speedy recovery.

"In his absence we are lucky to have Mr. Cliff Janeway, who came to Boston just this week to buy a very special book. And I should add that this is a show, despite its spontaneous scheduling, that I have long wanted to do. As fascinating as the world of new books can often be, the world of older books, of valuable first editions and treasures recently out of print, has a growing charm for many of our listeners. Mr. Janeway, I wonder if you would answer a basic question before we dive deeper into this world. What makes a valuable book valuable?"

This was how it began: with a simple, innocent question and a few quick answers. We talked for a while about things I love best, and the man was so good that we soon seemed like two old bookscouts *hunkered down together after a friendly hunt. I talked of supply and demand, of classics and genres and modern first editions: why certain first editions by Edgar Rice Burroughs are worth more than most Mark Twains, and how crazy the hunt can get. I told him about the world I now lived in, and it was easy to avoid the world I'd come from. This was a book show, not a police lineup, and I was an antiquarian bookseller, not a cop.*

"I understand you live in Denver, Colorado."

"When I'm hiding out from the law, that's where I hide."

Again the polite laugh. "You say you're no expert, but you were featured this week in a very bookish article in The Boston Globe."

"That guy had nothing better to do. He's a book freak and the paper was having what they call a slow news day."

"The two of you met at a book auction, I believe. Tell us about that."

"I had come here to buy a book. We got to talking and the next thing I knew, I was being interviewed."

"What book did you come to buy?"

"Pilgrimage to Medina and Mecca *by Richard Burton.*"

"The explorer, not the actor."

We shared a knowing laugh, then he said, "What is it about this book that made you fly all the way from Denver to buy it? And to pay—how much was it?—if you don't mind my asking . . ."

Auction prices were public knowledge, so there was no use being coy. I said, "Twenty-nine thousand five hundred," *and gave up whatever modesty I might have had. Only an expert pays that much money for a book. Or a fool.*

I might have told him that there were probably dozens of dealers in the United States whose knowledge of Burton ran deeper than mine. I could have said yes, I had studied Burton intensely for two months, but two months in the book trade or in any scholarly pursuit is no time at all. I should have explained that I had bought the book with Indian money, but then I'd need to explain that concept and the rest of the hour would have been shot talking about me.

Instead I talked about Burton, master linguist, soldier, towering figure of nineteenth-century letters and adventure. I watched the clock as I talked and I gave him the shortest-possible version of Burton's incredible life. I couldn't begin to touch even the high spots in the time we had left.

"You've brought this book with you tonight."

We let the audience imagine it as I noisily unwrapped the three volumes in front of the microphone. My host got up from his side of the table and came around to look while I gave the audience a brief description of the books, with emphasis on the original blue cloth binding lettered in brilliant gilt and their unbelievably pristine condition.

The man said, "They look almost new."

"Yeah," I said lovingly.

"I understand there's something special about them, other than their unusual freshness."

I opened volume one and he sighed. "Aaahh, it's signed by the author. Would you read that for us, please?"

"'To Charles Warren,'" I read: "'A grand companion and the best kind of friend. Our worlds are far apart and we may never see each other again, but the time we shared will be treasured forever. Richard F. Burton.' It's dated January 15, 1861."

"Any idea who this Warren fellow was?"

"Not a clue. He's not mentioned in any of the Burton biographies."

"You would agree, though, that that's an unusually intimate inscription."

I did agree, but I was no expert. The man said, "So we have a mystery here as well as a valuable book," and it all began then. Its roots went back to another time, when Richard Francis Burton met his greatest admirer and then set off on a secret journey, deep into the troubled American South. Because of that trip a friend of mine died. An old woman found peace, a good man lost everything, and I rediscovered myself on my continuing journey across the timeless, infinite world of books.

BOOK I DENVER

If I wanted to be arbitrary, I could say it began anywhere. That radio show moved it out of the dim past to here and now, but Burton's story had been there forever, waiting for me to find it.

I found it in 1987, late in my thirty-seventh year. I had come home from Seattle with a big wad of money from the Grayson affair. My 10 percent finder's fee had come to almost fifty thousand dollars, a career payday for almost any bookman and certainly, so far, for me. All I knew at that point was that I was going to buy a book with it. Not half a million books riddled with vast pockets of moldy corruption. Not a million bad books or a thousand good books, not even a hundred fine books. Just one book. One great, hellacious, *killer* book: just to see how it felt, owning such a thing.

So I thought, but there was more to it than that. I wanted to change directions in my book life. I was sick of critics and hucksters screaming about the genius of every new one-book wonder. I was ready for less hype and more tradition, and almost as soon as I fell into this seek-and-ye-shall-find mode, I found Richard Burton.

I had gone to a dinner party in East Denver, at the Park Hill home of Judge Leighton Huxley. Lee and I had known each other for years, cautiously at first, later on a warmer level of mutual interest, finally as friends. I had first appeared in his courtroom in 1978, when I was a very young cop testifying in a cut-and-dried murder case and he was a relatively young newcomer to the Denver bench. That gulf of professional distance between us was natural then: Lee was far outside my rather small circle of police cronies, and I could not have imagined myself rubbing elbows with his much larger crowd of legal eagles.

Age was a factor, though not a major one. I was in my late twenties; Lee was in his mid-forties, already gray around the temples and beginning to look like the distinguished man of the world that I would never be. He was by all accounts an excellent judge. He was extremely fair yet sure in his decisions, and he had never been overturned.

I saw him only twice in the first few years after my appearance in his court: once we had nodded in the courthouse cafeteria, briefly indicating that we remembered each other, and a year later I had been invited to a Christmas party in the mountain home of a mutual friend. That night we said our first few words outside the halls of justice. "I hear you're a book collector," he had said in that deep, rich baritone. I admitted my guilt and he said, "So am I: we should compare notes sometime." But nothing had come of it then for the same obvious reasons—I was still a cop, there was always a chance I would find myself on his witness stand again, and he liked to avoid potential conflicts of interest before they came up. I didn't think much about it: I figured he had just been passing time with me, being polite. That was always the thing about Lee Huxley: he had a reputation for good manners, in court and out.

A year later he was appointed to the U.S. District Court and it was then, removed from the likelihood of professional conflict, that our friendship had its cautious, tentative beginning. Out of the blue I got a call from Miranda, his wife, inviting me, as she put it, to "a small, informal dinner party for some book lovers." There were actually a dozen people there that first night, and I was paired with Miranda's younger sister Hope, who was visiting from somewhere back East. The house was just off East Seventeenth Avenue, a redbrick turn-of-the-century three-story with chandeliers and glistening hardwood everywhere you looked. It was already ablaze with lights and alive with laughter when I arrived, and Miranda was a blonde knockout at the front door in her blue evening dress. She looked no older than thirty but was elegant and interesting in her own right, not just a pretty face at Lee's side. The judge's friends were also considerate and refined, and I fought back my natural instincts for reverse snobbery and liked them all. They were rich book collectors and I was still on a cop's salary, but there wasn't a hint of condescension to any of them. If they saw a $5,000 book they wanted, they just bought that sucker and paid the price, and my kind of nickel-and-dime bookscouting was fascinating to them, something they couldn't have imagined until I told them about it.

Miranda was a superb hostess. The next day, as I was composing a thank-you note, I got a call from her thanking me for coming. "You really livened things up over here, Cliff," she said. "I hope we're going to see lots more of each other."

And we had. I hadn't done much rubbernecking that first night, but the judge's library later turned out to be everything it was cracked up to be. It was a large room shelved on all four walls and full of wonderful books, all the modern American greats in superb dust jackets. At one point Lee said, "I've got some older things downstairs," but years had passed before I saw what they were.

From the beginning there were differences to their most recent dinner party. For one thing I was no longer a cop, and the manner of my departure from the Denver Police Department might have chilled my relationship with any judge. I had roughed up a brutal thug, and the press dredged up my distant past, a childhood riddled with violent street fighting and close ties to people like Vince Marranzino, who later became one of Denver's most feared mobsters. Never mind that Vince and I had only been within speaking distance once in almost twenty years; never mind that I had lived all that down and become, if I do say so, a crackerjack homicide cop—once you've been tarred by that brush it's always there waiting to tar you again. By then there were rumors that Lee was on a short list of possibles for a U.S. Supreme Court nomination, and though it was hard to picture Lee and Ronald Reagan as political bedfellows, I had no real idea what Lee's politics were. All I knew was this: if there was even a chance for him in the big teepee, the last thing I wanted was to mess that up. I had been front-page news, none of it good, for most of a week, but if Lee worried about his own image and the company he kept, I never saw any sign of it. He called and asked for my version of what had happened, I told him the truth, and he accepted that. "Not the best judgment you've ever shown, Cliff, but this too shall pass," he said. "I'm sure you're busy right now keeping the wolves at bay. As soon as this settles down, we'll get together."

But then I was gone to Seattle, and suddenly several months had passed since I'd seen them. I came home with a big stash, my Indian money; I book-hunted across the midwest with Seattle friends, and when I returned to Denver one of my first calls was from Miranda.

"Mr. Janeway." Her icy tone sounded put-on but not completely. "Are you avoiding us for some reason? Have we done something to offend you?"

I was instantly shamed. "Not at *all*," I said, answering her second question and avoiding the first. "God, you can't believe that."

"Then kindly get your ass over here, sir," she said. "Friday night, seven o'clock, no tie, please, no excuses. Come prepared to liven up what promises to be a rather drab affair."

"You wouldn't know how to do a drab affair."

"We'll see about that. This one may be a challenge, even for a woman of my legendary social talents. One of Lee's boyhood chums is coming to town. Don't tell anybody I said this, but he's not exactly my cup of tea. So, will you come help me make the best of it?"

"Yes, ma'am, I'd be honored."

"It's been so long since we've seen you I've forgotten your face. Are you married yet?"

I laughed.

"Going steady with anyone?'

"Not at the moment."

I knew why she was asking. Miranda loved informality, but at a sit-down dinner she was a stickler for a proper head count. "I've got the perfect lady for you on Friday," she said.

I paused, then said, "Thank you for the invitation."

"No, Cliff, thank *you*. I know why you've been so scarce, and I just want you to know we appreciate the consideration but it's not necessary and never was. We've stopped by your bookstore any number of times but we've never been able to catch you."

I knew that, of course: I had seen their checks in the cash drawer. "I'm always out hunting books," I said.

"Apparently so. But Lee and I would be pretty shallow people, wouldn't we, if we wrote off our friends at the first sign of trouble."

"That was some pretty bad trouble."

"Yes, it was, but it got you out of being a cop and into the book business. So it wasn't all bad, was it?"

This was a smaller group than they'd had in the past, with only eight of us, including the Huxleys, at the table. Lee's boyhood pal turned out to be Hal Archer, the writer and historian who had won a Pulitzer prize six years before, coming from far left field to snatch it away from several favored and far more academically endowed candidates. At the time I was glad he had won: I always pull for the underdog and I had truly admired his book. It was a dense account of two ordinary families in Charleston, South Carolina, during the four years of our civil war. Using recently found documents, letters, and journals, Archer had managed to bring them to life despite having to deal with a mountain of detail. He told, in layman's words and with the practiced eye of an artist, how they had survived and interacted among themselves and with others in the shattered city. It was an epic story of courage and hardship in the face of a stiff Union blockade, an unrelenting bombardment, and three years of siege, and he told it beautifully.

Archer had published only historical fiction before turning out this riveting true account, but even then I considered him a major talent. I had read him years earlier and had earmarked him at once as a writer who would never waste my time. He had a towering ability to make each word matter and he never resorted to showy prose. He made me live in his story; his work was everything I had always loved about books. With all that going for us, why did I dislike him so intensely the moment I met him?

Such a strong negative reaction often begins in the eyes. Archer's eyes were dismissive, as if his superiority had been recognized much too late by fools like me and he had paid a damned stiff price for my ignorance. He was right about one thing: it is fashionable to adore an icon after he has become one, but it's also easy for a writer to become a horse's ass when fame and riches are suddenly thrust upon him. It was screwy to think that Archer had instantly made me the point man for all the years he had worked in obscurity, and I wanted this impression to be wrong because I had always liked his stuff. But it held up and deepened throughout the evening.

He was the last to arrive, forty-five minutes late. Miranda showed him in at a quarter to eight, accompanied by a pretty young woman she introduced as Erin d'Angelo. I saw Ms. d'Angelo make a gesture of apology to Lee when Archer wasn't watching, but it was brief and his response was even more so. Miranda was unruffled at the delay in dinner: it would be perfect, I knew, because it always was at her house. She knew her guests and planned for their little quirks accordingly, and that told me yet more about Mr. Archer and his ways. A man who will keep an entire dinner party waiting for most of an hour has a pretty good opinion of himself.

Archer took center stage at once when he arrived; even Lee stood back with what I thought was a look of quiet amusement while his old friend held court. There was some talk about a new book coming but Archer turned that quickly aside, implying that whenever it came, it would certainly be important but he couldn't talk about it now. A national booksellers association was having its annual meeting in Denver that year and the great man was in town to speak at the banquet, receive an award, and do local media appearances. Ms. d'Angelo was his escort, one of those super-competent people provided by publishers for writers on tour, and occasionally for writers between books if they are important enough and their business is

somehow career-related. The Pulitzer had locked in Archer's importance for the rest of his lifetime, and so he got Ms. d'Angelo to drive
him—not forever, I hoped for her sake.

Her name suggested an Irish-Italian clash of cultures but to me
she looked only like the best of America. She might have been a
freshman college student straight from the heart of the country, a
professional virgin with taffy-colored hair, a lovely oval face, and
big eyes that radiated mischief. "She's actually a thirty-year-old
lawyer," Miranda told me during a quiet moment in the kitchen.
"She's extremely bright and as tough as she needs to be."

"What does that mean?"

"She could go very far in law is what it means. Sky's the limit, if
she wanted to."

"That sounds like pretty deep exasperation I hear in your voice."

"Yeah, it is. It's really none of my business, but Erin's like the kid
sister I never had and she's been like a daughter to Lee. She lived with
us after her father died and we love her like family. We want the best
for her and she could have it all. She's got a great legal mind; she
could climb the heights and make a ton of money while she's at it."

"Maybe she just wants a quieter, gentler life."

"I should have known I'd get no sympathy from you. You
couldn't care less about money."

"Long as I've got enough to keep my act together."

"Erin's father was like that. Until one day when he really needed
it and didn't have it. Knock wood and hope that doesn't happen to
you."

"Hope what doesn't happen?"

"Oh, don't ask. It's a story with a bad ending and I never should
have brought it up."

I didn't say anything. She gave me a sad look like nothing I had
ever seen from her. "D'Angelo and Lee were partners very early, a
pair of idealistic young eagles right out of law school. Mrs. D. had
died. I was a silly adolescent worshiping Lee from afar and Erin was
just a child."

She wavered, like maybe she'd tell me and maybe she wouldn't. "I really shouldn't have gotten into this," she finally said. "Do me a favor, forget I said anything about it."

"Sure."

"Promise."

"I promise, Miranda. I will never breathe a word to anybody— not that I have any idea what you're talking about."

"It's not important now. If Erin ever brings it up, fine. I'd just rather it didn't come from me. She's a great girl and we're very proud of her. What's not to be proud of? She got perfect grades all through college and look at her now, working in a big downtown law firm."

"What's she doing schlepping writers around? Can't be much money in that."

Exasperation returned in a heartbeat. "See, *that's* what I'm talk-ing about. She's been doing that since her days at the DU law school, and she won't give it up. Suddenly she's tired of law. Now what rings her bell is lit-tra-ture. She's even been writing a novel, God help her, in her spare time."

"I can't imagine she's got any time to spare."

"She works by day and drives by night, writes when she can. Are you interested, Cliff?"

"I don't know—would you want me to be?"

Miranda gave me a long, wistful look. "You're a good guy, Janeway, and I mean that. But I'm afraid you'd only reinforce all her bad ideas."

The woman she had invited as my opposite was certainly nice enough—a ravishing redhead named Bonnie Conrad—and we spent much of the evening, when we weren't listening to Archer, in a pleasant exchange of views on world events. But my eyes kept drifting back to Erin d'Angelo, who provided such a cool presence at Archer's side. Once she caught me looking and her eyes nar-rowed slightly, as if she had picked up a whiff of my thought and found it as welcome as a fresh dose of herpes. Then she must have seen the beauty of my inner self, for she smiled, and in the heat of that moment all I could think was, *Oh, mother, what a wonderful face.*

Rounding out our party were Judge Arlene Weston and her husband, Phil, a plastic surgeon who had carved up some famous Hollywood noses before moving to Denver in the sixties. It was Phil who brought up the Supreme Court. "Arlene says you had an interview with Reagan."

"You're not supposed to talk about that, sweetheart," Arlene said. "It's bad luck to bring it up before the fact."

"I don't think it matters much," Lee said. "It was just a visit, certainly not what I'd call an interview. Tell you the truth, I'm still not sure what started it all."

"Somebody gave him your name, that's pretty clear. Must've been a hell of a recommendation from one who's very close to that inner circle."

"Maybe he's looking for a pal to come in on slow afternoons and keep him company while he watches his old movies," Phil said, joshing.

"All his afternoons are slow," said Archer.

"Whatever it was, it's pretty hard for me to take it seriously at this point," Lee said.

"I don't see why," said Bonnie. "You'd make a great justice."

"That's not how they choose them," Archer said. "Politics is what counts in that game, not legal acumen."

"Hal's right about that," Lee said. "I imagine it's the same in academia. The good teachers get lost in the shuffle, while those who play the game get ahead."

"And the same in books," Archer said. "Them that sits up and barks gets the awards."

"I never saw you barking for anybody."

"Maybe the Pulitzer committee's above all that," Archer said. "Or maybe I just got lucky."

"Maybe you'll both get lucky," Arlene said. "Wouldn't that be something? A Pulitzer prize winner *and* a Supreme Court justice from that one graduating class in college."

"High school, actually," Archer said. "Lee and I have known each other forever."

"We graduated from a tiny high school in Virginia," Lee said. "Our graduating class had twenty-two boys and twenty-two girls."

"Isn't that romantic?" Miranda said. "I just love that."

"That's because you got somebody's guy," Arlene said. "You're so *evil,* Miranda."

"Yep. I love to think of the poor, weeping wench, doomed to a life without Lee."

I said nothing during this light exchange, and it went on for a while before the inevitable swing to books came, at around ten-thirty. "So," Miranda asked privately at one point, "how do you like Mr. Archer?" I told her I had always loved his books and prepared to let it go at that. The Westons left in the next hour, and then we were six. Miranda had sensed the spontaneous hostility between Archer and me, and now she did her heroic best to overcome it. "Cliff has been a big, *big* fan of your books forever, Hal," she said, but this only made things worse. Archer's comment, "How very, *very* nice of him," was a startling breach of etiquette, too pointed and caustic even for him. He barely saved himself with a weasely "of course I'm kidding" smile, but the private look that passed between us told the real story. How dare I pass judgment, good, bad, or indifferent, and who the hell needed my approval anyway?

Normally at this point I would take off my kid gloves and bring up my own verbal brass knucks. I almost said, *And listen,* Hal, *that was even* before *I knew what an accomplished asshole you are . . . now I've got two things to admire you for.* I would have said this with my pleasantest smiling-cobra demeanor, and then, into the shocked silence, I'd have had to say, *Yes siree,* Hal, *you're way up there on my list of favs, right between Danielle Steel and Robin Cook.* Damn, I wanted to say that. I wanted to say it so badly that I came *this* close to really saying it. In my younger days I'd have let it rip instantly, in any crowd. I caught the eyes of Erin d'Angelo, who still seemed to be reading my mind from afar with a look of real mischief on her face. *Go ahead, say it, I dare you,* her look said. But I had my host to consider. I gave a little shake of my head, and Erin rewarded me with a soft laugh that no one could hear and only I could see.

Then she mouthed a single word and pulled me into the screwiest, most extended repartee I have ever had with a stranger. I couldn't be sure, but the word looked like *coward.*

I gave her my Tarzan look, the one that said, *A lot you know, sister, I eat guys like him for breakfast.*

She made a show of her indifference. Glanced at her nails. Looked away at nothing.

I stood up straight, my face fierce with my savage cavemanhood.

I had the feeling she was laughing at that; I couldn't be sure. In another moment, people would begin noticing what idiots we were, and I looked away, cursing the darkness.

Round one to her, on points.

We were in the library by then and Bonnie was ogling the books. Suddenly Archer said, "My goodness, Lee, don't you ever show anyone your real books?" Lee seemed reluctant, as if this would be much too much ostentation for one evening, but the cat was out of the bag and down the stairs we all went. We came into a smaller room that was also shelved all around, the shelves glassed and containing books that were clearly from another time. Archer stood back while the rest of us marveled at pristine runs of Dickens, Twain, Kipling, Harte, Hawthorne, Melville, so many eminent Victorians that my head began to spin as I looked at them. There wasn't a trumped-up leather binding in the room, and the sight of so much unfaded original cloth was gorgeous, inspiring, truly sensual.

"This is how my book fetish started," Lee said. "I inherited these."

"From his good old grandma Betts," Archer said. "Ah yes, I remember her well, what a dear old gal. Show them the Burtons, Lee."

And there they were, the greatest works of their day. With Lee's permission, I took each book down and handled it carefully. Archer talked about Burton as we looked, and his own zeal lit a fire that spread to us all. He seemed to know everything about Burton's life, and at some point I figured out, at least in a general sense, what the new Archer book was going to be. You can always tell with a writer: he gets that madness in his eyes whenever his subject comes up.

The room had gone quiet. Then I heard Erin's soft voice.

"There aren't any men like that anywhere in the world today."

I gave her a challenging look. She rolled her eyes. I said, "He'd go crazy today," and she cocked her head: "You think so?" I said, "Oh yeah. Ten minutes in this nuthouse world and he'd be ready to lie down in front of a bus." She said, "On the other hand, how would a man of today, say yourself as an example, do in Burton's world— India, Arabia, or tropical Africa of the late 1850s?" I said, "It'd sure be fun to find out," and she looked doubtful. But a few minutes later she slipped me a paper with a telephone number and a cryptic note, *Call me if you ever figure it out.*

Round two to me, for brilliant footwork.

It was one o'clock when I left the judge's house. All my annoyance with Archer's arrogance had dissolved and I was glad I hadn't retaliated at his stupid insult. I felt renewed, as if the pressing question in my life—what to do now?—had just been answered. Sometimes all it takes is the touch of a book, or the look on a woman's face, to get a man's heart going again.

I opened my eyes the next morning thinking of Erin and Burton together. Neither gave ground to the other; each grew in stature throughout the day.

I called her number. Got a machine. Her voice promised to call me back.

I let Burton simmer.

She called the next day and talked to my machine. "If this is a solicitation call, I gave at the office. But I'm a registered Democrat, I'll talk to anybody."

"Nice line," I told her machine. "I liked it almost as much when Jim Cain used it in that story he wrote thirty years ago."

"*Very* impressive," she said to my machine later that day. "I wondered if you'd catch that Cain heist. My God, aren't you ever home?"

"I'm home right now," my machine said to hers. "Where are you?"

"I'm off to Wyoming, dear heart," was her final attempt, hours later. "We're heading into what looks like a long, long trial. The environment of the very planet is at stake and the partners need my young, fertile mind far more than you seem to. Good-bye forever, I guess."

My machine said, with an incredulous air, "Wy*oming* has en*viron*ment?"

Then she was gone, a loss I hoped to hell was temporary. But Burton kept perking away like a stew in fine wine. On the morning of the fifth day I commenced strategic reconnaissance. In military terms this means a search over wide areas to gain information before making large-scale decisions. In bookscouting it's exactly the same: I got on the phone. I ordered some reference books. I fished around for cheap Burton reading copies. Strategic reconnaissance indeed: it was the bookman's madness, and I was hooked again.

2

Within a week I had read Fawn Brodie's Burton biography and had skimmed through three of Burton's greatest works. I began to read Burton slowly, in proper chronological order. I read Norman Penzer's Burton bibliography from cover to cover and I started a detailed file of points and auction prices on Burton first editions.

To a bookman a good bibliography is far better than any "life" pieced together by even a diligent scholar like Brodie—the subject is revealed through his own books and not through the eyes of a third party. Burton had been unfortunate with his early biographers. Long before Brodie made him respectable in 1967, he had been presented as a scoundrel, and sometimes, because of his frankness in translating the sexual classics of the East, as a pornographer. He was luckier with his bibliographer. Penzer was a fierce Burton advocate. His 1923 bibliography contains superb scholarship on Burton's books, and Penzer added pages of color on Burton's character, unusual in such a work. Penzer considered Burton the greatest man of his century, but a tragic man who could not suffer fools and was damned for all but his greatest accomplishments. Knighted near the end of his life in an empty gesture, he was treated shabbily by his government. He lived in the wrong time, said Penzer: "His queen should have been Elizabeth rather than Victoria."

Burton's story is a grand one in the most sweeping tradition of the book world. He was a Renaissance man long before the term came into popular use: master of twenty-nine languages, perfecter of dialects, great explorer, student of anthropology, botanist, author of thirty books, and in his later years translator of the *Arabian Nights* in sixteen volumes, of *The Kama Sutra,* and other forbidden Oriental classics. He was an excellent swordsman, a man of great physical and mental strength. He would need it all for the hardships he would face in unknown deserts and jungles around the world. His knowledge of human nature was vast, his powers of observation both panoramic and exhaustive, his memory encyclopedic. Wherever he went, he saw and noted everything, so that he was able to produce, almost immediately after a whirlwind trip across the American desert to Utah and California in 1860, a dense, seven- hundred-page work describing the flora and fauna, the people, the customs, and the land, and follow this two years later with a book of advice to the prairie traveler. His observations on the American Indian, with a long description on the practice of scalping, are classic passages of travel writing. Penzer believed Burton stood with the greatest explorers of all times: compared with Burton, he said, Stanley traveled like a king. Burton's expeditions into unknown Africa would read like myth except for the prodigious mass of detail he recorded about everything he saw there.

These accomplishments alone should have made him a giant of British folklore, but he was also "one of the two or three most proficient linguists of whom we have authentic and genuine historical records." He taught himself and was fluent in Arabic, Hindustani, Swahili, and Somali; he spoke Persian and Turkish, Spanish, Portuguese, and Greek. Of course he knew Latin. Wherever he went he soaked up languages, often perfecting dialects in a few weeks. *And,* Penzer reminded, he was a master of ethnic disguise. That's how he was able to go among natives as one of them, risking his life to breach the ancient holy cities of Mecca, Medina, and Harar.

He wrote of his travels in the Congo, Zanzibar, Syria, Iceland, India, and Brazil. He wrote books on bayonets, swords, and falconry. He was one of those brilliant swashbuckling wizards who comes along rarely, who understands life and writes exactly what he sees without pandering to rules of propriety or knuckling under to religious tyranny. His kind does not have an easy life. He is resented and shunned by churches and genteel society; if he's lucky, he may escape being burned at the stake. In Burton's case, he was victimized after death by his pious, narrow-minded Roman Catholic wife. Lady Isabel torched his work, burning forty years of unpublished manuscripts, journals, and notes in her mindless determination to purify his image.

This is why I am not religious. If and when we do learn the true secret of the universe, some kind of religion will be there to hide it. To cover it up. To persecute and shred, to burn and destroy. They stay in business by keeping us in the Dark Ages.

Darkness is what they sell.

By the middle of the second week, I had a good grasp of Burton's life and times; by the middle of the third, I knew what I wanted to do with my fifty grand. All I needed was to find the right copy of the right book.

I sent out feelers. Booksellers around the country began calling me with tips. By the middle of the fourth week, I had been touted to the Boston Book Galleries and an upcoming Burton that was rumored to be everything I wanted. I made plans to fly East.

How can I describe the joy of pulling down those sweetheart books for twenty-nine thousand and change? I knew I'd probably have to pay what the trade considered a premium. Dealers dropped out of the bidding early, and the contest winnowed down to two collectors and me. When it went past twenty I thought the hell with it, I wasn't buying these books for resale, this was food for the soul and I didn't care if I had to spend the whole fifty grand. The Seattle stash was found money, in my mind. People who gamble in casinos on Indian reservations sometimes call their winnings Indian money. They put it in a cookie jar and give themselves permission to lose it all again. But a book like the Burton set is never a gamble. I wasn't about to throw my bankroll at a roulette table, but thinking of it as Indian money made me instantly more competitive and ultimately the high bidder. There was a time when it would have been unthinkable to spend so much on a single first edition. I laugh at those days.

I laughed a lot in the wake of Boston. I was amazed at how far my Burton story had been flung. It surpassed even Janeway's Rule of Overkill, which goes like this: getting the media's interest can be so much more difficult than keeping it. Reporters and editors are such pessimistic bastards—everyone wants a few inches of their space or a minute of their time, and they put up walls that are all but impregnable. Editors will send a grumbling reporter many miles to cover a man with a butterfly collection and ignore some shameful injustice that's been growing in their own backyards forever. Out-of-town experts thrill them, but anyone who openly tries to lure them will get brushed off faster than a leper at a nudist colony. The key to the gate is your own indifference. Be shy enough and the media will swarm. At that point anything can happen.

I was indifferent, I was almost coy, and overnight I became the most prominent Richard Burton specialist in America. I didn't claim to be the best or the brightest: I probably wasn't the wisest, whitest, darkest, wittiest, and listen, this part's hard to believe, I may not have even been the prettiest. The events that put me on the map were arbitrary and embarrassingly unjustified. A single piece in *The Boston Globe,* passionately written by a rabid Burton fan on his day off, led to my appearance on NPR, and to far greater exposure when a Boston wire-service bureau chief ordered a light rewrite and put that *Globe* piece in newspapers around the country. I didn't kid myself—they were all using me as a modern hook for the story that really interested them, because Burton's story had been history, not news, for more than a century. But this is how I got my fifteen minutes of fame: I was carried there on the broad shoulders of a man who died sixty years before I was born.

At home I had twenty calls on my answering machine, including one from Miranda. Because of the Denver angle, both local papers had carried my AP story from Boston. Lee had seen it, and of course he wanted to see the books. Miranda invited me for "supper" that night, making the distinction that this was not "dinner," it was family, and there would just be the three of us. It was a weeknight; we'd make it a short evening for the good of us all. Lee was in the middle of a complicated trial and I had lots of work to do. Even Miranda had an early date the next morning, at a neighborhood old-folks' home where she worked as a volunteer.

We ate on their patio, laughing over my close call with Archer the last time I had seen them. "I was holding my breath," Miranda said: "For a minute I thought you were going to take him apart before God and all of us." She glanced at Lee and said, "Not that Cliff wouldn't have been justified, sweetheart. I know the man's your oldest friend, and it's certainly not my habit to apologize for my guests. But that one's a real bastard and I just don't like him."

Lee smiled in that easy way he had. "Hal's had a hard life. That's what you need to understand about him before you judge him too harshly."

"Why is it *me* who's got to understand *him*? I like people I *already* understand."

"Give him just a little break, Miranda. His family was against his writing career from the start and he had to struggle all through his life. His early books—all the ones that people are now calling modern classics—were rejected by everybody for years. He has suffered the tortures of the damned—the truly gifted man whose talent was ignored for decades, actually. If he's bitter it's because of the bestseller mentality and what he sees as the dumbing-down of our literature."

"I know that but it's such an old, tedious story. He's hardly the first writer to feel unappreciated. How many talented people never do get recognized? You don't see them whining about it, or causing a fuss when all someone wants to do is admire them. There's just no excuse for boorish behavior. He should cut off his ear and enjoy some real pain."

I asked for a truce. "I'm sure he didn't mean anything by it. Really, I barely noticed it."

Abruptly, thankfully, Lee changed the subject. "Let's look at your books," he said, and we went back into the house. He studied the three volumes in awe, as if he couldn't believe what he was seeing. "My God," he said. "Where on earth did these come from?" Ultimately, I didn't know: the auction house wasn't required to disclose consignors' names. Miranda wondered who Charles Warren had been, how someone who had received such a warm inscription could remain so unknown to Burton's biographers. Finally Lee brought up his own volumes to compare. There was no comparison. Lee's were near fine, more than good enough for most collectors of hundred-year-old books. Mine were a full cut above that: unblemished, stratospheric, factory-fresh. Placing the two sets side by side gave new meaning to the words *rare books*.

"I'd say you did well, even at thirty thousand," he said. "In fact, if you want to sell them and make some instant money . . ."

"I'm going to hang on to these, Lee. They're going into my retirement fund."

That night I had a message from Erin on my machine. "I am going crazy on some planet called Rock Springs. Now I know what happens when all hope dies—rock springs eternal. My desperation simply cannot be described! It's so bad that I'm actually calling *you* in some misguided hope for relief. Of course you're not there, but I guess that *is* my relief."

I left an answer on her home phone—"I warned you about Wyoming, kid"—and in the morning, when I turned mine on, she had already replied: "I beg your pardon, you certainly did *not* say I was being sent to *Mars*. It looks like we'll wrap it up here in a couple of weeks, but that sounds like eternity on this end of it. I will need some very serious pampering when I get home."

I thought about her a lot that day. We were having some fairly intimate bullshit for two people who had yet to touch, feel, probe, or say more than a few direct words to each other. At bedtime I launched a new attack on her hated answering machine. "Look, let's make a date. You. Me. Not this gilhickey you make me talk to. Us, in the . . . you know . . . flesh. Didn't mean that the way it sounded, it just popped out. Didn't mean that either. I promise to be civilized. I swear. White sport coat. Pink carnation. Night of the thirtieth. Come by my bookstore if you get in early enough. Call me if you can't make it."

She didn't call. But soon the crank calls began.

For days after Boston I had crackpots calling at all hours: people who claimed to have real Burton books and didn't, fools who wanted me to fly to Miami or Portland or Timbuktu on my nickel to check them out, wild people with trembling voices who needed a drink or a fix and had battered copies of Brodie's biography or cheap Burton reprints that could still be found in cheesy modern bindings on chain-store sales tables. One man, certain that he was Burton's direct descendant, had talked to Burton for years in his dreams and had written a twelve-hundred-page manuscript, dictated by Burton himself, with maps of a fabulous African kingdom that remained undiscovered to this very day. A woman called collect from Florida with a copy of Richard Burton's autobiography, in dust jacket, signed by Burton, Elizabeth Taylor, and some woman named Virginia Woolf. All she wanted for it was $1,500, but I had to take it *now,* sight unseen, or she'd get on the phone and after that it was going to the highest bidder. There were calls from Chicago and Phoenix and Grand Rapids, Michigan. An old woman in Baltimore said my book had been stolen from her family. She talked in a whisper, afraid "they" would overhear her, and when she insisted that the man in the inscription had been her grandfather and that he had been there when Richard Burton had helped start the American Civil War, I moved on as quickly as I could without being rude. One thing I knew for sure—there'd be another hot item in the next mail, and another with the next ringing of the telephone.

Packages arrived without notice at my Denver bookstore. Most contained worthless books that I had to return. A man in Detroit sent a nice box of early Burton reprints, which I actually bought. But the strangest thing was the arrival of a true first edition, Burton's *City of the Saints,* in a package bearing only a St. Louis postmark— no name, no return address anywhere on or inside the box. I waited for some word by telephone or in a separate letter, but it never came.

By the end of the month the clamor had begun to calm down. The thirtieth came: the crackpots had faded away and my new friend in Rock Springs still had not called. My suspense was delicious. I was thinking of all the places I might take her, but then the old lady from Baltimore arrived and the mystery of that wonderful inscription came to life.

3

She was not just old, she was a human redwood. I got a hint of her age when her driver, an enormous black man in a military-style flak jacket, stepped out of a Ford Fairlane of mid-sixties vintage and stood protectively at her door. A bunch of rowdy kids roared past on skateboards: six of them, all seventeen or eighteen, old enough to be frisky and not quite old enough to know better.

East Colfax is that kind of street: common, rough, unpredictable. I heard one of the kids yell, "Look out, Smoky!" and I cringed at the slur and was shamed again by the callous stupidity of my own race. I could hear their taunting through my storefront, but the driver stood with patient dignity and ignored them. He had an almost smooth face with a short, neat mustache, and I liked his manner and the way he held himself. Sometimes you can tell about a guy, just from a glance.

The kids clattered away and the driver opened the car door. A gray head appeared followed by the rest of her: a frail-looking woman in a faded, old-fashioned dress. She gripped his arm and pulled herself up: stood still for a moment as if she couldn't quite get her balance, then she nodded and, still clutching his arm, began the long, step-by-step voyage across the sidewalk to my store. She had to stop and steady herself again, and at that moment I saw the driver look up with a face full of alarm. Another wave of reckless kids was coming, and in that half second the first of them whipped by just a foot from my glass. The driver put up his hand and yelled "Stop!" and I saw the old lady cringe as a blur flew past and missed her by inches. I started toward the door, but before I could get there, the big man had stiff-armed the next kid in line, knocking him ass over apex on the sidewalk.

I opened my door and several things happened at once. Another fool swerved past, I got my foot on his skateboard, tipped him off, and the board shot out into the street, where it was smashed by a passing car. The first kid was up on his hands and knees, bleeding at the elbows and dabbing at a bloody nose. I heard the ugly words, "nigger son of a bitch," and two more of his buddies arrived, menacing us on the sidewalk. The car had pulled to the curb and now a fat man joined the fray, screaming about the scratch on his hood. In all this chaos the big fellow managed to get the old lady into the store, leaving me alone to handle the fallout.

The bloody nose was flanked by his pals. "I oughta beat your ass."

I laughed at the thought. "You couldn't beat your meat without help from these other idiots. Maybe you better haul it on out of here before you get in real trouble."

I juked them and they stumbled over one another as they backed out to the curb. It was hard not to laugh again, they were such colossal schmucks, but I let them put on a little face-saving sideshow, to which middle fingers were copiously added, and even-tually they sulked away.

Now I had to go through another song and dance with the fat guy. He said, "What about my car, wiseguy, you gonna pay for my hood?" I asked if he knew how to read, pointing out that my sign said BOOKS, not STATE FARM INSURANCE. He suggested throwing a brick through my window and we'd see how funny that was. I took obvious note of his plate number and told him I'd be inside calling the cops while he was looking around for a brick. I heard him leave, putting down a foot of rubber as I opened my door and went inside.

The old lady sat in a chair with her eyes closed. I spoke to her driver, who had a name tag sewn military-style on his jacket. "Mr. Ralston, I presume."

"Mike'll do."

I shook his hand, said, "Cliff Janeway," and gave a small bow in her direction. "Welcome to East Colfax."

* * *

The phone rang and I had a brief rush of business. The old woman sat still through it all, her balance eerily stable in what appeared to be a light sleep. Occasionally I made eye contact with Ralston, arching my eyebrows and cocking my head in her direction, but he shrugged and waited for the calls to subside. When it got quiet again I motioned him over to the end of the counter. "So . . . Mike . . . what's this all about?"

"Beats me. I think she just got to Denver last night."

"Just got here from where?"

"Back East somewhere. I don't know how she made it all alone. You can see how shaky she is, and she's got almost no money. That had to be one helluva trip."

"What's your part in it?"

"Let's call it my good deed of the month." He smiled, a humble man embarrassed by his own kindness. "Look, I'm no professional do-gooder, but this woman's at the end of her rope. She's staying in a tacky motel not far from here. My wife works there and I can tell you it's not a place you'd want your grandmother to stay. Or your wife to work, either . . . not for long."

"So?"

"So Denise calls and tells me she's got a lady there who needs some help. Denise is my wife." He said her name so lovingly that I could almost feel some small measure of the affection myself, for a woman I had never met. "You married, Janeway?"

I shook my head.

"Well, this is one of those things you do when you are. As the line goes, to ensure domestic tranquillity. You'll understand it someday."

I laughed and liked him all the more.

"All I can tell you right now is, this lady came a long way to see you, and she almost made it. The least I could do was get her the last few miles over here."

I liked Mr. Ralston but I sure didn't like what I was hearing. The arrival of an ancient and penniless woman at my door charged me with responsibility for her welfare. Maybe I owed her nothing—that was the voice of a cynic, and I am the great cynic of my day. I can be a fountain of negative attitude, but from that moment she was mine to deal with.

"I wonder if I should wake her."

"Up to you, friend. I'm just the delivery boy."

It was unlikely but she seemed to hear us. Her eyes flicked open and found my face, and I had a powerful and immediate sense of something strong between us. I knew that in some distant past she had been an important part of my life, yet in the same instant I was certain I had never seen her. Her face was almost mummified, her eyes watery and deep. Her hair was still lush and striking: now I could see that it was pure white, not gray, swept across her forehead in a soft wave that left her face looking heart-shaped and delicate in spite of the deeply furrowed skin. I pulled up a stool, said, "What can I do for you, ma'am?" and her pale gray eyes, which had never left my face, struggled to adjust in the harsh late-afternoon sunlight from the street. Suddenly I knew she couldn't see me: I saw her pupils contract and expand as she lowered and raised her head; I saw the thick glasses in her lap and the lax fingers holding them but making no effort to bring them up to her eyes. The glasses were useless; she was blind. It was impossible but she had come across the country alone, trembling and unsteady . . . virtually sightless.

I couldn't just shake that off, and I still felt some vague sense of kinship between us. It was probably simple chemistry, one of those strong and instant reactions that certain people have when they meet, but it had happened so rarely in my life that its effect was downright eerie. And this was doubly strange, because I now began to sense that her reaction to me was almost a polar opposite. Her face was deeply apprehensive, as if I had some heaven-or-hell power and she was finally at the time in her long life when the accounting had to begin.

"Mr. Janeway."

Another surprise: her voice was steady and strong. She put on her glasses and squinted through the heavy lenses, confirming my original guess. She could make out colors, shades of light and dark, shapes moving past on the street; she could assess enough of my appearance to see a fierce-looking, dark-haired bruiser straddling a stool before her; she could find her way along a sidewalk if she didn't stumble and fall. But by almost any legal definition, she was blind.

"My name is Josephine Gallant. You have a book that belongs to me."

I thought at once of that mysterious *City of the Saints* that had dropped in my lap from St. Louis. This was actually going to be good news: I could pay her a thousand dollars for that copy; hell, I could give her *two* thousand and sell it at cost. Maybe that would make a small difference in her life and I could go back to my own life knowing I had given her my best. Then she said, "My grandfather was Charles Warren," and at once I remembered that phone call from the crazy woman, surrounded by spooks in Baltimore. This is how quickly good news can turn into *oh shit* in the book business.

Before I could gather my thoughts she said, "What I meant was, it *once* belonged to me. Even after all these years I still think of them as my books."

"Them?"

"There were more where that set came from."

Again I felt her chemistry. She felt mine too, and suddenly she trembled. "You're a formidable man," she said; then, in a much smaller voice, "Aren't you, Mr. Janeway?"

For once I was flabbergasted into near-speechlessness. She repeated it, more certain now—"You *are* a formidable man"—as if she half expected me to haul back without warning and knock her off the chair. Softly I said, "Ma'am, I am no threat to ladies." After an awkward pause I went on in a silly vein, trying my best to lighten her up. "I haven't robbed a bank all week. I don't do drugs. Don't kick dogs . . . well, maybe little ones, but I never eat small children. That's one good thing I can say for myself."

She stared. I said, "Honest." She lifted a shaky hand to her eyes and I gave up with a soggy punch line. "Those are all rumors that got started by an angry bookscout."

I had a flashing moment of insanity when I almost told her the actual truth. By nature I am a cavalier with women, but I was afraid if I said that I'd have her for life.

Then she spoke. "When I called you on the telephone that day you were busy. I should have considered that. I only realized later that I must have sounded like a fool."

"I think it was just that business about not letting *them* hear you."

I felt a hot flush of shame but my cutting remark didn't seem to offend her.

"I live in an old folks' home in Baltimore. I'm on Medicaid and I'm not supposed to have unreported money of my own. That's why I didn't want them to hear what I was saying. It took everything I had hidden away to get here."

This was not going well. Her answer for *them* had been annoyingly believable, so I threw her another one. "I was also a little puzzled when you said Burton had started our civil war."

"You thought I was crazy."

I shrugged. "No offense, ma'am. I was getting a lot of crazy calls then."

"Well, of course he didn't *start* that war. If I said that I didn't mean it literally." She was agitated now, whether at me or herself I couldn't tell, but the trembling in her hands had spread to her face. For a moment I thought she was going to faint.

"Are you okay, ma'am? I've got a cot in the back if you'd like to lie down."

She took a deep, shivery breath. "No, I'm fine."

She didn't look fine: she looked like a specter of death. She said, "I know I'm not going to make any headway trying to convince you about what Burton did or didn't do," then almost in the same breath she said, "How much do you know about his time in America?"

"I know he went to Utah in 1860 to meet Brigham Young. He was interested in polygamy and he wanted to see for himself how a polygamous society functioned."

"That's only what the textbooks tell you."

It was what Burton himself had said in his books, but I nodded. "He had to get away from England for a while. He had been double-crossed by Speke, who took all the glory of discovering the African lakes for himself. I don't know, maybe there was some truth to the story that he just wanted to come here and fight some Indians."

"You know of course that he was a master spy."

"I know when he was in India he often spied for the Crown."

"And when he came to America, he disappeared for three months. What do you think he was doing here then?"

"Nobody knows. It's always been assumed that he was on a drinking spree in the American South with an old friend from his days in India. But there's no documentation for that time: the only evidence is Burton's comment that they *intended* to do this. All Burton said was that he had traveled through every state before suddenly arriving at St. Joseph for his long stagecoach trip to Utah."

"That's not entirely true anymore. I heard that some pages from a journal have been found in England, supporting the view that Burton and his old friend Steinhauser were together after all. According to this account, they spent more time in Canada than in the Southern United States."

"Well, there you are."

"What if I told you there was *another* journal of that missing period, one that tells a far different story?"

"I'd have to be skeptical. A dozen biographers never uncovered it."

"Maybe they didn't know where to look."

This again was possible. A man travels many roads—even a diligent biographer like Fawn Brodie never finds everything—but I still didn't believe it. "I thought Mrs. Burton destroyed his journals."

She simmered behind her old-lady face. "Well, this would be one she never got her bloody little hands on."

"If such a book exists, I'd love to see it."

"It exists, all right. Don't worry about that."

She fought her way through another attack of shakes. "It exists," she said again.

"That's pretty definite, ma'am . . . almost as if you'd seen it yourself."

She nodded dreamily and I felt the hair bristle on the back of my neck. "A very long time ago," she said. "A long, long lifetime ago. I don't expect you to believe me. I just thought you might want to know that your book came out of a collection that was stolen from my family. But I guess that wouldn't matter either."

"Of course it would. But you've got to have proof."

Outside, an ambulance went screaming past. In those few seconds I decided to take an objective and academic interest in what she was saying. Her great age demanded at least that much respect, so I ordered myself to go gently and save the assholery for someone who needed it.

I picked up a notepad and felt almost like a cop again. "How big a collection was this?"

"Large," she said, and I could almost feel her heartbeat racing at my sudden interest. She had my attention: this was why she'd come, this was what she wanted.

"It was quite large," she said. "You'd probably consider it the makings of a library. A good-sized bookcase full of books. A cabinet full of letters and papers."

"A library like that isn't easy to steal," I said. "A man doesn't just walk away with that in his hip pocket."

"This was not a thief in the night. It was done through lies and deceit."

Immediately I asked the vital legal question. "Did money change hands?"

She said, "I don't know, I'm not sure," but her answer was too quick and her eyes cut away from mine. I knew she was lying and she knew I knew. But what she said next only made it worse. "What difference does that make, if it was a crooked deal?"

That's the trouble with a lie, it usually leads straight to another lie. A question rooted in a lie is a lie itself. I figured she knew quite well what a difference it could make, and a lie is a lie is a lie, as Gertrude Stein, that paragon of the lucid profundity, would have gushed. Ms. Josephine Gallant dodged it by retreating into her own dim past, and there, so surprisingly that it surprised us both, she saved herself.

"That collection was put together by my grandfather more than a hundred years ago. My earliest memories are of my grandfather and his books. I remember the colors of them . . . the textures. I remember that room, in a house that exists only in my memory. The pale blue walls. The plaster beginning to crack in the far corner, over the kitchen door. The shiny oak floor. Me, sitting on my grandfather's lap while he read, and outside, the sounds of horses in the street. The garbageman, with his speckled walrus mustache . . . nice old Mr. Dillard, who drove a wagon with a horse named Robert. Our windows were always open in the summer and there was noise—all the noises of the street—but it never disturbed my grandfather when he was reading. He could lose himself in a book. If I asked him, he would read aloud until I fell asleep. And if I awoke—if I nudged him—he would start reading again."

She took a long breath. "If you've read Burton's books, you know they can be difficult. But there are places where they bring a landscape to life, even for a child. My grandfather admired Burton tremendously. The cabinet was full of letters from Burton, written over twenty-five years. All of our books were inscribed to him by Burton, and he had many more that Burton had not written but had sent him over the years, on exotic topics that Burton had found interesting. There was always a little note inside, with some mention of the time they had spent together, and many of the books were extensively annotated with marginal notes in Burton's hand."

She smiled. "He often asked me, my grandfather, if I liked his books, and I always said oh yes, I loved them, and he said, they will be yours when you grow up."

She cocked her head as if to say, *That's all I have. I'm sorry it's not enough.*

"These are my fondest memories. Listening to my grandfather read, in Burton's own words, of his adventures in India, Africa, Arabia, and the American West."

Her smile was faint: fleeting and wistful, lovely in the way a desert landscape must be from the edge of space. In that moment her small untruth seemed trivial and the general unease I had been feeling sharpened and became specific.

She wasn't talking like a crazy woman now.

Not at all.

Suddenly I believed her.

I had spent years interrogating people, and in most cases I could smell a lie as soon as it was said. The good cops are the ones who know the truth when they hear it.

The little things were what got me. The particulars, like the blue plaster . . .

The *pale blue* plaster. The crack in the ceiling, just *over the kitchen door.* The garbageman with his *speckled* mustache and his horse named *Robert,* for Christ's sake. Who the hell thinks of Robert as a name for a horse? Unless it's real.

Suddenly she was getting all the benefit of my doubt.

Suddenly I had to give her that much simple justice. Suddenly the choices were no longer mine to make. Suddenly I had to hear what she really knew: I had to separate what she *thought* she knew from what she wanted to believe, and keep what I wanted to believe out of it. Suddenly I had to figure out what the truth was, because, that suddenly, I might have to ask the auction-house people to figure it out for all of us.

I could just imagine what they'd say. There are seldom any guarantees in a book auction, and at first there'd be icy disdain, the kind of ivory-tower, holier-than-thou bullshit that book people dish out better than anyone. Maybe if I made enough noise they'd have to look at it. The Boston Book Galleries was an upscale auction house with a fine reputation, and the book had been sold with a provenance that looked spotless. But in recent years even the most prestigious auction houses had been duped. Some of them had sold their souls and participated in the duping, so nothing was sacred if the book had to be checked. The inquiry would go all the way back to the day when Richard Francis Burton had signed it to some man named Charles Warren.

The old woman looked at me hard, trying to see me through her haze, and again it was as if she knew things that had not been said. She knew how close she had come to losing me. She had broken through a chink in my defenses and she knew that too, even if she didn't quite know how. She had come with little hope on a journey that must have seemed endless, and in just these few minutes we had reached a turning point. She took a deep breath and we were back to that moment of truth she had sidestepped a moment ago. She tried to smile but didn't make it, and in the end there was nothing to do but to say what she had come here for.

"My grandfather died in 1906. His library was pillaged immediately after his death, all of it whisked away in a single evening. It's never been seen since."

I coughed, politely, I hoped. But the chemistry between us was sizzling now, and I knew exactly what she wanted. She wasn't just after my book, she wanted it all. Her grandfather's library had been missing for more than eighty years and Ms. Josephine Gallant, at the end of her life, wanted me to find it for her.

4

The only sound in the next half minute was the ticking of the clock. She sat waiting while my mind ran through the worst possible implications of what she had said.

I knew enough about the law in these matters to know how murky it could get. Common law says title can't be acquired even from a good-faith seller if there's theft hidden somewhere in the property's history. The term *caveat emptor* may be part of a dead language but there are excellent reasons why it is still universally known. Richard Burton in his earliest childhood would have had a perfect understanding of it.

Things are seldom that simple in modern American law. State statutes may vary wildly on the same set of circumstances, and the passage of enough time can erode original rights in defiance of legal intent. People die, decades slip away, and what was once clearly their property can acquire a valid-looking new history of ownership.

Eighty years was a good long time, but this old lady had not died. She sat before me, a human relic, waiting tensely for some indication of what I would do. All she had going for her was a faint hope and the tiny matter of my conscience. If I chose to go happily among the world's most notorious assholes, what could she do about it? I had bought the book fair and square: hell, I could stonewall her forever. Even if she'd had money and the law was ultimately on her side, its process was not. Given her age and the way lawyers jack each other off, she'd never live long enough to see her book again.

I had a hunch she knew these things as well as I did. Even Ralston knew: I could see him in my peripheral vision, out at the end of my art section, keenly interested in us now and no longer making any effort to hide it. Was there such stuff as three-way chemistry? Maybe so, but that didn't account for everything. We all knew what I could have done. Only I knew what I had to do.

"What are you thinking, Mr. Janeway?"

"Just groping around the edges of a moral dilemma, Ms. Gallant."

I could almost see her mind churning, hunting for any small thing that would make my dilemma less groping and my choice more moral. But she didn't know how to get there, and all she could do was ask a blind question. "What can I tell you?"

I picked up my notepad, which had dropped to the floor beside my chair. "His name was Warren, yours is Gallant. You can start with that."

"Warren was my mother's name. Gallant was the name of the fool I married, more than seventy years ago. I kept it because I always loved the regal sound of it."

This too sounded real, but she was still reading doubt into my questions. "Does it seem far-fetched that I might've found someone to marry me once, Mr. Janeway?"

"Not at all."

"I wasn't always a withered old prune. There was a time when even a young buck like yourself might've found me comely. But that was so long ago it might have been on another world." She touched her cheek as if searching for a tear. "The first time I heard it I thought the name Gallant had the loveliest sound. Tucker Gallant. My God, he's been dead almost sixty years. I wonder if I didn't marry him just for his name."

"You don't strike me as the type who would do that, Mrs. Gallant."

"Who knows what type I was? I was barely a grown woman when I met him."

Her hands had begun to tremble and she looked away, squinting at the light from the street. Hope was fickle and it faded now as reality settled in. "I knew I was coming here on a fool's errand. You're being very kind, Mr. Janeway, but I'm not under any illusions about anything. Even if I could prove everything I say, where would I be?"

"In an ideal world, I would return the book and get my money back. Then the auction house would give it to you as the rightful owner."

"Your tone tells me that's not likely to happen."

"It's not theirs to give. Their position would be that all sales are final. In that ideal world, maybe you could discover who consigned it. But then you'd have to fight it out with him."

"How do they think I'm supposed to do that?"

I shrugged. "Not their problem."

"So much for the ideal world. Now what?"

I didn't say anything. Hell, I was no lawyer: it wasn't my place to tell her what to do. If I made a good-faith effort to find out about the book, nobody could ask more than that.

"This is some situation," she said.

Yes, it was, but I wasn't going to advise her.

"If you keep the book, I lose. If you give it back, I still lose."

So far she had an excellent grasp of it.

"I guess my only recourse is to persuade you to give *me* the book."

There was a touch of self-ridicule in her voice, like, *That'll be the day, when cows milk themselves dry and the ghost of Richard Burton comes back to take it away from you at the point of a sword.*

"No one but a fool would do that," she said.

She had that right. In our dog-eat-dog world, she was nothing to me. She was trouble and pain, the embodiment of bad news. But my heart went out to her.

"I shouldn't joke about it," she said. "That's a lot of money to joke about."

"Tell me about it."

I hadn't been aware she'd been joking—how could I tell?—but now in her self-deprecating laugh I caught a glimpse of the girl she'd been: a heartbreaker, I'd bet, in the springtime of the Roaring Twenties with her life just beginning and the world opening up. In that moment the money seemed crazily irrelevant. It was still only Indian money: If I had to give up the book, I'd miss it like a severed kidney, but how much would I really miss the stupid money? I shifted my weight on the stool and said, "I don't know what I'd do," and she took in her breath and held it for a moment.

"I just don't know, that's all I'm saying. If we could verify everything—if there were no doubts—then I guess that would be one of my options, wouldn't it?"

She shook her head. "You're out of your mind."

"We're not breaking any new ground there, Mrs. Gallant."

She squinted and peered, said, "I wish I could see you better," but her apprehension was gone. Her fear was gone, and what was left between us was a strange and growing harmony. Was that trust I saw in her face?

"I had no idea what I'd find when I came here. I certainly didn't expect to meet a man of honor. I thought such creatures were extinct today."

"Don't get too carried away, ma'am. I haven't done anything yet."

But there was no getting around it: in those few minutes, something fundamental had changed between us. She gave a small shiver and clutched at the collar of her dress. I asked if she was cold—I had an afghan back in my office—but she shook her head.

"Mr. Ralston?"

"Yes, ma'am?" He came up to join us.

"Would you please get my bag from the car?"

I had my own chilling moment as Ralston brought in the bag and she directed him to take out what was obviously a book wrapped in cloth. What else would it be but a Burton? I fingered its violet cloth cover, opened it to the title page, and my last doubt about her vanished. A cherry copy, an exquisite *First Footsteps in East Africa*, London, 1856. I touched the inscription: *To Charles Warren, my best American friend Charlie, in the hope that our paths may one day cross again, Richard F. Burton.* It had been inscribed in 1860.

"That's an exceedingly rare volume today," she said. "I've had it hidden away, protected it for years. I understand it's unheard of to find one with the forbidden appendix intact."

The notorious so-called infibulation appendix. I turned to page 591 and found it tipped in, four pages in Latin. I remembered from Brodie's biography that it had contained material then considered so salacious that the printers had refused to bind it into the book.

"The sexual practices of the Somalis," she said. "All spelled out for the public horrification and secret titillation of proper old hypocritical England. Penis rings, female circumcision—things they couldn't talk about then and we can't get enough of today."

"Burton never did have any inhibitions when it came to describing what he saw."

"For all the good it did him. I understand only a few copies survived."

"How did you manage to save this one?"

"I was lucky. Charlie had taken this volume out of his library to look up something. It was upstairs where it wasn't supposed to be the night he died. Later my mother found it and hid it. She kept it secret until she died, and it was found among her things. A few worthless relics, some worn-out old clothes, and this—the sum of her existence, but to me it was a symbol of what we'd been, who we were."

I flipped my notepad to a new page. "So tell me who you were."

"We were never rich, I'll tell you that. We were always comfortable, solidly in the middle class while Charlie was alive, but people were more apt to be either rich or poor then, and the middle class was a much smaller part of the population. You could live very well in the middle class in those days."

She slipped back into her dream face. "Everything we were in the good times began and ended with my grandfather. He was such a loving authority figure to me when I was a child. His friends called him Charlie, but of course to me he was always Grandfather; it would have been a sacrilege to think of him any other way. But on my eightieth birthday I suddenly realized I was older than him—when he died, you know, and got stuck at seventy-nine forever. That's when he became more like a dear old friend and I started thinking of him as Charlie."

"What about your father?"

"My father . . ." She struggled for a word but couldn't find it. The moment stretched and became strained. "What do you want to know? I tried to love my father . . . but he wouldn't let me. He wasn't a bad man . . . just a weak one."

"Did he drink?"

I saw her recoil in surprise.

"I'm not a mind reader, ma'am, it just figures."

She fidgeted. She could feel me hemming her in, taking her into places she had avoided for a long time. At last she answered the question. "His drinking put my mother in the poorhouse after my grandfather died. That's where *she* died, alone in a consumption ward. They all died within a few years of each other—Charlie . . . Mama . . . him."

I decided to leave her father's drinking for the moment, but I knew we'd get back to it. "So you were alone in the world at what age?"

"Thirteen."

"This was in Baltimore?"

"Yes, but when Mama got sick I was sent to live with her brother in Boise, Idaho."

"How did that work out?"

"It was horrible. He was a common laborer; he made very little money and his wife took in wash to help make ends meet. They already had five children, the last thing they needed was another one. I was resented by all of them; they never said it in so many words, but I knew. They put up with me because I was family, that's what good people did then. I hated being an obligation, so I ran away after two years and I never saw any of them again. I'm sure they all said good riddance when I was gone."

Her eyes drifted to the street, as if moving images from that old life had begun to play on my storefront window. "They'd all be dead now, wouldn't they?"

"That's hard to say. You're still here."

A pregnant pause: I flipped a page. "What happened then?"

"A lot of things you don't need to know about. Just say I soon learned how to take care of myself and we'll leave it at that. I went back to Baltimore and married Gallant in 1916. I've had an amazing ability to go from bad to worse all my life, and this was just another case of it. That doesn't matter now, it's all a very long time ago. Let's just say Gallant didn't live up to the promise of his name."

She made a nervous gesture. "Let's talk about something else. Those were hard times and I'd rather not think about it. Anyway, Gallant's got nothing to do with this. I doubt if I ever said the word *books* the whole time we were married. But I never stopped thinking about them. They were on my mind all through those hard years."

"Sounds like you had a few of those. Hard years, I mean."

She made a little laughing sound. "Oh honey, I could tell you stories that would curl your toenails. The twenties weren't half-bad; we had some good days then and some money too. But Tucker lost his shirt along with everybody else in 1929. Then he . . . died . . . and I lived in a cardboard box at a garbage dump all through the winter of 1931. The dump was the only place where the cops would leave me alone. I went to sleep every night with the smell of rotten meat in my nose and the sounds of rats in my ears. All I had was that little silver key to Tucker's deposit box, where I kept my book. But what does that matter now? I lived through it and I'm still here, fifty-eight years after Tucker Gallant was laid out with two fellas throwing dirt in his face."

She swallowed hard and looked off into the dark places of the store. "The tough part is when I think how different my life might've been if those books hadn't been lost. Knowing all the time they were meant to be mine."

"What would you have done with them then, sold them?"

"That would've been hard. They were such a part of my life."
She shrugged. "When you get hungry enough you'll sell anything.
They sure weren't worth then what they'd sell for today, but I bet I'd
have gotten myself a fair piece of change even in the thirties. Maybe
put myself through college. I always wanted to go to college. Always
wanted to study . . ."

"Study what?"

"You'll laugh."

"No, I won't. Of course I won't laugh."

"It just seems silly now, but I always wanted to study something
grand. Like philosophy."

She rolled her eyes at her own folly. "My gosh, philosophy. Of all
the silly things."

I didn't laugh: she did.

"Now I ask you, Mr. Janeway, have you ever heard of anything
as silly as that?"

Two customers came in, high-rollers from Texas who passed through
Denver once a year, and for a while I was busy showing them some
high-end modern books. They bought a slug of stuff that I was
thrilled to see hit the road, passing over two immaculate Mark
Twains to throw about the same amount of money at Larry
McMurtry, Hunter S. Thompson, and a few others whose names will
be toast when old Clemens is still a household word. Ralston
watched them peel off eight crispy bills from a roll of hundreds and
saunter up the street with their small bag of books.

"Man, I'm in the wrong business."

"Yeah, well, it's not always like that."

"Doesn't need to be."

Almost an hour had passed since I had last spoken to Mrs. Gallant. She looked exhausted, her eyes wide open, staring at nothing.
I thought, God, I'd like to crawl inside your head, but if I'd had one

wish, I'd liked to have been there when her grandfather died. I had some drippy, cavalier notion that I'd have rescued her life: that, one way or another, I'd have stopped her father from selling her books.

"Mrs. Gallant." I pulled up my stool. "I know you're tired, but can we talk about your father for just a minute?"

Suddenly she cupped her hands over her face and wept. I touched her shoulder and we sat like that, and after a while, when she was ready, she told me what had happened. Of course the old bastard had sold her books: to him they were nothing. "He never read a book in his life," she said. "He couldn't have cared less. He got thirty dollars for all of them and drank that up in a week."

"Was there a paper, any kind of legal document?"

"None that I ever saw."

Of course not—who makes up a paper for a thirty-dollar deal? But if money had changed hands it was legal, and who after eighty years could prove that it was not?

"He was told they weren't worth anything—they were just junk books. Doesn't that make it a fraud? And what *right* did he have to sell them? They weren't his to sell."

This was yet another legal mess. What had the law said in 1906, when a woman still couldn't vote, about a man's right to his wife's property? Specifically, what had the law in *Maryland* said in those days of such enlightenment?

I felt the beginnings of a headache. There were still questions to ask, all leading nowhere, I knew, but I had to ask them. I made some notes and when I looked up, Mrs. Gallant had begun to teeter in the chair. I put my hand on her arm and then Ralston was there, holding her steady. "That's all for now, Janeway," he said, and there was no nonsense in his voice: we were finished.

We talked for a moment about what to do. "She'll come home with me," Ralston said. "It ain't the Brown Palace, but she can rest easy till Denise gets home."

We helped her out to the car. Ralston gave me a paper with his telephone number and told me to call him later. I leaned down and spoke to her through the open window. "One last question, ma'am. Do you have any idea who bought those books?"

"Yes, of course. He was looking for fast money, so he sold them to a bookstore."

There it was, the only ray of light in what had so far been a damned hopeless story. If a book dealer had bought that entire library for thirty dollars, even allowing for the much cheaper values of the time, it had certainly been one hell of a fraud. But what did that matter now? Like Richard Burton and Charlie Warren, like her mother and father, the garbageman and his horse, Gallant, the Boise relatives, and all the others, that bookseller would have died a long time ago.

Then she said something that hit me like a slap. "When I think of those awful book people—those Treadwells—how can they live with themselves?"

It was the hint of present tense that turned my head around.

"Mrs. Gallant . . . are you telling me that place is still in business?"

"Of course it is, it's been there forever. Haven't you ever heard of Treadwell's? It's a den of thieves, passed down in the same rotten family for a hundred years."

If I had spent more time on the road I might have known about Treadwell's. A bookman who travels always picks up local scuttle-butt, and one who travels constantly eventually knows everything about everybody. The notorious get reputations, and booksellers do love to talk candidly with a colleague they can trust.

In an hour I had made six calls to dealers I knew around the country, and I had several pages of notes on Treadwell's Books. I had its address, its phone number, and a good description of its general lay-out. Its Yellow Pages ad boasted of two million books on three large floors in an old redbrick building on Eastern Avenue just off South Broadway, in an area of downtown Baltimore not far from Johns Hopkins Hospital. Over the years I had been in so many bookstores like that, I could almost see it. Dark stairwells, creaky floors, narrow aisles, deep and dusty shelves. Books double- and triple-shelved, books stacked on end, piled on top of the overflowing bookcases, with another overflow on the floor at the end of each section. Books on every conceivable subject and a few on topics nobody could have imagined. It was possible in such a store that some of the titles in the back rows of each section had not been touched in decades.

The store's history was colorful and long. It stretched back across much of the century and had spawned generations of bookpeople, beginning with old Dedrick Treadwell, the king of knaves in that turn-of-the-century book world. The Treadwells had always had a dubious reputation in the book world. "They'd pay as much as any-body if they were bidding against other dealers and the books were good," said a bookman in the D.C. area who knew them well. "But if it's just them and some poor know-nothing who's just inherited a houseful of books . . . Well, I'm not one to call another man a crook . . . let's just say I've heard stories, and let it go at that."

In his early days, old man Treadwell had operated out of various hole-in-a-wall shops. In the early thirties he had leased the building on Eastern Avenue with an option to buy. He had clearly set his sights on bigger game, and soon he and his son were sucking up books by the tens of thousands, all over the East Coast. They were voracious buyers, insatiable raptors of the book trade. "God knows how many books that we now consider classic and sell for four figures were blown out of there for nickels and dimes then," one dealer said. They were of the turn-'em-fast school: buy cheap, sell cheap, get the cash, move on, and buy some more.

I love stores like that: I can spend hours and thousands of dollars in those dusty, half-lit book dungeons. But they are becoming severely endangered as rents go ever higher and downtown space is consumed by high-traffic, high-profit enterprises. Soon they will be like the people of Margaret Mitchell's Old South, no more than a dream half-remembered.

The first Treadwell must have imagined the trends decades ago. He bought the building and his son had sons and flourished there. They rode out the Depression, the war years were good, and the postwar even better. The second generation died and a third came along. A few of them stayed in the trade; most left to find, they hoped, a brighter future elsewhere. Today the managing partners were brothers of the fourth generation, Dean and Carl Treadwell. I got good descriptions of both from a dealer in Chicago. "Dean is a big, burly fellow with a beard," my friend said. "Carl is a smaller guy, quieter, but you get the feeling there's a lot going on with Carl—some anger, maybe even an occasional original thought. Carl gives you the feeling of still water running deep, and Dean would rather come off as a hail-fellow-well-met, salt-of-the-earth type. Dean likes to pretend they're just rubes, but make no mistake, there are two cunning minds under all that bull-shit he puts on. And they do know their books."

Maybe so, but in the current generation, Treadwell's had suddenly fallen on hard times. "Carl's the culprit," said the guy in Washington. "You didn't hear it here, but he's gotten himself into bad company—gamblers, thugs, the Baltimore mob. Gangsters may even own a piece of that store now. I heard Carl lost his pants in a poker game last year."

"You should get out more," said my friend in Chicago. "Everybody knows about the Treadwells."

For another hour I meditated over what I had learned. There have always been a few crooks in the trade. As one old bookman put it, there's a bad apple in every town. Sometimes he's an obvious con man dripping with charm. He may be the cold thief who walks casually out of a bookstore with a ten-volume Conan Doyle tucked into every inch of his pants, coat, and shirt, the signed volume crammed desperately into some dank body cavity, and immediately finds another bookseller eager to hold his nose and buy it, fifty cents on the dollar, no questions asked. He is also that rival bookseller who must know a hot book when he sees one. He wears more faces than Lon Chaney in the best of his times. He's the sweet-faced kid who jacket-clips worthless book club editions and sells them as firsts to the Simon Pure collector. Occasionally he's a renegade, thriving on intimidation and operating from the trunk of a car. He may be any kind of personality, but that glitch in his character keeps him working the shady side of the street forever. His spots never change.

As I grew into my business I learned how gray it all is. There is such an eye-of-the-beholder mentality in the book trade that it plays perfectly into the hands of the enemy. What *must* be paid as a rock-bottom minimum to keep it just above the level of fraud? Should it matter if a two-hundred-dollar book is in tiny demand compared with a book that sells easily for the same two hundred? How much may be deducted for condition, and by whose standard must condition be measured? We don't like to admit it but the flimflam man has a trait that's all too common to the rest of us. The degree of his crookedness is a wild variant, and our own generosity can vary as much from one of us to the next.

It's no wonder that the trade is such a warm, fertile place for pond scum; what's amazing is how little of it you actually find there. Most dealers pay 30 to 40 percent, straight across the board, which is certainly decent, considering the overhead. Many do scale back what they pay because they may have those books for years. Some of them may never sell. And there's one thing that will always separate us from a cheese-pushing hose artist: we never lie on either end, buying or selling, and he *always* lies—on either end, both ends, and in the middle.

How different my own life might have been. Only some quirk in my character had kept me from becoming what I now despised. I could be rich now on crooked money. I had seldom seen Vince Marranzino since the old days but that possibility had been rife between us. On another night he had stepped out of a big touring car with a wicked-looking sidekick. I'd opened the door, hiding the apprehension I felt, and Vince embraced me like some godfather out of Mario Puzo. I'd slapped his back. He was still hard and tough, and the scar on his face had deepened where long ago a young hood had gashed him with a broken beer bottle. Thinking of him now, his scars reminded me of Richard Burton.

The muscle had waited on the sidewalk while Vince and I talked. Now he was called Vinnie, but I could still call him Vince. He remembered old debts and I could call him anything I wanted. *Only you can call me that old name, Cliffie.*

He knew his presence made me uneasy. But he'd had to come: he'd seen the newspaper stories about my fall from grace, and he wanted to help me square things.

He'd looked around him and said, *You like this book racket?*

Yeah, I do.

You wanna buy some real books?

I dunno, Vince. What would I have to do for 'em?

Just let me throw a little work your way. I've got a job now, you could do it in a week. Make you fifty, seventy-five grand. Buy all the goddamn books you want for that.

Well, I'd said, smiling. *That would be a start, anyway.*

But I'd said no thanks without hearing what the job was.

Vince had looked disgusted. *Hey you, you big bazooka, when are you gonna let me square accounts with you?*

We're square now, Vince. You don't owe me anything.

But I had once saved his life and he shook his head sadly. To a man like Vince, that account could never be squared with words alone.

He'd gripped my arm. *Strong as ever, ain'tcha, Cliff? Bet I can throw your ass.*

I'd laughed. *I'll bet you can.*

When I looked up again the afternoon had faded. It was five-fifteen and no word from Erin. I faced the fact that she wasn't coming.

It was two hours later in Baltimore, probably too late to call Treadwell's—assuming I had some valid excuse, or could think of one, or could say anything that sounded at all real. I was caught up in an old cop's impulse: I wanted to hear the man's voice, so I picked up the phone and punched in the number.

It rang, five times . . . six. Nobody there, just as I thought, and just as well. Then I heard a click on the other end, and a woman's voice. "Hi, Treadwell's."

"Is Treadwell there?"

"Which one?"

"Whoever's handy."

She said, "Justa minute, hon," and I was put on hold. Well, I was into it now: nothing to do but hang up or play it out. There was no elevator music, nothing but that dead-flat line to help me while away the hours. How many times had I done this as a cop, made a cold call with no plan of action and only a hunch to go on? Sometimes it worked out fine, and if there was a compelling reason to pussyfoot around with these guys, I couldn't see it.

Long minutes later I heard the phone click again, and suddenly there was a faint hum on the line. Almost at once the man spoke: "This's Dean."

"Hey, Dean," I said in my best good-old-boy voice. "I was referred to you as a possible source for some books I want to find."

"Well, whoever sent you got one thing right—I got books. You buying 'em by the pound or the ton? Or are you interested in something particular?"

I laughed politely. "The last book I bought by the ton was an Oxford textbook on erectile dysfunction."

He bellowed into the phone, a raspy laugh followed by a hacking smoker's cough. "Buddy, if you've got that problem, ain't no book gonna cure it. Might as well slice off the old ginger root and donate it to medical research."

"Jesus, Dean, don't jump to that conclusion. That book was for a friend of mine."

He laughed again. "Yeah, right. So listen, what the hell can I do for you?"

"I heard through the grapevine you might have some books by Richard Burton. I'm talking about real stuff, you know what I mean?"

I thought the pause was long enough to be significant. He coughed again and said, "What grapevine did you hear that through?"

"Oh, you know . . . here and there. The main question is whether it's true."

This time the pause was long enough to be halftime at the Rose Bowl. After a while I said, "Dean? You still with me?"

"Yeah, I'm here. Just trying to think what I might have. We got a lot of books here, pal. I gave up long ago trying to keep track of it all."

"I don't think you'd have any trouble keeping track of this stuff. You got a rare book room, I imagine you'd know what's in it, right? I mean, this isn't like the two million books you put out on the open shelves."

"Easy for you to say. You got two million books?"

"Hell no, thank God."

I waited. I heard the sound of a cigarette being lit. I heard him blow smoke. "Where you calling from?"

"I'm on the road. Trying to decide if it's worth my time and energy to come all the way out to the coast."

"And you're a serious buyer, right?"

"Serious enough to make your day." I decided to lie a little for the cause. "Maybe your month, if you've got what I want."

"We might still have something, I'm not sure."

Still? A damned significant word, I thought. He said, "I'll have to check and call you back. What's your name?"

Screw it, I thought: let's see where this goes. "Cliff Janeway."

"The guy in Denver?"

"I can't believe how that story got around."

"Yeah. You'll have to tell me who the hell your press agent is."

"His last name's luck. First name's dumb."

"I could use some of that."

"Maybe you're having it right now, Dean," I said with a nice touch of arrogance.

"Yeah, we'll see. I'm sure you know if I did have something like that, it wouldn't be at any dealer's prices. I wouldn't want you to come all the way here thinking there'd be a lot of margin in a book like that."

"I'm used to that. I didn't pay a dealer's price in Boston, either."

"Okay, so where are we? You want to call me back?"

"Yeah, sure. You say when."

"How about tomorrow, about this same time."

"You got it. Good talking to you, Dean."

I hung up and sat there quietly, thinking about it.

About ten minutes later the phone rang. When I answered it, nobody was there.

Actually, somebody *was* there. For a moment I could hear him breathing, then he covered the phone to cough. And there was that faint hum on the line.

Dean.

My new old buddy, Dean Treadwell. The last of the good old boys, checking up on me.

Now he knew I'd been lying. I wasn't on the road at all, was I?

I heard the click as he hung up the phone. The hum went away and the line went dead.

It was now twilight time, the beginning of my long nightly journey through the dark. For the moment the Treadwell business had played itself out. I didn't want to leave it there, but there it sat, spreading its discontent. I didn't want to go home. I didn't want to call a friend, catch a movie, do a crossword puzzle. I sure as hell didn't want to sit in a bar full of strangers as an alternative to Erin d'Angelo's luminous presence. When all else fails I usually work on books, but that night I didn't want to do that, either.

In fact, I didn't know what I wanted. I seemed to have reached a major turning point in my life as a bookman. I look back at that time as my true watershed, more significant than even the half-blind leap that had brought me straight into the trade from homicide. Today I believe I was shaped by that entire half year. Even then I sensed that I was moving from my common retail base into something new, yet for most of my waking hours I had doubts that I would ever get anywhere. This must be what a writer goes through when he's groping his way into a book. I think it was Doctorow who said that about the writing process—it's like driving a car across country at night and all you can ever see is what's immediately in your headlights, but you can make the whole journey that way. Maybe the book trade was like that. I had always been a slow learner, but already there had been wondrous moments when suddenly I *understood,* after months of plodding, some tiny piece of the enormous world I had come to. *A-ha! A bit of knowledge!* A leap of faith so striking that it sometimes took my breath away.

This was never greater than in those two weeks of 1987. I had

bought the Burton, which I now know was the catalyst. Millie, my
gal Friday, was off on vacation and I had been forced into the
annoying business of minding the store. Richard Burton had fired
me up and old Mrs. Gallant had stirred me up, but on a conscious
level all I had was the annoying hunch that I might work till dawn;
that, and how I'd explain to Dean why I'd lied to him, when I called
him tomorrow.

My working domain was normally the back room, but in my
solitude I wanted to be where I could at least see the lights of the
street. I brought up my stuff and sat at the counter, but I couldn't get
my mind into it. I stared at my reference books and for a long time
I just sat there and waited for my mood to change.

The book world was very different then. In 1987 it was real work
to research even simple book problems. We were still in the earliest
days of the Internet: the vast, sweeping changes that have come over
us had barely begun, and none of us knew how crazy it would get.
Points and values on unfamiliar books still had to be searched out the
old way, in bibliographies and specialists' catalogs, and with some,
you finally had to go on a gut feeling. Knowledge was rewarded by
the system: you put out your books, took your chances, and if another
bookseller knew more than you did, he scored on your mistake.
Today any unwashed nitwit can look into a computer and pull out
a price. Whether the price is proper, whether it's even the same
edition—these questions, once of major importance, have begun to
pale as bookscouts and flea markets and even junk shops rush onto
the Internet to play bookseller. They love to say things like "The Internet has equalized the playing field," but all they do is cannibalize the
other fellow's off-the-wall prices for books of dubious lineage and
worth. They want to play without paying any dues, now or ever. They
have no reference books to back up their assertions and they'd never
pay more than pocket change for anything. They wheel and deal but
they care about nothing but price. The computer may have leveled the
playing field in one sense—it's a great device for revealing what people around the world are asking and paying for certain books—but in

this year of grace it will not tell you, reliably, how to identify a true American first of *One Hundred Years of Solitude*.

In those early Internet years I posted an epigram over my desk: *A book is a mirror. If an ass peers into it, you can't expect an apostle to look out.* That was written two centuries ago by a German wit named Lichtenberg, but I think the same applies today to a computer screen.

I had just ordered my supper from Pizza Hut when I heard the tap on my window. I turned and there she was, the Gibson girl incarnate. Those incredible eyes. That lovely smiling face, so loaded with mischief. I leaped up and toppled my stool. My crazy heart went with it, a mad tumble that had happened with only one other woman. The great adventure of love, more thrilling and perilous than a man with a gun: I had given up the notion of ever knowing it again.

6

I fumbled with my keys and dropped them. Lurched over to pick them up, missed them in the dark, and almost fell on my ass. Had to go back for them, groping around on the floor. So far my performance was falling far short of the cool image I always project to the opposite sex. She stood outside, striking a pose of vast impatience. Looked at her watch. Tapped her foot while I got the key into the hole and opened the door.

"Sorry, I'm closed," I said, regaining my cool.

"That's okay, I'm just the gas girl, here to read your meter."

I almost laughed at that but recovered in time to make a phony cough of it. "You'll have to make it fast, I'm expecting someone."

"No one special, I take it, from the look of you."

"Just read the meter, miss, and let's hold the fashion critique. This has been a hard day."

"Obviously. A white sport coat indeed."

"I wore it till the pink carnation began gasping for air and turning green around the gills. There came a point when I had to figure that the girl of my dreams just wasn't going to show."

"You have no faith. I had you pegged from the start. All pop, no fizz."

"My faith was like the Prudential rock until an hour ago."

"That's not nearly good enough when I expected so much more of you. I take it from your wardrobe that we're going someplace fancy. Burger King or Taco Bell? Do I get to choose?"

"Actually, I just . . . um . . . kinda . . . ordered a pizza."

She laughed out loud at that.

"I'll bet I can cancel it," I said. "I just this minute ordered it."

"A *pizza*! And I'll bet it's a pizza for *one*."

"I can have them make another one," I said in the wimpiest voice I could put on.

She sighed deeply. "I guess you might as well. Oh, chivalry, where art thou? I'll tell you this much, sir, Sir Richard Burton rests unchallenged in his tomb tonight."

She browsed my shelves while I made the call.

"No anchovies," she yelled from New Arrivals.

I appeared suddenly at her side. "How'd your case go?"

"We lost but we knew we would. Anything else would have put us all in the hospital from shock. Now we've got something we can appeal, take it out of cowboy heaven."

"Want to tell me about it?"

"Maybe sometime. Right now I'm so happy to be out of there I don't even want to think about it. I drove straight through from Rock Springs. As of this time last night, I'm on vacation . . . three glorious weeks to write, contemplate, and recover."

After a moment, she said, "I thought of calling around three o'clock, in case you actually were standing here in some goofy white sport coat. Then I thought no, this would be more fun. Arrive when all hope is lost. See if you're still here. Razz you a bit. How's it working so far?"

"I'm getting pretty damned annoyed, if you want to know the truth."

"Miranda should have told you, I'm a card-carrying member of Lunatics Anonymous. We Loonies see the world as one big insane asylum. Our goal is to laugh at everything. If I don't find some kind of laughter in all this chaos, I've got to cry, and I hate that. So I make fun of the handicapped. Tell racially insensitive jokes. Put down those who are already oppressed."

A moment later she said, "I'm kidding."

"I knew that."

"I figured you did. Right from the start you seemed to be as crazy as I am."

"I must have compared wonderfully to the stuffed shirt you were driving that night."

When she said nothing to that, I said, "Did I step on professional toes there?"

"Would it matter?"

"Of course. Mr. Archer may be a jerk on a world scale, but I no longer feel any uncontrollable compulsion to say so."

"Don't bite your tongue on my account. Just be aware that an escort who speaks ill of her client soon has no clients to speak of. So I may not participate in the verbal dismemberment."

"Whatever you say, my lips are sealed."

"In that case, yes, Archer's right up there among the most pompous asses that the ill winds of New York have ever blown my way."

"As much as it grieves me to say it, he's actually a very good writer. He was one of the modern authors I liked best . . ."

"Until you met him."

"That does take away some of his sex appeal. What're you doing driving authors around?"

"Didn't Miranda tell you? She told me you asked."

"Miranda is proving to be an untrustworthy confidante."

"Oh, it doesn't matter. I got into the author tours early, for spending money in college. Now I don't need the spending money so it must be the intellectual stimulation."

"So if you're driving the author of *The Hungry Man's Diet Book,* or the guy who wrote *Six Ways to Profit from the Coming Nuclear War,* what kind of stimulation do you get from that?"

"I don't drive those authors."

"Must be nice to pick and choose."

"The woman who owns the agency became one of my best friends. When I see who's coming through, I can put in a request if it's someone I like."

"But this time you got stuck with Archer."

"No, I asked for him."

"Couldn't be his personality. Must be because he's an old friend of the judge."

"I don't remember saying that. You sure jump to a lot of conclusions."

"I'm trying to get you properly placed in the cosmos and you're giving me no help at all. Are you saying you knew Archer was a pompous ass and still you asked for him?"

"Life is strange, isn't it?"

She found a layer of dust, flicked it away, and said, "You need a woman's touch in here."

Before I could answer that, she said, "If it wasn't Archer I wanted to meet that night, who could it be? God knows it couldn't be you."

I did a beating heart gesture that made her smile.

She said, "I had already met Mr. Archer on a couple of occasions. I lived with Lee and Miranda for several years when I was growing up, so I already had a pretty good line on Archer. Didn't Miranda tell you that?"

I made a gesture: *I don't remember.*

"Oh, you're impossible," she said.

"Depends on what you've got in mind." I cleared my throat. "So what happens if you think you'll like an author, then he gets here and you can't stand him?"

"I try to show some class. Sometimes it's tough but I try to remember who I'm working for, just as you considered Lee and Miranda that night when you were so tempted to call Archer whatever you were tempted to call him. I never put the agency in an embarrassing position."

"So you get your choice of jobs, and still you drive Archer."

"Be nice to me and maybe someday I'll tell you why."

"Then let's move on, as you lawyers like to say. You look at my books while I walk up the street and get us a really cheap bottle of wine to go with this grand feast we're about to have."

I bought a fine bottle of wine, but the liquor store, which always stocked corkscrews, failed me tonight and I had to settle for a cheap bottle with a screw top. I kept the good stuff to prove my intentions but I knew I was in for some joshing. So far I was batting a thousand.

We ate in the front room with only a distant light, a pair of shadows to anyone passing on the street. The screwball mood had deserted us for the moment, and what we now had was a spell of cautious probing. Was she really writing a novel? Yes, and she was serious about it, she had fifty thousand words as of yesterday. She was a light sleeper and there had been lots of time to work on it in the middle of the bleak Rock Springs nights. The law filled her days and she escorted for a woman named Lisa Beaumont, who usually had others she could call in a rush.

She had always loved books—new, old, it really didn't matter. Even as a teenager she'd had dreams of doing what I did. "I knew a fellow long ago who showed me the charm of older books. He wanted to be a rare-book seller, just like you." But what about me? What was it really like in the book trade? It could certainly be boring, but you never knew what might walk in the door the next minute and turn the day into something extraordinary. She cocked her head in bright interest—*Like what, for instance?*—and the next thing I knew I was telling her about Mrs. Gallant, the whole bloody story beginning with my trip to Boston. "Wow," she said at the end of it. "So what are you going to do for her?"

"Whatever I can, which won't be much. Eighty years is a long time."

"A long time," she echoed. "But wouldn't it be great if you could find those books?"

"Oh yeah. It'd be great to win the Nobel Peace Prize while I'm at it."

"Don't make light of it. You could actually do this, if the books are still together. Then you could retire in utter glory. What else would you need to do in your career after that?"

"Oh, just the little stuff, like make a living."

"That's the trouble with the world today: there's too much emphasis on money."

"Spoken like one who has money to burn."

"Don't harass me, Janeway, I'm composing your mission statement."

We slipped back into cautious probing. Yes, she said with pointed annoyance, she did have a little money saved up. They paid her well at Waterford, Brownwell, Taylor and Waterford, where her office faced the mountains on the twenty-third floor and she was said to be on the fast track to make partner. They liked her, they were doing everything they could to keep her happy, but her heart wasn't in it anymore. "I wonder how I'd like what you do."

Who could say? Some of the smartest people never do get it—they have no idea about the intrigue that can hide in the lineage of a book, or the drama that can erupt between two people when a truly rare one comes between them. I quoted Rosenbach—*The thrill of knocking a man down in the ring is nothing compared with the thrill of knocking him down over a book*—and she smiled. But there are many quieter thrills in the book world. The bottomless nature of it. The certainty of surprise, even for a specialist. The sudden enlightenment, the pockets of history that can open without warning and turn a bookman toward new fields of passionate interest. Wasn't that what had just happened with me and Richard Burton?

"I think I'd love it," she said. "You want a partner?"

"Sure. I figure a fifty percent interest should be worth at least, oh, thirty or forty bucks. But you won't have an office on the twenty-third floor."

She asked for the grand tour as if we were serious, and I walked her through the store. I pointed out its attributes and shortcomings, and it took us twenty minutes to see every nook and cranny. We ended up back in the dark corner of the front room, where my best books were.

She looked up at me. "I guess before we seal this partnership we need to know more about each other. I'll start. How much has Miranda already told you?"

"Nothing."

"Lying's not a good way to begin, Janeway. And you don't do it very well."

"Actually, I'm a pretty good liar when I need to be."

"You're good at stalling too."

"You must be a killer on cross."

"I sure am, so stay on the point: what Miranda told you and why."

"She told me nothing. Nothing, as in no real thing, *nada*, caput."

"Why do I get the feeling she told you about my dad?"

"I don't know, maybe you're a suspicious creature whose instincts are to trust nobody. All she said was that Lee and your father were partners and you lived with them after he died."

She leaned into the light. "My father was an embezzler." Then she was back in the shadows, her voice coming out of the void. "My dad was a crook."

"Those are mighty unforgiving words, Erin."

"There can be no forgiveness for what he did. He stole from his client."

She took a deep breath and said, "When I was little my dad was my hero. He was funny and smart: he could do no wrong. I never wanted to be anything but a lawyer, just like him."

I told her I was sorry. Sometimes people fall short of what we want them to be.

"I was thirteen when it came out. The worst possible age. In school I heard talk every day. The humiliation was brutal. I wanted to run away and change my name but Lee talked me out of that."

"Lee's a smart man."

"Lee is a great man. He knew what I needed was not to deny my name but to restore it. I don't know what I'd have done if not for him. Did you know they put me through law school?"

I shook my head. "Miranda did say they couldn't be prouder of what you've done."

"Well, now I've done it. I made all the honor rolls, got a great job, paid them back. My father's not just dead, he's really buried, and I don't need to do it anymore."

Abruptly she changed the subject. "Your turn. Bet you're glad you're not still a cop."

"There's nothing wrong with being a cop. There are some fine people who are cops."

"I know that."

After an awkward pause, she said, "Look, I know what happened to you back then. I read all the stories and if any of it mattered to me, I wouldn't be here now. I like you. You make me laugh. And just for the record, I like the police too. Most of the time."

"Then we're cool."

She flashed me that lovely smile. "We're cool, man."

I wondered how cool we were, but at that moment the phone rang.

It was Ralston, taking a chance I'd still be here. "Can you come up to my house? Mrs. Gallant wants to see you."

"Sure. How about first thing in the morning?"

I had a dark hunch what he would say, just before he said it.

"You'd better come now. I think she's dying."

7

The address he gave me was in Globeville, a racially mixed North Denver neighborhood, mostly Chicanos and blacks who had escaped the stigma of being poor, if they actually did, by the skin of their teeth. Globeville had none of the fashionably integrated charm of Park Hill, but at least it had avoided the ethnic rage that simmered in Five Points a few years back. The area had its own distinct character: bordered by Interstates 25 and 70, formed by people struggling to get along, defined by a school of architecture best described as modern crackerbox provincial, it was a few dozen square blocks of plain square houses and cyclone fences, crammed tight for maximum efficiency.

Erin knew Globeville well. "I had a client who lived in that house," she said, gesturing as we turned off North Washington Street. "Classic case of a woman who desperately needed a man gone from her life. But *no*body was gonna tell *him* what to do with *his* woman."

"Until you came along," I said with genuine admiration.

"Me and the Denver Sheriff's Department. She already had a restraining order, they just didn't want to bother enforcing it. Because she was black, because she was poor, because, because, because. I just became her instrument to get them off the dime."

"That doesn't seem like a case for Waterford, Brownwell."

"It was pro bono. They were less than thrilled when I took it, but I do that once in a while. It keeps my head on straight, reminds me why I got into law in the first place, and lets them know they can't send me to places like Rock Springs without consequences."

She had offered to ride along because she found Mrs. Gallant's story fascinating, and second, she said, "to see where your idea of a real date finally takes us." Ralston's house was on North Pennsylvania, half a block from East Forty-seventh Avenue. By the time we arrived, not a trace of light remained in the western sky. I pulled up behind his car and saw his bearlike silhouette in the doorway. He pushed open a screened door as we came up onto the porch.

I introduced Erin as a friend and her hand disappeared into his. We walked through a small living room with the sparest imaginable furnishings—no television, I noticed—and on into the kitchen. There was a rickety-looking table, four plain chairs, a cupboard, and straight ahead the door to the backyard. Off to the right, a short passageway led to the bathroom and beyond that was apparently the only other room in the house, their bedroom.

"Is she in there?"

He nodded. "Denise is in with her. Sit down, she knows you're here."

We sat at the table and Ralston offered coffee. He caught me looking around at his raggedy surroundings. "I told you it wasn't the Brown."

"It's fine," I said. "I was just wondering where you two planned to sleep tonight."

"We'll get by. Won't be the first time we bagged it on the floor."

I nodded toward the door. "What happened?"

"She just all of a sudden gave out. Her old heart decided it had enough."

"Did you call a doctor?"

He shook his head. "She didn't want us to."

A long moment passed.

"I know what you're thinking," he said. "It seems indecent to let her die when help is just a phone call away. But you've got to ask yourself what the hell you're saving her for—to be sent back to that place, just so she can die next month instead of now? She hated it there, you know."

"That's not exactly what I was thinking. In fact, I agree with everything you're saying. But I used to be a cop and in situations like this, I still think like one."

"Are you saying we could be *prosecuted*? Man, that would figure, wouldn't it?"

"I never had a negligent homicide." I looked at Erin. "Isn't that what this would be?"

She nodded. "Criminally negligent homicide would probably be the statute."

"Jesus." Ralston looked at Erin and said, "You a lawyer?"

She nodded and I said, "She's a real lawyer, Mike. Be glad she's here."

"It's a fairly straightforward law," she said. "If you cause a death by your failure to act, it could conceivably be prosecuted as a class-five felony. That's very unlikely to happen, but you should be aware of the possibilities." She shrugged. "An aggressive DA . . ."

"Jesus," he said again. "The woman just wants to die a natural death, for God's sake, without having tubes running out of her nose for three months. What's the law got to do with that?"

"You're like me," I told him: "all fire, no ice. You leap before you look. You do a pretty good job of keeping the fire contained, but it's always there simmering, isn't it?"

He walked to the window and looked out into the backyard.

"Sit down and talk to me," I said. "You make me nervous, pacing around."

He sat and I made the universal gesture for *Go ahead, speak*. But when he did, it was not about the old woman's life, it was about her quest. "Have you asked yourself what she really wants? I mean, what can she hope to gain from this search she's taken on? Even if she found it all tonight and could legally sell it, what good would it do her?"

"It's hard to tell what she's thinking. Maybe she's got someone to leave it to."

"But in the end it doesn't matter, does it? It's pretty hopeless, what she's asking you to do."

I sighed. "Yeah, it is."

I brought him up to speed on my talk with Dean Treadwell, but we both knew that the odds of anything coming from that bookstore were less than the snowball in hell. It was still raw speculation, we were spinning our wheels, but at the moment there was nothing else to do. There was no hint yet that Mrs. Ralston was ready to let me into the bedroom.

"This is great coffee," Erin said. "What do you do to it?"

Ralston smiled. "That's my secret, miss. I'm a gourmet cook by trade."

"I'm learning all kinds of stuff about you tonight, Mike," I said. "So what's the story of you two? You and the missus."

Again he gave me that humorless laugh. "How much time you got?"

The question seemed to beg itself out of easy answers, but then he had one. "The easy answer is, I screwed up everything I ever touched. I drank, gambled, lost everything. Hell, look around you. We are starting from scratch. I've got nothing but that woman sittin' in there at the old lady's bedside, but that's enough. And that's the story of us. Since you asked."

I heard a stir and Denise appeared in the doorway. She was at least in her late forties, a good ten years older than Ralston: tall, gangly, black as night, homely as hell yet lovely in an exotic way that had nothing to do with what the world thinks of as beauty. She had a satchel mouth to rival Louis Armstrong's, and when she smiled, she lit up a room.

"Mr. Janeway. I'm so glad you're here."

I got to my feet. "Mrs. Ralston."

I introduced Erin and they had a warm exchange. She insisted at once on being called Denise. Her hand was warm in mine and I liked her eyes. I liked her face, which reflected a heart that I knew I'd also like. She said, "I think we'd better go right on in," and her voice managed to ask and tell at the same time, *steady as it goes, boys,* with just a hint of a French accent. "I don't think we have much time," she said.

Erin backed away from the door. "I'll just sit out here at the table."

The bedroom was cool, bathed in a soothing orange light from a lamp at the side of the bed. Mrs. Gallant lay with her eyes half-closed, but again that second sense, her instinct, *something* told her I was there. Her eyelids fluttered. I felt Denise at my side and for a crazy moment I had a sense that I had merged with these remarkable women, all of us standing in some single spirit outside ourselves. Denise touched my arm, moving me to the bedside. Mrs. Gallant said, "Mr. Janeway," and I sat in the chair beside her.

"Hey, Mrs. G. You're not feeling so hot, huh?"

"Not so hot. I've really messed things up here, haven't I?"

"You have made life very interesting for all of us. We're very glad you came to us."

"I can't imagine. But somehow I believe you." She turned her head. "Is Denise here?"

"She's right behind me."

"I can't see that far. Mr. Ralston?"

Ralston loomed out of the shadows. "Yes, ma'am?"

"I want you to promise me something. It's none of my business but that's one of the prerogatives of very great age—you get to meddle in other people's affairs."

"You meddle all you want, ma'am."

"Just . . . take good care of this wonderful girl. She is very special."

"I do know that, ma'am."

"Denise?"

She came up and took the old woman's hand.

"Did you tell Mr. Janeway about the picture?"

"Not yet."

"There used to be a photograph tucked into my book. A picture that proves what I'm saying. It shows Charlie and Richard together, in Charleston."

"What happened to it?"

She looked distressed. "I don't know. It vanished long ago, like everything else. But I remember it. Koko knows."

"Koko?"

"Yes. Koko can tell you."

She turned her face up to Denise. "You're such a grand girl. I wish you were my daughter."

Denise grinned. "Maybe I am."

Mrs. Gallant made a sad little laughing sound. "Wouldn't that have shocked the stuffing out of my proper old Baltimore family?"

A moment passed. The old woman said, "Besides, you're not old enough."

Another moment. "Where's my book?"

"It's right here." Denise got it from a table beside the bed.

"Give it to Mr. Janeway."

I took the book and put it on my lap.

"It's yours now."

I started to protest, but Denise squeezed my arm and shook her head. Mrs. Gallant said, "I want you to have it, but it's not an outright gift. I want you to make an effort to find the others."

"Okay," I said cautiously.

"I always had an idea they should be together, in some library in my grandfather's name. If you do that—exhaust all the possibilities you can think of—you may keep this book. But I want you to share what you get for it with Denise."

"Okay," I said again.

"That's all," she said.

But it wasn't all. A huge weight had settled over me, and it wasn't enough to sit here stupidly and say okay, okay, okay. I had a chance to make a dying woman's death so much more peaceful, if I had the guts to do it. I mustered my courage and said, "I'll find those books, Mrs. Gallant, I promise. I will find them."

She smiled. "I knew you would."

Suddenly she said, "I'm very tired, Denise."

She reached for my hand. "It was good knowing you, sonny."

These were her last words. She slipped into sleep and died three hours later.

8

There is always red tape when someone dies. First a doctor must be summoned: someone who can certify that the person is in fact dead and has died of natural causes. The coroner must be called, and if all goes well, the body is released to a funeral home. I was impressed with the Ralstons' personal physician, first that he was reachable and then that he was willing to make a house call at that time of night. He arrived at midnight, a youngish black man radiating competence. He and Ralston were old pals: like Lee Huxley and Hal Archer, they had been kids together, and maybe that explained his willingness to go that extra mile.

Denise showed him into the room while Ralston and Erin and I sat at the table and worked on a second pot of coffee. I asked Erin if she wanted me to call her a cab but she seemed not at all tired and she wanted to stay. When they rejoined us, the doctor and Denise had obviously been talking and the doctor had a good grasp of why the old woman was there and what had happened. There were a few questions for me and I told him about the Burton, which lay on the table in open view through all the talk.

"This is a valuable book?"

"It's quite valuable," I said. "My best guess would be somewhere around twenty, twenty-five thousand."

"And she gave it to you—the two of you to split equally? But there was no paper signed."

"George," Denise said in a long-suffering tone, "could you really see me doing that—asking that dying woman for a paper?"

"No," the doctor said, smiling. "I'm just trying to head off trouble. If there are any questions about why you did what you did . . ."

"I'm a witness," Erin said. "I heard everything she said."

The doctor made some notes and seemed satisfied. Then came the call to the coroner's twenty-four-hour hot line, and on the doctor's say-so the body was released. Nobody was going to question the death of a woman in her nineties unless there was something very suspicious about it. The doctor made another call and soon a man arrived in a hearse. I asked if he needed any help and he said, "Oh, I got her, gov." He took up the old woman in his arms, as fondly as if she'd been a favored great-aunt, and carried her to the hearse.

Next came the paperwork. Who would be responsible for the bills? "I will," I said. "You'll probably have to check with the home where she was living; they may have made some kind of arrangement or legally binding contract. But I will guarantee payment."

We talked about what kind of funeral she would have if Denver turned out to be her final stop. She might have gone to an unmarked plot in a potter's field with a plywood coffin, but I wanted her to have a plaque and a place of her own. This was strange since I had never cared much about funerals. I don't care where they put me; in terms of eternity, it doesn't matter much, but suddenly the tariff had leaped into four figures and I was okay with it. The man took my credit card number, the doctor went home, and for now that was that. Erin and I stood on the street with the Ralstons in the early morning and watched the hearse drive away.

None of us wanted to separate: not quite then, not quite that way. Ralston suggested a simple wake. "I don't mean to be disrespectful of the departed," he said, "but I am hungry as hell."

We all were. The pizza I had shared with Erin seemed like a distant meal indeed, and I suggested we all go down to Colfax, where the all-night eating places were. Denise wouldn't hear of it. "We will cook something. Michael is a gourmet cook, did you know that?"

"I told them," Ralston said. "It's gonna be hard to make anything decent with what we've got. We got some eggs and milk; I could make a simple omelet but that's about all. If y'all don't mind waiting, I could go out and get some better stuff."

"I'll get the stuff," I said. "You fire up the stove, give me a list of what you need, and I'll be back in a while."

He directed me to the nearest all-night Safeway. "You won't get any gourmet makings there, but do the best you can."

Forty minutes later we said our farewells to old Mrs. Gallant. We had known her only for a few hours but she had touched something in each of us. Even Erin, who had not known her at all, had been moved by her story.

"I should apologize for eavesdropping at the bedroom door," she said. "But I had a hunch those questions might come up. It never hurts to have an impartial witness to what was said."

This got grateful looks from the Ralstons. Then, in the best tradition of a real wake, we ate an incredible omelet.

"Damn, you really are a gourmet cook," I said. "You oughta do this for a living."

"I do, when I can find work. I should say, when I can keep it."

"Michael has a problem with arrogant authority," Denise said.

"Isn't that amazing, so do I," I said. "We seem to be more alike all the time."

"Except you don't have to worry about getting fired. That's what happened to me this week. Been thinking of changing jobs anyway, but I'd rather have done it on my own hook, after some bills have been paid."

"Well," I said casually, "now you'll have the money to pay your bills."

I motioned to the Burton, still on the table where I had put it hours ago.

"When you sell it, you mean," Ralston said.

"I may never sell it. But I'm willing to pay you half of what I think its retail value might be. We can do that tonight if you want to. Like I told your friend the doctor, I think it's a twenty, twenty-five-thousand-dollar piece. Say twelve-five to you."

"Holy mackerel, Batman," Ralston said, but Denise gave a tiny head shake.

"I just bought the *Pilgrimage* at auction for twenty-nine and change. That's widely considered to be Burton's greatest book. It's a very important piece, but so is this. The condition of both is outstanding, and that's actually a huge understatement. Old bookmen like to call everything the world's best copy, but I truly can't imagine better copies of either book anywhere in the world today. The inscription is intriguing, and I think it gains by having the two of them together."

They looked at each other.

"Listen," I said, "there's no pressure on this. You do what's right for you. Bring in another bookseller, get his opinion, I'll pay half of whatever he says. If and when I do sell it, if it goes over thirty, we'll split that difference as well. Whenever that might be."

"Couldn't be fairer than that," Ralston said, looking hopefully at his wife.

Denise was looking at me. "I trust you. That's not what's bothering me."

I knew what was bothering her. The deathbed promise I had made lingered in the air. "Nobody expects you to find those books," Ralston said.

Denise shook her head. "Oh, honey, that's where you're wrong."

A long quiet moment later, I said, "I didn't give that promise lightly. If those books are there to be found, I will find them. I'm just thinking how much easier it might be if this book is in my hands alone. We can let it ride, if that's what you want. But I get the final word on where the hunt goes and how I want to conduct it."

"He used to be a cop," Ralston told his wife.

"Really? That surprises me. You seem like such a gentle soul, Mr. Janeway . . . it's hard to believe you were ever part of any violent world."

"I've been called lots of things, but a gentle soul isn't even close to the list. Maybe I'm making some headway."

"Why did you leave the police?"

"Long story. Goes to my attitude, which isn't always so gentle. Let's just say I like the book world better."

"You should've seen him wheeling and dealing those two cats from Texas," Ralston said. "Two fat cats came into his store and he pulled eight bills out of their pockets slicker than hell."

"They knew what they wanted," I said. "They got what they paid for."

I asked if either of them knew who or what Koko was.

"I can't imagine," Denise said. "Probably some childhood friend."

"Who's been dead forever," Ralston said.

Denise touched the book, opened it carefully. "This is all so far from my own life, from any kind of experience I've ever had. Until now I couldn't have imagined such a book." A moment later, she said, "Would it bother you if I kept it overnight? Maybe for a couple of days? I'd just like to . . . I don't know . . . get a feel of it . . . if that wouldn't bother you."

It bothered me a lot, but what could I say? What I said was, "You'd have to be very careful."

"I know that."

"I mean *really* careful, Denise. A spot on the cover could be five grand."

"I hear you."

Now an extended silence fell over us. Denise walked to the window and looked out into the yard. Ralston cocked his head and smiled at me, a quizzical expression that said, *You'll have to wait for her, man, it's the only way.*

But he was the one who squirmed as the minutes dragged on. "That's a whole bunch of money, doll," he said to some crack in the floor. "We could get a great new start with that."

He looked up at me and found another reason to take the money and run. "The answers you want won't be here in Denver, will they? There'll be expenses, and they'll come out of the book's value, right off the top. That's only fair."

Denise took a deep breath, as if the same thought had just

occurred to her. I could quickly eat up the entire value of the book traveling, and for what?

Erin was watching me intently. I smiled at her, then at Denise, who had just turned from the window. "It's your choice," I said. "You could take your money and be done with it. Speaking just for myself, I've got to try."

"Wherever that leads," Ralston said. "Whatever it costs."

Denise looked at me and her face was troubled. She said, "This isn't easy, is it?" A moment later she said, "I'm sorry, Mr. Janeway . . . could Michael and I have a few minutes alone?"

Erin and I went out on the porch and stood quietly at the edge of things. "Well, old man," she said. "You do make for an interesting first date."

"Next time I'll take you on a tour of Denver's best pawnshops."

"That would be good. I've been wondering where I can hock my virtue."

Half a dozen crazy answers wafted up from my funny bone, but the moment trickled away: the mood was different now. I looked back at the door and said, "I wonder what they'll do," and Erin said, "Trust me, they are going with you. If I know anything about people, they're going all the way. That woman in there's got more heart and soul than I've ever seen in a stranger."

I tried to look hurt in the moonlight. "Hey, I've got heart, I've got soul."

"Yes," she said, "but you were no stranger. I had heard so much about you from Miranda that I knew you long before we met." And I thought, *wow*. Round three to me for heart. Extra points for soul.

"Denise is special," Erin said. "I don't know how to describe it, it's just something I know. Goes way beyond class. She has already decided what needs to be done and now she's got to break the bad news to him. But he will do whatever she says. He would lie down and die for her."

"He's smart."

"Yes. And they're both very lucky."

A moment later I said, "So what's next now that you're back from the wilderness?"

"Tomorrow I'm going to disappear for a week into the real wilderness. I have a cabin in the mountains, where I shall write, eat very little, drink lots of liquids, meditate, and commune with nature. It's a serious hike just to get up there. No roads, no electricity, best of all, no telephones. If I take a bath at all it will be in very cold water."

"Can I come?"

"That would defeat my purpose, wouldn't it? And you've got plenty enough to do here."

"I'll think about nothing all week but you getting eaten by a bear."

"Oh, I can take care of myself. I do this every year."

I pretended to sulk and she said, "I'll call you when I get back."

"That's what they all say."

I walked out into the yard and looked up at the sky. The old lady was still on my mind. She haunted me and I cursed myself for not listening to her better. I believed she had been trying to tell me something important, but I had heard only half of it and now none of it made any sense. How could Burton have had anything to do with our civil war? He had come to the States in 1860, a year before the war began. What could he have said or done that had gone off like a time bomb a year later?

It was crazy, almost impossible to believe.

But what a story if it were true.

I imagined Burton walking up into the yard. I saw him as a young man, just arrived from that other time, straight from the jungles of unknown Africa. How would we like each other? The first minutes would tell that tale, as they must have done with Charlie Warren. Burton formed his opinions quickly, and so did I.

Erin came down and stood beside me. For a long time we watched the sky. It was a night like I hadn't seen in Denver since my childhood in the late fifties, long before the big buildings came with the big lights, before crowds of people flooded into the state from California and Mexico and the East Coast, leaving crud on the landscape and poison in the air. In those days I could stand in City Park and look deep into the universe. From Lookout Mountain I could see everything the big god saw before she broke it all apart and hurled it into that endless expanse of empty space. I must have had faith then. I certainly had something. How had I lost it? When had I stopped believing the god thing? I didn't need to worry it to death, I knew when it was: the night I looked down into the blood-less face of the little girl who had been raped and strangled by her father.

I had grown cynical and easy with my disbelief. But in that moment I thought of Mrs. Gallant and, I swear, a meteor streaked across the western sky. I watched it disappear beyond the mountains and I shivered in the warm morning air.

9

Erin and I parted company at the store, where she picked up her car and headed wearily home. I sat for a while watching the empty street and thinking about restraint. The word had become almost extinct in the sexual sixties, when I was coming of age and everybody groped everybody at first sight. I had done my share of that but time and age had dimmed its appeal. In my younger days I might have made too much out of Erin's verbal horseplay and groped my way into hot water. I knew something strong was brewing between us and tonight, that was enough.

I got to my house at dawn, only four hours before I had to open for business, and I did what I always do after a sleepless night: put on my sweats and went for a torturous run in the park. I did my three miles in well over twenty minutes, then I jogged out another two miles and walked myself cool. All along the way I thought of Denise and how personally encumbered she had felt by the promise I had given in her home. I knew she'd keep pushing me until there was no margin left in the book for any of us, and I was okay with that.

We had agreed to meet again tonight, to formulate some plan of action. Denise would expect me to have some ideas, but everything I considered was immediately swamped on the rocks of the great time barrier. Eighty years! Jesus, where would I start? I could get on an airplane and fly off half-cocked to Baltimore. I could waltz into Treadwell's and ask a few stupid questions, and then what? As soon as they figured out how little I knew and what I really wanted, I'd be laughed out of there and jeered down the street into the harbor.

But even a fool must start somewhere. At eleven o'clock, having disposed of a few customers and rung up a few sales, I decided to defy the odds and call the home in Baltimore where Mrs. Gallant had been living. Maybe something she had left there would lead to something else. Neither of the Ralstons knew or remembered the name of the place, and when I called Baltimore Information I was told what I already knew. You don't just ask for the number of Shady Pines: there are dozens of entries under "Assisted Living Facilities." This would be a substantial trial-and-error job that could take days to pan out.

I went in another direction that might have been just as futile. From Information I got to Social Services, and from there I bumped my way from one extension to another until I got to the old woman's caseworker. I had hoped and assumed she'd be in the system, and there she was.

I knew the caseworker wouldn't blurt a client's affairs to a voice on the phone, but I had to try. I got a woman named Roberta Brewer and I told her the straight story, beginning with the news of Mrs. Gallant's death in Denver. No one had called her on that as yet, and she was sorry but grateful for the information. Then I told her what I wanted and why: I explained about the book and why I was searching for the others, and she understood it the first time and seemed to believe it. "Let me call around and check you out," she said. "Then I'll call the home where Jo was living and they can call you if they want to."

This was the best I was going to get, so I thanked her, hung up, and hoped for some luck.

Two hours later I got a collect call from a woman named Gwen Perkins at a place called Perkins Manor in Catonsville, Maryland. Ms. Perkins was defensive, uneasy that Mrs. Gallant had simply walked out of there. Of course they had been worried sick over her, and yes, of *course* they were distressed at her death. Ms. Perkins was obviously worried about her liability: she assured me that no one was a prisoner at Perkins, people often went out into the care of relatives or friends, and I said I understood and I said this in my caring voice, full of understanding. At last I got to ask a question.

"Did Mrs. Gallant leave any diaries or letters among her possessions?"

"There were no possessions, except for the clothes she had. Usually by the time they get to us they don't have much left."

She made it sound like a charity she was running, as if the state wasn't paying her nearly enough. I asked my next question on a wing and a prayer. "Is there a worker there who took care of her regularly? Somebody she might've told about her family?"

"We have volunteers who come in from the community. Some of them form very close friendships with the residents." She paused awkwardly, as if she had said too much, and finally she finished her thought. "In Josephine's case, that would be Ms. Bujak."

"Ah. Would it be possible for me to speak to Ms. Bujak?"

She thought about that. I sensed she didn't like it but there was no good reason to stop me.

"Wait a second, I'll get her number for you."

I waited through some elevator music. It seemed to take a long time and I figured she was calling the volunteer and covering her bases.

"I'm back," she said suddenly. "Sorry for the wait."

She read off a phone number. "Her name is Bujak. *B-u-j-a-k*."

"You have a first name?"

"Yes, it's Koko."

She answered on the first ring, like she'd been sitting over the phone waiting for me to call. She said "Hi," not "Hello," and her voice was gentle and soft. She might have been twenty or fifty.

"Is this Koko?"

"And you would be Mr. Janeway."

"I take it Mrs. Perkins told you what happened."

"Yeah, she did. Not the best news I've had all year. Jo was a good person."

"I didn't know her long, but I sure liked her spunk. That was some trip she took on alone. Apparently nobody at Perkins had any idea."

"They're all pretty uptight this morning. I think they're concerned about losing their standing with the state."

"Over one incident?"

"Oh, there's always something. All those places are understaffed. That's why I volunteer. I go out there twice a week. It's not their fault when something like this happens—at least it's not all their fault. Actually, I like Mrs. Perkins. She tries, which is more than I can say for some of them."

"But there've been other incidents?"

"Mr. Janeway." Now there was a slight edge to her voice. "Are you putting together some kind of file for someone, like maybe for a claim? That's how it's beginning to sound, and I just want to make sure we both understand why we're having this conversation."

"Let's start over. Forget the questions about the facility; I'm not out to sandbag anyone. What I want to talk to you about is Mrs. Gallant. And her grandfather."

"Charlie," she said, and I sat up straight in my chair at the real affection in her voice.

"You sound almost like you knew him. Like she sounded when she talked about him."

"I do know him."

"You talk as if he's still alive."

"That's how he seems. I've spent a good deal of time digging through her memories of him. I've got lots of tape—the two of us, just talking."

"Tape," I said densely.

"I'm writing her story," she said, and I felt my heart turn over.

She said, "I taped everything," and my battered old heart flipped back again.

Then she said, "We used extensive hypnosis to get at what she knew."

"Hypnosis," I said in the same inane tone of voice. "You hypnotized her?"

"Does that bother you?"

"No, it just surprises me a little. Did it work?"

"I guess that would depend on how you define *work*. If you're asking whether she could be put under, then yes, it worked wonderfully. Hypnosis is actually an old technique, goes back two hundred years. I've used it all my adult life: self-hypnosis, age regression, autosuggestion. I used it to quit smoking years ago. I quit cold, and I was a three-pack-a-day addict. Now I use it to record their stories. The old people."

"You do this for what, a hobby?"

"If you want to call it that. I retired two years ago and this seems to be worth my time."

"You don't sound old enough to retire."

"Flattery will get you nowhere. I'm probably old enough to be your mother."

"I doubt that. So what did you do? In your career?"

"I was a librarian. In my last ten years I was head librarian in a smallish suburban branch. I moved over here when I retired."

"Where's over here?"

"I live in Ellicott City now. It's just across the river, a few miles from Mrs. Perkins's house."

"And you hypnotize the old people and record their stories. That's fascinating, you know. Can you tell me about it?"

"We could be here all day. I'll tell you this much: a good subject can be sent back to almost any part of her life. She can relive it and describe everything that went on. People have been known to remember letters in detail, even from their childhood. There's nothing supernatural about it, it's all stored right there in the brain. This is all very well documented and I shouldn't be defensive about it. Take it or leave it."

"I'm not doubting you, just being educated. So Josephine was a good subject?"

"She was great. She got to where she could go under almost as soon as she sat in my chair."

"You did these sessions at your place?"

"Oh, sure. It would've been impossible to do it there, so once or twice a week I'd go over and pick her up. She loved coming out and she came to love our sessions. Afterward I would play the tapes back for her and she'd laugh and say, 'My Lord, I'd forgotten that.' So from that standpoint, it worked very well. Now what I'm trying to do is get hard evidence that what she told me was real."

"How's she holding up?"

"Amazingly well. We've done the same session a number of times and I haven't caught her in a discrepancy yet. And we're not talking about something you could write out and memorize. These were lengthy sessions, an hour or more at a time. You'd expect her to trip up somewhere if she were trying to pull a fast one, wouldn't you, Mr. Janeway?"

I took in a deep breath. I couldn't believe my luck.

"Aside from her memories," she said, "I've gone through many pages of records that tell who the people in her family were. How they lived."

"Ms. Bujak—"

"Call me Koko."

What a great name, I thought. Koko Bujak. A great and elegant name indeed.

I told her the long version of the story I had given the social worker, beginning with Josephine's arrival in my bookstore the day before. She said nothing while I flashed back to my own infatuation with Richard Burton, the auction, and how Mrs. Gallant had discovered me. Then she said, "I knew something was going on with her. I wish she had told me about it, I'd have taken her to Colorado myself."

"Why would she not tell you?"

"Who knows? Maybe she was afraid I'd try to stop her. We had a good working friendship but I think I still represented the state to her."

"For what it's worth, I think she'd have died anyway. Whether you had come or not."

"Yes, she sensed the end coming and so did I. She had lost a lot of ground in the past six months. I was working hard to get her memories transcribed, so she could see what I had."

"What are you going to do with it now?"

"Finish it, of course. I didn't get into this just to patronize her."

"What happens when you do finish it?"

"Depends on what I've got and how good it is. If it's good enough I might try to find her a writer to put it into a book. Otherwise I'll leave it with the state historical society. They're always interested in records that tell about local people."

"How will you decide . . . you know, whether to turn it over to a writer?"

"The obvious standard would be whether there's national interest or if it's strictly local. If what she thought was even partly true, I think it could be a significant book. Don't you?"

"I sure do. And if I may say so, it sounds like she left it in good hands."

There was a pause, as if she didn't quite trust the compliment. Then she said, "I do have a sense about it. It goes way beyond what I've done with other life histories. I can't think of a better use of my time right now. But there are some things I can't do from here. I may have to go to Charleston to chase down some facts. I've been avoiding that, but—"

"Can I ask how much you've been able to verify so far?"

"Quite a bit, actually," she said, and I felt my heart rumble again.

"How much of it really involves Burton?"

"Well, that's the mystery, isn't it? How much of what she thought was real really was, and how much can be nailed down at this late date."

We were at a sensitive point and I knew it. "Your name came up last night, just before she died. She was talking about a photograph of Charlie and Burton that had been taken long ago in Charleston. She said you knew about it." I suffered through an awkward pause, then said, "I guess I've got to ask for your help, Koko. I know it's asking a lot—you've done so much work on her story, and all I can do is promise you that nothing you share with me will get out before you decide how you want to go."

"In the end, though, I would have to take your word for that."

"That's what it would come down to."

"This couldn't be done on the telephone; you'll have to come back here. I want to see your face before we get any deeper into it."

"That's fine. I'm happy to do that."

"Just understand that this is still very much a work in progress. I'll talk to you but that's all I'm promising at this point."

"I'll take that chance. I might be able to come next week."

"I'll be here. I live on Hill Street, fifth house on the right. My name's on the mailbox."

Reluctantly, almost painfully, I let her go.

By then it was after six. I was late for my call to Treadwell's, so I punched in the number and waited. The same spacey-sounding woman answered. This time she asked who was calling. When I told her, she said, "Justa minute, hon," and I was put on hold.

I decided to play it by ear: I wouldn't mention my deception if he didn't and we'd see what happened. I sat listening to the hum on the line.

I heard the click of the phone on the other end. But the voice that answered wasn't Dean Treadwell's. It was a deep voice, and flat: the coldest voice I had ever heard.

"Yes?"

"I'm holding for Dean."

"Dean's not here."

"I'll call him back."

"Who is this?" he snapped gruffly.

"Who are *you*?" I said with a smile in my voice. A quiet few seconds passed. I asked, "Is this Carl?" but he had hung up.

A real friendly boy. So far both Treadwells were living up to their advance billing.

That night I ate with the Ralstons and gave them a report. Denise was elated that I had found Koko so quickly and was hopeful that this might be an early break. "Now what?"

"I'll fly back there next week, see Koko, rattle the Treadwell cage. See where that gets us."

She put on her pleading face. "But next week seems so far away."

"The woman who minds my store will be back then. I've got a flight out next Monday."

We talked for a while longer. Denise had brought out the old woman's book and she returned it to me now with a grand gesture. "You will note that there are no spots on the cover, I did not leave it out in the rain, or earmark any pages, or write my name inside with crayons, much as I wanted to."

"Thank you, ma'am," I said sheepishly. "I had to make the point."

"Oh, you made it, Cliff. I'd liked to've kept it another day, but Michael was a nervous wreck just having it around the house."

None of us had any brilliant new ideas and I left around eight. I went to bed early, knowing I had made some progress, even if I still didn't know what I was progressing toward or how far I might have to go to get there.

10

Just before noon Ralston came into the store and asked if it would bother me if he sat with some of my modern first editions and looked them over. When the morning trade petered out I joined him at the round table.

"You thinking of becoming a bookscout?"

"I'm thinking of getting a job, man. But between things, I don't know . . . this might be fun."

"Can I help you figure it out?"

"Tell me what this first edition stuff means. I see these are all marked 'first edition,' with your pencil mark, but the publishers don't always say that."

"Some do, some don't. Most of 'em are starting to put the chain of numbers on the copyright pages. But even then there are some pitfalls, and in the old days publishers all marched to their own drummers. Usually they were fairly consistent within their own houses, at least for a few years at a time, but with some it could vary from one book to the next."

I asked if he wanted a rundown and for the next hour I led him publisher by publisher through the grotto. I showed him the vagaries of Harcourt-Brace and its lettering system, how the words *first edition* were almost always stated with an accompanying row of letters beginning with a *B* until 1982, when for some screwball reason they began adding an *A*. "Some significant books, like *The Color Purple,* came out during that crossover year," I said. "It still began with a *B,* and there was a gap, as if there might have been an *A* in an earlier printing, only there'd never been one. This is important, because even some bookstore owners don't know it. They assume, they get careless, and you can pick up a three-hundred-dollar book for six bucks."

I told him about the usual dependability of Doubleday and Little Brown and Knopf, and how Random House stated "first edition" or "first printing" and had a chain of numbers beginning with 2— except for a few notables like Michener's *Bridges at Toko-Ri* and Faulkner's *Requiem for a Nun,* which had nothing to designate them in any way. We looked at every book in my section and I talked about the eccentricities of each publisher. When we were done he said, "Okay, I think I've got it now. I'm goin' out and find you some books. Tell me where's the best places to go."

I gave him a junk-store itinerary and a warning. "Take it easy, Mike. Remember, there are days when there's just nothing out there. You can waste a lot of money in this business, and it'll be a while before you remember all these publishers."

"Oh, I'll remember 'em," he said with vast confidence.

Five hours later he pulled up to my front door and unloaded two boxes of books. I didn't expect much for his first try and when I saw Sidney Sheldon and John Jakes on top of the pile, it didn't look promising. He had bought twenty books. Ten were worthless but eight were decent stock, and two—nice firsts of *The Aristos,* by John Fowles, and John Irving's *Garp*—made the day worthwhile. I paid him $130 and he did the math. He had spent $22.50 plus tax and gas, which netted him a bill for less than a full day's work.

"And you didn't make any mistakes with the publishers," I said. "That's pretty good."

"If I've got any kind of gift, it's a super memory. I can read a recipe and cook it a week later without ever looking back at it."

"That is a great, *great* gift for a bookscout."

It was after five but he wanted to go out again. "If Denise calls, tell her I'll be home after a while, but don't tell her what I'm doing." He fingered my check. "I want to surprise her."

I gave him a new route, this time across the southern reaches of the city, where a few places I knew stayed open till nine, and he left with a high heart.

Much later I pieced together what happened next.

The hunt was not as good the second time out. For some reason this often happens: a break in the continuity of a good day chases Lady Luck away, leaving the bookscout high and dry until she comes back again. There is no logical reason for this, but I know from my own experience that it happens. A bookscout's luck runs hot and cold, just like that of a player in a gambling hall, and a savvy player never leaves the game when it's running good.

He worked his way south on Broadway, then west on Alameda, where a pair of competing thrift stores faced each other across the street. I had once pulled two copies of *The Last Picture Show* out of those stores just five minutes apart, a coincidence that borders on spooky, but I had not found anything remotely that good in either place ever again. The juice wasn't working for Ralston that night, and he moved on west.

He drifted all the way out to the edge of Golden, where a few flea markets had sprung up in old supermarket buildings. Soon he would learn for himself that places like that are always slim pickings. Give a bookscout a booth of his own and a little rent to pay and suddenly he starts thinking of himself as a dealer, with prices to match. Ralston poked his way through several of these. He called me at home and asked about one book, a fine copy of Robert Wilder's *Wind from the Carolinas,* which would cost him ten dollars, and I told him to pass. He had found just one book since six o'clock, a fine copy of *Two Weeks in Another Town.* No big deal, but okay for a quarter.

He tried Denise from the pay phone just outside the store, but their line was busy.

By then the streets were dark. He had gone on a long, circular drive and was heading back to Globeville with almost nothing to show for it. There were still a couple of stores on the list I had given him, and he was lured on by his success of the afternoon. He wanted to find one more. *Just one good one.* The bookscout's curse.

The stores closed at nine and he picked up Interstate 70 and headed east toward home.

He felt good about the day in spite of the evening. Maybe this could turn into a new line of work, an avocation that would give him the freedom he hungered for above all else. If he got good at it, he might get Denise out of that crappy motel job and not have to kiss the Man's ass to do it.

He turned off the highway on Washington and a few minutes later rolled into his block. The lights were on, giving him a warm feeling of anticipation. He came through the gate and clumped up onto the porch.

He opened the door and heard Denise's favorite music on the classical radio station. The phone was off the hook but this was not unusual: she often left it off when she had a headache. But in that moment he felt the dark man cross his path: the same Grim Reaper Mrs. Gallant had seen was still in the room, and he shivered, then he quaked, and had his first vivid sense of the unthinkable.

"Hey, doll," he said to the empty room, and his voice broke in his throat.

He crossed to the hall quickly now. He looked into the bedroom and felt his life drain away at what he saw.

11

I was just reaching for the phone to turn it off for the night when it rang under my hand. "Hey, Cliff."

"Who is this?" I said belligerently.

I knew quite well who it was: I could pick his laid-back voice out of a crowd, but this late at night it could be nothing but trouble. Neal Hennessey had been my partner in homicide. We had been close friends a few years ago, and for a while after my abrupt exit from the Denver cops we had kept up the pretense that nothing had changed between us. Occasionally I bought him a lunch for old times' sake; sometimes we would go for a beer in a bar we liked on West Colfax near the *Rocky Mountain News*. But those times had become fewer and farther between. Months had passed since I'd last seen his beefy face, but I was an outsider now and that's how cops are.

"We got one on the north side," Hennessey said. "It's not my case but your name came up and the primary officer remembered what a dynamic duo we used to be. So I got a call on it."

I still didn't put it together. Who did I know on the north side? A few years ago it had been a hotbed of local mobsters and I had helped put one of them away, but how could that come back to haunt me after all this time?

Then Hennessey said, "Do you know a fellow named Ralston?" and suddenly I felt sick.

"What happened?"

"His wife's dead."

I sat numbly and in a while Hennessey read my silence.

"I take it you actually do know these people?"

"Sure I do. Jesus Christ, this is awful."

Now came a second reaction, disbelief, and slowly by degrees I felt diminished by what Hennessey had said. He was still a homicide cop; I knew he wouldn't be calling if her death had been a natural one.

"What happened?" I said again.

"Well, the boys are still trying to figure that out. The husband's not in any kind of shape to be helpful. Apparently he hasn't said ten words to anybody."

"That's because he's in *shock,* Neal. Hell, *I'm* in shock, I can't imagine how he feels."

I heard Hennessey breathing on the other end. After a moment, he said, "You got any ideas who might do this?"

I thought of Denise, her smiling face, and my voice quivered. "No," I said.

"If you've got anything you think might help, they'd like to see you downtown."

I stared into the dark corners of the room.

"Tonight, if you think of anything. They'll send a car for you. Otherwise they'd like you to come in tomorrow."

"Who's the primary?"

"Randy Whiteside. Your favorite guy."

Wonderful, I thought. Mr. Personality.

I looked at my clock. "Where's Mike now?"

"Who's Mike?"

"Her husband, Neal. Who the hell have we been talking about?"

"Hey, don't bite *my* head off. All I'm doing is making a phone call."

I heard myself say, "Sorry," and a moment later, "Damn, this hits hard."

"You knew these people well?"

"No."

I felt him waiting for some reason.

"I don't know how to explain it," I said at last. "Denise was . . ." I gave up after a moment and said, "I just met them recently."

"Well, to answer your question, I don't know where the husband is. They're probably still trying to talk to him out at the scene."

I felt a wave of sudden anger. "Goddammit, Hennessey, I hope you boys aren't treating this man as a suspect."

I could feel him bristle. "Of *course* he's a suspect. What would you think if you got to a scene and nobody's there but the husband and he won't talk?"

"I told you why."

"Yeah, well, maybe you know that for a fact, but me, I never met the man. Maybe he is overcome with grief, and maybe the grief's a hundred percent real and he still did it. Come on, Cliff, you've seen enough of these things to know that. I could tick 'em off on my fingers, the number of times the grieving husband did it and you and me brought the bastard in and you got him in the box and ripped the confession out of his lying ass."

I remembered those times: all the faces of the guilty and the damned came back in one shivery moment, and now I felt my skin crawl at the thought of someone like me, the cop I had once been, tearing at Ralston's open wounds. I remembered another case: Harold Waters, who had signed a confession for me and had been on the brink of a life behind bars until the real killer made a mistake. Harold Waters had signed everything we put in front of him. Why? He simply didn't care what happened to him after his wife was murdered.

Hennessey knew how that case had always haunted me. "Do me a favor, Cliff," he said. "Don't give me that Harold Waters shit. How many times has that ever happened?"

"It happens, though, doesn't it?"

"It happened *once*."

"All right, I'm interested in Ralston now. And I don't want him browbeaten."

I heard him cough softly, turning his head away from the phone.

"I mean it. There's no way he could've done this."

Hennessey said nothing. Exactly what I'd have done under the circumstances.

"Help me out here," I said.

This was an offensive thing to say to a cop and Hennessey was properly offended. "You know better than to ask me something like that. I told you it's not my case, I've got nothing to say about how it's run. I'm making a courtesy call to an old comrade-in-arms and that's all I'm doing. I should've just stayed out of it and let them drag you out of bed at midnight."

"All right," I said in a softer voice. "Are you interested in my opinion?"

"I'm sure Detective Whiteside will be, at the proper time."

There was a gulf between us now and Hennessey was as bothered by it as I was. I heard him sniff, then he said, "One thing about your opinion, Cliff, you always had one. They were pretty good too, as opinions go. But the man has said nothing to us, just that he walked in and found her sprawled across the bed. The only other word any-body recognized out of him was your name."

"He was talking to me on the telephone not thirty minutes before he went home. He was way the hell out in Golden at the time. I don't know when she . . ." I took a deep breath. "I don't know when she died but he couldn't have gotten home in less than half an hour."

"Assuming that's really where he was when he called you."

Again the moment stretched. Hennessey was saying what I would have said in his place.

"I'm sorry this wasn't better news," he said.

"It was bound not to be, wasn't it? But thanks for the call."

"Sure. We should grab a beer sometime." But I was thinking of Denise and I barely heard him.

I knew he wouldn't tell me but I tried anyway. "Any idea of the time of death?"

"That'll take some time. The boys are still out there and will be for a while."

"Do they know yet what the cause of death was?"

"Nothing you can take to the bank."

Then he gave me this for old times' sake. "It looks like she was smothered."

12

Ralston's block was full of cars, the usual scene when something bad happens. There were two patrol cars and some unmarked vehicles, a green Chevy belonging, I knew, to an assistant coroner named Willie Paxton, and Ralston's old Ford Fairlane. No obvious sign of news coverage. The TV idiots had taken a pass on this one: no wires or cams or blow-dried hairdos cluttering up the block. A Cherry Hills murder would have brought them out at midnight but this just wasn't that important. There were two seedy types in jeans, guys I knew from the Denver Post and the Rocky Mountain News, and plenty of plain people milling around. Even at that hour word had spread across the neighborhood: two dozen neighbors watched from the distance and a row of kids sat gawking on the roof of a house across the street.

A young uniform stopped me at the sidewalk. "You can't go in there, sir."

"Is Whiteside here?"

"He's busy right now. You got something to tell him?"

"I might, yeah. My name's Janeway."

The cop summoned another cop, a guy I knew. "Go inside and tell Detective Whiteside that Mr. Janeway is here to see him, when he gets a break."

I waited.

Minutes later the cop came out and motioned to me from the porch. The first cop nodded and held open the gate. On the porch the second cop said, "I know you know the routine, but I'm supposed to tell you anyway—don't touch anything." A moment later, to my own amazement, I was in the living room, sitting on a chair well out of the way.

It looked different now—not at all like the place where I had met Mike and Denise Ralston in the beginnings of friendship just a few days ago. Tonight it was cold in the harsh white strobe lights and loud with impersonal voices of the men who probed through its cracks and corners. I saw Whiteside pass the open doorway and he met my eyes before he disappeared in the crowd of people gathered around the bed. I tried to push away my prejudices and hope for the best. Whiteside had always seemed like a good enough cop; hell, his record of clearing cases was at least as good as my own and maybe that was at the root of it, why we had never liked each other much. He had come in five years ago, trading on a big reputation from some department back East, but to me he was a hot dog from day one. In a way he was like Archer. His badge was his Pulitzer and somehow that set him above the sorry race of men. I could still hear my voice and the words I had said to Hennessey years ago: "I'll bet he sleeps with that shield pinned to his nightshirt."

After a while he came out of the back room. "Well, goddamn, Janeway, imagine meeting you here." He loomed over my chair but I knew that technique and I didn't let it bother me. I looked up at him from the darkest part of his shadow, his face in silhouette, framed by lights behind him and above. "So what've you got to tell me?" he said, and I told him what I knew about Ralston's day hunting books. I told it to him short and direct, wasting none of his time. "He called me at nine o'clock," I concluded. "He was still out in Golden and he'd just found a book." I knew what he'd ask next and he did. "What book did he find?" I told him and he said what I knew he'd say: "Then that book might still be in his car." He called the uniform over and told him to go out to the car and see if there was a book by somebody named Irwin Shaw in it.

I was playing a wild card, a little too sure that the book would be there and would easily be traceable to that store in Golden. If we were lucky there'd be a receipt with a date and maybe even a time printed on it, and there'd be a price sticker on the spine, color-coded to tell approximately when the book had been put out for sale. Each week in stores like that, books were marked down according to the sticker colors. It wouldn't be conclusive: just another small piece of evidence that the man was telling the truth.

So far I had been playing Whiteside's game his way. Now I said, "Where is Mr. Ralston?" and Whiteside backed out of the light and looked at my face, keeping his own in shadow.

"He's where I want him to be."

"Okay," I said pleasantly.

"What's your connection with Ralston? Other than this hunt for books you sent him on, what's he to you?"

"I'm his friend."

"I guess that's good. He's gonna need a friend."

I felt my anger boiling up but I kept it in check. I heard a movement and the uniform came in carrying the book, suspended from a pencil under its spine like a pair of pants draped over a clothesline. I saw the blue thrift-store sticker on the jacket and the receipt peeking out of the top pages, and I thanked the book gods that it hadn't dropped out when the cop picked it up that way.

I said nothing for a moment: it would be far better to let Whiteside discover these things for himself. But when the cop continued holding the book that way, I said, "I imagine that's the receipt sticking out of it." Whiteside said, "Bag it," and the cop dropped the book, receipt and all, into a plastic bag.

"Well, Mr. Janeway, it was swell of you to come in. If we have any more questions, we'll be in touch."

I knew I was being dismissed with malice but I nodded, still the soul of reason, and said, "I'd like to see Mr. Ralston, if that's okay."

Whiteside gave a dismissive little laugh and that's when I knew it was going to turn ugly.

"Are you charging him with something?"

"That remains to be seen, doesn't it?"

"Well, until you decide, you have no right to detain him."

"I don't have to charge him with anything in order to question him."

"You've got to inform him of his rights if you intend to detain him. And he doesn't have to answer anything if you come at him with a hard-on. Come on, Randy, we both know the rules."

I had never called him Randy in my life. I held up my hands in a peace gesture. "Look, I'm sure he'll talk to you, I know he will. But the man just lost his wife, for Christ's sake. Give him some time to get the wind back in his sails. Can I see him?"

"Not till I've talked to him first."

"Then how's this for a deal? You talk to him in my presence. You be civil and I promise to be quiet."

"No way. I can't believe you'd even ask me something like that. How long were you a cop, Janeway?"

Long enough to know a prick with a badge when I see one, I thought. But I said, "Look, I promise you this man didn't do this. His heart's just been ripped out and I can't sit still while you rip it out again."

"You've got jackshit to say about what I do."

"Maybe not, but I can have a lawyer downtown by the time you get there. Then you can go piss up a rope and talk to nobody."

"Shit," he said. But he thought about it a moment.

"You just sit there and keep your fuckin' mouth shut. That the deal?"

"Absolutely," I said with my great stone face.

I moved out to the kitchen table and watched as they wound up their work. The house seemed incredibly small for the number of people bustling about. I looked into the bedroom and felt an almost crushing wave of sadness. I could see Willie Paxton in the other room talking to a woman I knew, Joanne Martinson, also from the coroner's office. I could see Denise's arm, flopped over the edge of the bed, and the sight of it filled me with heartbreak. Son of a *bitch,*

I thought. Some miserable son of a bitch did this, probably a cheap neighborhood spider looking for pocket change. How many times does it happen? Someone returns home, walks in on a thief, and bingo. Suddenly in my mind I was a cop again.

Paxton came out of the bedroom and Martinson was right behind him.

"Hey, Cliff, how ya doin'?" they said almost in the same voice.

"Ah, you win some, lose some." I had lost this one big-time, but I left that unsaid. I kept up the bullshit until Whiteside went into the bedroom. Then, in a low voice, I said, "So what's the story, guys?"

"Smothered with the pillow," Paxton said. "We'll know more later, but that's how it looks."

"How long?"

"I dunno. My guess is somewhere between five and seven o'clock."

"No later than seven, though, huh?"

"Not much chance of that. Rigor was already setting in when we got here."

Joanne looked at Paxton and said, "Look, I know you boys go back a ways and I love you too, Cliff, but Jesus Christ, Willie, this is inappropriate as hell."

"It's all gonna be in the report," Paxton said.

"Then let him read it like everybody else."

I nodded at them. "Yeah, don't get your tit in a wringer on my account, Willie. But thanks."

It had still been light on the street at seven o'clock. People had been coming home from work. That meant there was a chance the perp had been seen, and maybe Whiteside already had a witness under wraps.

Now there was nothing to do but wait. Cops can take hours at a murder scene and these guys were in no hurry. I thought of Ralston, alone on the hot side of Mercury, sealed off in his own private hell. This was the first of many hellish hours, and all I could do for him was try to make it less awful than it had to be.

After a while two men brought a stretcher into the bedroom and they lifted the body off the bed. I didn't want to watch this part—

you never do with a friend—but I stood up and without moving from the spot looked into the room. I didn't think of her as Denise now: Denise was gone and this shell was what she had left behind. Paxton directed the loading of the body, taking care to leave the dangling arm in the same position as it was when they'd found her. Joanne said something and he looked at the bed, took a long forcepslike instrument and peeled back the covers. Then he said, "Hey, Whiteside, look what she was lying on," and still using his forceps, he plucked what looked like a dollar bill from the folds of the rumpled sheet. But my eyes were good and I could see the picture of Franklin clearly from where I stood. It was a C-note.

Whiteside appeared at once with a plastic bag. Paxton reached over to drop it in. Joanne said, "Here's another one," and Paxton pulled it gingerly from the covers.

"Here's some more," Joanne said.

"I thought these people were supposed to be poor," Whiteside said. "Looks like she had something going on the side."

I held myself onto the chair. I hated Whiteside in that moment but I watched quietly while they bagged the other bills. With the body gone there was a general combing of the room. The bed was vacuumed for fibers and hairs, the floor around the bed was examined, and the small throw rug vacuumed as well. At some point Whiteside looked at his watch and said, "I'm going on in, see what the man's got to say."

I followed him out into the yard.

"I'll see you down there," Whiteside said without enthusiasm. "You know the way?"

"If I get lost I'll ask somebody."

"Remember, you're only there by my permission. You keep your mouth shut, just like you said."

I had never seen Whiteside work but I didn't think much of him so far. There was no way I'd have let him sit in if I had been in his shoes and he'd been in mine. I wouldn't have let him into the crime scene in the first place. I wouldn't have crumbled under any threat of bringing a lawyer in. They'd have talked to me on my terms or I'd have found out why. It was obvious that Whiteside had something up his sleeve: he was confident he could handle me or maybe even show me up, and the chance to get a quick confession and clear this case in hours was too much to resist. Some cops are like that. I met a reporter once who said it was like that in his business too. The two biggest hot dogs were battling it out in the front-page derby, just like some cops who always wanted to be number one in clearing their cases. I wondered who the other hot dog was now that I was gone.

At the station Whiteside showed us into an office that suggested the atmosphere of an interview rather than an interrogation. I sat off to one side while he and Ralston faced each other across a desk. Whiteside offered coffee but Ralston made no response at all. I thought of the Harold Waters case and the similarities were chilling. Waters, a big black man; his wife by all accounts articulate, the joy of his life. I looked at Whiteside and in that half second he seemed almost predatory.

A stenographer came in and sat just behind Ralston in a corner of the room. "We're making a tape of this conversation as well as a transcript," Whiteside said, glancing at me. "The young man who just came in is Jay Holt, and he will take down everything we say. This is routine."

Ralston's wet eyes moved around the room and found mine. I nodded what I hoped was encouragement. Ralston said my name, first just "Janeway," then "Jesus, Janeway," and his tears began again. Whiteside said, "Speak to me, please, not to Mr. Janeway," and the interrogation that was supposedly only an interview got under way.

The first questions were routine. State your name and address for the record, please. Where were you today and tonight? When was the last time you heard from Mrs. Ralston? What time did you get home? Had there been any hint of trouble prior to tonight? Had you noticed any strangers who seemed to have a special interest in your home? This went on for a while, and Ralston answered in words of one syllable. Twice he broke down and Whiteside called for a police-woman to bring him some water.

Whiteside asked about their finances. Ralston, in that same breaking voice, told him in a few words. They were dirt poor. They had almost nothing.

Then Whiteside said, "Eleven hundred dollars was found at the scene, Mr. Ralston. Can you explain that?"

"That's impossible."

"Uh-huh. Did you know your wife kept a diary?"

Ralston nodded.

"Please answer verbally."

"Yes."

"Are you aware what's in her diary?"

Again Whiteside had to repeat the question. Ralston said no, he had never read it.

"It was there in the open on the dresser," Whiteside said. "Is that where she usually kept it?"

Ralston nodded, then said, "Yes."

"It was there in plain view, just a plain little notebook," Whiteside said. "It wasn't locked away, there was no lock on the book itself, and yet you were never tempted to look inside."

Ralston looked somewhat dumbfounded, as if the question made no sense to him.

"You're saying you never looked at it? Not once in all the time you were together?"

Ralston shook his head. "That would've seemed . . ."

"Seemed what, Mr. Ralston?"

"Wrong."

"Wrong," Whiteside said. "Well, you know what, I believe you. I believe exactly what you're telling me when you say you never looked at that book. I believe it was such a habit *not* to look in that book that it just wouldn't have occurred to you to do that, no matter what else might have happened in your lives. You just wouldn't do that, would you, Mr. Ralston?"

"No."

"No." Whiteside shook his head. "That's why you didn't know what she wrote there."

He got up and came around the desk, pulled up a chair, and faced Ralston from a distance of less than two feet. "What she wrote in her diary, just two days ago, was how this old woman just died in that bedroom of yours, and how she gave you all this great deathbed gift, this rare book which Mr. Janeway says is worth a lot of money. Have I got it right so far?"

"Denise wanted . . ."

Whiteside waited. Ralston faltered again and dabbed at his eyes.

"You were saying, Mr. Ralston? Denise wanted something. What did she want?"

"She wanted to do what the old woman asked."

"Find the other books, is that right?"

"That's right."

"But you didn't want to do that, did you? You wanted the money. And you two quarreled about it, didn't you?"

"We never quarreled about anything. Not ever."

"What would you call it then, when she wrote these lines?" He fished a notebook out of his pocket. "'Michael wants so badly to take the money. So we have our first strong disagreement, but he'll come to see this was the right thing to do.' How would you interpret that, Mr. Ralston?"

Ralston shook his head. "That wasn't any quarrel."

"Maybe that's not how it started. Maybe it was just a disagreement at first, then it got to be more than that. Hey, I know how it is: I have disagreements with my wife all the time. Sometimes I'd like to shut her up so bad I feel like pushing a pillow in her face."

"Hey, Whiteside," I said. "None of that shit."

He turned on his chair. "Another word from you and you're out of here." He turned back to Ralston. "That's what happened, isn't it?"

"Don't answer that, Mike."

Ralston looked dazed, horrified.

"Hell, if you didn't mean for it to go as far as it did, I can understand that," Whiteside said. "You're a big, strong man—once something gets started, it can be hard to stop."

"Don't say another word, Mike. This guy has no honor, he's trying to sandbag you and he'll twist anything you say. He's an asshole and a bad cop besides."

Whiteside leaped up from his chair and grabbed my arm. "I warned you. Now you can get the fuck out of here or spend the night in jail. Go ahead, call a lawyer if that's what you want."

I pushed him away. "Touch me again and I'll leave your ass on the floor."

"As if you could."

"Try it and find out." I looked at the stenographer. "You getting all this down, Jay? I want the record to show that Mr. Whiteside is throwing charges around and he hasn't even read Mr. Ralston his rights."

"Goddammit, get out of here," Whiteside said.

"When you make up the transcript of this, I want to see every word of it in the record."

"You're obstructing justice, Janeway. I'm giving you five seconds to get out of here."

"You wouldn't know justice if I chiseled it on your dick."

"Jay, tell Matthews to get in here."

"What are we doing now, calling the A-team? Hey, I'll make it easy on you. I'll walk out, but not quietly, pal, and I'm coming back with one helluva savage New York lawyer who is going to make buffalo chips out of you and your tactics. You hear that, Mike? Don't say a word to this prick. Write that down, Jay. Janeway wants it on the record, this man was not Mirandized, and it better be there. Randy Asshole Whiteside can kiss Mrs. Ralston's diary good-bye."

I kicked over the chair and pointed at the stenographer. "Do you know how to spell *asshole*, Jay? It's *your* ass if it's all not in there."

I got right into Whiteside's startled face. "Because you know what, asshole?" I patted my pocket. "I've got a tape of this whole sorry interview."

I pushed my way past him. Ralston sat in wide-eyed disbelief. I had his attention at last. I looked down at him as I passed. "Remember, Mike, don't sign anything, don't say anything."

I walked out and slammed the door, and the spirit of Harold Waters walked out with me.

Outside, I took a deep breath and touched my empty pocket as if I'd really had a tape there.

13

My pal Robert Moses came from an old New York family of lawyers. Named after a public official who had transformed New York's parks in the La Guardia administration, he had moved to Denver years ago and I had met him when I was still a motorcycle cop. He always sounded wide awake and ready for battle, even when I woke him in the middle of the night.

"You should've called me right away. The minute you heard they wanted to question your friend, that's when I should've gotten this call."

"When have you ever known me to do what I ought to do?"

"This isn't funny, Cliff. Do us both a favor and don't try to play lawyer, please; you're not that good at it. Do you know how lucky you are not to be in jail now?"

I said I did know that. I had known that possibility even before the dance got started. But I had been on the cop's side of the table enough to know that Whiteside was after more than background information, and somebody had to be there to get Ralston a fair shake.

"You made Whiteside a promise and you broke your word. You said you'd be quiet. You call that quiet?"

"I said I'd be quiet if he'd be civil. You call that civil?"

He sighed loudly into the telephone. "All right, I'll go down and see what they think they've got on your boy. With luck we'll both walk out of there."

An hour later he called me from downtown. The cops had released Ralston even before he had arrived. There were no charges pending; the evidence consisted only of motive, which the police still considered strong. Twelve thousand-five was a lot of money to a man with Ralston's checkered past.

"Have they even asked along the block if anybody saw any strangers?"

"They weren't about to tell me that. You've got to assume they did, and found nothing."

"Which only means nobody was looking, nobody noticed, or nobody's talking. Or they haven't found the one who was, did, or will. But it gives them an excuse to stop looking, doesn't it?"

"They think Ralston wanted the money so he could go back to his gambling, womanizing ways. The missus wouldn't budge and things got out of hand. Frankly, Whiteside is having a hard time believing that a strapping young guy like Ralston, with his past, would form a personal attachment to a very plain older woman. *Ugly* I think is the word he used."

"The son of a bitch had better not use it around me."

"If he does, you smile, look in his pretty face, and say, 'Thank you, Constable,' on advice from your attorney."

A cop had taken Ralston back to his home, Moses said, and it was assumed that's where he was now. I thanked him and told him to send me a bill.

Then I drove back up to Globeville. Ralston's car was no longer parked at the curb where I had seen it earlier, and now the street was quiet and dark. I went up onto the porch and banged on the door. Nothing. I came down into the yard and stood there for a moment wondering where he might be. Finally I realized I didn't know him well enough to even begin such a hunt.

I was about to leave when I saw a shadow move on the porch next door. Then I saw the darting orange motion of a lit cigarette.

I walked over to the fence and said hi.

"Hey yourself," came the gruff voice. A black male: not a kid, an older guy.

"You know Mike?"

"Yeah, I know him."

"You know where he went?"

"Maybe I do. Who're you and what do you want?"

"I'm his friend Janeway. I'd like to help him."

"I don't think anybody can do that."

Before I could react, he said, "That man's bleedin'. He's bleedin' out of every crack and sweat hole. Awful damn thing, what happened."

"Yeah, it was. Denise was great. I didn't know her real well, but I sure liked what I knew."

He said nothing.

"You know them well?" I said.

"About like you. Not long but long enough. They ain't been livin' up here real long, and people here tend to mind they own business."

"Did the cops talk to you?"

"Oh yeah. They talked to everybody."

"You able to tell them anything?"

"Not a damn thing. I was sleepin' all afternoon. The Salvation Army marchin' band could've come through here and I wouldn'a seen 'em."

There was a pause. "I work nights, sleep days," he said. "This's my night off."

"Well," I said. "You feel like telling me where he went? I want to help him if I can."

"Then you better have one helluva fast car, friend. Mike said he was gettin' out of here, goin' to Vegas."

BOOK II BALTIMORE

Eastern Avenue was the color of a Confederate uniform and just about as empty in the pale light before dawn. The Treadwells' building squatted in the block like a brick fortress. At one time it might have been respectable, with its tiled portico and the leaded glass in its front door. Now the tiles were cracked and worn, the tiny glass pieces in the door replaced with glass that matched poorly or not at all. The sign said BOOKS, and just inside the portico another sign, equally peeling, equally faded, was mounted on the door. TEN A.M. TO SIX P.M., SEVEN DAYS A WEEK. I had more than four hours to kill.

I cupped my hands against the one clear window, but I could see little more than the dim outline of the front counter, a rickety-looking bookcase with a sign hawking sale books at a dollar each, and just inside the door a poster advertising book fairs in Wilmington next week, Washington next month, and Baltimore later in the summer. Shadows of more substantial bookshelves loomed in the darkness beyond.

I walked back to South Broadway and went down toward the harbor. I was looking for a café that might be open that time of morning, and what I found was a dingy place across from the market, which even then was beginning to come to life. I ordered a plate of grease and sat over coffee with my *Baltimore Sun* untouched on the vacant chair beside me. I could feel the weariness in my bones: the payoff for a general lack of sleep, compounded by the bumpy evening flight from Denver and the loss of two hours over the Mountain to Eastern time zones. It had been after midnight when I checked into a hotel not far from the bookstore. The events of recent days still played in my head, but I slept almost four hours, waking just before dawn.

I heard Willie Paxton's voice like a broken record: *smothered with the pillow . . . smothered with the pillow . . . smothered with the pillow . . .*

I saw Ralston's despair and felt my own.

I never know quite what to do at a time like that. I knew I could find Ralston if he had actually gone to Vegas. A man like that stands out. Give him time to settle and he'd be no problem.

Denise was another matter. If Whiteside didn't find her killer, and I didn't think he would, I would have to give it a try. Brave thoughts for an ex-cop who had just burned most of his bridges downtown. Brave thoughts when in all likelihood my first hunch had been the right one, that some two-bit burglar had killed her when she'd walked in and found him there. A spider, maybe a transient: a stranger, in any case. Those guys can be hell to catch, even when you've got the resources of a big-city department behind you. Even when you get prints, who do you match them to?

The guy jumps a train and he's in Pittsburgh tomorrow.

Or he stays pat, right under your nose, and you still can't find him.

I knew I couldn't expect any help from the cops. Cops stick together, and I'd be an outcast after news of my snit with Whiteside made its way through the department.

But two days after Denise's death I had walked along Ralston's block, knocked on every door, and talked to everyone I saw. In my own police career I had sometimes found that two-day wait productive. It gives talk time to ripple through the neighborhood; it can smoke out a reluctant witness and bring new facts to light. I know the theory of the trail gone cold and most of the time it's true. But more than once I had found something forty-eight hours later, just by walking the same walk and talking to the same people. In the third house across and down from Ralston's, I found a kid, about twelve years old, who had seen a man come out of the house just before dark. He didn't remember much but he was sure of two things: the man was in a hurry and the man was white.

On Saturday night, after brooding about it for another two days, I called Whiteside and left the kid's name and address on an answering machine.

Thus had the weekend passed. On Monday I had this flight to Baltimore, bought and paid for, so this was what I did.

I walked for a while, found a little park and settled on a bench, where I recovered an hour of sleep. At ten o'clock I walked back to Treadwell's, timing my arrival well after they'd be open and thus, I hoped, I'd be inconspicuous. But the CLOSED sign was still out and the place was still dark. I cursed Treadwell's work ethic and waited some more.

Eventually, from the window of another café near the corner, I saw a young woman turn briskly into the block. She was the living, breathing manifestation of that telephone voice, a bleached blonde in her late twenties with skintight leather pants and a scandalously thin T-shirt glorifying the local ball club in scarlet letters. Her unhaltered breasts held the Orioles scoreless at both ends, bouncing freely as she walked by.

I had more coffee and gave her time to open the store and get her act, whatever that might be, together; then I moseyed up the street and went into the store.

"Hey, hon," she said. "You need some help?"

I faced her breasts and fought back the urge to say, *I do now.* I shook my head and said, "Thanks, I'll just look around," and immediately she went back to whatever she wasn't doing and forgot I was alive. I moved on into the store. It was dusty, dog-eared, and immense, everything I had imagined when I'd first heard about it that day on the telephone. In the lower front room someone had long ago made an attempt to classify, with sections marked off by possible fields of interest. Whoever had done that had probably

been dead at least two generations, buried in the Treadwell graveyard with all the old bookpeople. There was a sign that said FIRST
EDITIONS, but if that was supposed to mean literature, the section
had died or moved somewhere else years ago. I did find firsts of
Marcia Davenport's Mozart biography and the New York edition of
Zorba the Greek mixed in with a bunch of thirties-era science and
technology, but their condition was nonexistent and dust jackets
weren't even a fading memory.

I went upstairs and up yet another flight, moving from one dark
row to another, ostensibly browsing but in fact getting the lay of the
land. Sporadic lightbulbs hung in each row but most of the light
came from the enormous windows that faced one another on each
floor from opposite sides of the building. The floors creaked as I
walked on them. The place had a musty, dusty smell to it from top
to bottom.

Slowly I worked my way back downstairs and came out into the
room where Blondie was holding the fort. I stayed behind the stacks,
watching her through the bookshelves as she went about her work.
This was mostly sand-sifting, marking the sale books and putting
them out, putting others aside for the Man to see if and when he
decided to come in. There was no business as yet: no customers, no
telephone calls, no people lined up to sell their treasures. But it was
Tuesday morning and that could be dead in any bookstore in any
city. I walked along behind the shelves, mainly to keep my feet moving and my blood pumping. I tried to stay away from the creaking
boards: if the lady had forgotten me, I wanted to keep it that way.

A few customers finally came in. Two books bought, one sold.
Always more coming in than going out, and again, that was the way
of the trade, the nature of things.

Dean arrived sometime before noon.

He was a big man, hulking and bearlike behind his thick red
beard, impossible to read at first glance: the kind of guy who could
be palsy, intimidating, or anything in between. Something had been
missing from the descriptions I had collected of Dean Treadwell,

and I had also missed it in his voice on the phone. On second glance I made a guess at it: Dean was an actor, a chameleon who never showed anyone his real nature.

He said nothing by way of greeting to the blonde and she went on pushing books around behind the counter as if he wasn't there. He browsed his own shelves, looking critically at the dusty rows of books that stretched away toward the back of the room. Abruptly he said, "You ever think of straightenin' this fuckin' place up, Paula? Maybe we'd sell a book once in a while if you did."

"So where'm I s'posed to start?"

"Throw all this shit out in the street would be a good place."

He came behind the counter and looked at the one receipt, then at the books she had bought. "*The Girl Scout's Book of Dildos,*" he read. "Is this a goddamn joke?"

"I thought it might appeal to ya," she said, smiling brightly.

He thumbed through the book, pausing over what seemed to be a triple-paneled foldout illustration. "How damn much money did you pay for this thing?"

"Buck and a half. I'll keep it if you're not int'rested."

But he took the book and walked away, disappearing into a room that looked like a private office, deep in the back of the store.

Carl came along about forty minutes later and the blonde's demeanor changed in a heartbeat. I saw her stiffen, craning her neck as he came to the door. From where I was I could see that he had stopped outside with a man who had been walking with him. They huddled together in the portico, as if what they had been discussing had to be finished now and kept strictly between themselves. Carl was about what I expected: a weasel. The guy with him had the hard look of a real hood, and he did most of the talking. My radar sensed the iron he carried under his coat and I knew this was a seriously bad dude. Not a pretender, not a man you could easily bluff. I knew this at once, from an old cop's experience. Blondie was right to be wary.

They finished their talk and came into the store. Carl went straight back to the office and Capone drifted to the counter, where he could ogle the blonde's tits. She looked up at him and tried to smile. "Need some help, hon?"

He leaned over the counter and his coat flopped open. "I dunno, *hon*," he said. "What kinda help you givin'?"

She saw the rod and chilled.

"I thought I asked you a question," the hood said.

She paled then, so visibly I could see it from across the room. "You know," she said. "Books and stuff."

"Oh, books and stuff," he said. "Do I look like I need books and stuff?"

"No, sir."

"Why not? You think I can't read?"

"No, sir. I mean yes, sir. I'm sure you can read."

"You don't know what the hell you mean, do you?"

"No, sir."

Then she looked up over his shoulder. That spooked him and he turned away from the counter like a cat had crossed behind him. Our eyes met through the stacks. I looked away, too late. I heard his footsteps coming. I took a deep breath.

"Hey, you."

I turned and looked at him down the row of books.

"Yeah, you. What the hell are *you* lookin' at?"

"Nothing."

"Is that right? Am I nothing?"

"I wasn't looking at you."

He took a couple of steps into the aisle and I felt my gut tighten. *Here we go.*

"What am I, a liar?"

"I was looking at the books. I just happened to glance up."

"I don't think so," he said in a singsong voice.

"Well," I said. "Sorry if I offended you."

"You better be. And you better keep your fuckin' eyes to yourself unless you wanna go around with a cane and a seein'-eye dog. You got me?"

"I got you."

He took another step forward as if he hadn't liked the tone of my voice.

"I don't think you got me at all."

"Yeah, I did." I made a slight laughing sound, hoping to put a layer of respectful unease into it. "I really got you."

We looked at each other. It could have gone either way in those few seconds but then Carl came up from the back room. "Dante?"

He turned his head slightly. "Yeah, I'm comin'."

He pointed a finger at my face, then he turned and the two of them left the store.

I came out from behind the stacks. The blonde had sunk onto a chair and had a white-knuckle grip on the arms as if she feared falling out on the floor. She looked at me and in a trembly voice said, "I'm gonna quit this goddamn job."

"You okay?"

"Hell no, I'm not okay. Did you get a look at that guy? Did you see his eyes? Did you see that goddamn gun?" She blinked. "Jesus Christ, what's wrong with him?"

"He just likes scaring people. He likes to watch 'em cringe, that's how he gets his kicks. His shtick is to always take offense no matter what you say."

"I'm not talking about *that* guy. I mean what's wrong with Carl, bringing people like that around?"

"I guess you'll have to ask Carl that," I said. Then I nodded a silent *good afternoon* and left the store before Dean could come out and find me there.

Out on the street I stopped for a minute and took stock. A dark mood followed me down the block and into the same café as before, where I sat at the same window so I could look back at the block and the bookstore. I ordered a light lunch and took stock again. The last time I had backed away from a bully like that I had been in grammar school, about to learn one of the great guiding lessons of my life: *never blink first, never let the bastards intimidate you.* But I hadn't come all the way from Denver to get in a deadly brawl at Treadwell's on my first day in town.

Deadly was right. You don't take on a guy like that unless it's for keeps. And once it starts, you've got to be willing to do anything.

Dante.

You and I will see each other again, Dante.

I hoped not. But I had a hunch.

I ate my sandwich, then went to the phone booth and tried calling Koko Bujak. No answer. I went back to my table for some real coffee, strong and black, none of that decaf crap after the night I'd had. I sipped my way through three cups, took stock for the third time, and pronounced myself okay.

Business at Treadwell's had improved by early afternoon and now they had a steady stream of book-toting traffic going in and out. A bookscout with a heavy backpack came out with his load no lighter. Things were the same all over.

Dean appeared at two o'clock. He stood on the street and scratched his balls for a moment; then he came on down the block, passed my window, and hustled himself across Broadway. I left three dollars on the table and hustled on after him.

He walked north a couple of blocks, went west on Gough, and on into a lively section of Italian restaurants and bars. He turned into one of the bars. I waited outside but that soon lost its charm so I went in, lingering in the dark place just inside the door. The room was crowded with afternoon boozers and I didn't see Dean anywhere. I started to move deeper into the room, but suddenly I stopped and jerked back against the wall. I had seen someone sitting at a table just a few feet away, someone who couldn't be here but was, who would know me on sight. I eased myself out and took another quick look.

It was Hal Archer.

I had to move away from the door. People were now coming in a steady stream, so I walked behind Archer to the end of the bar, where I could hopefully blend into the heavy afternoon crowd. I had just taken the last available stool when Dean came out of the john, went over to Archer's table, and sat down. They had a long powwow that ran into the happy hour, through half a dozen beers for Dean and two slow-sipping cocktails for Archer. I sat, watched, and nursed my own beer, thinking of these two odd bedfellows and what a small world it was. Small world, my ass. Seeing them together made everything murkier, but it left no room in my mind for coincidence.

Archer left first. He got up, said something to Dean, hit the boys' room, and walked out of the bar a few minutes later. Dean had ordered another beer and seemed to be settling in for the night. I decided there might be more to gain by tailing Archer than watching Dean get drunk, so I followed him out into the street. I had to be careful now: one mistake and my cover would be blown. But on second thought, how much did that really matter? My time here was short: I would have to confront them all at some point.

I half expected Archer to hop a cab and leave me gaffing on the street, but for once I was lucky. He kept walking and he never looked back. Five minutes later he went into a hotel. I followed him into the lobby, just in time to see him get into an elevator and go up to the tenth floor.

What now?

I would wait, at least for a while: sit in the lobby with a newspaper, and if my luck held nobody would bother me till Archer came down again. Again I was lucky. The desk clerk had just begun eyeing me suspiciously after an hour when the elevator opened and Archer stepped out.

He had changed clothes and now wore a dark evening jacket and a bright turtleneck. I watched him over the top of my newspaper as he turned in to the dining room. The old Murphy's Law derivative ran through my head. *If something jams, force it. If it breaks, it needed replacing anyway.* A plan, whole and devious, unfolded in my mind. *Hit him where he lives—in the book he's writing. Don't wait for it to grow cold. Just do it.*

I followed him in. The hotel offered a buffet in addition to the regular menu and Archer had opted for that. I got into the line a few people behind him.

I was close enough now to hear him giving the cashier his room number. He took a table in the far corner of the room, a solitary figure with all his glory unrecognized. The Pulitzer prize may have its charms, but it's a lousy bedmate.

I paid with a twenty and headed across the room toward him.

"Well, Hal Archer, imagine seeing you here."

He looked up. "Do I know you?"

He knew me, all right: I could see it in his face. But I said, "Cliff Janeway. We met at Lee Huxley's." I said this warmly, as if we had become buddies at once that night. Boldly I put my tray down on his table and sat down. "Do you mind?"

"Actually, I'm waiting for someone."

"Oh, listen, I'll get out of your hair as soon as she gets here. I've just got to tell you something that's been on my mind since Miranda's party. I never should've fawned over you like that; I know it must be a drag being set upon by strangers. I'll bet it gets tiresome as hell, being told how great you are every minute of your life."

"That's all right," he said coldly.

"How generous of you to say that. But I was a boob and I need to say so."

"Well, you've said it." His face remained passive, indifferent, distant, and finally tinged with annoyance. "Now if you'll excuse me."

But I had already started to eat. "I really did mean it when I said I liked your stuff. I was your biggest fan, long before you won anything."

"Look," he said. "If I've written something you liked, I'm happy for both of us. But at the moment—"

"In fact, I owe you a big favor."

He looked at me with doleful eyes, like a man afraid to ask.

"You're the guy who turned me on to Richard Burton."

He said nothing but his eyes wondered where the hell *this* was going.

"I'm a book dealer, you know."

"I remember."

"Because of you, Burton has become one of those burning passions that comes along just a few times in a bookman's life."

He looked at me coldly.

"I've done a lot of homework on the man and his life and times since that night, and I'll bet I can even tell you a thing or two. I know you've been researching him for years and you've got a book in the works, but I've come across stuff nobody else knows."

The plan was suddenly on track: I had rattled him. For a moment he kept staring at me, then he said, "Who told you that?"

"What, that you're writing a book? Oh, come on, it was so obvious that night even a blind man could see it. But your secret's safe with me. I know how writers are. Just let it be known that Hal Archer is doing Sir Richard Burton, and half a dozen wannabe writers will rush into print with warmed-over retreads. And of course that'll cut into your market even if their books are lousy. Which they will be, right?"

"Listen . . . Janeway . . ."

"It's o-*kay*," I said warmly. "I won't tell a soul."

"All I ever said about Burton was what a grand figure he was. I *never* said I was writing about him."

"I understand completely. My lips are sealed."

"You don't understand anything. There's nothing to seal. Get that? Nothing."

"Sure." I put on my best look of phony camaraderie, guaranteed to let him know that I knew bullshit when I heard it. I did everything but wink at him. Then I said, in a masterpiece of my own bullshit, "Look, I've taken up way too much of your time."

I started to get up. But he said, as I knew he would, "Just as a point of curiosity . . . what the hell *are* you talking about?"

"You mean about Burton?"

He looked at me like a scientist studies a lower-life form. *No, about the queen's sex life, you bumbling goddamn ignoramus!*

I leaned close, as if spies were everywhere. "I've found a great source of untapped Burton material. Somebody with a direct link to his time in America."

"And who might that be?"

"Mrs. Josephine Gallant. Does that ring a bell?"

"Not at all," he said.

"Well, since your interest in Burton is just academic, it doesn't matter anyway."

The silence stretched. I nibbled at my cornbread, then said, with lighthearted malice, "Looks like your friend's gonna be late. Maybe she ran into traffic."

Again I made as if to rise. He said, "So who is this woman?"

"Josephine? Oh, she died last week in Denver."

"Well, then."

"Mmmm, I wouldn't say that. She left behind some interesting stuff."

"Such as?"

"Way more than we can discuss here and now. But listen, if you ever do write that book you're not writing, you'd better get together with me before you send it in."

He gave me a bitter little half-smile. "For which you would want . . . what? Assuming there was anything to any of this, which there isn't."

"Oh, Hal, I am *hurt* by the implication that I'd do this for money. I'm a bookman! All I want is to see a great book come out of it. *I* can't write it, but somebody sure needs to. If that's really not gonna be you, maybe I should talk to somebody else."

"Such as . . . who?"

"Oh, there's no end of writers around. I know lots of 'em. Some really good ones. That's one of the things about the book business, you meet writers."

I saw the flesh sag a little around his cheeks and that alone was worth the price of my ticket to Baltimore.

"I gotta go," I said abruptly.

It cost him a million in trumped-up arrogance to say this, but he said it. "You haven't finished eating yet."

"Yeah, but I'm going to another table now." I looked away at an absolutely stunning brunette who had just come in alone. "I think your date is here."

"That's not who I'm waiting for."

"Well, *that's* a damn shame. Jesus, what a dish. Anyway, I'm sure your friend will be along any minute, and I've taken up way more of your time than I intended to."

Before he could say *Stop, Wait a minute,* or *Get up from that chair and I'll kill you,* I was gone. I went clear across the dining room to a place near the window, but not so far away that we couldn't see each other. I ate hungrily while Archer picked at his food, and every so often our eyes would meet and I'd smile at him and nod pleasantly. A roving waiter came by and asked if I wanted coffee and I said yes, thank you, even though I'd had three times my caffeine allowance for the day. I went back to the buffet for dessert, something else I didn't need, but at least I stayed away from the cheesecake. The stewed apples were sensational.

Archer didn't seem to be eating much at all. After a while he pushed back from the table and got up. The moment of truth had arrived. He was coming my way.

He was sitting at my table.

"You should try these apples," I said. "Wanna bite?"

When he spoke again, all the bullshit between us was suddenly gone.

"You really are an annoying bastard, Janeway. Do you have any *idea* how annoying you are?"

"Yeah, I do. It's my one real talent, so I work at it."

He seethed while I ate the last of my apples.

"So, Hal . . . what does this mean? Do you want to talk real now?"

"Come up to my room. The number is 1015."

"I know what the number is."

"I need to make a phone call. Give me fifteen minutes."

"Okay. But listen very carefully to what I say. Don't try any funny stuff with me, Hal. If Dean's brother shows up with his gangster bodyguard, I promise—are you listening to me, Hal?—I *promise*, Hal, the first casualty of the evening will be you."

Fifteen minutes later I stepped off on the tenth floor. Archer opened the door to a midpriced plastic hotel room, indistinguishable from every Holiday Inn or Ramada the world over. I looked in the bathroom and closet, I opened the balcony door and looked outside; I barely resisted the urge to look under the bed. I checked the lock on the door, slipped the security chain into its slot, and sat on the bed. Archer watched in annoyance, but there was also a trace of alarm on his face. "What's wrong with you? You act like a man on the run from somebody."

"Let's just say I've lived this long partly because I make most of my mistakes on the right side of caution. I had the pleasure of meeting Dante this afternoon."

"Who's Dante?"

"You're not helping us much here, Hal. I hope I don't have to reinvent the wheel with every question."

"I don't know what you're talking about."

"Then just this once I'll draw you a picture. Big, ugly-assed thug who goes around with Carl Treadwell. An intimidator. A genuine bone-cruncher. Attila the Hun would cut him some real slack."

"I don't know anything about Carl's friends."

I looked dubious.

"Believe what you want, but I stay away from Carl."

"What about Dean?"

He went over to the bureau, picked up a pint bottle of scotch, and poured himself a short one. He was putting the bottle away when I said, "I take mine straight, thanks," and he looked at me again with that mix of bitter amusement and contempt. But he poured me the drink.

I took a sip. "I believe we were talking about Dean."

"Why don't you refresh my memory about why I'm talking to you at all."

I sighed. "This is gonna be a toolbox-and-coveralls conversation all the way, isn't it? You're gonna make me work for everything I get."

At last he said, "Dean Treadwell helps me find books that I need in my work."

"Are you still living in Charleston?"

"What's that got to do with anything?"

"This seems like a long way to come, just to find a bookseller."

"That's my damn business."

I sipped my scotch.

"You try finding books in Charleston," he said. "See how long it takes you to turn up a copy of anything truly rare."

"So you're saying you stumbled upon Dean, way up here in Baltimore, and he performed for you. He found the books you wanted and that's all there is to it."

"If I'm saying anything, that's probably what I'm saying."

"Who'd you call on the phone just now?"

"What possible business—"

"Maybe I'm making it my business. Maybe I'm suddenly starting to see a whole scheme unfolding and it's making me nervous as hell."

"What scheme? I don't know what—"

"How long have you really known about Mrs. Gallant and her books?"

"I never heard that name in my life before tonight."

"Now see, Hal, that's a lie. If you've got to lie, at least try to develop some style to go along with it. People appreciate honest bullshitters like Dean and me, but nobody likes a cold liar like you, Archer. Nobody."

"How dare you," he seethed.

"Yeah, right. Maybe you can sell that indignation in polite society, but to me you just look like another scared street rat."

"How *dare* you!" he shouted.

"Gosh, Hal, I seem to have offended you, and just when you were beginning to like me so much. Could it have been something I said?"

"You're wasting my time. I don't think you know anything."

"About what? Is that why you invited me up here, to find out what I know? I've got startling news for you, Hal. I came up here to find out what *you* know."

He swished his drink, buying himself a moment to think. In a calmer voice, he said, "Let's get this straight. I don't care anything about your little old lady, or her . . ."

He blinked, as if he'd just saved himself from a stupid blunder.

I smiled at him. "Or her what?"

"Or her books. Isn't that what we're talking about?"

"Nice try, but I think you were about to say something else."

"I can't be held accountable for your silly hunches."

"Hal, please. I know you're much the superior being here, but do I really look that stupid?" I cleared my throat. "Obviously I do. It's amazing, dense as I am, how I picked right up on that crack in your story."

"What crack? You're talking in riddles."

"Are you still trying to tell me that what you were going to say was you have no interest in my little old lady or her *books*? Isn't the whole reason you brought me up here *because* of Josephine and her books?"

We stared at each other.

"Oops," I said.

He went on, blindly stonewalling. "I have no idea what you're talking about."

"Could it be you were about to say my little old lady and her *grandfather*? Or my little old lady and her *mother*, who was screwed out of what should have been her daughter's by a shyster bookman and her drunken husband?"

"You should be the one writing fiction, Janeway. My interest is purely academic. *If* there's Burton material that has never been seen, and *if* you have some kind of access, which based on this conversation so far looks goddamned doubtful, then yes, I would be interested in knowing about it."

"Even though you're not doing Burton."

"Yes! Jesus Christ, do we have to go *all* the way through this stupid dance? Of course I'm interested. What historian wouldn't be interested in seeing material like that?"

"Then maybe we can work out a deal."

"I don't even know what you've got to deal with. Why should I *deal* anything with you when all you're probably doing is wasting my time?"

"Bluster all you want, Hal, but these questions won't go away. What are you doing with the Treadwells? Don't you know how suspicious this is, given the history of that bookstore and its double-dealing with Mrs. Gallant's books? Don't you realize how far beyond chance it is that you went looking for a rare-book dealer and just happened to stumble over Dean Treadwell, six hundred miles away, at exactly this moment in time?"

"What double-dealing? What coincidence?"

"Are you actually trying to tell me you don't know about the

Treadwells? You don't know how Josephine was robbed of those books eighty years ago?"

He tried an artificial laugh but it came out shrill, like a hyena's bark. "Eighty years ago! Jesus, you *are* out of your mind."

"Do you really think you're fooling anybody with this bluff? I didn't kick your door down, you're the one who brought me up here. If you want to talk, talk, but don't try feeding me any more of that bullshit about Dean looking for rare books on your behalf. Do I look like I just leaped out of some bookstore in far left field? What rare books? What books do you need that only Dean Treadwell can find for you? Old Dean must be a killer bookman. I saw him in action this morning and I didn't think he could find his own cock in a pissing contest, but hey, maybe I was wrong. Give me the titles of a few books he's finding for you. I'm prepared to be knocked out by Dean's brilliance, so go ahead, give me his best shot."

"I don't have to give you anything."

"Tell me just two titles you've been looking for and only Dean can find them."

"Who the hell do you think you are?"

"Just *one* title, Hal. One lousy title and I'll believe anything you say."

"This conversation is over."

"Have we been having a conversation? I couldn't tell."

"Get the hell out of here! Get out now or I'll call hotel security."

"I've got to improve my manners, I'm getting thrown out of everywhere these days." I tried for a look of contriteness. "Can I finish my drink first?"

The room went suddenly quiet, and only in its void did I realize how completely I had been thinking and acting like a cop again. It had started last week with Whiteside, with Denise, and it wasn't just the nature of my questions or my interrogative manner, it was part of my heartbeat. A good cop suspects everybody of everything.

In that minute the case swirled through my mind and I saw them all: Josephine, Ralston, the Treadwells, and Denise, carried out of her bedroom on a coroner's stretcher. The thought I'd just had was so farfetched it had come only as an impression, lacking even the words to give it substance, but almost at once it became specific. I thought of the kid who had seen a fleeting white man leaving Ralston's house. Archer was a white man. So were the Treadwells. So was Dante. And Denise had had Josephine's Burton: for one night only, but who would have known that?

What if these sons of bitches had been following Josephine? What if they knew she'd died at Ralston's? What if they'd killed Denise?

Denver's three hours away. They hop a plane, bingo!

I leaned forward on the bed and riddled Archer with my eyes. "Where were you this time last week?"

"That's none of your business either, but I was in South Carolina, working."

"Can anybody verify that?"

"What kind of question is that?"

"It's a really, really simple one, Hal. It means, did anybody see you there?"

"I *know* what it means. Why are you asking? Why do I have to verify anything?"

"Obviously you don't . . . yet. I'd still like an answer."

"The answer is no. When I'm working I see no one and I don't pick up the telephone. Does that satisfy you?"

"Sure. I admire that intensity, that's why you're so good. But I couldn't help wondering if you were in Denver last Wednesday night."

"Why would you wonder that?"

"I don't know, just a wild hair. You're sure you weren't there?"

"Of course I'm sure. Do you think I wouldn't know if I'd just been halfway across the goddamn country?"

"You'd know, all right."

"Why would I hide that? Did somebody rob a bank last Wednesday?"

"Yeah, that's what happened, Hal, I'm trying to pin a bank robbery on you."

He walked to the window and looked out into the night. "I think I'd like you to leave now," he said softly. "This meeting hasn't exactly been productive."

"I was just thinking the same thing."

I got up and went to the door, betting he'd say something.

"What are you going to do now?" he said.

I looked back across the room. "Oh, I don't know, screw up your life as much as possible, I guess. I've got a friend at *Publishers Weekly* who'll be interested that you're doing Burton. She'll call you to verify. Of course you'll lie, but I'll tell her to expect that. It won't be much of a story, just a little squib. 'Is he or isn't he?' Enough to let the world know."

"Damn it, Janeway, will you please listen? I am *not* doing Richard Burton."

"Then whatever I say won't matter, will it?" I reached into my distant past and pulled out a name, a freckle-faced kid with pigtails I had loved madly in the third grade. "My friend's name is Janie Morrison. If you read *Publishers Weekly,* you've probably seen her byline. She'll love you, Hal, you're such an awful liar. Janie cut her teeth on the *New York Post,* so she knows a bad liar when she hears one."

I pulled the chain out of its slot and looked through the peephole at the empty hall. I could feel his eyes on my back, and when I turned for a final look, he had moved away from the window and was regarding me with a pitiful, whipped-dog look. "I'm really sorry, Hal," I said. "I'm sorry you're such a flaming fucking dickhead, because I really did love your books. You've got the rarest of all rare gifts, and you've got it by the bucket. If you'd just get your head out of your ass, maybe you'd even be happy."

"What would you know about happy? Are you happy?"

"Hey, I'm doing what I like, why wouldn't I be happy? So what if it's not perfect, I don't believe in perfection. Maybe happy's as good as it gets."

He said nothing.

"C'mon, honey, talk to me. It's not too late, we can still be friends."

He looked up and met my eyes. "Don't hold your breath."

"I never do. But if you change your mind, I'm at the Bozeman Inn."

I watched the floors tick off as I went down in the elevator. It stopped on three and I braced back against the wall, expecting . . . *what?*

An elderly couple got in, eyeing me suspiciously.

I was not just nervous, suddenly I was very nervous. What had seemed like a good idea had become, in Archer's continued silence, heavy and tense, fraught with peril. I had had that sudden hunch, and once it was there I couldn't shake it.

Let it settle. See if it sticks.

How many murder cases had I solved just this way? I'd get an idea, some harebrained notion that had no facts or logic to support it, and I'd start growing a case around it. How many times had I gone after a killer with nothing more than a wild hunch, and suddenly had the whole ball of wax fall into my lap?

Long ago I learned that murder isn't logical. Sometimes it is but those are the easy cases: the old man kills the old lady, the kid cuts his father a new orifice, the hooker shoots her pimp. The tough ones almost always go against the grain of common sense.

I walked out into the cool night air. The world looked peaceful, serene: all the synonyms for tranquillity. I walked west, then south, around the Inner Harbor toward Federal Hill. I finally settled on a bench overlooking the harbor.

The thought came again: What if these sons of bitches had killed Denise?

How could they have known about her? The book was the only possible motive and no one knew Denise had had it. Just Denise herself, Ralston and his doctor, Erin, and me.

I had another hunch, dark and full of trouble. Suddenly I feared for Koko. Koko knew things no one else knew.

My cop juice was finally perking. What if Denise's killer had not been a two-bit Denver cockroach looking for pocket change? If the Burton had been the motive, the killer had turned into a much bigger cockroach. What if it had all begun here, not in Denver? Almost surely, then, Archer was in the middle of it. So were the Treadwells. Dante was their enforcer, and I had just put out big pieces of myself as roach bait.

And what about Koko?

The night was no longer young but under the circumstances, I didn't care much about propriety. I stopped at the first phone booth I saw and punched in her number.

"Come on, Koko, answer the damn phone."

I let it ring twenty times before I gave up, cursing the darkness.

16

Forty minutes later the cabbie looked back over his shoulder and said, "What part of Ellicott City you want?"

"I don't know. How big is it?"

"Not big—few thousand people, one main drag, buncha winding little streets. But it helps if you know where you're goin'. It can get dark here."

I held up a paper and read my own writing in the glare of oncoming lights. "Where is Hill Street?"

"I can take you there."

"Just wondering if it can be walked from downtown."

"If you like to walk. It's uphill both ways, as my kid likes to say."

We crossed a river and were suddenly in Howard County. We clattered over a railroad track, passed a large stone building, and started to climb. "My wife comes from around here," the cabbie said. "Her dad had a gas station."

If I expected just another sprawling suburb, this was a surprise. Everything seemed to be narrow, winding, carved out of stone and at least a century old. Frederick Road had become Main Street, with stone buildings on both sides. What I could see in the night reminded me of Colorado. The town made me think of Central City.

The road took a turn and a moment later the cabbie said, "This is as downtown as it gets. Hill Street's straight ahead on your left, maybe a quarter of a mile. It's no skin off my nose to drive you there."

"Thanks." I thought about it, then said, "I'll get out here and go on my own."

I stood in the shadows of Main Street as the taxi disappeared back down the hill. It had to be eleven o'clock by then: pretty late to go groping through a strange land. I still felt jittery and I couldn't shake the notion that I was being followed. I walked along a street flanked by pubs and eateries and various shops that had closed hours ago. Night-lights shone through darkened windows, and beyond the street I could see an occasional light higher up, as if on a hillside. The Central City image grew stronger as I walked past something called Church Road and continued up the hill.

I passed a fire station and a bar. Stopped for a moment and looked back. A few cars were there on the street behind me, a few people were out on the sidewalk. No one who seemed to care, no one who watched, no one who followed.

Near the top was an old church. Hill Street led away to the left, looking like a lithograph, like a country lane in the moonlight.

The climb continued with only the moon as a guide. Occasionally I could see lights from a house but most were dark, their people asleep for the night. I had no flashlight but I remembered what Koko'd said: the fifth house on the right and her name was on the mailbox.

I saw it then, a low, flat dwelling on a large piece of land, surrounded by trees. Surprisingly there was a light, a faint glow that might have come from a lantern or a gas lamp. I stepped along her walk and clumped up onto her porch. Knocked on her door.

I heard a bump. The house was quiet then for what seemed a long time.

A shadow passed at the side window. I saw a hand, then a face in silhouette.

The porch light came on. I saw a dark figure looking at me through a small window. The shape looked female but I couldn't be sure yet.

"Koko? It's Janeway, from Denver."

The shadow backed away from the window and a moment later the door opened just a crack. I saw nothing of a face, only the rims of her glasses reflected from the porch light. But when she spoke, I recognized her voice.

"Mr. Janeway?"

"I know it's late. I'm sorry. I did try calling earlier."

"I was meditating. I can't hear the phone when I'm in that room."

"I should come back tomorrow."

I hoped she would counter but she said nothing.

A moment passed. I took a chance. "Listen, Koko, what I really need is to talk to you right now, tonight. Some things have happened since we spoke on the phone."

I heard her take a breath. "This can't be good if it brings you here at midnight."

"A friend of mine has been killed."

She leaned closer to the door and said, "I'm sorry." I saw the shadow of her face move across the crack in the door and she regarded me with her right eye.

"How was he killed?"

"She. The police think it was just a neighborhood burglary."

"Sounds like you don't believe that."

"I don't know what I believe. It's not like me to make up spooks, but I've been thinking all kinds of crazy things since I got to Baltimore."

"Things that have to do with Josephine."

Before I could confirm that, she said, "My manners are terrible. Come in."

I stepped into a dark hallway. The entire house was dark except for the dim orange lamplight in the room off to my right, and Koko was still nothing more than a shadow. She led me toward what was apparently a living room and I had a vision of a slender girl with a shawl over her shoulders, surrounded by books. The shawl was dark, I saw in the lamplight from the doorway; the girl, from her own description on the telephone, would be a woman somewhat older than me, but the girlish image persisted as she crossed the room into the light.

There was a hint of incense in the air. The room was slightly hazy, like a scene in an art film. She turned and motioned me to a chair. She was indeed slim. Her face was young and unwrinkled, her age just hinted by the glasses and her hair, which now in the orange light

looked to be black speckled with either white or gray. Even with the
salt-and-pepper hair she looked no older than thirty-five. Her face
like the rest of her was thin, but warm in the fuzzy light. I could see
a line of sweat on her forehead, though the house was cool. She said,
"Please sit," and she took a chair facing mine.

I looked in her eyes, which seemed to be blue. "You're younger
than I thought."

She smiled slightly. "I'm afraid that's a huge illusion. If I look
younger than I am, it's because I've been doing the right things for
about thirty years now. It's no great secret—just do what they all tell
you."

"Who are they?"

"Herbalists, medicine men, a shaman or two. I stretch, I walk, I
get violent, fierce exercise at odd moments of the day. Just before
you came, as a matter of fact. I eat right. And I don't smoke. That's
the absolute worst thing you can do to yourself."

She had a kind smile, which began in her eyes and radiated through
her face. She smiled now and said, "I'll be sixty-two next month."

"Get out of here!"

"You look pretty fit yourself."

"That's because I'm young at heart."

"You look like you're thirty-five and you talk like a wise guy."

"I'm thirty-seven. I run obsessively, drink occasionally, take in
way too much caffeine, and dispense more verbal trash than you'll
get from a dozen other sources in a month of Sundays. That's the
wise guy part of my nature. But I don't smoke."

"Good for you. Can I get you something? I was just about to
have tea."

"At midnight?"

"I'm retired, Mr. Janeway. I have no clock to answer to, so I sleep
when I want, stay up all night if I feel like it, and drink tea whenever
it pleases me."

"I would love some tea at midnight."

"Good. I'll be right back."

While she was gone I got up and looked around the room. She had books shelved everywhere, works on Eastern philosophy, on India and Egypt, Sufism and hypnosis; some poetry, some literature, a few fascinating individuals. The works of Rabindranath Tagore, the life of Gandhi, all the obvious books by and about Richard Burton. She had tacked a small framed quote from Tagore on the end of her bookcase: *Modern civilization has gathered its wealth and missed its well-being.* I looked into a dark hallway and I could see more books on both sides.

"I read a lot." She stood behind me, holding a tray with cups and a steaming pot.

"And you move like a cat."

"It's a solid house. Not many creaking boards. And I never wear shoes inside."

I looked back at her books. "Interesting collection."

"Does it tell you anything about its owner?"

"Sure. There are no better indicators of character than the books you have."

"What do you look for when you go into a house and there are no books at all?"

"I don't know. Whatever's there, I guess. But I always feel a sense of . . . what's the word I'm looking for?"

"Pity's the word."

"That's a strong, judgmental word." But I thought about it and said, "Yeah."

"I couldn't live without books. What amazes me is how many people can. I know *writers* who have no books at all, if you can believe that."

I not only believed it, I knew some of the same writer types. Glory seekers who want to make lots of money writing books but would never think of buying one.

"Come drink your tea before it gets cold."

I took a sip and said, "What is this? It's not tea."

"It's an herbal concoction. Do you like it?"

"Yeah, I think I do."

"It'll put hair on your chest."

I laughed. "Never had that problem, actually."

I asked her what kind of name Koko Bujak was.

"My father was what's called a White Russian. My mother was from Baltimore."

We looked at each other. "So what can I do for you?" she said.

I owed her the truth and I told it all: facts, suspicions, everything.

She didn't say a word the whole time. She barely moved in the chair. Her eyes were riveted to mine, a compelling gaze that made me keenly aware of her hypnotic skills as I talked. She must have blinked during the half hour but I never saw her do it. After a while her eyes were like pinpoints of energy and the rest of her went out of focus. I wasn't telling this story, she was pulling it out of me, but that was okay, none of it was against my will; I never had the feeling of going under or being out of my own control. If I wanted to I could get up any time, in the middle of a sentence, walk out, and fly back to Denver. It was almost pleasant except for the reality that someone had killed Denise and my sudden hunch that the killer might be in Baltimore, not Denver.

"That's why I'm here at midnight," I said as her face came into focus.

I didn't know what I expected her to do with it. What I didn't expect was how the conversation went from there.

"So you think I may be on someone's list, is that what you're saying?"

"I don't know, Koko. That sounds pretty goofy, doesn't it?"

"A week ago, maybe. Now, it doesn't." She took a deep breath, let it out through her nose. "I've had a feeling for the past week that someone's been watching me."

"Have you seen anybody?"

"I had a prowler last night. But I felt someone there long before that happened."

"What kind of prowler? Noises?"

"No, not just a sound. Someone I actually saw in the yard behind the house."

"How much of a look did you get?"

"Not much. He was back there in the trees, just for a moment."

"What time of day was it?"

"Middle of the night. Just about this time."

"How'd you happen to see him?"

"Felt a cat cross my path. Went to the back door and there he was, in the yard."

"Did he see you?"

"Oh yes. He was crossing the yard, looking toward the house when I came to the door. I couldn't have been more than a silhouette from where he was but we saw each other. He stopped in his tracks, then he veered into the trees and ran off that way."

"Did you call the cops?"

"What good would that do? He was gone before I could even get to the phone. Besides, the police would only blame the blacks."

"Why would they do that?"

"There's a black housing project up on Mount Ida Drive. Lots of low-income black families, lots of crime. The police are always over there about something."

"This prowler you had, were you able to see him well enough to—"

"He was white. It never crossed my mind that he might be some local kid. Maybe I couldn't see him well enough to identify him, but there was moonlight, like tonight. I know what I saw."

"Anything else?"

"You mean other incidents? No, nothing that obvious."

"Anything at all."

"Like I told you, I've been restless for about a week. Actually, it's been more than a month now, but for the past week since I talked to you it's been more . . . intense. I'm not sleeping well, and that's unusual. I wake up after a few hours with a feeling that my life's been invaded. That probably makes no sense at all and I can only tell you that it makes as much sense to me as seeing that man in the yard. I'll get up at, say, two o'clock in the morning and go straight to the back door, as if someone had knocked on it."

"But there's never anyone there."

"Except that one time, no. But on Tuesday . . ." She shivered suddenly.

"What's wrong?"

"Nothing. I felt it just now. It's probably talking about it that gives me the creeps." She got up and went to the window. "See? Nobody there."

She came back and sat in her chair, but I could see she was still nervous.

"You were about to tell me what happened Tuesday."

She smiled wanly. "You're pretty serious with your questions. Almost like a policeman yourself."

"I was one, for a long time."

I told her a bit about it, hoping to gain her confidence. Then I asked her again what had happened on Tuesday.

"I went to the store out on the highway to get some groceries. I was gone maybe an hour. When I got home I had a feeling even before I got out of the car. Like, *somebody's here,* only it was stronger than just a feeling. For a few minutes I was absolutely certain someone was in my house. I sat in the car for a long time, working up the courage to go inside. When I finally did, there was nothing . . . and yet the feeling wouldn't go away." She looked at the window. "Obviously it never has gone away. I still have it."

"Did you look through your stuff to see if anything was missing or out of place?"

"I looked through everything. If I'd had a burglar, he was a very good one. Nothing was missing. And the first thing I did was look at the Burton material."

"Why'd you do that?"

"I had a hunch. If you haven't figured it out yet, I follow my hunches."

"So you thought all along that this had something to do with Burton and Josephine. Is that what you're saying?"

"There's more to it than that. Did Jo tell you about the Treadwells?"

"She said one of the old Treadwells stole her Burton books eighty years ago."

"She always believed that. One of the first things that came out of our sessions was the name Treadwell. I was surprised to learn about that store, how it's still in business, and Jo was haunted by it. I don't think that's too strong a word—she was just *haunted* by the idea that something they did all those years ago might have had such a negative effect on her life. It became such an obstacle that I knew we'd have to confront it, so one day I suggested that we go down there and see the place, look around. She leaped at the chance. I never thought we'd be in any kind of danger."

"So what happened?"

"One afternoon we went and at first it was just what I thought— a look around. She had me carry her bag, which was heavy. I didn't know what was in it then. There was a woman running the place. Jo asked if the Treadwells still owned it and the woman said yes. Jo asked if she could speak to them, and a minute later a man came out of the office."

"What'd he look like?"

"Small . . . cold."

"Carl."

"You know him?"

"I've seen him—talked to him, so to speak."

"Well, at that point I didn't know what was going to happen, what she was going to do. 'Show him my book,' she said, and I looked in the bag and there was this exquisite old book—it turned out to be the African book. I was as surprised as Treadwell; I had no idea she had anything like that. 'What'll you give me for this?' she said, and Treadwell got all shaky and tense. I mean, truly, you could see it all over him. 'Where'd you get this book?' he said, and it was almost like an accusation. 'What'll you give me for it?' Jo said again. He looked at her hard, like he was trying to size her up. Then he said, 'Two thousand.' Jo smiled. It was a bitter smile, not funny, and she said, 'I thought so. You're still a den of thieves.'"

"Wow."

"Yeah, wow. But what happened then still shivers my timbers. He reached over and put his hand on the book and said, 'I've got to tell you something: this looks like a stolen book to me. I'll have to confiscate it till we learn where it came from.'"

"Wow. Then what happened?"

"I snatched it away from him. Said, 'Don't you even think of trying to take this lady's book. I'll go to the cops so fast it'll make your head swim.'"

"What'd he say to that?"

"Nothing. I put the book back in the bag and we walked out. But he saw us drive away, got a good look at my car."

"And maybe the plate number. So was that when . . ."

"That's when it started—that spooky feeling I had. For a while I thought it was just nerves, but I'm not usually like that."

"So that day, when you went to the store, you had good reason to worry about your Burton stuff. But nobody had touched it?"

"I have it well hidden."

"Here in the house, though, right?"

She took her time answering that. At last she said, "If somebody wanted to tear the house apart, he could find it. Whoever was here had decided—at least for the moment—not to do that. He wanted to keep me thinking no one had been here. I don't know how he could even get in without breaking something, but somebody was here. That's what I think, since you asked. I think someone *was* here. And he looked through my Burton books, the ones on the open shelf. He went through my things, then very carefully he put them all back. Then he left, just a few minutes before I got home. But his aura—his *heat*—was still here. That's what I think."

She looked at me hard. "What do you think? And don't humor me."

"No, I think that's all very possible. People can get into houses—I could pick this lock myself. So I think you'd better get that stuff, wherever it is, and get it the hell out of here. Make copies. Put it in a safe deposit box. You might not be so lucky next time."

She nodded. "I hear what you're saying."

"Good. So what'd you do after the prowler came?"

"I bought a gun."

I felt my backbone stiffen. "What kinda gun?"

"Little thirty-eight. I had it in my hand when you came to my door."

"Where is it? Can I see it?"

"Why?"

"No reason. Forget I asked if it makes you uncomfortable."

"No, I'm fine with you." She unfolded her shawl, took out a wicked-looking snub-nose, and put it in my hand. "It's loaded."

"I see that. No offense, but do you happen to know how to use this thing?"

"The man who sold it to me told me a few things. About the safety lock or whatever you call it. Other than that, what's to know? You cock it, point it, and make someone very sorry he's come into your house."

I handed it back to her. "That's basically it. As long as you don't shoot me or the paperboy, the mailman, or some Jehovah's Witness who's only trying to save your soul."

She pursed her lips. "That's pretty strong disapproval I hear in your voice."

"Hey, I wish you didn't need a gun. I wish the world could be a better place."

"But you don't like it."

"I don't like it that some clown sold you this thing with you not knowing any more about it than I know about transcendental meditation. You should see what this baby will do to a pound of flesh." I made a fist about the size of a human heart.

Her look said she could imagine. "Well, don't worry, I'm not going to kill anyone with it. I thought it might scare someone off."

"Jesus, Koko, that's even worse. If he gets it away from you, you've just armed your enemy."

Nothing was said for a moment. Koko put the gun down on the table.

"You never want to pull a gun on a guy unless you mean it, that's all I'm saying."

She looked frustrated. "I know you're right. I've been uneasy with that thing in the house. But what am I supposed to do? You don't get Jehovah's Witnesses at two o'clock in the morning."

"You never know. Those birds never stop trying."

The gun yawned up from the table between us. She started to say something but again her eyes drifted nervously to the window.

"I was pretty careful when I came up here," I said.

"Why? Did you think you were followed? Did the same cat cross your path?"

"I was careful, Koko. You know the reasons."

"Maybe so, but I think you *were* followed." She got up and went quickly to the window to peep through the curtains. "See? He's there. He's out there now."

I came up and we stood together, close enough to touch.

"I don't see anything."

"I saw someone, across the road. He went back in the trees."

"Same guy?"

"I don't know. I think so. I can't be sure."

"I'll go take a look."

"No. Don't do that."

"I'll be okay."

"You don't know that. I'll call the police."

"Whatever you want. But it's different seeing a guy in your back-yard and seeing one out on the road."

"The police will laugh at me, is that what you're saying?"

"They'll have a harder time taking this seriously."

"What about you? Do you think I'm imagining things?"

"I think you saw somebody. Who that was, we may never know."

"What if it's him?"

"He'd have to be pretty good to have followed me here."

"But if he is pretty good, it could be done."

"Anybody can be followed."

"No matter how careful you think you are. And it would be a lot easier if he knew ahead of time where you were going. Or thought he knew."

"Sure. He wouldn't need to follow me at all then, would he?"

"Just wait for you. But what would that prove?"

"That you and I have made contact. He'd have to assume that you now know what I know. And that I've put you on guard."

"So the next time he breaks in . . ."

"He won't pussyfoot around."

She stepped away from the window and sat looking down at her gun.

"None of this may happen," I said. "But you've got to play it safe now. I'll help you if you want."

She looked up at me. "We're in this together, is that what you're saying?"

"We are if you want us to be."

"I'm not sure what that means. But right now I sure would welcome your help."

"Then you've got it, no strings attached, for as long or short as you want it."

She gave me a grateful look. Then she looked uneasily around the room. "I guess there's nothing we can do till morning. But this house has been violated. I think I'll go crazy just waiting here."

"Well, the alternative is to get out now. Where's your car?"

"In the garage behind the house."

"Get all your stuff together, if that's what you want to do. Gimme your keys; I'll get the car and bring it up close to the house. Then we'll stash the stuff in the car and get it out of here."

"Where will we go?"

"Down to Baltimore where there are people and lights. Maybe we'll just drive around till dawn. At nine o'clock we'll go to your bank and get a safe deposit box. The bank should be able to copy your notes. Later you'll want to get dupes made of the tapes as well." I shrugged. "This isn't the greatest idea since Poe invented the detective story, but it's the best I've got. Unless you want to change your mind and stay here till dawn."

"No, that doesn't feel . . . I don't know how to explain it."

She gave me her keys and went away. I heard her footsteps on a stairwell going down, then I heard her moving around under my feet, and I walked from window to window, looking out into the yard for trouble. The backyard looked peaceful in the moonlight, the garage a ramshackle building in the center of it, the whole property ringed by trees and underbrush. From there I couldn't see any sign of a neighboring house.

I went out through the kitchen, through a small porch to the backyard. Nothing there either: no movements or sounds, no shadows darting away into the trees. It would be easy to find Koko guilty of an overactive imagination, but now I had a dark hunch of my own. I leaned back against the porch and wondered if we were doing the right thing. But I told her we'd go, it was her choice, so I finally moved uneasily away from the house toward the garage.

Halfway across the yard I froze. Something had moved, back in the trees. Might be a man, maybe a dog: probably nothing more than my own imagination competing with Koko's. A breeze had come up, fluttering the leaves, and maybe that's all it was.

I egged myself on. *Come on, boy, you're acting like a spooked kid.*

I reached the edge of the garage and looked around it. I could see the door a few feet ahead: a double door for the car and a walk-in at the side. There was a small window and the interior looked pitch-black. I eased along the wall. My dark hunch had grown into a monster and I wished I had brought a flashlight, or Koko's gun.

The door creaked loudly as I opened it and stepped inside. It was dark but I could see part of the car in the moonbeam coming through the window. It glinted off one of the fenders and fell against an empty wall.

I moved quickly away from the door and stood against the opposite wall, listening. This is damn ridiculous, I thought. Koko would wonder where I'd gone. But I didn't move.

Someone was in here. I *felt* him breathing: I *sensed* his spirit. Nothing moved, there was no sound from any part of the garage, but by then my internal alarm was going crazy.

Then he did move. A slight bump, small enough to be nothing more than a rat.

A shadow crossed outside the door. Nothing imaginary about that. I leaned forward and peered out as something flitted past toward the trees. Another shape flicked past the window. There were three of them now, at least three. I eased along the wall, my fingers probing around for anything that might work as a weapon—a tire iron, a wrench, a hammer—but all I picked up was a layer of dust.

Nothing to do but go ahead. I took two quick steps away from the wall, touched the hard, cold door of the car, found the handle, and jerked it open. I was ready for what happened next; he was not. The car's interior light came on and I saw him, in a crouch about three feet away. He shouted and came at me. I swung from the hip, caught him with a solid left just above the belt, and he dropped like a congressman's ethics. He rasped out two desperate words, "Jesus . . . *Christ,*" and the other two charged into the garage. I slammed the car door shut—we all might as well be in the dark—and spun away as a dancing shadow moved around me. I swung and hit nothing.

Suddenly a powerful flashlight went on in my face. I smelled a gunnysack just before it was thrown over my head and jerked down over my arms. "Now, you son of a bitch," a voice whispered. "Now we'll see how frisky your ass is."

I took a killer kidney punch. Someone wrapped me in another sack, my arms were pinned by some kind of rope or belt, my feet

were kicked out from under me, and I tasted the floor, a burlap sandwich garnished with blood. I felt a searing pain and saw red streaks
behind my eyes. One of them had stomped on the back of my head.
I knew I was hurt; for the first time in years I feared for my life, and
I fought like a wild man to get up and get out of that straitjacket.

I never made it. He went to work with his feet, not caring much
what he hit or how hard. I took half a dozen in the gut, a bad one to
the groin, and again he found my head. At some point I went under.

The next thing I heard was Koko's voice. I felt her hands as she
pulled off the gunnysack and rolled me over. It was still dark. I
looked up and saw her shape behind the tiny flashlight.

"Are you okay?"

"I don't know." I tried to sit up. "I may have some broken bones."

"I'll go call a doctor."

"Let's see if I'm still alive first."

"Lie still for a while. Your lip's split open and you've got a broken tooth."

I touched the tooth with my tongue and felt the ragged break. My
lip was busted down to the cleft in my chin.

I tried again and did sit up. But I ached in joints I never knew I had.

"I suppose they took your stuff," I said.

"You shouldn't worry about that now."

"Did they hurt you?"

"Nothing I won't get over. You got far worse."

"What'd they do to you?"

"One of them slapped me around, just to get my attention, he said.
He put a gun to my head and said there'd only be one warning."

I took the flashlight and played it on her face. She'd have a shiner
in the morning.

"What was the warning?"

"Not to go to the police. If I do, they'll be back and I'll be dead."

I got up from the floor and moved around.

She said, "Does anything feel permanently ruined?"

"Just my pride, Koko." But as I reached out for the wall it seemed to slip away. When I looked at her by flashlight there were two of her. "Never been kayoed before. Had plenty of chances but never had the pleasure till now."

"At least your morbid sense of humor's in one piece. Sit down here, I'm going to call a doctor."

"Not yet."

"I don't want to argue with you. You really do need some attention."

"I'm a fast healer when I need to be. And I don't have time for a doctor."

I figured I had a concussion but I could live with that. I reached out and squeezed her arm. "If you really want to do something for me, go inside and make half a pot of the blackest coffee you can brew. When the spoon stands up in it, call me."

"There isn't any coffee. I'm sorry, I don't use it." Her voice was distressed, as if she had failed me in my darkest hour. In a smaller voice: "Would you like some tea?"

"Oh God, no." I covered my face and laughed, and my laughter was the blood brother of tears. "Your tea is lovely, Koko, but please, God, no tea. Thank you for the thought."

She squatted in the light from the open door and looked up at me like a mother hen. "I'm so sorry this happened to you."

"It's not the first time. Based on past experience, I think I'll live."

We sat with each other, just breathing and happy we could.

"What'd you do with that gun?" I asked after a while.

"It's still in there on the table."

"They didn't see it. That's good, I'm gonna need it."

"Why? What are you going to do?"

"Go get your stuff back, I hope."

She didn't believe me. I smiled and moved away from the wall. She put an arm around my back and I hobbled across the yard to the house.

17

From across the street I could see the faint light far back in Tread-well's. Just as I had figured: they were in there trying to dope out what they'd got. I hadn't needed the brains of a Rhodes scholar to solve this one. One and one are two; two rats plus one rat equals three rats. There they were: Carl and Dante and some other rat.

"What if you're wrong?" Koko said. "What if it wasn't them?"

"Then I'll be a monkey's uncle."

It was still well before the dawn: the deadest part of the early morning, when anyone on the street would be noticed a block away. I had parked out on Broadway and we had walked boldly up East-ern Avenue, finding a crack between the buildings across from Treadwell's. We huddled there now, sharing our body heat just out of a cold predawn wind. I had draped the bloody gunnysack over my shoulder and it was an effective poncho in the wind. But I had a powerful do-unto-others streak in me, and I thought it might have another use before the dawn.

I had to hand it to Koko: not once had she tried to hide her hor-ror at what I was about to do, nor had she mounted any kind of argument against it. She had only insisted on coming along, and that was her call. They had taken her stuff and slapped her around and that made it her call, as long as she understood the risks.

In the hour since Dante and his boys had left me battered and bleeding on the floor, I had made a good comeback. The double vision had not cleared up, but most of my dizziness had. My bones ached and so did my muscles, but nothing was broken. The old bones would perform well enough when the moment came. That pain would melt away and the stiffness would be gone, but I'd pay a helluva price later.

"Time to go."

"What do we do if you're wrong?" she asked again.

"I'll tell you why I'm not wrong, Koko. They're back there now, so full of arrogance they're not even trying to hide from us. They're so sure they put the fear of God in you, and their boy Dante knows he put it in me the first time we met. That boy plays hardball and if I don't impress him or kill him, he's going to be a danger to both of us forever. He holds grudges and he doesn't forget."

I gave her a hug and we split up. She went back for the car; I crossed the street to the front of the bookstore. I scrunched down inside the gunnysack and came into the foyer and peered in through the window. The light was coming from the same back room Carl had gone into when I'd first seen them yesterday. The door was closed but it had an old-fashioned transom, well lit and cracked open. I could see their shadows moving on the ceiling. Three distinct rat-shadows.

I walked down the block and around the corner to the back alley; groped through the dark till I could see that guiding light from Carl's office. Two cars were parked there, a late-model Chevy and a new Ford. These boys bought American: true patriots, born on the Fourth of July, the sons of bitches.

I turned the doorknob. Talk about arrogance, they hadn't even locked the door.

I had to take them by surprise. Lose that edge and I might as well just walk in, hand them my gun, and let Dante kill me. I had to strike first, fast and hard.

I stepped inside and heard their voices. I recognized Dante's, then Carl's, over the transom. The third guy was probably one of Dante's sidekicks, some extra hired muscle. If I could get him out of the way fast, my attitude would improve. You can't plan those things, but at that moment, almost eerily, I heard footsteps. I got back between two shelves just as the door opened and the third man came out. He walked past me, opened the back door, and went outside. No chance to get him from there, and a few seconds later I heard one of the cars start. He pulled into the alley and drove away. My common sense said never mind him, he's just some dummy who does what he's told. I wanted Edgar Bergen, not Charlie McCarthy. But I was angry that even one of them had escaped, and it took a minute for that craziness to go away.

He had left the door open and now I could see into the office. Dante and Carl were sitting at a table with a cassette player between them. I could hear Josephine's voice droning in the room. Carl was listening intently and Dante with a look of impatience, as if he didn't know quite what to do with this voice from the dead, this old lady who couldn't be roughed up or intimidated to make her talk faster.

Dante was sitting across the table facing the door. That would make it tough to get any kind of jump on him. Maybe I could reach the door before he heard me but I doubted it; guys like Dante all seem to have some built-in radar as part of their defense systems. Even if I made it to the door there'd be a moment before I could get at him across that table: plenty of time for him to go after his gun. I could walk in with my own gun ready, but Dante might go for it against the odds, and a gun battle was not what I wanted. Or was it?

I ran my tongue along my split lip and I thought, Kill the son of a bitch now and worry no more. But I waited, God knows why.

Josephine's voice was the only sound in the room. Then Dante's voice rose from nowhere. "Man, this is bullshit. What the hell are we doing with this stuff? We're wasting our time."

I couldn't see Carl's face, couldn't tell if he agreed or begged to differ. A moment later he said, "We've been through her things. There's nothing else there. Whatever she's got, the answer's got to be on these tapes. Why else would they get ready to haul freight out of there and just take this box?"

"It's all bullshit: just some cock-and-bull travelogue from a hundred years ago."

"There's a lot of tape here," Carl said. "It'll take time to hear it all and know what's here."

"For *you* to hear it all. Me, I got better things to do."

"That's okay, I'll take it home and spend the day with it."

"Don't you get it yet? This is all it is, there's nothing else to hear."

"Maybe, but it's got to be done. Anyway, I got a feeling all of a sudden, like we'd better not sit around here too long. Where the hell did Harlow go for that coffee?"

Dante laughed. "What, are you afraid they'll sic the cops on us? Those two ain't callin' nobody, pal; I made sure of that."

"Still, there's no sense taking a chance."

Carl began putting things away: the tape player in its case, the notes and cassettes in their cardboard box. Dante got up from his chair and came around the table. I had less than twenty seconds to make my move. If you wait long enough for something to get better, it doesn't, but it happens to you anyway.

I slipped around the bookcase toward the office door. Dante's radar, if he had it, was off tonight: he had turned toward the far wall, looking up at a clock that I could now see said quarter to five. Dawn must be breaking, I thought irrelevantly. All over town people are getting up, taking showers, getting dressed, making love. That's what all the normal people are doing. In those two seconds I saw a parade of women from my life: Rita McKinley . . . Trish Aandahl . . . Erin. The ones I had and the ones I hadn't.

I had to get his gun: my top priority. He wore it inside his coat, well back on the left side. That's how I remembered it and I hoped I was right.

Carl came through the door and walked right past me. I couldn't see it but I knew he'd be carrying Koko's box and I had to get that too before he had a chance to run with it. The gun and the box, with no time-outs in between for a Tennessee waltz with Dante.

It took Dante hours to clear the door. In real time he was just two steps behind Carl, I was standing to his right, and in that half second I think he saw me. If he did, his reaction was lost between darkness and disbelief. He never broke stride till I hit him. I threw the hardest right I had, a jawbreaker. He was still standing as my hand frisked along his belt for the gun. He tried to lurch forward with his hands up and I got him on the other side with a good left. I jerked his gun free and it slipped, clattering on the floor as he went down. I let his face say hello to my kneecap in his free fall and I pivoted and kicked the gun away and ripped the box out of Carl's hand.

"Hello, asshole," I said seductively. "Welcome to hell."

Carl made a pitiful whimpering noise. "W-wait a minute," he croaked.

"Y-you w-wait a minute. Here's something to suck on while you wait." I hit him in the mouth and he joined Dante on the floor.

I shivered. That was way too easy.

Then I heard the car door slam. This would be Dante Jr., the one named Harlow coming back from wherever he'd gone, just when they were about to give up on him. I felt a wild surge of crazy elation as I stepped up to meet him.

He opened the door. I could see by the moonlight that he was carrying three giant Styrofoam coffee cups in a little cardboard tray.

"Hi, Harlow, make mine black," I said, and I clobbered him.

Coffee flew everywhere. Its first stop was on Harlow's face, but he never felt it.

I stood trembling. "Sons of bitches."

Dante groaned. I turned on the light and saw him trying to get to his feet. I threw the gunnysack over his head and kicked his legs out from under him, banging his head on the floor.

Prudence told me to get the hell out of there. I had what I'd come for but the elation was gone. There hadn't been much satisfaction in the love taps I'd given them, not after what they'd done to me. Besides, I had a blood enemy now and I should at least try to impress him.

I leaned over him. "I don't think I've had the pleasure. Cliff Janeway from Denver. We haven't been introduced, but I'm the poor, shivering bastard you scared half to death in here yesterday. And you would be the rough-and-tough Mr. Dante."

He tried to roll over again and I kicked him hard enough to break his hip. "Don't do that, Dante. Not unless you want a lot more pain than you pricks gave me."

I leaned over and talked to him through the burlap. "I'll bet you're thinking right now how much fun it'll be when you kill me. Big mistake if you are, because two things will happen if you try it. First, *I* will kill *you* if I ever see your face again. I will kill you the minute I see you, in a dark alley or a Pizza Hut or in a crowd at Rockefeller Center."

I cocked the gun and put it against his head. "How do you like this? Do you like the feel of it?"

I cracked him on the temple, hard enough to sting. "Just in case you do manage to kill me, here's the other thing you can look forward to. A pal of mine—a fellow I won't name but he's way tougher than I am—has already been put on your case. If anything happens to me—*anything, Dante*—your ass is grass. If I get a hangnail and get hit by a truck while I'm standing in the street trying to chew it, you can assume the fetal position right then and kiss your ass goodbye. You'll be dead in twenty-four hours."

I breathed down at him. "You'd better hope I live a good, long life, Elmer."

I stuck the gun in my belt, grabbed a handful of burlap, and hauled him to his feet. "That goes for Koko as well."

Suddenly in a new fit of rage I ripped off the gunnysack and got him with a brutal open-hander that slammed him into the wall. "That's for Koko. Touch her again and I'll cut your heart out."

We stood two feet apart, seething primal hatred. Slowly I backed to the door. "Remember, you only get one warning and this was it."

I picked up the box, slipped out of the room, and hustled down the alley, where Koko waited with the motor running.

18

She listened to my account with her eyes wide open and I gave it to her straight. She touched my battered face and said my name. "Oh Cliff. Oh God, Cliff, what a night." Almost a full minute later, she said, "May I call you Cliff?"

I laughed painfully. "You really are a piece of work, Ms. Bujak."

We were sitting in some common breakfast joint well away from downtown. She had struggled mightily to find something she could eat and I had eaten whatever came out of the dingy-looking kitchen. I was working on my third cup of real coffee.

"I thought you were a bookseller. I thought you were a scholar. Then you come out here and turn into some warrior straight from the Middle Ages."

I smiled and she said, "I meant that in a good way."

"I know how you meant it."

"Does it make you uneasy, being a hero?"

"Nah. My favorite song is 'The Impossible Dream.' But it's got to be sung in a deep baritone, not some wimpy tenor. I heard a tenor try to do it once. Disgraceful performance. Comical, in fact." I drank some coffee. "A good bass could really do it up right."

She smiled, almost lovingly, I thought, and said, "Do you always do that?"

"Do what?"

"A comedy routine whenever someone tries to say nice things about you?"

I shrugged. "You haven't even seen my old bullet wounds yet."

"See, that's what I'm talking about."

It was fun being her hero but the fun soon went away. She still didn't understand what had just happened. To her the story was over. We had won.

So I told her. "I wasn't trying to impress you, Koko. You need to know what you're up against. Everything I did to Dante was calculated for an effect."

"Sounds like you're not sure it'll work."

I didn't have a quick-and-easy answer for that. I sipped my coffee.

"Like maybe you're afraid you've put me at some kind of risk."

"You were already at risk. I just hope I didn't make it worse."

"What choice did we have?"

"Slink away in the night and let them keep your stuff."

She flushed and shook her head. "No way."

I liked her decisiveness but Boot Hill is full of decisive heroes. Vast new questions yawned before us.

"They may try to kill us. Does that change your mind?"

She shook her head, this time a little tentatively. But a no is a no, I thought. I said, "I don't think you should go home. Not till I have a better read on it."

She looked solemn at this news. I had her focused now.

"Where will I go?" Almost in the same breath she said, "Maybe I'll go to Charleston. Sooner or later I'll have to, I told you that. Maybe this would be a good time."

I felt nothing but relief at this news. "Maybe it would. Maybe I'll even go with you."

She brightened. "Do that," she said. "Please do."

"Why not? It looks like I'm finished in Baltimore. I think my cover has been blown."

"If I find what I hope to find down there, it might help you as well."

"Want to give me a hint?"

"You can listen on the plane. Charlie tells it better than I do."

I paid the tab and we retrieved her car.

"Can't I even go home for some clothes?"

"I wouldn't. Not just yet."

"How long am I supposed to hide out like this?"

"Not forever. If something doesn't happen after a while, I'll force his hand."

We made a quick swing by my hotel, got my stuff, and headed toward the airport.

"Is the tape player still in the box?"

"Yep. It's even got earphones."

We didn't say any more till the unmistakable signs of runways and aviation rose up around us. She went to long-term parking and we got a shuttle to the terminal.

"What do you really think they'll do about us?"

"I don't know. Dante's an animal. I gave him my best shot."

"What do you think, though?"

In the end I still didn't know. "Maybe it's fifty-fifty. If I had to lay money . . . I don't know. I'm just glad you're getting out of here."

We got on standby to Atlanta. From there we could get passage on Soapbox Airways to the coast.

"You must put on the world's greatest bluff," she said at some point.

But my silence told another story.

"You weren't bluffing."

"You don't bluff a guy like Dante."

"You would kill him."

"He's lucky he's still alive and I hope he knows it."

"What about your other promise?"

"He'd better believe that one too." I looked at her sadly, hating the notion that I was becoming a tarnished hero. "Don't ask questions if you don't want to know the answers, Koko."

"How do you know people like that? People you can just call up and order someone killed?"

"Please," I said impatiently. "I am not a friend of killers. We're talking about an old boyhood chum. He went his way, I went mine, but he still thinks he owes me. Something that happened long ago when we were kids. Maybe now I'll let him get that off his chest."

After a while I said, "I'm not ordering Dante killed. He'll be fine as long as we're fine. If anything happens to him, he does it to himself."

But I still didn't call Vinnie. Something in my heart wouldn't let me.

Instead I called Erin and got her answering machine. "Hi," I said. "I'm out of town. Not sure when I'll be back, but we need to talk. Leave a message on my machine."

No jokes this time around.

An hour later Koko and I looked down on the East Coast from 35,000 feet. She got out the player and rigged me up, picking among half a dozen fat folders and two dozen recorded tapes until she found what she wanted. "This is the best one. This is Charlie. All we'll ever have of him."

The tape began to play—an old man's voice, recounting the times of his life. An old man's voice, but as I listened the tone sounded vaguely familiar.

"Is that . . . *Josephine*?"

"Just listen. She's trying to tell us what he told her—and what she read in his journal years ago."

I looked at her.

"There's nothing supernatural about this. Jo was in a deep trance that day. And this is what he told her. This is it, word for word. It's been stored there in her head for eighty years. She's even trying to tell it in his voice."

"What'd she say when you played it back for her?"

"Nothing. She just cried."

She pushed the rewind button and ran it back to the beginning.

"You'll hear me on here, asking a few questions. All the rest is Charlie. Just forget me and listen. Just sit and listen and keep an open mind."

A hissing sound came through the earphones; then, Koko's voice.

"Who are you? What's your name?"

There was a pause, followed by the high-pitched voice of a child. "Josephine."

"Josephine who?"

"Josephine Crane. My friends call me Jo. *J-o,* like in *Little Women.*"

"That's a good, strong name. May I call you Jo?"

"Yes, of course."

"How old are you, Jo?"

"It's my birthday. I'm nine years old."

"What day is this?"

"September third, nineteen hundred and four."

"You sound *very* grown-up for your age."

"Thank you."

Another pause. Then Koko said, "Do you want to tell me about your grandfather?"

"What do you want to know?"

"What's his name? We can start there."

"Charles. Charles Edward Warren."

"Tell me a little about his life."

Now came a long pause. The tape went on hissing for two or three minutes. At that point there was a click followed by several bumps, then Koko's voice came across in a whisper.

"I've moved the microphone back from Josephine's presence to add a footnote and a description of what's happening. She seems to be trying to gather her thoughts. Her face is very relaxed, more so than when I have asked this question in the past. Today I will ask her to tell me more about her grandfather's life, but she can't go outside her own persona unless she is relating something she personally has heard or read. I would expect her to be limited to what she knew about him at that age, but at times she seems to go far beyond her stated age. She has knowledge and uses words that I would not expect her to know at nine. I think what she's giving me here are things she has heard him say about himself, coupled with what she read in his own diary after his death."

From some distance I could hear the child's voice. There was more scurrying as Koko moved the microphone closer.

"I'm sorry . . . I missed that."

"I asked where you went," Jo said.

"Nowhere, I just needed to move something. Can you tell me about Charlie now?"

There was a pause. I heard a labored breath.

"He's retired now. When he was younger he was a draftsman. That's a mapmaker, you know. He says it was a good trade then, there was so much expansion. He worked as a cartographer in and around Baltimore all his life."

"For a time he worked for the government in Washington, is that correct?"

"Yes." Another long pause. "He was in the War Department during the administration of President James Buchanan."

"What were his interests?"

"In his youth . . . long ago . . . he liked opera and history, philosophy, nature. He was a bird fancier. Eventually he became an accomplished ornithologist—good enough to write a book and several scientific pamphlets. He liked playing card games. Poker with his pocket money and whist for fun."

"His picture reminds me of a college professor."

"He is often told that. My mother sometimes says so."

"What else can you tell me about him?"

"Ummm . . . he's a book collector."

"Is that how he discovered Richard Burton?"

"Yes. He knew about Mr. Burton long before they met. Even then he had copies of Richard's earliest books. Some of them went through many editions and lots of revision, but Grandfather always wanted the first British editions. When there were reprints with textual changes, he collected both. We have all those books, with notations in Mr. Burton's own hand. Grandfather also kept a thirty-year correspondence. The letters referred to the texts, to Mr. Burton's problems with his publishers, and to his joys and frustrations in writing his books. From 1861 onward, Grandfather had a standing order, with a request that Mr. Burton himself send two copies of each new work as it came off the press, or as soon thereafter as possible. This he did for more than twenty-five years."

"Can you tell me how he met Mr. Burton and what they did in May of 1860?"

There was another long breath. "They went to Charleston."

"Yes, but would you share the story of that trip with us?"

There was another long silence. Again came the bumping: more clicks. Again Koko's voice dropped to a whisper.

"I expect, based on earlier sessions, that this story of their trip south will emerge in a stronger, less hesitant voice than what we have just heard. I should note that we have done this identical experiment several times, and it's always the same, almost to the word. Comparisons can be made with the tapes numbered seven, twelve, and thirteen.

"In all these sessions, Jo displays adult knowledge that may taint the proceeding for a skeptic. Charlie seems to tell her things—such as Burton's carnal interlude with the inn girl named Marion—that a grandfather of that era would hardly relate to this nine-year-old child. Burton swears at one point and Charlie reports it, another place where he'd surely censor himself if he were talking to a child. When I asked her about it—find tape ten—she confessed that she had read those passages in her grandfather's journal of the trip. So what we're probably getting is a mix of what he told her and what he wrote. His own journal was unfortunately lost in the plunder of their library after Charlie's death."

More bumps. More clicks.

"I'm back," Koko said in full voice. "Are you comfortable now?"

"Yes. Thank you for the water."

"Can you tell us about Charlie now?"

"What he told me, you mean? Or what's in his journal?"

"Whatever feels right to you. Can you tell me in his own words? As you read it? As he told it to you?"

"Maybe."

When the voice began again, almost a minute later, it was the old man's voice.

"It started on a warm day in May 1860. I was thirty-three years old. The world was a brighter, more exciting place then. I was young and there were so many things yet to do. . . ."

I closed my eyes and Koko let me listen.

"I was thirty-three," the voice said. "I was six years younger than Burton when we met. This is how it happened. . . ."

BURTON AND CHARLIE

19

BURTON

had come to Washington to see John B. Floyd, Buchanan's secretary of war. This much we know. What went on in that room no one will ever know.

I had admired Burton from afar but I never trusted Floyd. Yes, I worked for him but I had always considered him a rogue. In the daily job my opinion didn't matter much, for I did my job diligently and our paths seldom crossed. My work required little contact with the secretary, and I functioned well and was reasonably well satisfied. But I was not at all surprised when history put Floyd in a traitorous light—a man who used his position to transfer tons of arms and materiel to the South, then fled to join the Confederacy when the war finally began. In the department I kept my distance.

Even so, I could not possibly stay away when I learned of Burton's appointment with Floyd that morning. I must have looked exactly like what I was, a nervous young man waiting in the hall with his hat in his lap. Then the door opened and Burton stepped out, and all that unease disappeared. I walked up boldly and said hello. I told him I had followed his adventures and had ordered his books and read them all. This cheered him enormously. As I later learned, he was particularly open to an admirer after the cutting disappointment of Speke and his own relative eclipse in England. Of all the strange and unexpected things, my sudden appearance flattered him and brightened his day.

To me Richard was the salt of the earth. We liked each other immediately.

He put his hand on my shoulder. Like an old confidant, he drew me to him and I stood tall and felt myself a man among men.

"Say, Charles—"

"Oh, please! All my friends call me Charlie. I'd be honored if you would too."

"The honor is mine. Is there a grog shop nearby? I'll buy you a glass of ale."

"There's a good water hole just up the street, and a free lunch comes with the brew. But I'll do the buying, sir—you are a guest in my country."

"We'll fight that out at the bar."

The history books say that Burton intended to leave Washington at once. But he disappeared that spring in 1860. Three months would pass before he surfaced again, in St. Joe, Missouri, to begin his long stagecoach journey west. Of these missing weeks, Burton later said only that he traveled through every state.

But he stayed a week in Washington. He lived in our house. All that week we ate together and were constant companions. We argued politics, history, and the great questions of American slavery, secession, and war.

Burton always hated slavery, but he was no great admirer of the Negro. I was something of an apologist. We had differences that were deep and vast, and still we became fast friends at once.

I knew that something extraordinary was happening. I sensed a great adventure, mine for the taking if only I had the courage to open my hand. On the third day he said as much. "You should travel with me for a while. I'll change your mind about things."

"Maybe I'll change yours," I said, and he laughed.

I was awed by him and he knew that. But I was never cowed and that was my saving grace. I know he respected me. If I had been a toady or a bootlicker, he'd never have made such a suggestion. Burton was quickly bored by those who fawned.

On the fourth day we had a fierce argument. It ended in red-faced laughter.

"I must leave soon," Richard said on the fifth day. "Come with me on a journey."

How many of us ever reach such a clear crossroad? How many shrink from the bold path when they come to it? A hundred will pass before one takes the turn.

I had to follow it. To shy away would have been a betrayal of my life.

All my years I had been cautious. We had some money put away. I had my trade: a dozen private firms in Washington, Baltimore, and New York were eager for my services. I was tired of War Department politics, of bureaucrats pulling every string. If I disappeared for a time with Richard, who would be the worse for it?

I gave my employers short notice and said good-bye to my wife and daughter. I left Washington with Burton on Monday, a week after we met.

* * *

On the train for Richmond I asked where we were going and Burton, without hesitation, said, "Charleston."

My question had been rhetorical. I didn't care where we went: I was in the throes of a glorious sense of freedom and excitement the like of which I had not known since my graduation from college, long before my marriage and the commencement of my career. If Burton had said "Africa," I swear I'd have gone, even though I was still thinking like a tourist. I had assumed we'd be going by steamer only because that way was easier. The railroads in 1860 were still fragmentary, with many lines incomplete. An overland passage would require connections on stagecoaches, along roads that could turn impossible in even a moderate rainfall. A ship would avoid most of that. We could board at once, steam down the Potomac, catch the train at Acquia Creek, board another steamer at Wilmington, and go the rest of the way in relative ease. But Richard wanted to see the land. He was not interested in ease for its own sake, or in traveling as a tourist—after all, what fears could even the worst travel in America hold for a man who had just survived that horrific two-year trek across unknown Africa? So we would take the train to Petersburg, on into North Carolina, and from Wilmington depart from the recommended route and instead go inland, into South Carolina.

During this time Burton was a most affable companion. We had many mutually interesting conversations, but there were also times when we each left the other to his private thoughts. At every stop on the long rail journey, Burton sought out the local newspapers and devoured them before passing them on to me. There were tiny towns where the train stopped to take on water and coal, and smaller hamlets through which we sped in the blink of an eye. People everywhere came out to watch us: fools who stood so close to the track that they took their lives in their hands, laughing and refusing to step back even at the angry blast from the engineer. In the smallest towns children and old men gathered and gawked as we whipped through in what must have been a blur. Occasionally I would pick out an individual face and get some notion of character, or perhaps make one up, in the half second it filled my window and then vanished forever. A general impression of poor simpletons began forming in my mind, and in the years since the journey I have often thought of those people and the injustice I did to them. We underestimated them. They were the heart and backbone of the South, and I now believe that my Yankee condescension, repeated on a broad national scale, was a factor in the near-destruction of our great Union.

Whenever our stop was of sufficient duration, we would get off the train and mingle with the natives, who were noisy and anxious to share their outrage at the national government. Often we were challenged on our political beliefs, but Burton billowed among them like a kite of many colors, always getting more than he gave, and I had at least enough good sense not to stir them up with my opinions on their peculiar institution and their absurd noises of secession and war. I had never been south of Fredericksburg and I found the press full of rabble-rousing nonsense. But as we went deeper into the country, I began to understand a little of what they cherished and why. The landscape was singularly beautiful. I saw peach orchards and cotton farms stretching away in the distance, and now and then we came upon the edges of a great plantation with long dusty roads and enormous live oaks and slaves working in the fields. But much of our journey was through dense wilderness, across vast pine forests with occasional swamps.

Everywhere we went Burton used up all his spare moments making notes.

At Wilmington we bought our passage only as far as the village of Marion, which I remembered as a spot on the map about thirty miles into South Carolina. Soon we were in a dismal swampy area of lower North Carolina. I couldn't help seeing the land in terms of cartography, but I quickly realized that Burton had also studied his maps and had committed them to memory. Until now I had said nothing: I had come as his traveling companion, content to let him plot our course. But this stoppage in such a small hamlet seemed curious and at last I said so. "What's in Marion?" I asked. "And why are we taking such a roundabout route?" For the first time, I had begun to feel slightly superfluous, almost enough to laughingly add, "And by the way, why am I here?" But this would have been much too pointed, even as a jest: there would be time enough later if the notion persisted. I do remember it was in that swamp, a few miles from the Rebel state, when the thought first crossed my mind that I might have a purpose other than what had been stated, to be merely a friend for the road. Burton gave my question a halfhearted reply.

"I imagine there's a tavern and an inn at Marion, where we can stay and browse among the people, get a tolerable supper, and then get pleasantly drunk together. In the morning, or the next day, we can go on to Florence."

I must have still had a quizzical look on my face, for Burton then said, "Are you getting impatient, Charlie? Are you becoming anxious to see the nest of rebellion that is about to bring so much grief to your country?" In fact, I *was* curious, and a year later when Burton sent me the two volumes of *The Lake Regions of Central Africa* just before the war broke, I found an amusing handwritten footnote in one of the page margins that I believe refers obliquely to Speke: *You reminded me, but only briefly, of another traveler I knew, who always wanted to get there, wherever there happened to be, and as a result missed what was all around him at the time.*

There wasn't much to see of Marion. My memory is of a muddy street and a collection of crude buildings along it, but Burton found it satisfactory. As he predicted, we did find an inn, taking a pair of rooms upstairs facing the street, and that evening we had a surprisingly good supper. It took Burton no time at all to become acquainted with other travelers and with the town's natives: he was extremely gregarious, but again I noticed his way of telling them nothing about himself, of asking questions and becoming alert whenever the volatile issues of slavery and secession arose. He had also begun speaking in a much more Americanized English. Completely gone was his British accent, and when I remarked on it later, he said, "That's just my way. Wherever I go, I make an attempt to learn the language." We shared a laugh, but then he said, "Don't be surprised if I change even more as we go along. I like to experiment with words, and these crackers, as they are called down here, do have a language of their own."

It was at that moment when I had the first vague thought that would change things between us. I suddenly wondered if he was slipping into some kind of disguise. After a while this led to a far more unsettling thought, that I might somehow be an unwitting part of it. Years later, in biographies by his widow, Isabel, by his niece Georgiana Stisted, and by a man named Thomas Wright, there were references to the nature of his intelligence work in India. He alludes to this in his own early books: how he would pass among the people as one of them, having fluently learned their language in a few weeks or even days, darkened his skin, made himself up to look the part, and ply his secret service work. And already in print, of course, was his account of the epic journey, in the flawless disguise of an Arab, to Mecca and Medina. Richard could be anyone, and this fact led to a disturbing new thought. Could he now be spying on my country—was that what this journey was? Had he been sent here to assess the likelihood of civil war, when it might come, and how England could exploit it? Such a mission made chilling sense. On the surface, relations between England and the United States had been warm enough since our last war had ended in 1814, but it was common knowledge that many in the British government still seethed with anger and wished us ill. Lord Palmerston, for one, had never forgiven us for that last defeat, when he had been secretary of war. Now that he was prime minister, was he plotting, after all these years, to get his revenge, and was Burton the advance scout for his ambitions?

I felt a great anger come over me at such a thought, and I decided to confront Richard and have it out. I was ready to declare our brief friendship finished if he had undertaken such a deception, and to catch the next steamer north out of Wilmington. But when the moment came, I wavered. As we sat over dinner, I tried and failed to formulate the question, which could result in a grave insult and ruin a friendship that might in fact be innocent. Burton had said or done nothing specific to justify my suspicion: only what he always did, as he said himself. By the end of the evening I had decided to say nothing. But I remained uneasy and several times I caught him watching me, as if he had read my thoughts and suddenly knew what I suspected.

There was one incident worth noting in the tavern that night. It almost seems superfluous but its importance came to bear much later. We were sitting with a small group of new acquaintances near the bar when a large, boisterous man named Jedro Fink joined our group. He was clearly a Yankee hater, already well fortified with ale, and the more he drank, the more he seemed to take offense at whatever I said. It was my accent: no one could ever mistake me for anything but a Northerner. Once in the general babble, the phrase "Yankee dogs" floated over my head, and when I looked, his bleary eyes were fixed on mine.

Richard had also consumed a vast amount of ale but his eyes were clear. I gave him an apologetic look and began seeking an out. At the first lull in the conversation I said, "I think I'll retire, gentlemen," but our Yankee hater said, "What's your hurry, mate, are we not good enough for Yanks to drink with?"

I felt two sharp stabs, anger and fear. I had never been in any kind of fight, and what frightened me most was not the prospect of being hurt but the spectacle of being beaten in front of the crowd. Still, I could not let this pass. I said, "That's an offensive thing to say, sir," and I steeled myself for whatever might come. But in the same moment Richard said, "I think I'll join you, Charlie. It is getting late."

The fellow across the table smirked as we pushed back our chairs.

Richard leaned forward. "You have something else to say, *mate*?"

The man scoffed again and Burton said, "Be careful, sir."

Fink made as if to laugh. "Maybe you're the one who should be careful. In case you don't know it, we have harsh ways of settling things here when insults arise."

Burton smiled warily out of his deeply scarred cheeks. "No one's been insulted . . . yet. We can all still go to bed and be on our way in the morning."

"That's true enough." Fink pushed himself back, slightly but ominously, from the table. "Unless we choose not to."

The smile faded from Burton's face. "That would be unfortunate, but it would be *your* choice. And I believe under your own code I would have the choice of weapons in any dispute that can't be resolved. And for what that's worth, I would choose swords."

Fink sat back. "What the hell, who carries a sword around?"

"I do."

They stared at each other. "Well, I don't have one," Fink said.

"I could provide a pair. If the occasion arose. Which it hasn't. Yet."

Suddenly the man laughed, not derisively as he had before but with a tavern laugh, in uneasy fellowship. Burton remained stoic, waiting.

"You're all right with me, mate. It's a good thing for all of us that we know where lines are drawn, eh?"

And on that nervous note, we went upstairs.

In the hallway, I said, "I would have fought him if it came to that."

"I know you would. I never had any doubt."

"You don't have to hold my hand, Richard. It's important that you know that."

"I do know it. And I apologize if that's how it appeared."

"Of course it is. How else would it appear? You don't have any swords at all."

"No. But he didn't know that."

"My God, what if he had called you on it?"

"Then the matter would have become far more serious, and the choice of weapons would have passed to him."

In my room I lay awake staring up at the black ceiling. All my thoughts of the afternoon came flooding back, and my anger returned with great, yawning doubts about the nature of our journey. I saw Richard on my ceiling and he was always making his notes. These I had assumed were for a new book but now I wondered what he was actually writing in that notebook. I felt our friendship had been seriously compromised—perhaps, maddeningly, by nothing more than my own imagination—and I knew then that at some point it must be discussed. I dreaded Richard's reaction, for in fact I did not know him well enough to initiate a talk of such sensitivity. I personally had never held any grudge against England, I had accepted Richard with wholehearted delight as my friend, but my years in the War Department had given me access to certain intelligence and rumors that had received little or no attention in the press. Now in my dark room all this intrigue swirled across the canvas of the ceiling. The sun never sets on empire, I thought, calling up an old quotation; the sun never sets on England. The only reason we are not serving the queen today is because of those long-dead boys in places like Bunker Hill and Saratoga and New Orleans. Were we really at peace now? Friction between our nations had never actually ceased since 1815, and Palmerston, that old devil, always seemed to be at the root of it. In his forty-year political career he had never ceased agitating. I could almost feel his acrimony invading my room, disrupting my sleep, and now I remembered incidents from my reading, from reports that had circulated through our government. I knew that years ago England had arbitrarily seized our ships and had forced our boys to serve in her navy. I had heard she had given aid and support to our Indians, encouraging them to attack our frontier settlements. Everyone knew how she had tried to keep Texas out of the Union, and there had been persistent rumors that she had helped finance Mexico's war against us. It was certainly no secret that England had had serious designs on South America since our Revolution, and she had always resented and tried to undermine our Monroe Doctrine. Why should she now turn timid when the upstart nation that so seriously rankled her was heading into deep trouble?

I felt a flush of shame at my suspicion, but it grew into the early morning, until sometime before the dawn, when I finally fell asleep.

I was in poor spirits in the morning: a lack of sleep had combined with my increasing doubts to put me on edge again. I would be much happier, I thought, when Marion, this mud hole of a village, was behind us. The train to Florence had been delayed, but Richard had arranged for passage on a coach, which would put us there late that afternoon. As we left the inn another tense incident occurred. Coming to the bottom of the stairs I turned to say something to Richard and collided with someone coming through on my blind side. At once I begged his pardon, then saw that it was Fink, my antagonist from last night. Suddenly, as if in the grip of some demon, I said, "Mr. Fink, I am sorry I jostled you, but at the same time I must tell you that your behavior last night was inexcusably rude. I can be good-natured enough at being made the goat of the evening, but your repeated insults to my country were intolerable."

He looked up at Richard, who stood behind me.

"Please speak to me, sir. Mr. Burton is not involved in this."

For a moment he wavered. I was certain we would come to battle, but he grinned and said, "It was the ale talking, mate. I get that way when I drink too much."

I took that as my apology and we left for Florence an hour later.

Another mud hole. What Burton saw in such places, or what he was learning from them, remained a mystery as we put up in another inn. But the inn was a pleasant surprise, a rambling building at least sixty years old, showing its age on the outside but warm and tidy within. It was called Wheeler's Crossing.

We had a marvelous dinner, a simple quail dish with wild rice and various ordinary accompaniments but prepared with such care that it was outstanding. It was easily the best meal I had had in any eating establishment in recent memory, beating the finest restaurants of Washington hands down. "Wonderful food," Burton said, and he called for the innkeeper to compliment the cook. The man was gracious but said we could tell her ourselves. A woman was summoned from the kitchen, and as she came through the doors I felt Burton sit up straighter beside me. She was truly a beautiful young lady. "This is my daughter Marion," the inn master said. Burton and I both stood and she gave a little curtsy, and Richard stepped away from his side of the table. He reached out with perfect propriety and took her hand. "Mr. Wheeler," Richard said without ever taking his eyes from her face, "your daughter is a national treasure. The town we just passed through must be named after her."

"After Francis Marion, more likely," she said impishly. "Our hero of the Revolution. My name came from my mother's side."

"Wherever it came from," Burton said, "the best establishments in London can barely do you justice."

She accepted this politely but as if she had heard it all before. Richard asked where she had learned her cooking and she said, "From Mrs. Simmons and Mrs. Randolph—from our servant Queenie, and from my grandmother." Mrs. Simmons and Mrs. Randolph turned out to be the authors of popular cookery books, which Marion had on her shelf in a back room. "We buy them for her whenever we can," her father said. "And my mother left her many good menus and recipes in an old notebook. She uses them all. An establishment like ours is only as good as its victuals." Burton, ever the charmer, said, "Yours is very good indeed," and Marion gave another bow and retreated into the back room.

"That's one reason why I stop in these little places," Richard said as we settled in again. "You never can tell what you might find."

It never occurred to me that we had "found" anything, certainly not in the sense that Richard obviously meant it. I was happily married: I would never have betrayed my wife by chasing around after other women, even such a lovely one as Marion. But I was no prude either, and I was anxious in my recent discontent not to be a wet blanket. Richard, in his thirty-ninth year, was still unattached, and a striking vision of bold manhood. Indeed, though he had already formed a strong bond with Isabel Arundell in England and would marry her before the year was out, I had no way of knowing this and in fact I had not yet heard her name. We sat in Richard's room and enjoyed a small brandy and he looked like the soul of contentment. "This really is a wonderful little inn," he said. "There's even a bath out behind the house, and *that* is not a luxury one takes lightly. I'm tempted to stay over for a day or two. Would you mind?"

I was actually warming to the place myself. "Not at all," I said. "Don't worry about me any: I'll find things to do."

I retired but again sleep was difficult. At midnight I awoke for the third time, burning with a thirst that comes over me when I drink too much alcohol. I got out of bed and groped my way into the darkened hall, hoping someone would still be downstairs who could fetch me a glass of water. I had just reached the top of the stairs when I heard their voices: Richard's soft laugh followed almost at once by hers. I moved to join them, then stopped short on the top step. I could see them from there: they were alone, seated at a table over cups of smoking bishop, Burton sprawled in his chair, Marion beside him in a pose that changed from moment to moment, servant, companion, and hussy all at once. His right hand clutched his drink; his left covered hers with such easy intimacy that I was shocked by the quickness of it. We had met her just six hours ago, yet there was an assumption between them that no one could miss. Already they were like old lovers together.

I began to creep back down the hall but a short snatch of their talk followed me. Marion had mentioned my name.

"Wouldn't your friend Charlie be shocked if he saw us now."

Burton laughed. "It's not Charlie I worry about. Your father is another matter."

"He's gone to bed hours ago. An earthquake wouldn't wake him once he hits the pillow, and he's a late riser as well. I can't remember when he slept less than ten hours."

"Well, if Charlie were shocked he'd get over it soon enough."

"If you say so. He still strikes me as a bit of a pill."

"Your mistake," Richard said. "He's a grand fellow, one of the best I've known. He has a lion's heart, even if he doesn't always know what to do with it. And the keenest sense of honor."

"I'll take your word for that. Even so, it's not him I'm interested in."

"My good fortune, I hope."

"And mine."

"Marion." Richard kissed her hand. "It is the fairest name, and you wear it like a birthright. As if Maid Marion of Robin Hood had suddenly been reborn."

"Oh, Sir Richard, you are *such* a shameless liar."

"Not Sir Richard . . . please, not that. You'll never hear that honor attached to my name. If the queen knows no better than to approve that coveted title so carelessly, there are many who have her ear and will be happy to tell her why not."

"Why not is clear enough. It is because you are a scoundrel."

"So they say."

Whatever honor Richard had seen in me would not let me eavesdrop another moment and I left them then. I lay in the dark, inflated with pride at his words. Conceit and a vivid imagination kept me awake for the second night running.

At first light I heard a noise outside my half-opened window. My room looked down into the yard, and the bath stall Richard had mentioned was directly below. It was a crude little wooden cage, circular with a canvas draped around it, a perforated steel tank suspended overhead, a pull rope that would open the vents and rain water down on anyone inside, and a set of makeshift steps for a servant to climb up and pour the water in. Now came a real shock! Richard appeared in the yard totally nude, a pale blur in the hour before the sunrise. He parted the canvas and stepped into the stall, and a moment later Marion, still wearing her dress of last night but with a far more disheveled look, came out carrying a large pot of steaming water. She climbed the stairs and dumped in the water, and I heard the tank open as Burton pulled the rope. He sighed deeply and she laughed at his pleasure. When he came out she was there with a blanket, draping it over his shoulders and rubbing him gently, affectionately, sensually.

We stayed in Florence another day, and another, and on after that. On the third day we walked over to the little cemetery together, Richard and Marion and I, and there we saw the plot where her mother rested. *Jennie Marion Wheeler,* the stone said simply: *Beloved Wife and Mother, 1812–1843.* "She died giving me life," Marion said, and something about her face, etched with deep sadness for a woman she had never known, moved me almost to tears. "What a damned shame!" I said in a trembling voice. "That's what happens with too many women. We're supposed to be so advanced, yet medical science hasn't come an inch in women's health since Caesar's day."

She looked at me and smiled tenderly, then reached out and squeezed my hand. That's what I remember best about her: aside from her liaison with Richard, the warmth of her, the feel of her hand and a smile that has followed me across three decades.

That night we sat on the back porch listening to the Negroes singing. The Wheelers had half a dozen blacks who worked around the inn, whether in bondage or as freemen, I never learned, though the father did not strike me at all as a slaveholder. Burton in particular was enchanted by these melodies: "Some of them are very similar to tunes of tribal songs I heard in Africa," he said. "The only difference here is the white man's addition, the inclusion of the Christian spiritual aspect." He wrote quickly by the firelight, trying to capture the words and compare them with his memory of their

African origins. He came out every night to scribble down the lyrics, and in odd moments throughout the trip I would hear him humming them softly, comparing them with others he was picking up across the Southern states.

We left early the following week. I looked back and saw Marion and her father watching our departure, but Richard never gave them a wave or a backward glance. I found that rather cold, considering the kind of friendship they must have had, and the certainty that they would never see each other again. "I said my good-byes earlier," he told me. "There's no sense going on about it."

Charleston now seemed close at hand. But we had to endure another night, and a wretched one it was, on the road. It was too much to expect another grand inn in backwoods country, and we stayed in the worst place ever imagined by the angels of hell. The road from Florence to Charleston was a hundred miles of near-total wilderness. I had never seen its like; the choking thickness of it was unbroken except for an occasional settlement with a few scruffy citizens and the equally unkempt shanties they lived in. There were moss-draped trees, swamps, and all around them that brooding black pine forest: vast, unrelenting, increasingly intimidating. I have forgotten the name of the place where we put up that last night before Charleston. Burton seemed satisfied with it, and I had to be, for darkness was falling rapidly and even he did not wish to be caught on the road in such a night as these trees would bring down on us.

The inn was run by an old woman and two hulking simpletons who were apparently her sons. She had a hag's face, gaunt and full of gaps where presumably teeth had once been; the men conversed in grunts and were well on the way to losing their teeth as well. The only name I heard for any of them was that one of the boys was called Cloyd. The woman tried to appear friendly but this had an effect that I found chilling. We were given a very poor stew, made of some mysterious stringy meat that I could barely manage to taste and Burton ate not at all. He had his suspicions even then, and we retired soon after our arrival.

"I don't trust these people," Richard said. "I think we should bunk together tonight and one of us stay awake at all times."

This was alarming and what he said next was even more so. "I'll bet there's more than one sinkhole, each about the size of a man, out in that swamp."

"What are you saying?" I asked stupidly. "That they would murder us?"

"Wouldn't be the first time an innkeeper has done away with a guest to steal his purse."

He volunteered to take either watch. It didn't matter: I was tired from my restless nights but unlikely to sleep after that. I took the first six hours, abandoning my own room to sit on a chair in Richard's. "If you get tired, wake me," he said. "Don't worry about the time. Six hours from now or six minutes, I don't care." By the light of a coal-oil lamp, he produced a gun from one of his bags. He slapped it into my hand and went to bed while I sat at the door and blew out the lamp. This was going to be a long, long night and I took my responsibility seriously. I must not, must *not,* fall asleep!

Richard was asleep at once. I sat in the most incredible black void listening to him breathe. He snored briefly and the minutes dragged by. I had no idea what time it was, and after a while time stood still.

At some point much later I heard the noise in the hall: a single footstep and the slight creaking of the floor. I stood with the gun in my hand. There was a bump outside the door and I turned the knob and opened it so slightly—just enough for a look into the hallway. I could see nothing at first, then the two hulks and the smaller one nearby. I heard them whisper, though what they said was much too faint to make sense. I pulled the door wider and cocked the gun. Its sound was loud and unmistakable in that quietude, and suddenly everything froze, all of us where we stood, except Richard, who was just as suddenly out of the bed and at my side. We waited but nothing happened: they had faded away and disappeared.

Inside again with the door closed, Richard lit the lamp. "Well, that settles that. We'll have to stay alert." I asked if he had slept, and he said, "Like a baby." I felt a great sense of camaraderie and pride in his trust. I asked if he had any idea what time it was—my watch had stopped at half past eight. "My sense of things tells me it's near midnight," he said. "Your turn to rest." I protested—I was not at all tired—but fair was fair and he insisted that I take the bed. So I lay down in the recess, still warm from his body, closed my eyes, and did sleep, soundly, for several hours. When the dawn broke I still felt that sense of kinship in what I foolishly imagined lingered from Richard's body heat.

The proprietress and her sons were nowhere to be seen as we left. "They have no real courage," Richard said. "They know we've figured them out and they will only return like vermin of the night, after we've gone. They remind me of Burke and Hare, the infamous Scottish murderers. One held while the other smothered, but I suspect these three had far quicker and more violent deaths in store for us."

So we were on the road again. I had already studied my maps: I knew that Charleston was located at the end of a long, crooked peninsula, with wide rivers on both sides emptying into a spectacular harbor. It was easy for a mapmaker to visualize it as an eagle might see it, like a long buzzard's neck. I was not surprised to learn that the upper peninsula was in fact called the Neck. We came down east of the river, on a road that would take us through the village of Mount Pleasant and within a few miles of Fort Moultrie. The road was alternately hard earth and planked, and I suppose we made good time by the standard of the travel Richard had chosen for us. The train would have avoided all this and got us there a day earlier, but this was so obvious I kept it to myself. When you traveled with Burton, this was what you did.

The skies threatened rain, which would have added greatly to our misery, for the road was rough and sloppy in places from another rain two days earlier. Charleston was on the horizon: Richard said that more than once, but in fact we now headed into the deepest forest on the trip and I saw nothing on the horizon but more of the same. There was a river crossing before we came out into land that telegraphed an approach to the sea. Richard spent the time talking earnestly to the ferryboat owner, about what I could only guess. "That was the east branch of the Cooper River," he said when our coach was under way again. "We are almost there."

I was ready to believe this, so delighted was I to be out of the dark and dreary forest. "Our luck is changing," I said: "It didn't rain after all." Richard smiled, noncommittally, as if it didn't matter to him either way. We had to cross again at the Wando River, with its broad expanses of marshlands, and now I saw the unmistakable signs of the sea: sloughs and creeks thick with sea oats, and there was a salty tang in the air. But night was coming and I feared we would still not arrive until tomorrow, an awful prospect. The sunset was spectacular, lighting up the cloud-streaked horizon as we put in at Mount Pleasant.

We managed to catch the ferry to the city. I stood out on the deck and watched the lights draw closer, but Burton seemed restless, circling, looking out to sea, making his notes in light almost too dim to see. He spent his time on the port deck, watching the dark, empty hulk of Fort Sumter, and aft, where he could see Fort Moultrie and the lights of the lonely federal garrison stationed there.

We got in at eight o'clock. "No more backwoods inns for us, Charlie," Richard said merrily. "Now we go first-cabin."

He instructed our driver to take us to the best hotel and soon we were on Meeting Street in front of an elegant blockwide, four-story building, gas-lit, with a marvelous facade. I had studied Greek architecture briefly in college, and immediately I loved that hotel and its magnificent colonnade: fourteen great white Corinthian pillars that reached from the second-floor balcony to the roof. The Charleston Hotel. That night I slept the sleep of the dead.

*   *   *

All the next day we were like tourists, walking the streets, talking to people we met, probing the babble of the marketplace not far from our door, strolling along the Battery. The Battery is a walled promenade around the tip of the city with a green behind it and some of the town's finest old houses in the background. The view of the harbor is spectacular. One elderly gentleman offered the pompous opinion that this was where the Cooper and Ashley rivers met to form the Atlantic Ocean. We should all have shared a hearty laugh except that the old bird seemed absolutely serious and might have been offended. Richard listened politely but I knew he was far more interested in the geography than in any local silliness advancing this city, as lovely as it was, as the center of the Western world. From any point on the Battery we could see Fort Sumter, that brick fortress sitting on its man-made shoal in the mouth of the harbor. On both sides the land curved in tight, with Fort Moultrie on Sullivan's Island to our left and Fort Johnson on James Island to the right, giving Sumter the appearance of a cork in a bottle. "Exactly right," Burton said when I put it that way. "It's a cork in a bottle."

"When it's finished it will make the city pretty much impregnable," I said.

"*If* they finish it. And *if* they get the guns mounted, and *if* all three forts are controlled by the same side."

"A lot of ifs."

"Indeed. And if the wrong side had it, speaking from their viewpoint, its guns could easily be turned on the city it was built to protect."

The fort was just a speck from there and I doubted that even the most powerful guns could reach that far. But Richard looked askance and said, "You don't know much about modern warfare, my friend," and I had to admit the truth of that.

We walked around the point and back again. The sun was warm and bright, a blessed relief from the miseries of the road, and again

I was so delighted I had come. I was in the company of an extraordinary man and he liked me: what else mattered? But then as I stood watching the waterbound fortress, Richard moved away, and when I looked around for him he was standing off at a distance, scribbling in that damned notebook. All my suspicion came back in a gush. What was he doing? If he wanted to spy, why bring me along? That part made no sense. But my doubt magnified and doubled again, and abruptly I walked up to him, quickly enough that I could see he was not making notes but a sketch of some kind.

"What are you doing there?" I asked, making the question sound as much as possible like idle curiosity.

"Just drawing a picture." He snapped his book shut. "To remember the day."

Again this was so plausible that it had to be real. Unless it wasn't.

We walked up East Bay, turned in to Chalmers Street, and saw a slave auction. The building had a platform on its second story where the Negroes were paraded and sold. Richard, who must have seen other such events in his travels around the world, still stood mesmerized for an hour as a family of blacks was broken apart and sent off with their separate masters. The pain in the mother's face was heartbreaking and I was angry and indignant on her behalf. "You must write about this," I said, but Richard only watched and kept his thoughts to himself. "These men are beasts," I said, none too quietly, and Richard gave me a withering look and said, "Try to remember, Charlie, you are in their country now."

We moved on. On East Bay near Queen Street we saw a photographer's studio—BARNEY STUYVESSANT, the sign said—and I asked if we might get a real picture made. "Something that will capture this day."

Burton's inclination was to dismiss this as silly, but before he could seriously object I went inside and made the arrangements. I didn't want a trumped-up studio shot; something on the street would be much better, a picture that captured some semblance of the city and her architecture. Burton did protest then—he wanted no part of it—but the photographer was so young and eager for the business that his equipment was already out on the sidewalk, and I so clearly wanted it done that he stood still for it at last. The photographer fussed over the light: it was high noon and the sun was harsh, and Burton was such a reluctant subject that the young man knew he couldn't keep us waiting long. He tried to chase away two little colored boys but Burton insisted they be left alone, and he gave each of them a penny. At last the photographer stood us on the walk near a palmetto tree, with the old Exchange Building rising dramatically behind us: Richard smiled and draped his arm over my shoulder, and there we were. The picture we took that day long ago was perfect, and remains one of my dearest possessions.

We lunched at the hotel, and I finally broached the dreaded subject. "You must know Lord Palmerston well." I said this innocently, I thought, but Richard looked hard in my eyes: there was no fooling him, and his answer was vague. "We've met a few times in social gatherings."

I pushed the point. "What do you think of him?"

"A colorful man. Not one you'd want to trifle with or have as an enemy. Rather like Calhoun was, I would imagine, like some of your fire-eating Southerners of today when he's opposed." A long moment passed while he leveled me with those eyes. "Why do you ask?"

Another long moment, and I saw that there could be no lying or evasion. "Richard," I said, looking straight at him.

He waited.

"I've become uneasy about a few things."

"I could sense as much."

I felt my insides trembling: my God, I did not want to lose him! In those few seconds a dozen thoughts flooded through my mind. I imagined him taking dire offense, wounded in the heart. I saw him getting up from the table, walking away without a word, checking out of the hotel and disappearing into the bright sunlight. I saw myself rushing along beside him, pleading, *I didn't mean it, you've taken me wrong!* But in fact if I offended him, he would be taking me exactly right.

I mustered myself and as calmly as I could said, "I would rather cut out my tongue than say this."

Then to my amazement, he said it for me. "You are worried that I am spying against your country."

"No," I lied quickly. "No, no, nothing like that."

"Please . . . Charlie."

"All right, yes. I can't help it, the thought crossed my mind and it won't go away. I just wouldn't have put it so bluntly."

"Sometimes bluntness is the best way. The only way."

"The thought never once occurred to me until we were in the backwoods, and you seemed so preoccupied with everything and everybody."

"I told you, I do that everywhere. It's my way."

"Of course it is and I know that. I know as well as anyone how your books were compiled and written. I know these things and yet . . ."

"No," he said. "You may *think* you know them, but you can't understand the volume of material that runs through my mind in the course of a work. In India, just as an example, I had to make my notes in conditions that only one writer in ten thousand would endure. Impossible working conditions, yet there I worked, sitting under a table in an endless rain, the air so hot I could barely breathe, the paper shredding and falling apart even as I wrote on it."

"You're right, I don't understand that. What's the point of it?"

"Discipline, Charlie, discipline! And it did serve its purpose. Once I had written it down I had it committed to memory, even if the notes themselves didn't survive."

Well, at least I could believe that. I smiled wanly and said, "All right," and we ate for a time in silence. I thought the discussion was over: if so, it had been wholly unsatisfactory from my point of view, for Richard had not yet answered the most difficult question in plain language. I decided to say no more about it, to forget it, but I had made such resolutions before and what had they come to? Once a dark thought crosses the mind, it is there forever.

Then Richard said, "I sympathize with your worry. This is a very bad time for your young nation, more so than I imagined from the other side of the sea. Anything could tip you into war."

England, for instance, I thought: Britannia, who could not defeat us in two staunch attempts when we were united but might have far easier pickings if we so stupidly divided ourselves. But I said, "Nothing will come of this. These people are noisy braggarts but they are not going to destroy the Union."

"If you think that, you are naive."

I shook my head. "In fact, I don't think that."

"No. This is a powder keg. It will take just one incident, and these people are itching for that excuse. It is inevitable."

I shivered at his words, knowing how right he was. Richard had coffee and I joined him across another silence. Eventually he said, "I will give you an answer, but for your ears only."

I felt myself blush again. "Richard, you know I can't accept that."

"Then let's put it another way. You must never divulge anything of what I say unless it compromises your own sense of loyalty to your country."

"And then?"

"Then you are free to do or say whatever you wish."

I was still uneasy. He smiled and said, "That leaves an awful lot to your own discretion, Charlie. I can't be much fairer or more trusting than that. And if you think about it, this says a good deal about my faith in your honor."

I was moved by his words, but I knew what he was really saying. My honor could be clear, for any reason of my own choosing, but I knew our friendship would be lost.

Burton sipped his coffee and said, "I'm not spying on you, my friend. It's just that there are personalities involved. Issues unresolved in England. Things I still haven't decided how to deal with—personal things that influenced my decision to come here. I don't want my business scattered about for everyone to know. Isn't that reasonable?"

"Of course it is," I said, but I knew my tone was unconvincing.

He made a small gesture of impatience and lit a smoke. "Damn it, you brought this up and now it must be dealt with. The alternative is fairly unattractive for both of us. We must part company in distrust."

"I cannot accept that. I won't."

"Then what do you say?"

I nodded warily.

For a time I thought he still would not tell me. Even when he did speak his talk was rambling and not obviously to the point.

"You may have heard that I came home from Africa as something of an outcast. If that sad news hasn't yet reached America, it will. And it will only get worse as Speke publishes his opinions. In my own forthcoming book I mention our differences only briefly. But Speke and I are at impossible odds: he has made his claim to the discovery of the big lake, insisting that this alone must be the source of the great Nile River. Never mind that he has no scientific evidence: he saw nothing more than a vast body of water, not even a visual sighting of a river flowing outward, to the north or any other direction. So it all remains unproved, unprovable, really, without another expedition. None of that mattered in the jubilation of the moment. People wanted a hero, and Speke rushed to get home first and give them one. At my expense, if that's how it had to be."

He sniffed derisively but there was no missing the hurt in his face. "We had an agreement: discussion first, before any publication or speech making. We would decide together what we had found and what it meant. But I was burning up with fever and Speke hurried home alone. His book, if he writes one, which I can't imagine—my God, the man is almost illiterate—but you watch, publishers will wheedle it out of him, and such a book will be calculated for one effect above all others: the glorification of Jack Speke. The public already believes it, hook and sinker, so what more does a publisher need? Damn the truth."

His eyes took on a faraway look. "The Nile," he said, almost wistfully. "Do you know how many centuries people have been wondering where it comes from? But no one could penetrate that wilderness until Speke and I did it."

He sipped his coffee. "I have many enemies in London, Charlie. One has to choose what to believe, and a great number chose to believe Speke's accounts. And his slanders."

"I believe you," I said. "I don't think it's in you to write an untrue word."

He smiled gratefully. "I'll tell you one of the truest and ugliest things about human nature. If a man betrays a friend, even a little, he must then turn completely on that friend and destroy him. That's what Speke must now do to me. I alone know what happened. I'm the greatest threat in his life so there's no other way to validate himself. And maybe get rid of a little self-loathing."

He looked down at his cup. "I swore I would never trust another man after Speke, but here I am, trusting you."

Yet another long silence passed, as if he of all people could not find the words he sought. "Listen, Charlie. This must not sound like any form of self-pity."

At once I said, "I would *never* suspect you of any such thing. Never, Richard."

He cocked his head slightly. "There is a woman I have decided to marry."

I gave him a heartfelt congratulation and predicted that he would greatly enjoy his wedded life. But he looked doubtful and said, "Her family is furiously opposed. Her mother is impossible."

My look told him how sorry I was.

He said, "This is how things are. If I had returned a hero, many things might have been different. But getting back to the prime minister."

"Yes."

"Lord Palmerston was not unkind to me, as some were. I was invited to his home. We had several confidential chats. It was he, in fact, who suggested that I come here."

I felt suddenly alarmed: we had moved perilously close to that point of leeway Richard had given me. But he said, "There was no intrigue about it. Palmerston simply said that in my shoes, under the circumstances, he would undertake a new journey, something completely unexpected. To the States, for instance."

He lit another smoke. "That was the first thought I had of it. But I warmed to the idea at once. Suddenly it felt very right. I couldn't bear London any longer."

"And that's all there was to it?"

"Almost all. The prime minister summoned me to his home again, just before I left, to say he'd be anxious to hear my impressions of America when I returned."

"But no specific expectations—no *assignments*, so to speak?"

He laughed softly. "No assignments, Charlie. I do have a list of people he wants me to see. To convey his respects."

"Southern people, you mean. Charleston people."

"And others. I am going on to the frontier. Your secretary of war was very helpful to me in that regard. He also gave me a letter to the commander at Fort Moultrie."

I let that pass. There was no use telling Burton of my own personal disdain toward Mr. Floyd. What difference did it make what I suspected or thought?

"But in the main this journey is for my own self-renewal," Richard said. "Something I needed badly. And am finding, by the way."

Pointedly he said, "I hope that satisfies you."

"Of course."

It had damned better, I thought.

With that we dropped it. But it never really went away.

Richard.

His eyes were so full of mystery, his presence so quietly formidable. He was nothing like I had imagined him to be. With me he was always gentle and respectful, and I found it difficult to imagine him as the intimidating and often feared presence that others saw in him. The pictures drawn by his biographers, by accounts in the press before and after his death, and even in the writings of his widow more than thirty years past the events I am describing, miss much of the Burton I knew. I cannot challenge them: Who am I to challenge anyone? What was I compared with Isabel, or with men who spent years studying his life? I was at best a shirtsleeve authority. Our time together was so brief, and all I can ever be is the authority on those few weeks. Today I see how random it all was: how easily we might have failed to meet and never known what each of us would bring to the other. But we did meet, and I know I had at least a small effect on Richard's life, and it would be impossible to overstate the vast effect he has had on mine. There has never been a day in forty years that I have not thought of him, written to him, reread favorite passages from his work.

It was only by chance, browsing through a dusty used bookstore in New York, that I first became aware of his name. There I saw in a bargain bin a small volume bound in red cloth: his 1853 book on bayonet exercise. Today it is a rare piece, but then it looked like just another book of narrow interest, to be thrown down among the sales items. What was it about this little book that drew me to him and ultimately led me to this marvelous journey? Was some hand of Providence at work? I remember thumbing through it, ambivalent, waiting for my companion to finish her Christmas buying from a shelf of leather-bound items behind the counter. I looked at the plates and, caring nothing about the subject, tossed it back in its place. I walked away and browsed the shelves, but eventually some compelling force—how else can I put this?—drew me back to the sales bin. I could see from the title page that the author was then a lieutenant in the Bombay army, that he had written of his travels in the Scinde, in Goa and the Blue Mountains. None of that had interested me then, but Burton had also written a book on falconry, and I was a birdman, so that did have some appeal. I bought the bayonet book on a whim, and as we left the bookshop my soon-to-be-wife looked at my purchase and said, "What on earth are you doing with that awful thing?" I joined her in a laugh at Burton's expense, saying, "It's no great loss, it only put me half a dime down." What I could never make her understand was how quickly and deeply my involvement with Burton grew. Even when she knew how and why, years later, she had no idea. Some things, like Burton making his notes under impossible conditions in India, simply can't be shared. A friend can be told, as I was told, of the table and the rain and the paper shredding as he wrote on it, but no one can ever truly know the experience of another. In the beginning I made light of it, but almost at once I searched out and read his falconry book, then his works on Goa and the Scinde. There was something bigger than life in his words, some mysterious sense of things, an attitude that drew me from one book to another. I sent away to his publisher, John Van Voorst in England, and obtained my own copies of the falconry title. But it was the monumental achievement of his travels to Mecca and Medina that captured my mind and thrilled my imagination. That's when I became a serious Burton collector.

The hand of Providence guided me to him, then him to me. Call me a self-serving sentimentalist, call me a fool, but that's what I believe.

We stayed in Charleston a week. On the third day Richard disappeared and was gone almost thirty-six hours.

He had complained of a headache after a night of too much alcohol, and I had gone walking on the Battery alone. In fact I went far beyond the Battery, around the entire city and out on a footpath that ran along the Ashley River. I spent hours walking, watching the people, talking to strangers, and soaking up the sun. I lost track of time with a gang of pickaninnies crabbing from the riverbank, fascinated by their strange language and delighted with their catch. The sun was low over the river when I finally turned back to the city: suddenly I realized I had been gone all day.

At the hotel there was a message in my box: *Looked for you and waited as long as I could. Gone to meet some people. Hoped you would return to join us. Opportunity arose suddenly and might not come again. Will see you tomorrow. Richard.*

This was disappointing but I had only myself to blame. Never mind: I would enjoy the evening without Richard's company. The city was exotic; I would explore its tastes and sounds and sights on my own. I dressed for an occasion and was determined to find one. At the desk I asked the clerk what entertainments might be available and he suggested a musicale and a melodrama, both within walking distance. I could catch either of these and still have time for a good dinner before curtain. He gave me the names of several restaurants; then, as I was turning to leave, he said, "There was a message for you from Mr. Burton this morning. Did you get it?" I said I had and thanked him. "It's too bad," he said. "You just missed him."

I was already out on the street when what he'd said brought me up short. I returned to the desk and asked him to elaborate. He said, "I only meant because he left immediately after you did," and my heart sank.

I was crushed by this proof that Richard had lied. He hadn't looked for me at all; he had *watched* for me to leave. If there was any truth in his note, it was only that he had gone to see some people. Yes, I thought bitterly. He's seeing some people he doesn't want me to meet or even know he's met.

I had opted for the melodrama but now I was in too sour a mood to enjoy it. I wasn't hungry either—normally I am a three-a-day man and I hadn't eaten since morning, but at that point the prospect of a meal was, to say the least, unappetizing. I walked the streets and I could see only one possible course of action. I must cut the trip short. No more fencing: I would remove even the possibility of further lies by removing myself from Richard's game, whatever it was. I would simply say that something about the Southern climate had begun to affect my health and I must catch the steamer north at my first opportunity—tomorrow if possible. I could lie if he could, I thought childishly. Richard, of course, would know the reason; he was far too intelligent to be fooled by such a lame excuse, but that was the best I could come up with. The alternative—to remain under pretense—would be intolerable.

I was bitterly disappointed, but once I had decided I felt surprisingly better. Not that I wanted to leave—far from it. I would have given much to have Richard appear that moment with a credible reason for his deception, but I couldn't imagine what that would be. What I now wanted was to salvage whatever I could of my personal regard for Richard and take my leave while I could still give him some benefit of the doubt.

But out on the street a new thought hit me. I would have to warn someone. Someone had to be told that England was already making plans against us. Someone in our government, high enough to matter, must be told.

Not the treasonous Secretary Floyd, that much was certain.

In the morning I walked to the offices of the steamship company and obtained a schedule. I could get a boat for Wilmington within the hour. But Richard had still not returned; I couldn't leave without at least saying good-bye, and so I lounged around the hotel waiting until long after the steamer had departed for Wilmington. I was quite hungry: I had not eaten since yesterday, and now I had a substantial lunch at the hotel, then waited over a glass of ale in the bar across the street. Well, I was stuck for another day. This fact brought an odd mix of clashing emotions—anger, dismay, anxiety, along with relief and a wild hope that at times overrode all the others. I was anxious to have it all behind me and be away from here but the thought of what must come filled me with despair. Above all I still wished desperately for some word or act that would save us from the ugly split that seemed inevitable.

I had another ale and sometime later, on my third, I felt my limit and switched to sarsaparilla. My anger had again dissipated, and again I sat groping for some innocent reason behind Richard's actions. There was none: he had lied, there was no doubt about that, there could be no excuse for it, I had to go, I should have gone at once and left him a note. But that would be a coward's way and we both deserved better. So I waited.

I saw him arrive at three o'clock. I crossed the street and came into the hotel behind him, but again I wavered. How could I do this? What could I say? I stood in the lobby and watched him skip jauntily up the stairs, and only when he had gone did I go up at a far slower gait. I walked softly past his room and went into my own. I lay on the bed in a state of deep trouble, and after a while I fell asleep.

I opened my eyes at his knock on my door. I didn't move.

He rapped again. He said nothing but I knew who it was. I heard him walk away, down the hall, down the stairs. I couldn't keep him waiting much longer.

At last I went down and saw him sitting alone at the far end of the lobby. He was reading a newspaper: the *Charleston Mercury,* Rhett's rabble-rousing sheet of traitorous innuendo and sedition. He looked over the edge of the paper as I approached.

"Charlie. I've been looking for you."

Immediately I started my lie. "I haven't been feeling well," I said, but my voice faltered and I knew I could not continue with it. How could I chastise Richard for lying if I was doing the same? Before I could go on, he said, "Sit down here, talk to me," and I sat in the lounge chair facing his. He looked in my eyes. "I want to tell you something."

I almost brushed him off in a wave of impatience. Please, I thought, no more lies. I felt my hands tremble as I prepared to speak. But he spoke first, offering a surprising confession. "I didn't tell you the truth in that note I left you."

I nodded.

"You guessed as much?"

Nodded again.

He regarded me for a long moment. "I don't lie easily to any man. It's almost impossible when that man is a close friend."

Please, Richard, I thought, how close can we be? We barely know each other. I wanted to say it but didn't.

"The fact is, I had to be away from you for a day. So I waited until you left the hotel. Then I left and called on some people."

"Am I allowed to ask why?"

"Because you would not have approved of what I did. And it had become necessary for me to play a role."

I looked up, met his eyes, and suddenly I found my voice, surprising myself at the strength of it. "You must know how this seems to me. You must know I can't sit still for it. I think under the circumstances—"

"At least hear me out. Then do what you must."

He spent no time gathering himself. He knew what he had to say, and at his first words I felt my anger melting away. Suspicion remained: it would take years for that bitter pill to completely dissolve. But what I thought I now heard in his voice was truth.

"I have been up to Mr. Rhett's plantation. I went at the request of Lord Palmerston, who had paved my way in a secret communication."

He looked at me directly. "There were many ultrasecessionists on hand, and a number of state officials, with lots of heated balderdash thrown about. Charlie, these fools are having the time of their lives. Strutting like cocks in a barnyard. So much self-aggrandizement, so much egotism, no regard at all for the tragedy they are about to rain down on their country. They have no idea how quickly the world is turning against state-sponsored slavery, and how difficult it will soon be for them to function with that as their calling card. They can't imagine how many of their boys will die for their foolish pride."

He took a deep breath. "Your presence would have been impossible."

Softly, I said, "What did they all think, having Richard Burton among them?"

"I didn't go as Richard Burton. To them I was a friend of a friend of the prime minister whose name they will quickly forget."

"Richard . . ."

"My only lie was the manner of my escape yesterday, and I intended to set that straight between us, whether you had guessed it or not."

"There's more to it than that. I asked you specifically whether you are on a spying mission."

"And I told you I'm not."

"I asked you specifically if you are under any instructions from Palmerston."

"Lord Palmerston asked me to make this call only as a courtesy and I've done that. When I return to England he will want my impression of the overall situation here and I shall give it to him. That's hardly what anyone would call grand intrigue."

He gestured impatiently. "I can't tell you what England will do when your war comes. I'm not the prime minister. All I can do is tell him what I think."

"Which is?"

"That we would be ill-advised to get involved in this conflict in any way. That the American spirit will not be defeated. That even if the South should somehow prevail—it won't—but even then there would be resistance groups at work to restore the Union, and that intervention or tampering by any foreign power, especially one based thousands of miles away, would be insane. That such a for- eign power can expect fierce guerrilla warfare, perhaps for years, with many casualties. The day is coming when no power, not even England, will be able to sustain such a war. If Palmerston brings us into it, it will be a quagmire and history will remember his name for that above all else. That's what I'll tell him."

He cleared his throat. "I apologize for the small deception."

"Richard . . ."

I think he knew then what I had to ask but he waited politely.

"Why did you bring me into it?" I said. "Why involve me in something that could only turn out badly for both of us?"

He smiled dolefully. "Charlie, don't you know that?"

I blinked at him and gestured impatiently. "Know what?"

"I came to America hoping for self-renewal. You gave it to me. You restored my spirit, almost completely, on the first day we met."

I couldn't imagine. I felt numb with surprise, and a flush of—oh God, was that *love* growing in my heart? I recoiled at once from such a thought.

"I was a wounded man when I left England. My spirits have never been lower, and by the end of that first day with you I felt like my old self again. You were a stranger, a strong and intelligent man far from my own land, who had collected and read my books, and even took time out from his day to come say hello."

"But that seems . . ." I groped for the words. "God, that seems so . . . *small*."

"Big gifts often seem small to those who dispense them."

A minute passed. Then he said, "I shall never forget that week we spent together in your home. You have a rare ability to make a man feel like a hero without pandering to him."

"How could I possibly have done all that?"

"Just being your own man. You had intelligent opinions and you stood up to me. That's how I came to value your opinion. And your company."

"Well, Richard," I said, still numbly. "I've never been much for glaring hero worship. To me, of course, you were a hero, and still are. But there had to be something more than that to create a friendship. I had to bring something of my own to it."

"Isn't that what I'm saying? I meet enough kowtowing idiots to know the difference."

He turned his palms up, the universal gesture for "That's all there is," and said, "So why did I bring you? You can be sure I never would have suggested it if I had been sent here on some spying mission. I brought you because I wanted you with me. And I thought I could slip away for a day without offending you."

He got up and squeezed my shoulder. "Give it some thought, Charlie."

*   *   *

That night we went out together as if nothing had happened. We visited bars along the market, from Meeting Street to the waterfront, and I drank more ale than I had consumed in any week of my life or have ever done since. Richard, far more practiced at imbibing, held his liquor well, but I became rather silly with the night still young. As midnight approached, Richard also began feeling the influence, and we sang bawdy seaman's songs with other merrymakers we met along the way. We laughed at everything: every drunken slur and slip of the tongue brought a riot of laughter from the crowd around us, which, in some of the taverns, numbered almost as many women as men. Richard charmed them all and they seemed willing to give my obviously Northern voice the benefit of doubt. We staggered out of the last open bar at some ungodly morning hour and made a tortuous walk back to the hotel. As we parted that night, Richard said, "Tomorrow we can see some more sights, if you want. And sometime before we leave I'd like to go over to Fort Moultrie and visit the garrison there."

I wondered through my alcoholic haze whether I'd be welcome on such a trip, but Richard said, "Wouldn't you like to see that, Charlie—see how it looks from the perspective of those poor devils who will have to die defending it?"

I said I would, and we left it at that.

The commanding officer at Fort Moultrie was Colonel John Gardner. I knew little about him before that day: Richard, in fact, knew much more. "He's an old man," he said as our steamer curled in toward the landing at the western tip of Mount Pleasant. "He served in the War of 1812 and in Mexico."

The former would make him at least sixty, not too ancient for command, but Richard said nothing when I voiced this. We docked and began the cumbersome voyage to Sullivan's Island. In the summer it would be easier: there'd be a direct ferry crossing from the city, used by wealthy families with island homes to escape Charleston's worst yellow fever months. But now in late spring it was a more tedious journey, across the marsh on a plank road and from there by small hired boats to the tip of the island.

The beach was lovely in the warm spring air. I remembered reading of this island in Poe, who had been stationed here some thirty years before and had set the tale of his gold bug partly in these dunes. It had changed little in that time. The fort was at least as dilapidated and run-down today, and as we approached it I could see what an untenable mission the garrison had been given. Huge sand dunes had accumulated against the walls, making its defense impossible: I could have walked up and over the walls with no effort at all.

There were no guards out as we approached, and we went on past, turning inland to trek around to the front gate. There, Richard presented our cards and asked if we might pay our respects to Colonel Gardner. We were taken into the fort, where we met Captain Abner Doubleday, who spoke with us briefly.

"Colonel Gardner is quartered not far from here, outside the fort," Doubleday said. "If you'll kindly wait here, I'll send someone to see if he can receive you."

When we were alone again, Richard rolled his eyes in the universal gesture of disdain. "He lives outside his fort. What does that tell you?"

"Nothing good," I said. "I wonder if he's a rebel Yankee like our Mr. Floyd."

"He's from Massachusetts," Richard said, surprising me again with his knowledge.

Doubleday returned fifteen minutes later and said Gardner would receive us after his lunch hour, which unfortunately was already under way. "You're certainly welcome to share mess here," he said, and we thanked him and accepted his offer.

Burton had made no attempt to conceal his identity, but if his name meant anything to Doubleday, that wasn't immediately apparent. Doubleday had just returned to the army after a long leave of absence and was in the earliest days at his new post. I wondered what he thought of this place in these times. He held his own curiosity with perfect military propriety, but when Burton asked who was running the day-to-day affairs of the fort, he said, with a touch of malicious irony, "The officer of the day. Today that seems to be myself."

We ate the simple fare and talked about small things—the weather, the potential danger of Burton's proposed trip across the continent, the Indians in the West, and the prospect of yellow fever in Charleston again this summer.

"Come, I'll show you the fort," Doubleday said when we were finished.

We walked around the walls, all of us carefully avoiding what was so painfully obvious even to me. The fort could not be defended. Burton finally ventured a gentle opinion. "Those dunes do make it difficult, don't they?"

"Yes, sir, they do do that."

"Why can't they be removed?" I asked.

"There's a worry that the locals might be provoked by it," Doubleday said. "They don't need much to provoke them."

"Even if the dunes were removed, defense would not be easy," Burton said.

"No. We are like a leaky raft, surrounded by sharks."

He was a bit easier now, with the two of us obviously kindred, at least in spirit.

We had come full circle. Doubleday looked out to sea and then at Richard. "So what would you do in this place, Captain Burton?"

Burton smiled, pleased to be recognized and acknowledged by his most recent rank. He looked off to sea and said, "I suppose that would depend on my authority and how I interpreted it."

A soldier came along then and said that the colonel would see us. Doubleday walked us to the gate and shook hands. "Drop by

again on your way out, if you have the time. There's a tavern up the
beach that you might enjoy."

We spent an hour with Colonel Gardner, who was an old man in
every sense. The talk quickly became political, and Gardner's sym-
pathies overrode his Northern upbringing, coming down much too
solidly with the Southerners for my liking. "You've got to understand their anger," he said. "They are being treated very badly on
the question of the territories. If Lincoln somehow gets elected and
slavery is outlawed in the new territories, their way of life will soon
be suffocated through the legislative process."

Burton was polite as always, expressing an understanding of
the Southern viewpoint without stating his own. But as we took
our leave and trudged back to the fort, he said, "It's not his age
that makes him unfit for this command, it's his attitude. Look at
the position this puts his men in. It's not bad enough to be surrounded by enemies and have the walls of their fort covered with
dunes that any five-year-old could climb over; now for a leader
they've got an old man who lives among the enemy and spouts the
enemy's dogma." He stopped in the middle of the road and beheld
the sorry fort. Loudly, with no attempt to hide his anger, he said,
"So, Charlie, how'd you like to be stationed here with your life in
the balance?" Then, under his breath, he said, "God *damn* such
authority! God *damn* such arrogance! God *damn* politics and
politicians!"

Captain Doubleday seemed happy to see us again, as if we represented some fading semblance of sanity in a world going quickly
mad. The three of us walked up the beach, chatting pleasantly in the
warm May sunshine. He needs our outside voices, I thought, even
though he can't admit that or commit himself to strangers. He's a
soldier; he can't criticize the politicians who have put him here, or
the seditious old man to whom they've entrusted his life. All he can
honorably do is hope to die well when the time comes.

We stood for a while and watched the sea, looking at incoming ships gliding past Fort Sumter and around the point to the city. Then Doubleday said, "Come, I'll buy you something to drink."

The tavern was just a short trek across the dunes: a cool, dark haven with a pair of cool, dark wenches as barmaids. The ladies were so closely matched that they had to be sisters, and Doubleday introduced them to us as Florence and Frances. I thought of Marion, the girl in the little upstate town that now seemed so far behind us: the town of Florence, I remembered with a shudder. I looked across the table and wondered if Burton was having the same supernatural thoughts.

Doubleday ordered ale for us and tea for himself.

I offered a toast. "To the Union."

Instinctively Doubleday raised his cup. Richard was tardy by just a couple of heartbeats.

We talked into the afternoon. Doubleday and Burton spoke of general military strategies, captain to captain. It all came down to the one thought, without ever getting more specific than they had already been: how to defend the defenseless.

It was after three o'clock when Doubleday said, "I should get back to my post and you have a boat to catch."

At the very last, he said to Burton, "I've been thinking about that question we left unanswered this morning. You said it would depend on your authority and how you interpreted it. I'm not sure what you meant."

"I meant that in your colonel's position, lacking specific orders to the contrary, I would move my men under cover of night to that new brick fort out yonder in the harbor."

If Doubleday had expected some theoretical, wishy-washy answer, this was a surprise. He stiffened, clearly shocked by what he'd heard. "You can't be serious."

"I wouldn't make jokes about something this grave, Captain."

"That would surely be taken as an act of war by the people who live here."

"Such a viewpoint has no logic. The fort is Union property, not the state's."

"Captain, you are speaking of logic in a land that does not know its meaning."

"Then the problem must inevitably become critical, no matter what you do to prevent it. You can't talk logic to madmen and you can't prevent a war if only one side is interested in doing that."

Nothing was said until Burton spoke again. "So in that situation my most immediate loyalty would be to my men. Assuming, as I said, no orders to the contrary."

"And you would move them," Doubleday said, still in disbelief.

"I would move them now—tonight if it were mine to do."

"Interesting thought," Doubleday said. "Depressing but interesting."

We walked down the beach and took our leave in a hazy afternoon sunlight. At the fort we wished Captain Doubleday and his garrison good luck. As we put it some distance behind us, Burton said, "Those men are going to need a hell of a lot more than luck," and this reality followed us over the marsh to the steamer and back across the harbor to the city.

That to me was the climax of our journey. All these years later I can still see Burton's dark face in the candlelight; I can feel Doubleday's surprise, as palpable as a slap in that dark, flickering corner, and I would bet my life that he had never given such a bold move a serious thought before that moment. The act that started our civil war may seem obvious now in its dusty historical context. But what seems obvious to historians might not have been quite so clear to the men who were living it. Yes, those Southerners were mad, hot-blooded and irrational, determined to have their war. If there had been no Fort Sumter they would have found another time and place to begin it. But the fact that it did start at Sumter makes the provocative act, first posed by Richard Burton on a quiet afternoon a year before the shooting started, of considerable historical significance.

* * *

The time was now coming for us to part. Nothing had been said, but I had already gone well past the days I had begged from my wife. Richard planned to go on to New Orleans and then catch the riverboat north to his jumping-off point into the Western territories. Over dinner he launched a spirited campaign for me to join him.

"Come at least as far as New Orleans."

"Richard, I can't. I'm a family man who has indulged himself long enough."

We had carefully avoided the subject of his disappearance, but he alluded to it now. "I hope things are right between us."

"Of course they are. I wouldn't have missed this trip for anything."

"Good. I'm glad to hear that."

He lit a smoke. Impulsively he reached through the smoke to grip my hand. "I'm not a sentimental man, Charlie. But in all likelihood we shall never see each other again, and I must say this. I've had damned few friendships that I value as much as yours."

"That's very mutual, Richard," I said over the lump in my throat.

"Then come with me to St. Joe. I wouldn't insist on anything beyond that, my word of honor. I don't want your scalp on my conscience if I run into Indians on west."

I resisted, he insisted, and at last we compromised on New Orleans. The next morning I sent a telegram to Baltimore, stealing another two weeks from my wife and young daughter, and we left Charleston that afternoon. Down the coast we went to Savannah, then west on a rugged overland trip that took us through the growing towns of Columbus, Montgomery, and Mobile. We spent five days drinking and laughing in New Orleans. My two weeks ran into a third, and as the time drew to its inevitable close, I felt a cutting sadness like nothing I've known before or since. When my wife died in 'eighty-three, my grief was crushing; this was different, but in its own way almost as overwhelming. I felt the loss of Richard as sharply as the slice of a knife.

We got roaring, hilariously drunk that final night. Richard drank more than I had ever seen one man consume, and we staggered into our rooms in a stupor that I can barely remember. In the morning we both paid the price: Richard was actually ill from the aftereffects, and it took him all morning, until just before his steamer departed, to begin to recover. I walked with him to the dock and we promised to write. I gave him a standing order for any books he might produce, "two copies of each, please, one inscribed to me, for as long as you write them and as long as I'm here to receive them."

I watched him, a lonely figure on the riverboat's deck, until he went out of sight. In that moment I'd have done anything to have him back. The city that night was full of tourists, but to me it was excruciatingly empty, and I knew the long voyage home would be solemn and bleak.

As I checked out the next morning, the clerk asked if my stay had been satisfactory. "And will you be seeing your friend again, sir?"

"I hope so. But he lives in London . . ."

"I only ask, sir, because the maid found something he left in his room."

He brought it out from behind the desk.

It was Richard's notebook.

Of course I wrote him, telling him I had the notebook and it was safe with me until such time as he could claim it. Did he want me to entrust it to the mails? That transatlantic passage could be perilous, but I would be happy to send it on if that's what he wanted. Otherwise I would hold it until we met again.

His reply when it came months later was enigmatic and brief. He would appreciate it if I would put the journal in a safe place, unseen by *anyone,* until he could retrieve it. "I must have knocked myself out that night," he said by way of apology. "I thought I packed it, but I drank like a fish."

Other than that I didn't expect much from his promise to write: Burton was a busy world traveler and in the gradual letdown after my homecoming, I had to be realistic. I was a minor character in his crowded life, an admirer he had met by chance. But one day a letter came.

It was everything I could have hoped for: detailed, packed with news of his journey to see Brigham Young, his trek to California and across Central America, and the steamer voyage home. Soon he would have a book, to be called *The City of the Saints,* describing what he had seen of the Mormons and his stagecoach trip across the American desert to California, and his book *The Lake Regions of Central Africa* was imminent from the publisher. "I have taken you at your word regarding two copies of each book, but don't hesitate to holler uncle if it becomes too burdensome." He said nothing about his journal, and though it sat on my shelf like some wicked temptress, I never opened it, I never peeped; I rose to the highest expectation of his trust and let it be.

I wrote him back at once, saying that not only did I want his new books as they came off the press but any new editions of his older works as well, especially if they contained new or amended material. I sent him news from the States. The little garrison at Fort Moultrie was living under a national microscope in the wake of Lincoln's election, anything could tip us into war, and if there was a chance that his books might fail to arrive through some difficulty with the mails, he should please hold them for me until the trouble was settled.

I followed the events at Moultrie and kept a diary of my reactions, with the silly idea of sending it to Burton at some point and perhaps egging him to do a book on our part of his journey. "Old Gardner has been replaced by a much younger commander, Major Robert Anderson," I wrote in December. "Captain Doubleday is his right-hand man." Later that month I wrote again, when the Moultrie garrison slipped into Fort Sumter under cover of night, exactly as Burton had suggested almost a year before. "You must have made far more sense to that captain than either of us thought at the time," I said. "Of course, having no alternative will change a man's mind."

"God help us all now," I wrote in January. "War cannot possibly be averted more than another two weeks." But the talks dragged on until April, when a blaze of fire sent us into four years of hell.

All that year the war news was bleak. Any hope for a quick end dwindled in a series of bloody battles that pushed us to new levels of hatred. November brought my severest test with Richard when a Union warship stopped the British mail steamer *Trent* and two Confederate officials on board were arrested. In London, Lord Palmerston thundered and roared. This was the excuse he had been waiting for. I trembled with rage as thousands of British troops, the vanguard of a certain invasion, were massed on the Canadian border. During those weeks I felt so wracked with suspicion that I decided to torch Richard's books and be done with him. If I sent him a box filled with their ashes, topped by a petulant note telling him what I thought of his honor and the worthlessness of his word, perhaps that would ease my conscience somewhat. But I couldn't light the fire: I couldn't even bring myself to read the truth in his journal, and at last I took it out of my room, out of sight, and, I hoped, out of mind. I waited into January, thank God, when Seward finally announced that the Rebels were being set free, and the crisis with England was defused.

One day a cryptic note came to me. It was months old, written at Christmas in the worst days of the *Trent* affair. It was only two lines and unsigned, but there was no mistaking that cribbed hand: *I made my best case*, it said. *Now we'll see what happens. You may be sure, that I join you in hoping for cool heads to prevail.* Again I felt riddled with shame. The bad friend had not been Richard but myself, and my lack of faith had nearly brought us to ruin. I made up my mind that I would keep his friendship for the rest of my days. No matter what happened, there would be no further suspicion. And to seal my decision I brought out his journal and put it up on my open shelf, where it has sat unread ever since.

* * *

I got nothing more from him until our war was over, but the cornu-
copia that followed was one of my great thrills of 1866. A vast collection arrived in two enormous boxes: *The Lake Regions of
Central Africa,* in two volumes, signed to me with an inscription
that never fails to warm my heart. *To Charles Warren—my dear
friend Charlie—I think of you often and hold very dear those days
we traveled together through your troubled American South.* I read
The City of Saints with great interest, wondering why he had written not a word on his time in the South. I knew he hated slavery;
why would he not take that opportunity to comment on its evils. A
trace of the old suspicion wafted up: *Because he was a spy, England
will invade us the first chance she gets, and I in my silence am her
accomplice.* But those dark thoughts I pushed aside: my trust in
Richard always returned.

There was more in the boxes: *The Prairie Traveler* was a book of
advice for hardy souls crossing the vast American continent.
Abeokuta and the Camaroons Mountains had a striking frontis por-
trait of Burton, charming despite the posed, formal nature of it. *Wan-
derings in West Africa from Liverpool to Fernando Po* and *A
Mission to Gelele, King of Dahome* continued his fascination with
and exploration of the great Dark Continent. *The Nile Basin* was a
small work that I was happy to have as a book collector but as his
friend found unfortunate in its continuation of his rivalry with
Speke, who was then dead by his own hand. Later I would learn that
its reception in England confirmed my own judgment: you can't win
an argument with a dead man, and Burton should never have published it. But *Wit and Wisdom from West Africa* was a charming collection of native beliefs, and *The Guide-Book: A Pictorial Pilgrimage
to Mecca and Medina (Including Some of the More Remarkable Incidents in the Life of Mohammed, the Arab Lawgiver)* summarized his
most famous journey. In the bottom of the second box was the
strangest book he ever wrote: a long poem in the form of a dialogue,
titled *Stone Talk,* ostensibly written by a "Frank Baker" but full of
Burtonian trademarks. It was a biting attack on religion, embracing

Darwin in crude and clever ways, and calling his homeland to account for her hypocrisy and crimes around the world. He penned a tongue-in-cheek inscription and signed it "Frank." *If it becomes known that I wrote this I will be run out of England and banished to the land of the Mormons forever.*

This remarkable output totals nearly three thousand pages in three years. Burton had become a veritable writing machine. Immediately I wrote him a laudatory letter and asked to hear from him if ever he could find a moment (pun intended) to write.

He did write. I got occasional notes from distant world ports, and once a year, more or less, he wrote long catch-up letters. These always closed with fond memories of the weeks we had spent together and the hope that our paths might someday cross again.

The years passed and his books kept the spirit of our friendship alive and well. I lived in his words, traveling with him in my mind to Brazil, Zanzibar, Iceland, and the gorilla land of the Congo, and when he was no longer the great explorer, I marveled at his philosophical works and translations. I always found it curious that he never wrote about our days traveling in the South. Never a line or a word, but I kept my silent vow not to doubt his motives again. The curiosity would remain, long after his death, and it remains today in my own old age.

I had my one opportunity to josh him into some kind of comment in 1877. Captain Doubleday, then brevetted to major-general, had just published his short memoir of Fort Sumter and I sent a copy to Richard. In my covering note I referred him to page 58. *See how profoundly you affected our history,* I wrote. *Our war was certainly inevitable, but the way it began was yours to tell.*

By Doubleday's account, he and others had repeatedly urged that the garrison be moved to Fort Sumter as the situation grew more critical. But Anderson had always replied that he was specifically assigned to Fort Moultrie and had no right to vacate it without orders.

At some point he had changed his mind. Either that, or he had hidden his true thoughts, even from his officers, giving them just twenty minutes' notice on the night they slipped across the harbor in rowboats.

Had Doubleday brought about this change of mind, which had seemed fixed on a very different course?

Did Anderson wrestle with the question of authority, and finally turn it on its head, as Burton had immediately done with the phrase "no orders to the contrary"?

Had Burton been the source of the act that started the war?

Richard never acknowledged it. He never mentioned the Doubleday book at all.

Richard's handwriting, never easy to read, became almost impossible in the last year of his life. I managed to decipher it with the aid of my daughter, the two of us hunched over a thick magnifying glass, sometimes for an hour with a single page. "I have not been feeling well," he wrote in 1890. "It would be grand to see you again and to laugh over those olden days when we were young and the world was ours to discover."

Halfheartedly I said, "I should go see him," and my daughter immediately took up this cause. "You *must* go, Daddy! You will regret it forever if you don't."

"It would be an indulgence," I said. "That's all been so long ago now."

But on the spur of that moment I decided to go to England. That afternoon I wrote Richard a long letter asking if I might visit, say in a month or two or perhaps in the spring. I sent it away on the first of October and waited for a reply.

Less than three weeks later I was shocked by the newspaper headline: SIR RICHARD F. BURTON, NOTED BRITISH EXPLORER, DEAD AT 69.

I was inconsolable. I hadn't seen him in almost thirty years and his sudden death was a deeper wound than even the loss of my younger brother all those same years ago at Gettysburg. I broke down in tears over the paper, shocking my daughter, who had brought it to me. I deplore displays of sentiment, and she had never seen a tear fall from my eyes except at her mother's graveside. But in that moment I felt I had lost the only friend who had ever mattered in my life, and I cried. She hugged my head and she cried also at my obvious distress.

How do I explain such a reaction? Burton was certainly not my best friend: How could he have been in so short a time? Still, time doesn't always tell a true story. You can know a man for years and not know him at all, and another man rises up in a brief acquaintance and is closer than a brother.

I thought of him constantly after his death: the young Burton who had come here defeated and renewed himself on a journey down and across this vast continent. I had been part of that. I know what we did and no one can take that away from me. Even today I hear his voice in the night, fascinated by the power and durability of music, humming Negro spirituals that reach across two continents.

In the spring I got a formal note from his widow. She had come across my letter suggesting a trip to London and had written to ask what it meant. She was intrigued by the familiarity in my lines, frankly because she had no idea who I was.

"Now you have your reason to write it all down, Daddy," my daughter said.

Over the next week I wrote Lady Burton a long reply. I told in detail how I had come to know Richard and most of what we had done together. But when I read it over I felt like a carpetbagger, a charlatan trying to trump up his own importance on the coattails of a far greater man, and instead I sent her a short note.

I never mentioned his journal and I never looked in it. It couldn't matter then, after his death, but there was something between us, his spirit and mine, that made me keep that trust.

Long after her own death, Isabel's question rings in my ears.

Who are you?

Richard never told her.

Who was I?

Well, I was one of his greatest admirers: that cannot be disputed. But he had many great admirers.

Who are you?

I knew him briefly and was deeply saddened when he died. Many were saddened.

We went on a journey once, deep into the lost kingdom of cotton. There, on a sunny afternoon in May, Burton might well have influenced the beginnings of our great civil war.

Might have, could have, maybe. Never mind that. What is real? What is certain?

I shrug. I never stopped wondering, since he never used any of it, whatever he was writing in that notebook. At some point in my old age I even entertained the fancy that he intended to leave it behind, in my care, as a record of what he thought and did in those crowded weeks.

But *why?*

I look at it there on my shelf and it looks unreal.

What is real?

Only Mrs. Burton's question is real. It is still there in my seventh decade.

Who are you?

I look in my mirror at a withered old man and find one answer. I am . . . nobody.

BOOK III CHARLESTON

20

We arrived in Charleston after dark, the ground crew rolled out an air stair, and we climbed down into another world. This was more than just an illusion and it was more than just the heat: the air smelled different—I could taste its salty tang—and the humidity was like a battering ram. As we walked across the runway to the terminal I said, "We're not in Kansas anymore, Koko," and she made a face and a go-away gesture with her hand.

I rented a car while Koko bought a street map, a guidebook, and a pictorial history. A few minutes later she navigated me out to Interstate 26 and turned me south toward the city. "We should stay at the Heart of Charleston," she said, leafing through pages. "That's a motel they built in the sixties on the site of the Charleston Hotel, where Burton and Charlie stayed. Won't that be cool? Maybe their ghosts are still lingering there."

I thought this unlikely, but if I couldn't share her view of the afterlife, at least I could agree that it would be cool to stay there.

The highway swerved down the Neck and Koko provided a running commentary. In the Civil War, batteries had been built across the peninsula to fight off an attack from the north. The city limit then was far south of here and this was mostly country. Like all cities, Charleston had spread far from its core and the sprawl was still going on. We passed through a grim industrial area and a few minutes later I saw the harbor, ablaze with lights to my left, and a spectacular pair of bridges spanning the river. I got off on Meeting Street and ten minutes later we reached the motel. We took two rooms on opposite sides of the motel and were lucky to get them.

There were three conventions in town and rooms of any kind were hard to come by.

By then it was well after ten. We were tired: we had to be after last night—but we were still in the throes of an artificial high, like a Coke sugar rush after a heart-sapping marathon. We met out on Meeting Street five minutes after check-in and found a pub a block away. Koko surprised me by having a beer. I said, "That'll put hair on your chest," and she laughed. "What else can I get in a place like this? One won't kill me."

She took her first cautious sip. "So what did you think of the tape?"

"I liked the feel of it. If the old lady was conning us she was a very skilled operator. We have to assume it's real until we learn otherwise."

"Wait till you hear the others. My case for real gets much stronger then."

"How much more do you have?"

"Hours and hours."

"Can you summarize it?"

"You won't need to listen to the other age-regression sessions. It's just duplication, repeated just for consistency. Jo tells it without any errors every time."

"I'll take your word for that and pass up the repetition. What about the others?"

"It's still a lot of tape."

"I didn't fly down here to sit in a motel and listen to tape, Koko. Where do we start?"

She shrugged. "We've got different goals. I want to prove Jo was authentic, you want to find the books."

"Those things aren't mutually exclusive, you know. They do have common roots."

Koko took a big gulp of her beer. I sipped mine and said, "I don't know why but I feel like my part of the hunt got suddenly warmer."

"What does that mean?"

"Just a gut feeling. Makes no sense at all. It doesn't seem logical that the books would be here."

"I don't know why not."

"For one thing there's the humidity. Humidity like this does terrible things to books. If they were here for any length of time, I'd expect to see some evidence of that on the pages. In a hundred years the paper would've become badly foxed unless they've been kept in an airtight bookcase all these years. In severe cases, foxing can eat up a book. The ones I bought at auction didn't have any of that."

I thought about it some more, then said, "So much for hunches."

"Don't lose faith. Please, we haven't even started yet."

"I never had much faith to lose. Remember, I just came here on a flyer with you. There never was any reason to think the books might be here, except they've got to be somewhere. If they're in Baltimore, none of those thugs knows where."

"There you are, then."

"Where am I? They seem to be divided into two camps: Carl and his gangsters, Archer and Dean. They're all hunting pretty hard. That must mean none of them knows any more than we do. They've got some reason to think they're in Baltimore, but that may just be because of that book Jo took into Treadwell's that day."

"Wouldn't it be a kick if they were here all along? Right in Archer's backyard."

I grinned maliciously. "That would be a real kick, Koko. Hey, your glass is empty. Want another beer?"

21

We were still up at midnight, fiddling with tapes in her room. She snapped a cassette into the machine and said, "This was done right after that session you heard on the plane."

Suddenly I heard Josephine say, in her natural voice, "Koko? Where'd you go?"

"Nowhere, dear. I'm right here."

"I saw him again."

"Your grandfather?"

"No. I mean yes, I always see him. But that stranger was with them."

After a long gap, Koko said, "Jo? Are you all right?"

"Yes, of course. Why wouldn't I be?"

"You've gone pale on us. How are you feeling?"

"What difference does that make? Holy Christmas, I'm almost a hundred years old, how do you think I feel?" A moment later: "I'm sorry. Bad temper doesn't become me."

"Don't let it bother you," Koko said. "Can I get you something?"

"Not unless you can rig me up so I can see again."

Koko adjusted the microphone. "Try that. Why don't you tell me what you remember and I'll try to be your eyes."

"That never works."

"Let's give it a try. Unless you'd rather not."

Another gap: forty seconds to a minute. Then: "I saw three of them. They were standing in some kind of fog, talking. Their faces were hidden by the swirling gray. But every so often it would clear up. Just for an instant a breeze would come through and lift the fog, almost enough to make their faces clear. But they were never clear enough."

"You recognized Charlie, though."

"By his voice more than anything. He was much younger than I had ever seen him in life. In my childhood, you know, he was always an old man."

"Did you get any kind of look at him in that awful fog?"

"Just for a few seconds . . . less than that. But enough to know him, I guess."

"What did he do?"

"He smiled at me and nodded."

"You must've seen him very clearly, then, at least in that split instant."

"No, I *felt* him smile."

"Isn't that the same thing?"

"Yes," said Josephine, obviously pleased. "He was *so* happy to see me again."

"I can imagine. Then what?"

"He said something to Burton."

"Ah. So one of the others was—"

"Richard. Charlie only called him Richard, but of course it was Burton. In a while I could see him, too. A fierce-looking man with mustaches and those awful scars."

"What did they say to each other?"

"I don't know. I couldn't hear."

But almost at once she said, "They were discussing what to do about the third man. It was fairly severe. Then they all moved back in the fog and that's all I saw."

"And you never did see the third man?"

"No."

"You know nothing about him?"

"I didn't say that. I know his name."

"How did you learn that?"

"Richard pushed him away and called him by name."

Again the tape seemed to finish there. It must have been two minutes later when Koko said, "What was his name, Jo? What did Richard call him?"

"Archer," Josephine said at once.

I heard her take a deep, shivery breath. "His name was Archer."

22

I slept nine hours and change, till Koko came pounding on the door at a quarter to ten. I rolled out of bed, sore all over, but I felt rested. My double vision had cleared, I was still alive. I took half a dozen Advils and a shower, and emerged for inspection at ten-thirty.

"You need some dark glasses," Koko said at breakfast. "That shiner you're growing matches my own. Together we look like Bonnie and Clyde."

Her first order of business was to find a department store and get some clothes. "Kerrison's looks like a good bet. This afternoon I'll get started in the library."

"Do you have any idea what you're looking for?"

"Any document that shows Charlie was here and they did what he said. This is a very old library: it was old even then. They have newspapers from the seventeen hundreds. It's a private library but I can use it for a small fee."

"I can't imagine what you think you'll find there. The press didn't exactly cover their arrival or departure."

"You never know. Sometimes the press then did take note when someone visited from abroad. Maybe just a paragraph, or a line somewhere."

"I wouldn't count on it."

"I'll try to pin down other things. Whether there was a photographer named Barney Stuyvessant on East Bay in May of 1860. That picture he took of Burton and Charlie is lost now, but just getting a definite yes or no on the photographer would be helpful."

My own day had begun organizing itself late last night as I listened to the Josephine tape. Like a bad penny, Archer just kept turning up.

"I wondered who he was when we made that tape," Koko said. "Jo had no idea."

"So she said. No offense, Koko, but you swallowed that story of hers pretty easily."

She did take offense. "Why shouldn't I believe her? I had never heard of Archer then."

"Well, you've heard of him now. Don't you find Josephine a little suspicious at this point? I know you don't want to hear this but that sweet old gal may have known more about all these people than she ever let on. Has it ever occurred to you that she may be manipulating us from the grave?"

Her temper erupted. "Oh, go away! God, you're *such* a cynic!"

"Somebody's got to ask the hard questions, Koko. Where do you think she got Archer's name? Did she just pull it out of thin air? Did she pluck it out of the phone book by chance?" I leaned over and stared in her face. "Maybe it *came* to her in a supernatural daze."

"No, it did not *come* to her and I've told you before, there's nothing supernatural about it. Listen, picklepuss, because I don't intend to say this again. I do not believe in the supernatural. At all. About anything. Do I have to say that again or did you get it this time?"

"*Pickle*puss?"

She glared. "If the face fits, wear it."

I countered with deadpan silence. Once in a while our eyes would meet across the table and I'd give her my crushed-dog-in-the-highway look and eventually I got her to laugh.

"That's better," I said soothingly. "Now isn't that better?"

"You mark my words, Cliff, and get ready to eat your own. You're going to learn there's a practical answer for everything. Jo heard that name somewhere—she heard it, read it—how and when she got it isn't important now. But it made an impression and later she dreamed about it. She was describing a *dream,* you fool, you know how mixed-up dreams are. This can't be *that* hard to understand, or are you still such a poopy old cop that you always think the worst of everybody?"

"That's a great way to leave it for now, Koko. You be the pure-hearted optimist, I'll be the poopy old cop."

"Poopy old cynical picklepuss cop," she said with sour amusement.

And on that note we split up.

At least I had a starting point, something to do with my day while she plowed through dusty archives. I prepared to battle pissant clerks who had never been told that public records belong to the public, but this time it was easy. It helps to know what questions to ask and how to ask them, and by late afternoon I had a growing file on Archer.

God, we have become such a depressing nation of numbers. Get a guy's number and you can get almost everything about him. From Motor Vehicles I had his address and phone number on Sullivan's Island. I had his Social Security number and the license plate number on his car. I knew he drove a Pontiac, two-tone blue, bought new in the year of his Pulitzer. But a check of his credit turned up a surprise. He had almost lost the car to repo boys in '85 and again last year. If the Pulitzer had put Archer on Easy Street, he wasn't there long. He needed another book, a big one, and soon.

I bullshat my way from office to office, the good-old boy who made people want to help. If a clerk commented on my battered face, I turned on the charm and yukked him around, concocting tall yarns that made him laugh. In the courthouse I learned that Archer had been sued several times for nonpayment of bills. None of these had gone beyond the filing stage: he always coughed up when the wounded party got serious. He was one of those infuriating stonewallers who will not pay even a bona fide debt until he absolutely must, and now he was considered a bad risk by his plumber, his mechanic, and the man who had painted his house after a near-hurricane a few years earlier. He had several ugly defaults and a history of leaving others hold-ing bags of various sizes. Some of them never did collect, and these days nobody loaned the famous Hal Archer money. He had kept up the payments on his beach house, but by then I had a hunch that it was always by the skin of his teeth. He had bought the property in 1983, leaving me to wonder why he had moved here from Virginia, where he had spent his entire life until then.

I stopped at the public library just off Marion Square. As I'd fig-ured, Archer was in the latest *Who's Who*. Son of Robert Russell Archer and Ann Howard Archer of Alexandria, Virginia, he had married and divorced long ago: a woman named Dorothea Hoskins, who had lived with him only long enough to have a son in 1957. In a vertical file of clippings the library kept on local notables, I learned that Archer had had little to do with his son, and today the boy was a man, living in California with his own family. Archer was a grand-father three times over and he'd never seen his grandchildren. The source of all this was a tabloid tearsheet, not great, but in Archer's case it had a ring of truth. Suddenly the bitter picture looked tragic: a life wasted, with the big prize little more than a hollow victory. I found it unimaginable that anyone could have a child and not die to be part of that kid's life.

There were no other marriages cited, no business affiliations, no memberships, and he did not seem to be religious. He had turned fifty-four on his last birthday. He had never served in the military, even though Korea was still causing trouble on his nineteenth birth-day. His residence was listed as his business address: the same Sulli-van's Island street number I had gotten from Motor Vehicles. There was a list of his books, unhelpful since I already knew them.

His father, Robert Russell Archer, had been a powerhouse Vir-ginia politician, prominent enough to earn his own entry in past *Who's Who*s. Born in Alexandria, Virginia, 1905, he was an acade-mic whiz, graduating from high school at sixteen and with honors from Rutgers in 1925. Married Ann Howard of Baltimore, 1926. Two children, the first named Robert Russell after himself and a few years later our boy Hal, William Harold Archer. Admitted to the Virginia bar 1928. Read law and studied under a prominent judge of the U.S. Circuit Court of Appeals. Public servant prior to starting own law firm: assistant DA in the mid-thirties; U.S. Attorney just before World War II. Too young to be killed in one generation's war, too old to be maimed in the next. Never a candidate in his prime but always a power behind the scenes: worked hard for Dewey against FDR, even harder for the same poor loser against Truman. Chairman of his state's Republican party in the early postwar years; a presidential elector from Virginia in 1948. The firstborn son, the namesake, died in 1945, at fourteen. I made a note to find out how.

Many honors were attached to his name. Slowly as I listed them I began to imagine a powerful patriarch, some Burl Ivesian codger from a Tennessee Williams play. He had come out of his shell to run for the U.S. Senate in the early sixties, but had served only five years of his term, retiring because of illness. He died in 1966, aged sixty-one years.

I read it again and thought, What's wrong with this picture?

The Archers had been like the Huxleys—money, position, power—but Hal Archer was the exact opposite of all that. Hadn't Lee Huxley described him as dirt poor when they were kids? Maybe it was the Depression. A lot of people lost a lot of money in those days.

I looked deeper and found an earlier Robert Russell Archer, also a lawyer, who had dominated his state's Republican party in the First War era, all through Prohibition until his own death in 1939. Grandpa, dead at fifty-three. The Archers had a nasty little gene in their makeup that did them in young. At fifty-four, Hal must be looking over his shoulder.

Born in rural Virginia, 1886, Gramps was a real log-cabin kinda guy. Put himself through the U of Virginia, then law school, and in 1907 married a woman named (I kid you not) Betsy Ross. *Damn, I love that—I can almost hear "Stars and Stripes Forever."* Only one child, the already mentioned Robert Russell Archer. Apparently the family never used "Jr." or "the third," so at least their kids didn't have to battle that all their lives. Like his son he missed the carnage of his day, 1914–18, but you knew he'd have gone in a heartbeat if he'd been a little younger. He was patriotic to the bone: tireless on Liberty Loan drives, a four-minute man always on the stump. Grandpa took a hand in everything that crossed his path. He never saw a civic need that he didn't just yearn to fill: worked on an impossible number of worthy campaigns, and later, with his law career in full bloom, was involved in trusteeships, arbitration societies, and a debating club. He held retainers from half a dozen major companies in the twenties. And with all this real life going on, the old boy had still found time for a hobby. I took in a long, slow breath as I read it.

The first Robert Russell Archer—Grandpa—had been a noted book collector.

By then it was almost dusk. Koko would be waiting for me at the motel but at the moment I had an urge to see Archer's natural habitat. I cruised over the newer spire of the Cooper River Bridge, on through Mount Pleasant, and then, pushed by an incredible sunset, headed east across a broad expanse of marsh. I crossed a drawbridge and came onto the long narrow island, yellow in the fading day. The road dead-ended at a continuous stretch of rolling sand dunes. I knew from my map that Fort Moultrie was a mile to the right, the beach lay just ahead, and Archer's place was two miles north. I turned left and drove up the island.

The island wasn't complicated—no more than half a dozen streets running north and south and a grid of short crossing streets, numbered from First to Thirty-second. Archer's house was near the far end, not far from the inlet that separates Sullivan's from a sister island called the Isle of Palms, and it took me less than ten minutes to find it. It was built on stilts, eight feet above the beach, with a grand wraparound porch, room under it to walk or park cars, and stairs on both the street side and the beachfront. As I drove past I saw a light somewhere inside and a car parked under the porch: couldn't tell from there if it was Archer's car, but all this made it look very much like someone was home. I parked my own car a block away, locked it, and walked along a path through the dunes.

In those few minutes the beach had gone from yellow to purple. The sea was rough, with whitecaps and large breaking waves closer in. I was pelted by heavy gusts of wind as I came abreast of the inlet. Far out at sea a light flashed from an incoming ship. The horizon was already dark, but the sky behind me was still showing a last spectacular sun splash through a thin layer of clouds. I went to the edge of the water and tried to look like some tourist out for a stroll.

I thought about what I had learned that afternoon and what it might mean. The editors at *Who's Who* had a standard for brevity, with no word ever wasted on trivial information. When they said Grandpa had been a *noted* book collector, they weren't talking about the Little Leather Library or *The Rover Boys Whistle Dixie*. Grandpa had been a *substantial* collector of expensive first editions, his collection worth mentioning to an international readership. Wouldn't this put Josephine's dream, if that's what it was, in a new light? If her reference to Archer had meant Grandpa, not Hal, that could make her dream, recalled under recent hypnosis, more than fifty years old.

I walked up a long stretch of hard, wet sand. Archer's house was just ahead. I could see only enough of the car to know it wasn't his blue Pontiac, and in the room facing the sea was a light, in addition to the one I had seen out front. As I stood still on the beach, someone moved past the window. I came closer, skirting the house yet drawn toward it, wishing the dark were a little darker but unwilling to wait for that to happen. I stepped into Archer's yard and went quickly into the dark place under his porch. From there I could hear the faint ringing of a telephone and someone moving around inside the house. The footsteps stopped: I heard a woman's voice but she spoke too softly for anything more than that fact to be clear. I had a hunch that whatever was going on in that room was germane, important enough to take a chance, so I moved into the pale light at the bottom of the stairs and started up.

She was standing just above me and a bit to my left; the window was open and I could hear soft music playing in the background. It covered what she was saying and what her voice sounded like saying it, so I moved closer. I took the stairs slowly, making no noise, and at the top I eased across the porch and flattened myself against the house. Whatever was happening, the other party was now doing all the talking. I heard an *uh-uh* and an *uh-huh* and more silence. I stood against the wall just outside the window, close enough to be charged with groping. She said, "Okay," and that single clear word turned my head around. I knew that voice and knew it well.

She said, "Yeah, right," and if I'd had any doubt I kissed it good-bye.

"He should be here soon," she said. "I'll let you know when there's something to report."

Oh, Erin, I thought.

23

I eased back toward the stairs, felt my way down, and stood under the house listening. I could hear her up there pacing. She was nervous. Whatever she was here for, the outcome was far from certain. And me, I had only two choices: announce myself or drop back into surveillance. Take the option while you've got one, I thought, and surveillance felt right on second guess. But cover your ass, Janeway. Get the car in case you need it.

By then it was quite dark: My cover was as good as it gets, so I walked away from the house, down the beach to the inlet, through the dunes, and up to the road where the car was parked.

A minute later I pulled into Archer's street and parked in front of the house. It didn't matter much where I parked: there were other cars along the road and my rental slipped in nicely among them. Archer would have no reason to know that I was within six hundred miles of here.

Nothing was happening on this side of the house. Erin had confined herself to that beachfront room and I played it boringly safe for now.

An hour passed. I watched the clock, imagining Koko tearing her hair.

Of all the jobs I had done as a cop I had always hated surveillance. It's bad enough when you have a partner to talk to; alone, it's a killer. But I waited, slumped in my seat, only my eyes moving from the road to the house and back again.

He finally came at ten-thirty. I saw his lights far down the road and I got down deep in my seat. Gradually his lights washed over my car and went away as he turned into his drive. I eased up and looked over the edge of the window. He had pulled under the house and his taillights shone out at the road. I heard the door slam and saw his shadow moving around to the beachfront steps.

When he had gone into the house I got out of my car and walked up the drive. I stopped at his car and opened one of the doors, just enough for the momentary flash of light to confirm the '83 Pontiac, two-tone blue. The literary lion had come home to his den. Now came the tricky part: getting close enough to learn something useful without getting caught.

Again I went up the stairs and across the porch. I stood flattened against the wall, two feet from the open window, but so far nothing was going on: no sounds, not even a hint of talk from some other room.

Suddenly the door opened and Erin stepped out. I held my breath. If she moved away from the house or went even partway to the edge of the porch, she couldn't miss seeing me when she turned around. But a sound drew her back into the room and I heard Archer say, "These goddamn airlines, it's getting so I hate to fly. How was your flight?"

"It was okay. It got me here."

"I guess I'm lucky mine was only two hours late. Did you have any trouble finding the key?"

"Right where you said."

I heard him move again, coming closer to the window: then the clink of a bottle on glass. "How about a drink?"

"Only if it's a very short one, please."

"Name your poison."

"Gin and tonic."

I heard the sound of pouring and ice. Someone sat down, probably Archer, in the easy chair just to the left of the window. "Come on, Erin," he said. "Relax."

I pictured them looking at each other over their drinks, fencing with their eyes.

"Cheers," Archer said.

A moment passed.

"Do you want to get down to cases now?" Erin said.

It had begun pleasantly enough but suddenly the mood got darker. Archer said, "*I'll* tell *you* when I do. I'll tell you how it's going to go too." There was no missing his intent: he was putting her in her place, letting her know who was boss.

"What's wrong with you?" he said. "You fly all the way from Denver and now you act like you can't wait to get out of here. Do I really bother you that much?"

It took her a moment to answer that. "I wouldn't drive you around if you did, would I?"

"As a matter of fact I've been wondering about that. The night of Lee's party, for example, how it came to be you who picked me up."

"You found that unusual?"

"Considering how we parted after my book tour a few years ago." She said nothing.

"I should apologize for my lack of manners back then," he said.

"There's no need for that."

"What if I feel a need?"

"Don't, please. It's not necessary."

"You must like having that to hold over my head. Does it empower you having seen me in a bad light? Do you think you'll get a better deal that way?"

"Let's just talk business, Hal."

"I am talking business and you're starting to make me angry again. Do you think it's easy for a man like me to apologize? About anything?"

"Look, Hal . . . I told you before, we're fine."

"But you're lying, precious. Besides, maybe you're not so fine with me."

"If that's the case, I'm sorry."

"You're sorry, all right. Because now I've got something you want."

"Which we haven't even seen yet. I don't know whether this was written by Richard Burton or the man in the moon."

This was followed by another awkward silence. Then Archer said, "I'm not gonna give anything away. You're good-looking, precious, but not that good," and the tone changed again.

"You know what?" Erin said. "I've just decided I'm not in the mood for this."

"Now *there's* the Erin I know. She takes no prisoners. She goes straight for the gonads."

"Do you want to talk or not?"

"I don't know, what's your offer?"

"You know what the offer is."

"It's not enough."

"Then let's hear your counteroffer."

"Double it for starters. And you be a lot nicer than you have been. A lot, *lot* nicer."

"That's not going to happen, Hal."

"What isn't?"

"Either condition. Double would be five times what anybody else would pay. And I will be civil and professional and that's all you'll ever get from me. I hope we're clear at least on that."

"Don't put too high a premium on it, sweetheart. It's just possible that I wouldn't want anything you've got."

"Then we're making progress. We have our first item of agreement."

"You really are one cold, calculating bitch."

"Another comment like that and I'm on the next flight back to Denver."

"So who's stopping you?"

I heard her get up. She moved across the room and came toward the door.

Incredulous, he said, "You'd actually walk out of here? With all that's at stake . . ."

"You've got a lot more at stake than I do. And the answer is yes. Keep a civil tongue in your head or I'm gone."

He laughed without amusement. "You really are something else."

She waited.

"All right, let's talk," he said.

She sat. "Start with the offer you've got. It's already generous, as I'm sure you know."

"That's your opinion. How much is a lifetime worth? And let's dispense with the notion that doubling it would be five times anything. There's no telling what something like this would sell for in a well-publicized auction."

"I've looked at recent auction records."

"There are no auction records for this and you know it."

Silence. Finally he said, "We're talking unique, precious."

"Maybe it's so unique it doesn't exist. You haven't shown me anything yet."

Archer laughed. "Now who's wasting time?"

"Then show it to me. I'll have to see it anyway, before anything real can happen."

"Let's get in the same ballpark first. If I put this at auction it'll go through the roof."

"It could also go for much less than you think."

"Then call me on it."

More silence.

"I didn't think so," Archer said.

"Not to beat a dead horse, but there are reasons why I don't want this to become public."

"That's why you're going to pay me, isn't it, precious?"

"I can go up some. Not a lot. Certainly not double."

"That's too bad. Double's where I start."

"You're wasting your time. And don't call me precious again."

I could almost see him shaking his head when he laughed. "I'll bet you are one tough cookie in court, cookie."

"You don't want to find out."

"That sounds like a threat. Are you threatening me, Erin?"

"Just agreeing with you." She sighed suddenly and said, "We're getting nowhere."

Abruptly she got up: I heard her walk across the room. "Thanks for the drink. It doesn't look like we'll be able to do business but it's always *such* a pleasure seeing you."

"You can't bluff me."

Her voice was hard now. "This isn't a bluff, *precious*. I'll negotiate within reason but I haven't heard anything out of you yet that sounds reasonable. By the way, the offer will only be good through noon Saturday. If I have to go back to Denver without a deal, all bets are off."

"I'm quaking in my boots."

"Don't quake yourself out of a small fortune, Hal." She moved across the room. "If this doesn't go well you could lose it all. This way you get your money and nobody's any wiser."

"Erin, my goodness, that sounds like you're talking tax-free money to boot."

"That's not what I'd advise if I were your lawyer."

"But the IRS won't hear about it from you."

"No."

She moved closer to the door. "Sleep on it but don't forget where I'm staying. Once I'm gone, I'm gone."

"I want to talk to Lee."

"I don't think so, Hal. That's a bridge you've burned pretty badly in recent days."

"I know him better than you do. He'll talk to me."

"Don't try to take either of those presumptions to the bank. I know Lee pretty well too. He's angry and he's wounded. He thought you were his friend. He's been a friend of yours all his life and this is what he gets for it."

I could feel the heat of the passing moment. Erin said, "I'm just telling you. Don't make the mistake of thinking you can get too high-handed with us, just because I came all the way out here."

"We'll see about that," Archer said. "Maybe I'll call you. Maybe I won't."

"Don't cut it too short. I'm not about to miss my plane for any more games. You've got to show me something or this whole deal may fall apart."

"Somehow I doubt that."

She moved to the door. I heard him say, "Erin," buying me just enough time to slip down off the porch.

From the bottom of the stairs I heard her say, "What now?"

"Go fuck yourself," he said.

I barely made it to the ground before she came out and started down the stairs. I dropped into the sand under the house and lay there. She got into her car and backed out toward the street.

What now, indeed? These are the times when you wish you could split yourself in two.

I abandoned Archer and hustled after her. She was still in sight on the long, straight road, and it was easy to follow her back into town.

24

She turned south off the bridge onto Meeting Street. For a few moments it looked like we might be staying at the same hotel: she kept going that way and I stayed close on her tail. We reached Calhoun Street just a few car lengths apart and I stopped behind her at a red light on Wentworth.

The light changed. She went on past the Heart of Charleston and across Queen Street to the Mills House, a classy old-world hotel rebuilt in its antebellum excellence, where, according to Koko's guidebook, Robert E. Lee had stood on the original balcony and watched the city burn.

She handed her keys to a valet and disappeared inside. I parked on the street and hurried up to the door. She was standing in the marbled surroundings just a few feet inside, reading some brochure on a table. From the street I could see no sign of a front desk; just a small room off to my right and a hint of a lobby around the corner to the left. What now? I knew if I let her disappear I might not see her again till I got back to Denver, but how would I confront her? I made the following decisions, all within seconds. I would speak to her now; act as if I had encountered her here by the most incredible chance. She would know better but that didn't matter; at the moment I was looking only to break the ice and get us going.

This wasn't great but in another moment she would go upstairs and the opportunity would be lost. I opened the door and followed her around to the desk. The clerk saw me at once: a street person, he'd be thinking, surely not one of ours. His eye went up, looking for the bellboy or the concierge.

"May I help you, sir?"

"I'm just the ghost of Robert E. Lee. Have you seen my horse?"

His scrutiny turned to alarm: not only was I a street person, I was a crazy one. But Erin had also turned at the sound of my voice. Her face showed a flash of surprise, which she bypassed at once. Deadpan, she said, "I saw a horse outside. What's his name?"

"Traveller. He's a big ugly stud with an attitude."

"Can't help you. The one I saw was a gentle sweetie named Buttermilk."

"I *scorn* such horses! That horse belongs to Dale Evans—only lets herself be ridden sidesaddle. Can you imagine what would happen if I rode sidesaddle into Gettysburg?"

"The North would win in one day instead of three."

She was quick but I knew that. She was also tense: I couldn't see that on her but I sensed it. She cocked her head and said in a soft voice, barely audible, "Six thousand lives would be saved."

The voice of the clerk cut across the room. "Do you know this gentleman, Ms. D'Angelo?" he said, and she smiled with a kind of comic disdain. "I'm afraid so. Don't throw him out yet, let's hear what he has to say for himself." She came toward me but stopped after a couple of steps. "What are you doing here, Janeway? What happened to your face?"

"I break out like this once in a while. Where can we find a place to talk?"

"Our lounge is still open for a while yet." The clerk looked immediately sorry that he had volunteered that but she thanked him and we settled in the lounge. The game began again.

"So what're *you* doing here?" I said.

"I asked you first."

"I needed a change of scenery after you dumped me and told me that fib about going off into the wilderness. I stuck a pin in a map and this is where I came."

"I didn't dump you and I didn't fib. Something else came up."

"A better offer," I sniffed. "So you went to the mountains where there isn't even a honey bucket to pee in, you planned to be gone at least a week, yet somebody managed to track you down and drop a bunch of new work on you."

"That's about the size of it."

I shook my head. "You really need to quit that job."

"I won't argue with you about that. But there's no way Waterford, Brownwell or God would've lured me down after the agonies of Rock Springs. I'm on a mission for a friend."

"Anybody I know?"

"Can't talk about it. The friend is also a client."

"And you don't talk about a client's affairs."

"Especially not to very strange people who wander in off the street. Besides being ethically shaky, it's not a good idea for practical reasons."

"Oh, I do understand. I'm here for a client as well, so I can't talk about it either."

"You have clients?"

"Sure. You're not the only one who knows how to pad an expense account."

"Well, shucks," she said. "That doesn't leave us much to talk about."

In other words, the ball was in my court. I said, "Maybe we can still find some area of mutual interest. Something that violates everybody's confidence but nobody knows where it came from. How about Richard Burton and his trip through here just before the Civil War?"

"Is that why you're here?"

"Maybe." I leaned across the table, serious now. "Actually, I'm pretty good at keeping secrets, Erin. When I was a cop I sometimes had life-and-death situations that depended on me being able to keep my mouth shut."

"Which means what? Just because you're not the world-class blabbermouth you seem to be, that doesn't relieve me from the ethical reality of protecting my client's business."

"'Well, shucks' is right, then. How's your drink?"

"Gin and tonic is like small talk. It's pretty much the same all over."

"So when do you go home?"

"Saturday afternoon. How about you?"

I shrugged. "Can't say for sure. Might be weeks yet. We may never get to have that date." I took a sip of my drink and played a card. "It can take a while to track down a killer."

"What's that supposed to mean?"

"Think about it for a minute."

She furrowed her brow and said, "Hmmm," to good comical effect.

"Think hard about who was killed in the last week or two. It'll come to you."

"I have no idea what you're talking about."

"Do you know how to spell *Denise*?"

That got to her. "You don't mean Mrs. Ralston?"

"The late Mrs. Ralston." I was watching her eyes, which never wavered. "It was in the Denver papers."

"I went to the mountains, didn't I just tell you that? I haven't seen a Denver newspaper since before I went to Rock Springs. What happened?"

"Somebody got in there and smothered her."

"Oh, *Jesus*. Oh, that elegant woman. Mr. Ralston must be . . ."

She turned her hands palms up and I said, "Yeah, he is."

"Oh, Cliff. Why would anyone hurt that lovely lady?"

"The cops think it was Ralston."

She shook her head, angry now. "The cops think, give me a break. Do they have any evidence against him?"

"Other than the fact that it's usually the husband, no. They were hoping to sweat a fast confession out of him. If they don't come up with something, they'll have to go with the unknown assailant theory."

"And it'll never get solved."

"That's the way to bet. Unless, by some hail-Mary piece of luck, I manage to do it." I gave her my miracles-do-happen look and the moment stretched.

"What would you do? Where would you start?"

"I think it might've had something to do with the book I left with her that night."

She weighed this and said, "And that would be why the police are looking at Ralston?"

"That's how one cop thinks. Unfortunately, he's the one running the investigation."

"Can you talk to him?"

I laughed dryly. "I did that."

"So it's one of those. Maybe he'd rather talk to me. Does Mr. Ralston have a lawyer?"

"Mr. Ralston went on the lam."

"It just gets better and better, doesn't it?" She sipped her drink. "So what happened to the book, did the killer get it?"

"I got it."

"Then what makes you think the book was behind it?"

"Just a hunch that got started. There's one problem with it, though. Only five of us knew they had it: the Ralstons, the doctor, me . . ."

"And me."

If ever there was a pregnant moment, that was it.

I said, "I didn't tell anyone."

"Well, I didn't. I went up to the mountains early the next day. Like I told you."

"It's conceivable that Ralston might've told somebody in the neighborhood. Maybe Denise did herself. If Whiteside's any kind of cop, he'll be looking at that now."

"Randy Whiteside?"

I nodded.

"Oh God," she said, rolling her eyes. "Oh God. God, *God,* that poor woman."

She thought a minute, then said, "If Ralston is arrested or contacts you in any way, I need to talk to him. Immediately, before he says something the cops can use against him."

I knew my friend Moses would be only too happy to step aside on this one. "If you take him on, it'll have to be pro bono."

Her look became prickly. "Did you hear me mention anything about money?"

We had another quick drink. There wasn't much time left: the lounge was closing.

"They're about to kick us out," I said. "Last chance for you to tell me your secrets."

She looked like she actually was giving this some thought. "I'll be talking with my client again tonight," she said. "We might be willing to share certain facts in exchange for the same."

"Okay," I said nonchalantly. "It might help if I tell you some of what I already know, just so we don't rake over stale material. For instance, I know you came here to see Archer."

She didn't blink at that, so I went on, hoping I was right. "I know you're representing Judge Huxley in an attempt to buy a book that Archer claims to have."

This time she did blink. Encouraged, I kept going: "I know Archer's being his usual enchanting self, I know he and Lee had a falling-out, and I know some other things as well. I tell you this so you'll know we'll have to start well beyond these points. No reinventing the wheel."

"I wonder how you learned all that. Assuming it's true."

"I was a pretty good detective, Erin."

She smiled wanly. "Unauthorized wiretaps are illegal almost everywhere, Janeway."

"Thank you, Counselor, for clarifying that so that even a poor old dumb-schmuck ex-cop nonlawyer understands it. For your information, I haven't done an illegal wiretap in at least a week."

She stared at me and I could almost see the wheels turning in her head.

"So what do we do?" I said. "Have your people call my people, as you lawyers like to say?"

"Let's just meet for breakfast, wise guy. Be here at eight and we'll see what happens. And comb your hair before you come over."

25

A note from Koko had been shoved under my door. It seemed to be an account of her day in the library. There were also several pages of photocopies, showing, I assumed, what she had found. I still didn't hold out much hope for her end: it was a very cold trail she was chasing, so I didn't read the note immediately, just tossed it on the table and sat on my bed for a few minutes, thinking about Erin. Tomorrow, I hoped, would reveal a lot more. I wanted her to be telling the truth and for the moment I believed what I wanted to believe. She had been genuinely surprised about Denise, I thought. Her explanation rang true. Lee Huxley had been closer to her than her father: he would have her cell phone number, and when his chance came up to buy Burton's journal, she would be a natural as his representative. He couldn't come to Charleston himself: his docket was always full and he'd be in the middle of a trial. What else had I learned? That Lee's relationship with Archer had begun to unravel. That this had happened only recently. And whatever piece of the Charlie Warren–Burton library Archer might have, and from whatever sources, he didn't have it all by any means. But he was ready to sell what he did have. Archer needed money and he wasn't above asking a highway-robbery price from an old friend. The book was unique—not even *rare,* the most overused word in the bookman's lexicon, adequately described it. Archer himself had said so, and I didn't have to like him to recognize his excellent command of the English language. He would not be one of those idiots who throw *very unique* at every common happening. *Unique* would mean to Archer what it meant to me—one of a kind. I thought of Burton's journal. What else could it be? And how did he get it?

Richard Burton's notebook. Burton's version of the Charlie War-ren story: the final word in his own hand, the incontrovertible proof that Josephine's memories of her grandfather were true or false. I felt tingly just thinking about it, and Koko . . . God, she'd be faint with excitement and hope.

And then there was this: Erin had hinted that Archer might face legal action. What could that mean? To me it meant that Archer had somehow obtained whatever he had in a questionable manner and that Erin and Lee knew it. Somewhere he was vulnerable. What *that* meant I couldn't guess. I couldn't imagine Lee buying hot goods: it just didn't jibe with the man I knew. And I couldn't picture him in such rabid pursuit of any book that he would allow himself to be yanked around, even to this extent, by a two-bit chiseler like Archer. I thought about that and it still didn't seem real when I applied it to Lee. I knew better, of course: the bookman's madness can get us all, even a distinguished judge. Some of us put on stoic faces, like expert poker players whose masks hide the fever, but I had known Lee Huxley for fifteen years and I just didn't believe it. He was a book collector but a sane one, and I'd bet my bookstore on that.

So where was I? I reached for straws and came up only with wild unlikelihoods. Lee was buying the book back for someone who had lost it, maybe years or decades ago. He was righting an old wrong. He was . . . what? What the *hell* was he doing?

It was late by then. I went to the table and looked at Koko's note. I thought I'd read it in the morning but there was an air of breath-less excitement in her opening words that drew me in. She had already found proof of something. One of the inns that Burton and Charlie had stayed in upstate had existed. It had been a notorious story: an old woman and her two sons had run a veritable homicide hotel, murdering and robbing wayfarers for God knew how long before they'd been caught and hanged in 1861. The inn had been just about where Charlie had described it—in the middle of nowhere—and the accounts she had read conformed exactly to Charlie's memory of it. The woman's name was Opal Richardson and her sons were named Cloyd and Godie. The only name Charlie had heard that night, huddled with Burton in the dark, was Cloyd, but how many Cloyds could there be in the world? To Koko this was proof that they had been there.

But slowly my own initial excitement was tempered by doubt. The fact that it had been so easy to uncover worked against it. That Koko, even with her long experience in libraries, had found it in one afternoon was not a good sign. It meant anyone set on promoting a fraud could also have found it. The thought that Josephine might have just come through Charleston to get background for some tall story was so unlikely it bordered on the absurd. But what if she had been here years ago, found the story of that old inn then, and saved it for another day? She might even have come to believe it. People do such things. When the stakes are great enough they will some-times believe their own lies. I had a vision of Josephine at forty, hunting feverishly through old documents and newspapers, building the tale in her mind, then chasing it in vain for the rest of her life. But how did that explain the books? So far we had just two, my *Pil-grimage* and Jo's *First Footsteps*. To me this was strong proof, but for Koko to publish anything serious we would need more than that.

I looked through the photocopies Koko had left. Just as I thought, writers had had their way with Opal Richardson and her dimwit sons for a hundred years. It had become a piece of Carolina folklore, with newspaper rehashes every few years for a new readership.

At the bottom of the last page Koko had written, *Where ARE you? Call me when you come in. I don't care how late it is, I won't sleep till you do.*

So I called her and got no answer. That old uneasy feeling began again.

I went outside and crossed the motel to her room. Knocked on the door.

Unease blended into anxiety and became worry.

I went to the desk. A man there told me she had been in and out all evening, asking for me. But he hadn't seen her for at least two hours.

I called her room from the lobby and let it ring ten times.

By then I was alarmed. Where would she go after midnight? Maybe she was giving me a dose of my own medicine: *If you want to keep in touch, picklepuss, you need to stay in touch.*

There is nothing quite so helpless as a situation like that. You're in a strange town. Suddenly you lose someone. There are reasons to be concerned; potentially, there are alarming possibilities, though it is unlikely that your enemies could have found you this quickly. You can't go to the cops when someone's been gone just a few hours. But you know something's wrong.

All I could do was wait.

I walked out into the pungent Southern night and stood on the sidewalk looking up and down Meeting Street. Finally I retreated to my room, where I tried to watch the TV.

I stared at the screen.

At two-thirty my telephone rang. I picked it up with a feeling of dread and was overjoyed to hear her voice. She said, "Hey," but her voice was flat. I could hear her tremble as she took a breath.

"What's going on?"

She didn't say anything.

"Hey, Koko, where are you?"

"In my room."

"Where you been?"

"Walking around." She sniffed. "Listen, I've got to go home."

Uneasily I said, "Okay."

But it wasn't okay. Something was wrong with her. "I'll go with you," I said.

"Cliff . . ."

"I'm coming over."

"I've got to go home," she said again.

Then she sighed, very deep, and said, "They've burned my house down."

26

We talked for an hour: Koko in her sadness, me as a release from the hot wrath I felt boiling inside me. Everything she'd had was in that house. Furniture handed down from her mother, books from her father and the books she herself had bought for years. Pictures, documents, the love letters of her parents: everything that told who she was and where she'd come from. I didn't argue with her: I listened to her plans, knowing I couldn't possibly let her fly back to Baltimore. It would be better if she realized that on her own, but I would restrain her if I had to.

She had called a friend, a woman she knew in Ellicott City. That's how she'd learned about her house. "I needed her to water my plants. Now there aren't any plants."

"Koko . . ."

She looked at me.

"It's a little late for me to ask you this," I said. "Do you wish now you had never heard of Charlie or Josephine or Burton? Or me?"

"No way."

I took heart from that, but I didn't push it. I let her see on her own what it meant and how it had inevitably led to this point.

"No," she said again when she did see it. "No way." Then she smiled and said, "Well, there are times when I can do without you."

I reached over and squeezed her hand. "You see what this means now."

"I can't go home."

"Not for the moment. It's a chance we can't take."

"What about the police? I could have them arrest those people."

"If they left any evidence. My guess is, they had a torch do it. A professional fire man who leaves no trace. And they will all have alibis for the time when it happened."

She just stared at the floor.

"It's hard being a cop," I said. "People don't realize. We've got to play by all the rules while thugs like Dante can do what they want. Unless they make a mistake."

"Won't the police at least protect me?"

"I'm sure they'll try. But they can't watch you around the clock forever. There'll come a time when you'll be vulnerable."

A moment later she said, "You're the one they really want."

I nodded. "They'll use you to get to me. But they won't be able to let it go at that."

"Then what can I do?"

"Let's take it one thing at a time. How's your insurance situation?"

"The house is covered. It's all my other stuff that's lost."

"Do you have a lawyer? Someone you can trust?"

She nodded. "My lawyer drew up my will. His father knew my father."

"Does he have your power of attorney?"

"I never gave it to him. There never was any need."

"You can do that easily enough. Then he can handle the house. Dealing with the insurance company, stuff like that."

"Will I ever be able to go home?"

"I think so."

It took another moment for the implication of that to settle. Her eyes opened wide and she said, "You're going to kill him."

"That's not something you should worry about."

"Oh please. Don't treat me like I'm some fool who's not involved."

"I told him what would happen. He decided not to listen. At this point it's him or us."

She shook her head, horrified.

"Don't waste your tears," I said. "He's a brutal man. He'd kill us without a thought."

But she couldn't get past the idea of it. "What if it wasn't him?"

"That's pretty unlikely, under the circumstances."

"But what if it wasn't? I don't even know *how* the house caught fire at this point."

"Yeah, you do."

"Cliff . . . what if you're wrong?"

"Then I'll be a monkey's uncle."

"Don't make a joke of it, please. This is too awful to joke about."

"It's him or me, Koko. Think about that."

"What about the others?"

"They don't matter. They'll fold up like a house of cards when Dante's gone."

Suddenly her eyes opened wide. "Oh my God."

"What?"

"I just remembered. I think I did something stupid tonight." She closed her eyes and muttered what sounded like a curse. "I told my friend where I am."

"Did you tell her not to tell anybody?"

"I didn't think of it." She put her hand over her eyes. "I didn't *think*!"

Almost a full minute passed.

"Oh, I am so *stupid*!"

"It's okay, Koko," I said softly. "We'll work with it."

27

The telephone rang at seven-fifteen. I rolled over on the bed, thanked the desk man for the wake-up, sat up, leaned over my knees, and stared at the phone. First thought of the day—call Denver. It would be like calling pest control for a rat problem. Call Denver from Charleston and a rat would die in Baltimore tonight.

I was first amazed by the detachment I felt and then by its slow reversal. It was as if only now had I begun to see the consequences, not for Dante but for me. To get this far, to be sitting here looking at that phone, I must have stepped naively indeed through the first half of my life and never thought about what such acts make of the men who do them. I had spent a lifetime on the right side of the law. Could I really be thinking now of becoming a cold-blooded killer? Never mind the reasons or the justifying. Never mind that someone far away would pull the trigger or that I had killed men myself in more forgivable ways. Make this one call and I'd be going all the way over to the dark side: I'd be an animal, just like him. And I knew that Dante, one of the real dark men, had seen this weakness in me that night at Treadwell's. For all my tough talk, he was betting I'd never make that call, and in the end it would just be him and me.

I shaved, took my shower, and dressed well. I combed my hair for Erin's sake.

It's a beautiful day, I thought as I stepped out into it. Not too hot, not too much Charleston humidity. I left Koko a note and let her sleep. She needed it and her presence would only inhibit whatever was about to happen with Erin.

I stood at a traffic light on Market Street and thought about

Dante. The light changed and I walked across Meeting and down the street to the Mills House.

Erin was at a table in the corner, looking through the *News and Courier.* She folded the newspaper and put it away as I came in. I sat across from her, waiting for her lead. The waitress hadn't even brought my coffee when she said, "Lee wants to talk to you."

"Okay. Any idea what's on his mind?"

"He's thinking of opening a bookstore on East Colfax and he wants your advice."

I laughed politely. "Ask a stupid question, get a stupid answer."

"We'll call him in a little while." She looked at her watch. "It's still only six forty-five back there. In the meantime you can eat your breakfast and talk to me."

"I won't complain about that. Is this going to be a business talk or pleasure?"

"All business, I'm afraid."

I snapped my fingers. "Alas."

She regarded me with quiet amusement, then said, "As you guessed, we are involved with Archer in a delicate negotiation for a book Lee wants. We're afraid your sudden appearance will complicate things and might make it impossible for us."

"Well, so far Archer has no idea I'm here."

"We'd like to keep it that way."

"I hope you're not going to offer me money to go away."

She shook her head a little, but I didn't think she meant no.

"That would be very disappointing, Erin."

I could almost see her changing tactics. "We certainly don't want to insult you," she said.

"Glad to hear it. I like Lee and I respect him greatly. As for you . . ."

She raised an eyebrow.

"I like you too."

"That's nice to know."

"Yeah. But it does make things difficult."

"I don't see why it should."

I smiled. "I think you do."

She said, "Look, would we rather you weren't here? Yes, we would. Would we rather you went away? Yes, we would. Lee likes you more than you know, but he will be very upset if you get into this and mess it up. So will I."

"Is that supposed to make me cut and run back to Denver?"

She looked unhappy, and this time I did not smile. I said, "So far you're not doing too well, Erin. I know you're a better negotiator than this. I know you know not to come into a situation and ruffle your adversary, unless it's some knucklehead like Archer who takes offense at everything. And at this moment I am your adversary. If you want me to be your friend I'll be happy to do that. But *my* friend is dead and, frankly, whether Lee gets another book or not doesn't matter much alongside that fact. If you want peace between us, you two had better level with me."

She leaned back in her chair. "God, you're touchy this morning. Did you have a bad night?"

"You might say that. I've got my own moral dilemmas to work out."

The waitress brought my coffee. I ordered lots of calories and she wrote that down and went away. Erin said, "The last thing we want is to get in the way of finding out who killed Mrs. Ralston."

"Now that's a much better start."

"But I don't see how we're doing that."

"That's why I'm here. I'll tell you if you do."

Abruptly she said, "Okay, we'll level with you. That's what I was told to do anyway."

"Told when?"

"Last night after you left I called Lee from my room. I told him you're here asking questions about the book. His instructions to me were simple. 'Tell him the truth,' he said. That's all."

"That's what I would expect from Lee. So why didn't you just do that?"

"My own judgment call. A lawyer never wants to tell a third party anything about her client's business, even when the client tells her to."

"See? Right has a way of winning out over treachery and guile after all. Now you can get off to an even better start by telling me what book we're talking about."

"A handwritten journal kept by Richard Burton when he was here."

"Gosh, that almost sounds like one of the Charlie Warren books."

"At this point we don't know whose it was, originally."

I looked dubious.

"Look," she said testily. "Archer has a book. He wants to sell it. He claims it's been in his family for generations. He says he has rock-solid provenance."

"And the thought of Mrs. G's books never occurred to you?"

"Of course it occurred to me, do you think I'm stupid? That's the first thing Lee and I did when the subject came up: I sat him down and went point by point over what had happened to the old woman, and what would happen if this turned out to be a stolen book."

"And what conclusion did you come up with?"

"That Lee would be at risk if that turned out to be the case." She shrugged. "He wants to take that chance."

"And give up the book if he has to."

"Yes, of course. That's the chance you take if you want to play the game. In all likelihood there'll never be a challenge. All the people are dead."

"As far as you know."

The moment stretched.

At last I said, "That would be a pretty good book, wouldn't it? It might even put a new slant on history. I don't think we're talking about a revision on the order of, say, the South suddenly wins the war, but you can bet historians as well as book collectors will be interested."

"Yes," she said.

"The book would get a lot of attention."

"Yes, it would. If the owner wanted it to."

"I can see a story like that on the front pages of quite a few newspapers. And that might make it worth a lot more as a rare book."

"That's been Archer's point all through the negotiations, and we *agree* with him. Where our negotiations break down is over how much that should be."

"What are you offering?"

She stared at me.

"I tend to ask impertinent questions," I said. "I guess that was one of them."

"Yes, it was. But Lee wants me to tell you everything, so our offer was $250,000."

"Wow."

"So? You're a bookman. Is that fair?"

"You want me to be your arbiter now? Somehow I don't think Archer will go for that."

"Not for attribution, just for my own information. I'm curious."

"A quarter of a million is a helluva price for any book. You could get *Tamerlane* for less, if you could find one to buy."

"Then you agree it's a fair price."

"I haven't seen the book. And remember, I'm no expert."

She looked annoyed.

I said, "Hey, I'm sorry, but content is everything. I'd have to read it to offer even an incompetent opinion."

"All right, forget I asked. We haven't seen it yet either."

The waitress came with my breakfast, set it nicely on the table, and left.

"Archer wants half a million," Erin said.

I laughed. "That's our boy."

"Certainly is. We should be glad he's not asking a full million, or two, or ten. It wouldn't matter. What he does want is still out of the question. Lee is not a poor man, as I'm sure you know, but he hasn't got that kind of money to throw around on something this shaky."

Abruptly I said, "I hear you were pretty hard on Archer last night."

She scoffed, "You hear, indeed."

"I hear you even threatened him, in an oblique way, with legal action."

"You'd better get your hearing checked. Whatever I might've said was nothing more than part of a negotiation."

"Tactics."

"Exactly."

"Still, you've got to have a valid reason for a threat like that."

"I never threatened him. If he thinks I did . . ." She shuddered. "The deeper I get into this deal, the less I like it. I wish Lee would just tell Archer to get lost and be done with it. But he thinks the book is so historically important that it's got to be bought."

"I understand that, all right. There are books like that, that *must* be bought. So does Lee think Archer might actually have stolen this book? How would he have done that?"

"That's the rub, isn't it? We just don't know."

"But they had a falling-out over something."

"Over Archer's greed. Lee thought they had a deal, then Archer got greedy. In Lee's mind, you don't do that to a friend. You know, as kids they were almost like brothers. But Archer was different then. He was a grand guy. I know that's hard to imagine, but if Lee says it was so, I believe him. Hal Archer was a kind, generous, wonderful friend in those days."

"So what screwed him up?"

"Everything, starting with his grandfather. He was never good enough, either for his father or grandfather. His older brother was named after the father and grandfather. *He* was the one who was supposed to rule the estate, like some stupid progression in royalty, and he would have if he hadn't been killed in an auto wreck. Hal's first mistake was being born second; his second mistake was not wanting to be a lawyer."

"So the Archers loved books but wouldn't let their son write 'em."

"I don't think that's so unusual. Would you want your son to be a writer? Or your daughter to marry one?"

"If that made them happy, why not?"

"Because most of the time it doesn't make them happy. Most writers I know lead difficult, hand-to-mouth lives. In the first place the odds against selling a book are enormous. A big New York publishing house may get twenty thousand manuscripts in a year and publish two hundred. Most of those slush-pile books are horrible, so there's an expectation of failure that's tough to overcome even with decent work. Those first-readers can't expect to find much, so they don't."

"And this is what you want to give up law for?"

"That's probably exactly what Archer's father said, in far stronger terms." She shrugged. "At least I've got some money in the bank. I'm not going to starve and I can always go back to law, but I'm still a good case in point. I suppose I'm like every other wannabe writer with a huge ego. I believe my talent and sheer persistence will overcome the odds, even when I know what the odds are. I'm facing a long, uphill battle, but at least I know it. That's why I can talk about Archer's life with some understanding even if I don't like him much as a man."

"So Archer was estranged from his family fairly early."

"To put it mildly. He was sent to the University of Virginia, the old man's alma mater, in the hope it would straighten him out. But he was put on notice and given no money for anything. He dropped out after a year and the family made him an outcast. In effect he was on his own from then on. He went to New York, lived in a hole in the wall, and started to write stories."

"And had a terrible time selling them."

"*Oh* yeah. Miranda's right: Archer's a real bastard, but what a great talent. That should have been evident from the start, publishers should have been clamoring to get at his stuff. Instead he met a wall of indifference that broke his spirit and finished the job his family had started. Can you imagine what it's like to write for *years* and get nowhere? To know in your heart that you're something special and watch your books get rejected and rejected and rejected, over and over till the paper they were typed on begins to come apart. I'll tell you what happens to writers like that. One day they wake up and they're old. All that promise just seems to flush away overnight and they've got nothing to show for it except a wasted life. It comes faster than they could've imagined. Archer was in his forties when he published his first book. It had gone everywhere and finally David McKay bought it. McKay was a small house and the book sank like a lead balloon. Then they rejected his next book, and there he was, starting from scratch, looking for a publisher. His book had made him less than three thousand dollars, and that was spread over several years. Try to live anywhere on that. Try living in New York."

She took some more coffee. "His next publisher was St. Martin's Press, a real mixed bag. They'll put money into a big book, but a lot of their fiction is nickel-and-dime, with half of a very modest print run going to libraries. Archer made nothing from them; he refused to send them his next one and they parted company in mutual anger. Archer had to start his hunt from scratch again and no one would touch him. He fired his agent, his agent fired him, or they each fired the other at the same moment. By then there may have been a grapevine at work, I don't know. It would stand to reason that publishers hear things, and why would they publish someone whose books come with a bad attitude and don't sell anyway? Those two factors will offset a whole *bunch* of literary excellence, even in the minds of dedicated editors. So Archer toiled away and began to lash out at everyone. Finally in pure desperation he let Walker have the book. You know about Walker."

"Yeah, there's a shaggy-dog joke in the trade about Walker and St. Martin's. Their print runs sometimes are so small that some of their authors become instant rarities. Those books are only a few years old and they sell for hundreds of dollars."

"What's the joke?"

"How do you become a millionaire in the used book business? Buy five copies of everything St. Martin's and Walker publish. How do you go broke in the book biz? Same answer."

She smiled. "As you can imagine, then, nothing happened with Walker. Archer's bitterness got deeper and he became even more unbearable. Hindsight may be twenty-twenty, but in fact he should've been published by Random House or Doubleday, with six-figure advances and book tours, the whole nine yards. But all he could see coming out of the big houses was trumped-up suspense junk and mindless bodice rippers."

"You sound bitter yourself, Erin, and you haven't even started yet. As if nothing good ever gets published. I know you know better than that."

"I'm talking as Archer now. You asked how he got screwed up and I'm telling you."

"So he turned to nonfiction and the Viking Press found him," I said. "But apparently the Pulitzer did him no good at all."

"Didn't do much for his attitude, did it? If anything it made him angrier. Instead of being overjoyed that he'd finally made it, he felt only rage that his whole writing life had been spent getting there. The Pulitzer was confirmation of his greatness, and of the stupidity he saw everywhere he looked."

"Hey, he's not dead yet. What about his new book? Viking's not chopped liver, I imagine they've given him a good advance."

"I don't want to talk about that. It was told to Lee in confidence. Nobody else knows, not even Miranda. I think you've got to ask Lee that question."

I ate my breakfast and watched her think. Over coffee I asked what her strategy would be if Archer continued to stonewall. She shook her head. "Can't talk about strategy. You'll have to ask Lee that as well."

"Then call him up."

* * *

She called from the table. "Hi, it's me. We're just finishing breakfast and I've got a couple of sticky points. You know where. He asked if I knew the status of Archer's new book. I still don't want to talk about that, for obvious reasons."

She looked directly into my eyes while she talked. "I know what you said, Lee, I just don't like it. He also wants to know what we'll do if Archer continues to be unreasonable."

After a short silence, she said, "I've got to tell you again, I wouldn't advise that."

She said, "If he gives his word, yes, I do think we could trust him."

I nodded superseriously.

"That's not the point," she said.

Lee said something and she shook her head. "I'm against it."

She frowned. "You're the boss, but I don't think we need to tell anybody, including Mr. Janeway, what we might or might not do. Especially what we *won't* do. That's hardly pertinent to anything he's doing, and it's just not smart."

She shook her head. "Well, I knew you'd say that. But I still don't like it."

She handed me the phone.

"Hi, Lee," I said.

"Cliff." Lee sounded tired. "I'm sorry you've been put in the middle of this mess. But it sounds like Erin's giving you what you need."

"She's great. She does have a couple of concerns, which are probably reasonable."

"She's being lawyerly, covering my flank. You know how it is. But she'll talk to you now."

For a moment I listened to the phone noise: all the distance between us.

"Erin said you wanted to talk to me too," I said.

"Just to make sure you get what you need and to tell you not to worry. Whatever you have to do, I understand. Your cause comes before mine."

"Thanks for that."

"We'll see you when you get back. And good luck with it."

I hung up the phone.

"I'll answer your questions now," Erin said, "but you've got to respect our confidence. This can go no further."

"I won't tell a soul."

"You asked about Archer's new book. When he was in Denver he got drunk, cried on Lee's shoulder, and told him some things he probably wishes he hadn't. Turns out the great one is suffering from the granddaddy of all writer's blocks. In the years since he won the Pulitzer he hasn't written a publishable line. Or if he has, he's second-guessed himself into fits of depression and destroyed whatever he's done. If the prize has done anything, it's given him a sense that nothing he does can ever measure up to his own . . . you know."

"Legend," I said sourly, loathing that dumbest of all modern buzzwords.

She looked sad, as if Archer's plight had suddenly touched her. "I told you writers are screwed up. Archer took a lot of money from his publisher on a two-page plan to produce a groundbreaking work in a specified period of time. That time has passed. Viking has been more than sympathetic: they even came through with more money. The Pulitzer is a powerful wedge and they really do want to publish him. But their patience will run out sometime, and as of now, six years later, Archer has nothing to show them."

All I knew about writers and their hang-ups was what I'd read here and there. But it seemed strange to get stuck over a work of nonfiction when most writer's blocks seemed to come over some creative lack of faith. "I wonder if he promised them more than he's got," I said. "He may still be doing that, only now Lee is the mark, not the Viking Press."

"Don't think I haven't thought of that. Lee doesn't worry about that nearly enough, but this journal will have to be meticulously examined before I allow him to give Archer a dime."

"Even then you won't like it."

She shook her head. "I think Lee is putting a lot of money at risk. What would you advise him, as his friend?"

"Check the provenance, six times over."

28

She leaned across the table and said, "Your turn, Janeway, talk to me," and I had to tell her about Koko and Baltimore. Then, with deliberate understatement, I told her about Dante and what had brought us to Charleston: how stealth, not electronics, had given me such insight into her dealings with Archer. She shook her head and tried to look disgusted, but a small smile gave her away. The smile faded when I told her that Dante had burned Koko's house.

"This is a bad man you're playing tag with," she said.

"I've been going on that assumption."

"What can I do? As a lawyer maybe I can give him some grief."

"Don't even think about it. I don't want you anywhere near this creep."

"I don't think you automatically get the final word on that."

"The hell I don't. I don't want him to even hear your name."

She looked angry but I cut her off with my own look. "Listen, goddammit, you make me more vulnerable, not less. I've got enough on my hands with Koko and myself."

She made a little arch with her fingers and held them up to her face like a woman praying. I looked at her fiercely and said, "Don't make me sorry I told you."

"Nice try, but I'm not buying that."

"You'd damned better buy it."

She came straight up in her chair. "Or what's gonna happen? Gonna take my dolls away?"

What I said next was stupid and false. "Erin, I appreciate your concern—"

She wadded up her napkin and bounced it off my head. "Don't give me that imperious male baloney. If you want me out of your life, at least be man enough to say so in plain language. Is that what you want? Yes or no."

"God, no."

"Then shape up. Behave yourself. Don't talk down to me. Don't try to protect me."

I thought about what to say and settled on this: "In your world every conflict has a legal answer. You think you can just file a brief in Denver District Court and force him to become human, but it doesn't work that way. Don't take this personally, but you're out of your league with this boy."

"And you're not?"

"I don't know."

She shook her head. "I can't just stand by and do nothing."

"Well, you've got to."

"And if he kills you, and there's no evidence, what am I supposed to do then?"

"Nothing. What can you do anyway but get killed yourself?"

"I can't accept that."

"What can you do about it?"

"I'll hold him down while you cut him a new one."

It was one of those crazy unexpected comments and at once we were convulsed. She dabbed her eyes and said, "Stop it, this isn't funny," and we laughed all the more. I said, "Listen, I'm going to handle this," and we laughed like idiots. "Don't you make it harder," I said, and we laughed.

I coughed. "I'm sorry, was that too much imperious male baloney?"

"Yeah, it was, but the groveling tone helps." She smiled at me from somewhere far behind her face. "How much time do you think you have before he finds you?"

"I don't know that either. There's no reason yet to assume he knows where we went."

"You hope."

I fiddled nervously with the saltshaker.

"Are you afraid of him?"

"I'm . . . wary. I've had enemies before, some of them real bad-asses. I just get the feeling there's no limit with this guy. My biggest fear is I may never see it coming."

She was sober now, the laughter of the moment gone and forgotten. "This makes our little rivalry pale by comparison, doesn't it?" A moment later she said, "I want to tell Lee."

"What good will that do?"

"I don't know, maybe none." She looked away, then back. "Three heads are better than two."

"Tell him, then. If he's got the good sense I think he has, he'll tell you to stay out of it."

"Lee doesn't own me and neither do you. You really are annoying when things don't go your way."

"That's why people want to kill me."

She gave the waitress a high sign and took out a credit card. "I want you to think about something else while you're still alive. The possibility that your old lady was a clever fraud."

"I've always been aware of that. Why bring it up now?"

"I don't know: just a feeling I have. Something's not right there. Did you ever have the handwriting on your book checked?"

"Not personally. The auction house is reputable and I know what Burton's handwriting looks like."

"But you're no expert."

I shook my head, suddenly aware of how much of my business is taken on faith.

"That might be worth doing," she said. "Something's afoot there, I can smell it. Doesn't it strike you as odd?"

"When you've been in the book business awhile, everything is odd."

"But you were primed to believe it. Look, I know she was a sweet old gal and I don't want to think bad things about her. But it's not something we can dismiss."

"She was in her nineties. That's pretty old to be pulling a scam. And who pulls a scam when they're dying? People who have lied all their lives tend to tell the truth on a deathbed. All she wanted was for the books to be put in a library in her grandfather's name."

"Maybe she was crazy, did you ever think of that? Maybe she heard that story years ago and transposed herself into it. Maybe Charlie became a grandfather in her mind."

"She had the book."

"She had *a* book. You don't know where she really got it, or when, or how. Maybe getting the book is what started it all. She may have had Burton on the brain for a long time."

"Koko checked a lot of this out."

"That may be well and good, but I don't know Koko from a sack of beans. She may have her own agenda, as the boys in the board-room like to say. Don't get defensive, just think about it."

I controlled my imperious male baloney and let her pay the tab. "I guess I won't see you again before you leave," I said. "What're you doing tonight?"

"I thought you'd never ask. I'm facing a miserably lonely hotel room."

"Want to test Charleston's restaurants?"

And that's how we had our first date.

When I got back to the motel Koko was gone. I tracked her down at the library, where she was searching through old records for some evidence of the East Bay photographer's existence. She had found nothing new since her discovery of the murdering innkeepers the day before and her mood was bleak. "I'm beginning to think this is all going to be a waste of time."

I stayed with her, following her instructions, reading my share of old newspapers and documents. Occasionally she would powwow with one of the librarians, the librarian would bring out another folder or have a bound volume of newspapers brought up from the basement, and we would start in again. At noon she called her lawyer in Baltimore and got things moving on her house. We started in again after a quick lunch, but the work was frustrating and by four-thirty we had nothing. "A waste of time," she said. "You got your head kicked in and my house got burned down, for what? And we'll never be able to go home again."

At the motel she showed me a chart she had made of the whole block where Burton and Charlie had supposedly been photographed. Every building along the street had a name written neatly in its square. "This is it," she said: "every tenant on that stretch of East Bay in May 1860 accounted for, and I don't see any photographers there."

There was a café and a beer hall, a glass shop, a blacksmith, a druggist. Some used only personal names: Phillips, Jones, Kelleher, Wilcox. "Phillips turned out to be a dealer in rugs," she said. "Jones was a butcher. Kelleher was a dentist and Wilcox owned a grocery store. If Burton and Charlie had their picture taken, where was the photographer?"

She received the news about Erin deadpan, but over the next hour her mood darkened. "I'm going out to Fort Sumter tomorrow," she said, "take a break from this monotony and let you have fun with your friend." She apologized reluctantly for the catty remark and tried to look ahead. "Don't mind me. If she's a lawyer, maybe she'll have some idea how we can get out of this mess."

"I think she wants to take on Dante in a bare-knuckles brawl."

"You already did that and look where it got us."

She tried to turn the talk back to Fort Sumter. "One of the librarians told me there's a ranger out there who knows something about Burton. Maybe he can shed some light." I didn't say anything but I doubted it. I asked her about tonight. "I'll be fine," she said. She had found a health food store and she planned to lock herself in, eat in her room, meditate, exercise, go nowhere, and not answer the phone. "Don't bother me unless there's an earthquake."

* * *

At six o'clock I retrieved my car and drove the three blocks to the Mills House. Erin came down looking lovely and I told her so. I was on my best behavior, somewhere between smarmy and suave, decked out in my dark coat and tie. I held the door for her and took her hand as she sank into the car, and for the moment there were no wisecracks between us. I had found a seafood place on Shem Creek in Mount Pleasant. We were early enough to get a spectacular table near a window facing a sweeping marsh. The food was good, fishing boats passed beneath us, and the setting sun turned the creek into a ribbon of fire.

It was the pleasantest evening I'd had in a long time and there were long, casual moments when the specter of Dante and his thugs seemed very far away. Outside, she said, "You know what I'd like to do? Take off my shoes and walk on a beach somewhere, without much risk of running into Archer." I consulted my map and a few minutes later we were heading back through the city, over the Ashley River and out to the coast. It was a good drive across miles of marshlands dotted with small wooded islands, and I could imagine what it had been like before growth, the scourge of our time, had turned too much of it into a long, continuous suburb.

Folly Beach is a little town with a few flashing neon blocks, a shooting gallery, a game room, pavilion, and rides. The carnival atmosphere disappeared at once as I turned south into the night. I found a place to park and we kicked off our shoes and went barefoot in the moonlight along the edge of the surf. The wind was strong and a little cold for the season; Erin curled her hand into mine and drew herself close. I draped my coat around us like a cocoon, she snuggled against me, we stood wrapped together like that, and at some point I lifted her chin and kissed her. She pulled us tighter and I buried my face in her hair. My old heart was going a mile a minute.

"Now look what you've done," she said. "We can never be friendly antagonists again."

"I thought that was pretty friendly, actually."

"Yes, but now what are we going to do about it?"

"That's a tough one. The answers can range all the way from nothing . . ."

". . . to everything."

"The prospects boggle the mind."

"But how to decide? Do we take a vote?"

"That would be pointless without some way of breaking a tie."

"I've never been much for casual sex," she volunteered airily.

"At the same time, I'm not getting any younger."

"Are you having trouble with your, uh . . ."

"No, I'm fine as of today. But the male body was not made for endless periods of celibacy. Deep, unexpected flabbiness can occur."

"Maybe I'd better talk faster."

I had to laugh at that.

She said, "If we eliminate casual sex, where are we?"

"Sounds almost like we'd have to get serious."

"If that turned out to be the case, what would you say?"

"What do you want me to say, I love you?"

"Not unless it's true."

"That's my point. If I did say that . . ."

"Yes?"

"How would you know it's not just some scuzzy male ploy to get my way with you?"

"I've got pretty good vibes."

"Experience will give you that."

"I *beg* your pardon! I don't just fall down for every dude I meet."

"Still, you must have some way of—"

"Forty days and forty nights."

I took that under advisement, then said, "I'll bet there's a clue there somewhere."

"Once we reach a certain point, we take forty days and forty nights to get to know each other. But back to the original question: If you did say 'I love you,' how would *you* know? Have you ever been in love?"

"Sure. Once."

"What was she like?"

"A lot like you, actually. Not as crazy but very quick. Smart as a whip."

"What happened?"

"My performance left something to be desired."

"Well, since we've already established that you're not physically challenged, I take it you were being your usual boorish and dictatorial self."

"Okay."

"That's not something you can answer okay to, Janeway. Either you were or you weren't."

"I didn't trust her."

"That's a biggie. Oh, that's very big. You don't ever want to let that happen again."

"I'll try," I said, but I couldn't help thinking how often history repeats itself.

She burrowed closer than I thought possible. I felt her fingernails through my shirt.

"You've got to give up your need to run things," she said. "I don't do well with that."

"Maybe I could work on it."

"Would you really?"

"Anything's possible."

"We'll see. I'm about to tell you something that will test you severely. Are you ready?"

I wasn't but she told me anyway. "I canceled my plane reservation this afternoon. I'm not going back to Denver, I'm staying with you. God help Mr. Dante if he bothers us."

She unwound herself, spun away, and stood shivering in the wind. "So what do you say, Janeway? You lost once because of your attitude—are you going to blow it again?"

She squinted at her watch. "Hey, I think our forty days and forty nights just began."

29

I remembered half a dozen moments in my life, crossroads where everything would be different if I had gone the other way. I could tick them off in no particular order. When I became a cop. When I stopped being a cop. When I discovered Hemingway and Fowles and those three lovely books by Maugham, all in the same month. When I became a bookseller. When I found, won, and lost an unforgettable woman. Now this. Suddenly my world was shaken. Everything in it was different.

We met again at dawn. My telephone rang in the darkness and when I lifted it she said, "You sound awake, I hope." I said, "I am awake." She said, "Have you had any sleep?" Not much, I admitted: not enough to matter. She asked for the time; I looked at the clock and told her it was four twenty-seven. That's what hers said too, as if clocks were suddenly untrustworthy. "Meet me on the Battery," she said. I told her I'd pick her up, I had to come past her hotel anyway, but she wanted to be met at dawn at the top of the steps where the rivers join and the wall gets higher. "It'll be so much more dramatic that way."

The wind of last night had blown dark clouds over the city and the day promised rain. I walked over, arriving at first light after a fifteen-minute hike. She stood looking out to sea like the French lieutenant's woman. She heard me coming: didn't turn but wiggled her fingers in an endearing "hi, there" gesture. I climbed the steps to the high wall and wrapped my arms around her. She sank against me and I kissed her neck. "How are we doing?" I said.

"So far, so good. Thank you for not pitching a fit last night."

I thought the jury was still out on that. Then she said, "Our lives are changing, old man," and I heard the jury coming back early.

"It looks like there are two of us now," she said. "That takes some getting used to."

"Yes, it does."

"I've been on my own forever."

"Never a guy to answer to. Never somebody to lay down the law."

"I've been way too career-minded. Maybe now I've got to be more . . . what's the word?"

"The word is reasonable," I said dryly. I spelled it for her, enunciating each letter clearly.

"You're a regular walking dictionary. What can this mean?"

"You talk tough and you make a lot of noise. You set your mind on something and that's it." I gave her arm a squeeze. "You've got a few good points as well."

"Do I tell you what to do?"

"Not in so many words."

"How, then? I expect you to make your own decisions. But once you've done that, then I get to decide what I'm going to do."

I could have said, *That's the same thing,* but didn't. I still had the feeling she was somewhere between loving me madly and walking the hell out of my life.

"This is why I actually believe in the forty days and forty nights," she said.

"That seems like a long time in these wild, permissive days."

"Does to me too. But it's a good, honest test. Separates the wheat from the chaff."

"Then it's a good thing. I wouldn't want to be mistaken for chaff."

"Never fear. I'm a little self-conscious saying it, but right now I feel . . . glorious."

"That's good," I said. "That's good."

"It is good, and don't look so troubled about it all."

"You know why. It's this business with Dante. Can we talk about that?"

"Of course. See how reasonable I am?"

"I want you to leave. And it's got to be soon, before anyone knows you're here."

"Now see, that's a dictator talking. How am I supposed to respond to that?"

"Let's start again from a more tactful place. Will you *please* go back to Denver?"

"Certainly. Shall I book a flight for two or will Koko be coming with us?"

I stood at the railing and stared despondently out to sea. Somewhere in that gray void, Fort Sumter would be showing off her ruins for the new day. Right here, Charlie Warren had walked up to Richard Burton and asked what he was drawing in his notebook. Erin put an arm over my shoulder and tousled my heavy head. "Cheer up. Interesting days lie ahead."

"That's one way to look at it."

"I'm giving up law," she said a moment later. "I plan to stay current and take on a case if it speaks to me, but my days working for a big law firm are over. I gave notice on Monday."

"What are you going to do, then? Aside from writing; I mean in real life."

"I thought we'd settled that. I'm going to buy half an interest in your bookstore." She tugged at my sleeve. "I've got a feeling there's a world of books out there at a whole different level than where you've been playing."

"Half a dozen levels, and they all take lots of money."

"I've got some money. If we can get past this bump in the road, life could be fun again. Will you teach me the book business?"

"From the ground up. So to speak."

Out on the harbor the sun had broken through and the fort appeared, a tiny black dot in a psychedelic mist.

"Koko's going out to Fort Sumter today."

"Have you told her about me?"

"Yes, I have."

"That's a pretty dreary-sounding yes. I take it she wasn't thrilled."

"She's a funny woman. Sometimes it takes her a while to figure out what she thinks."

"Tell me about her."

I told her and she said, "God, she hates me already."

"How could she hate you? She doesn't even know you."

"She's probably heard how unreasonable I am."

I pushed at her arm and pulled her back again.

"I think you should go to the fort with her," she said. "I'll stay here."

"What's that going to accomplish?"

"Archer may call, and you can pave the way for me with Koko. Do you like her?"

"Yeah, I do. She can be difficult, like somebody else I know. But she's got character."

"I think she likes you too. If you know what I mean."

"Erin, she's twenty-five years older than me."

"Just a hunch I have." She smiled wisely. "Anyway, do what you can. The three of us are going to be together for a while and it'll help if we can tolerate each other."

30

The threat of rain blew away and by noon the day was sunny. We caught the two-thirty boat, taking seats on the upper deck in a warm sea breeze. It was a thirty-minute ride, sweeping us past the city's most elegant waterfront homes and on across the harbor to Fort Sumter. Koko had called her lawyer and her insurance company. The wheels were in motion on her house; there was nothing to do but push ahead. Our pilot droned into the PA system about the notable places we were passing in the city and pointed out sites of Civil War action to the west, but I didn't hear much of it. I was thinking of the days to come, and where our trail might lead if everything here petered out.

Koko wanted to go north, to Florence. She was hoping some record might be found of the Wheeler family, where Burton and Charlie had spent those few days 127 years ago. Charleston had disappointed her. "I didn't think it would be this hard," she said. "These people put so much stock in their history, they keep records of everything, that's why I knew we'd find at least some evidence of that photographer. Now that doesn't look so good, does it?"

I told her to cheer up, we weren't dead yet. But that choice of words cast a harbinger across my path and I saw the Reaper's face in the white, billowing clouds. Whatever was coming between Dante and me was inevitable now, like a river pushing everything out of its path. If he didn't find me, I'd find him.

Today the harbor held a deceptive sense of tranquillity. Hard to imagine it filled with gunboats and bursting shells on this quiet day 120-odd years later; harder yet to understand the national lunacy that had led us there. For a moment I wondered what those Rebels, strutting around like peacocks, would have done if they'd known what a disaster they were bringing upon themselves and their sons, but I knew. Destroying themselves was just in their nature.

The fortress rose out of the water and took on color and life, a pentagon of red bricks turning pale with age. The boat made a circle and eased in toward the dock. It had a full load of passengers with both decks crowded, and we sat in the sun until most of the people were off. Two rangers met us on the pier. Koko told them she was looking for Luke Robinson, and we were directed inside the fort, where we found a uniformed man giving the tour.

What remained of Fort Sumter was the outer wall, and under it the shadowy gun rooms with vintage cannons, dark passages that went into black places under the wall, and the brick ruins of the officers' quarters. Running down the length of the old parade ground was a black battery, a fort within a fort that was obviously of a different era. The ranger was explaining it as we came in. It was called Battery Huger, built as part of the coastal defense system during the Spanish American War. Today it housed the museum, rest rooms, and a small living space for him and his wife. Nearby were the remains of a small-arms magazine that had exploded in 1863, killing eleven men and wounding forty, leaving the wall still blackened and leaning from the force of it.

We waited through the tour, about twenty minutes, then the crowd was sent off to explore on its own. Koko approached the ranger, a lanky man in his thirties with a grand mustache.

"Mr. Robinson?"

"Yes, ma'am, at your service."

Koko introduced us. "I was told you might know about the time Richard Burton spent in Charleston."

"Oh, wow, where'd you hear that?"

"In town, at the Library Society."

"I didn't know librarians talked about people's private research projects."

"I'm a librarian myself. I promised her it wouldn't go any further without your consent. We're looking for proof that Burton was here in May of 1860."

"Good luck. You're chasing a real will-o'-the-wisp. We haven't found a single thing you can take to the bank."

"You seem to believe it anyway."

"Whatever I believe, it's just my own opinion—mine and Libby's. She's my wife."

"Would you mind telling us why you believe it?"

He laughed lightly. "How much time you got? Never mind, I know when the boat leaves. It's just not something I can answer in twenty minutes."

"I'll take what I can get."

"Come on upstairs."

We climbed a narrow staircase to the upper level of the battery. There, in the smallest imaginable living space—a bed, a bookcase, a microwave oven, a table, two chairs, a small dresser and a closet, all in one tiny room—we met his wife. She was dark-haired and pretty in a crisp uniform, with a ranger hat in her hand, as if she had been about to go out. Instinctively my eyes scanned their books and found all the Burton biographies on the top shelf.

"Libby, this is Ms. Bujak and Mr. Janeway. They're interested in Burton."

She brightened at once and we had to go through it all again: how we got their names, what we hoped to find. It turned out that Libby had been the instigator of their Burton research, and only later had her enthusiasm spread to her husband. She was like a pixie, warm and giving, immediately likable. She said, "Sit down, stay awhile," and we all laughed. Outside, people were already moving back toward the dock. Our time was short.

They insisted that we take the chairs. Libby sat cross-legged on the floor and Luke leaned against the bookcase. "I've been inter-ested in Burton all my life," she said. "Even when I was a child I thought he was the world's most romantic figure. It was only by accident that I heard he'd been here."

"How'd you hear that?" Koko said.

"There's a Burton club here."

"You mean like a fan club for a dead man?"

"You could call it that. There are Burton clubs all over the world. That's one of the first things I did when we got assigned here, I went to the Burton club and we got friendly with some of the people. You know how it is: there are always a few in any group who have off-beat ideas. Most of it's folklore, theory, hot air. There was one old man in the Burton club named Rulon Whaley who was just like that. Very loud and opinionated, but there was so much energy in him that he made me listen. He'd been fascinated by the Burton myth for years. Rulon not only believed Burton had been here but that he spied on us for England. He was determined to prove it but he never did. He died this year."

"Do you know where he got that idea?"

"Heard it from another old gent long ago, I think. Once he got something in his head, he was almost impossible to defeat."

Most of the talk that followed was historical rehash, things we all knew. Koko and Libby talked, the ranger and I watched. I especially watched Libby. A certain tone had come into her voice. A look I had seen many times had come into her eyes. As a cop I called it the knows-more-than-she's-telling look. Koko had missed it because she had spent her life answering questions and I had spent mine asking them.

I asked one now. "Did you ever learn who the other man was?"

Libby shook her head. "He died years ago, so it always seemed rather hopeless."

"Maybe he left some papers, or some record."

"No way of knowing now. If he did, I guess I dropped the football."

Koko stood and said, "Well, thank you for talking to us."

I glared at her and my look said, *Keep still.*

"This is awful," Libby said. "There's not even enough time to offer you a cup of coffee. I'd love to sit around with you and kick at it for a while."

"Maybe we should do that," I said.

"Like when?" Robinson said. "The boat's going to leave them, Lib."

"Maybe they could come back."

"They'd have the same time problem. And none of us really knows anything." He looked at me apologetically. "You're certainly welcome to come back but I'm afraid it would just be a waste of your time."

"You could come back anyway," Libby said. "If you wanted to you could stay the night. We'd have plenty of time to talk then."

"Is that allowed?"

"Oh, sure. You'd have to bring sleeping bags. We're not exactly the Holiday Inn here."

I had a hunch and so did Libby: I could feel it, like some energy field growing between us. "What do you think he was doing here?" she said.

"Well, we know he wanted to see the States."

"Do you really believe he came only as a tourist?"

"No."

She smiled quixotically and I felt Koko stiffen beside me. Koko had come here for information, not to talk too much, and I knew she wouldn't like the way this was going. Stiffly, she said, "Of course that's just conjecture. We don't know any more than you do."

But Libby was looking at me, not Koko. I said, "Maybe together we'll all discover stuff we didn't know we knew. Sometimes you've got to give a little to get a lot."

"What stuff?" Libby said. "Do you actually know something?"

"He used to be a detective," Koko said dismissively. "Thinks he still is."

"Really?" Libby smiled at me as if she liked that idea.

"We think Burton came here with someone," I said.

"Oh, don't tell them that," Koko said. "My God, there's no proof of that at all."

"Then it doesn't hurt to tell them, does it? As an unproved theory."

"Tell us what?" Libby said.

"We think he met a man in Washington and traveled with him. They came through here in May of 1860 and went to New Orleans together. They became close friends."

Koko's face was red with anger. She turned away and looked out over the fort.

Libby said, "Do you know what his friend looked like?"

Now there's a strange question, I thought. I might have expected her to ask whether we knew his name, but who asks about the appearance of a man from a time when photography was so new that few had ever had their pictures taken?

"Do we know what he looked like, Koko?"

"Don't ask me. How would I know?"

Again Libby made eye contact. I shrugged and Robinson said, "You're going to miss your boat." Mischievously, Libby said, "Then they wouldn't have to worry about the time."

"That's her way of saying she wants you to come back," Robinson said.

"When?"

"Can't be tomorrow or the next day," Libby said. "I'm going to school. I'm writing a paper and I've got to study for a wicked test. It all hits at once."

"What about Tuesday?"

"Tuesday would work. Bring good sleeping gear. The ground here's hard."

They walked us down to the dock. At the pier we all shook hands. Again they apologized for the hectic schedule. At the very end Libby asked the question I had expected in the beginning. "Do you know the name of the man who came with Burton?"

Before I could answer, she answered it herself. "It wouldn't be Charlie, would it?"

31

On the boat, Koko said, "I wonder what she really knows."

"She's clever. She wants you to wonder that. She wants us to come back and she timed her bombshell so we wouldn't have even a minute to get into it."

"Right now I don't need clever. I just wish people would say what they mean." A moment later she said, "Anyway, you were right, I was wrong."

"Coulda just as easy been the other way."

"Thanks, but I don't think so."

We were sitting on the enclosed lower deck, out of a wind that had turned the harbor into a basin of choppy water. Koko sat near the glass, staring out at the whitecaps.

"I've been an old bear lately. Just want you to know I know that and I'm sorry."

"You've had a lot to think about. I didn't just lose my house."

She changed the subject. "What a strange day this is. Goes from rainy to sunny and back to rainy again. God can't get anything right."

"He's got a lot on his mind. It's got to be tough being God sometimes."

"What's that from? I used to know it."

"*The Green Pastures.* 'Bein' God ain't no bed o' roses either.'"

She smiled but it was a sad smile.

"Hey," I said, leaning over to look at her face. "What can I do?"

"Nothing. Go away. Jesus, I hate self-pity."

"They'll build you a new house, Koko."

"What good is that if I can't go back and live there?"

"I think you'll be able to go back."

"How?"

"We'll work on it."

She didn't look convinced. "It's not the house anyway, it's what I lost inside the house."

"I know it's tough," I said, and felt stupid saying it. She confirmed my stupidity with a frigid look. "You don't know anything," she said, carving me into a Mount Rushmore of dunces. "What do you know about my life?"

"Nothing. You're right, I don't know anything."

"Take a guess. Wildest guess you can think of."

"Jeez, Koko, I don't know."

"Old-maid librarian is what you're thinking."

"I never said that."

"But if someone asked you, that's what you'd think. Well, I had a husband once. We had two beautiful children. My son would be just about your age now. I was young and happy and not at all bad-looking. I had a very different life then. My husband was an engineer, I was working on a master's degree in literature, and I played the violin well enough to try out for our symphony orchestra. We had everything then, the whole world ahead of us, and in one crazy minute a drunk driver took it all away."

"Oh, Koko . . ."

"No, don't say anything." She turned her face to the glass and spoke to my reflection. "I'm not looking for pity. But don't tell me you know what I lost, because you don't know. The only pictures I had of my babies were in that house. I had film of their first steps and tape recordings of their voices. It's like he killed them all over again."

What can you say at a moment like that? I left her alone, but I thought of Dante and I felt a shimmering wave of real forty-karat hate. Another reason for us to meet again.

Late that afternoon I got in my rental and drove to a place I had looked up last night in the telephone book. It took me less than an hour to buy a good little gun and fire it on their range till it felt natural in my hand. I bought a snug holster for it, slipped it far back under my coat, and left hot but armed and dangerous, fully dressed for the first time in many days.

32

That night I got them together for the first time. Koko tried to resist, pleading a headache, but I reserved a table at one of the classiest new restaurants in town and threatened to lay siege to her room until she came out. "Want to drive or walk?" I asked. "It's an easy walk from here."

"Let's walk, then. Looks like that silly old guy, God, blew the clouds away again."

On the way over, she said, "I've had the weirdest feeling. Like I'm being watched."

I asked for specifics but she had none. "It's just the jitters. When I went out to the store, there seemed to be a man walking along behind me, on the other side of the street."

"Did you look at him?"

"At one point I did."

"But you didn't recognize him."

"No, but I'm not sure I'd remember any of those guys anyhow. It was night and I never did get a good look at them."

Erin was waiting in the lobby of her hotel. I had prepared her for Koko: that afternoon I had called and told her the story and she had immediately become cautious and considerate. "She sounds very fragile right now. I don't know her but she may be on the verge of some kind of nervous breakdown. She's been putting all her energy into this Burton hunt, and when that didn't seem to pan out she began to unravel. Now even the hunt may be losing its appeal. Don't ask me where my psych degree is, it's just one of those hunches like you seem to have all the time. I think we'll have to be careful with her, and the sooner we get this business finished with that madman in Baltimore, the better."

I made the introductions. Erin smiled warmly and said, "Hey, Koko, heard a lot about you." Koko said, "Hi there." They shook hands and we were off.

The restaurant was on Exchange Street near East Bay. We walked side by side, the wide sidewalk of Broad Street accommodating all of us. They talked about the charm of Charleston and the weather, the small talk of ordinary people who live out their lives without ever being threatened by violence or murder. I watched the people passing on both sides of the street.

The restaurant was noisy and already crowded, but there was a quieter dining room off to one side. We were seated in a far corner out of the din. Koko excused herself and went to the rest room and the waiter delivered us a wine list.

"So," I said. "What do you think?"

"I like her. And I revise my opinion. I think she's solid."

"She thinks she's being followed."

Erin dealt with that for a moment. "Maybe she is. Even if she's not, she's entitled to some frayed nerves."

"Question is, do we want to talk openly about this stuff?"

"Absolutely yes would be my vote. We have some decisions to make, and she's got a right to be part of that." She smiled as Koko returned. "I have some news to report."

Part of her news was about Archer, who had called with a counterproposal. "He may be willing to show me the journal. If he does, I'll try to browse it for content. Maybe I can pin down some things you're looking for."

"There must be something about Charlie in it," Koko said. "Even a mention would help."

"I'd give a year's pay to get Archer's fanny in court and ask him a few tough questions."

Erin had called Lee and told him everything. "He's concerned about us, of course. He thinks we should all get on the first plane for

Denver and coordinate our strategy from there. That's actually not a bad idea."

"It's not a great one, either," Koko said. "It means giving up on Burton."

"Only for now. It's not so bad if you think of it that way. This story's been there for more than a hundred years, it's not going away."

"You two could go to Denver," I suggested. "I could stay and see what the woman at Fort Sumter has for us. Then I'd come along in a few days."

Erin closed her eyes and made that praying motion with her hands. "What are we going to do with this man, Koko?"

"We could each carry around a two-by-four. When he tries too hard to protect us, we could just whack the hell out of him without warning."

"You bash him on that thick forehead, I'll get him from behind."

"Would you two like me to leave so you can talk freely?"

"Look, sweetie. If we don't do anything else tonight, let's dispense with the John Wayne routine. It's way out of date—John Wayne is dead—and it annoys me like crazy."

"You aren't going anywhere without us," Koko said.

"Because if anything happens to you, I will take this Dante on alone if I have to," Erin said. "Just think about that. I know he's strong, but I am not without resources and I will get him."

Koko shivered and laughed at the same time. "This is quite a girlfriend you've got here, Janeway."

The waiter came and we ordered our dinners. Koko gravitated toward the vegetarian items but we were now officially living dangerously and she chose the blackened grouper. We talked over wine and made some decisions. We would stay three more days in Charleston, giving Erin another crack at Archer and us a shot at whatever the Robinsons might know. Erin would move out of the Mills House and take a room near us in the Heart of Charleston. On Wednesday we would see where we were and go from there.

We walked back in a warm summer night. But in two blocks the air became heavy, the humidity bore down, and in the distance lightning flashed over the sea. We left Erin where we had found her, in the lobby of her hotel, and she hugged us both.

"We're gonna be fine," she said.

"Of course we are," Koko said. "Why wouldn't we be?"

Erin vanished into the elevator and Koko and I walked up the street together.

"I like her," she said. "I was determined not to, but she's a good girl."

"She likes you too."

At the motel a message had arrived from Koko's friend Janet in Baltimore. The fire department had officially classified her house as arson. Janet had talked to the reporter at the morning paper, who was still digging around. Yesterday he had put it in the paper that Koko had apparently gone to Charleston. "So they know we're here," I said.

We had to assume they had known for almost two days.

In the morning the rain finally came, a steamy downpour that billowed across Meeting Street and left the world slick-looking and empty. I talked to Erin soon after daybreak and she was moved over to our motel by nine o'clock. She circumvented the afternoon check-in by paying for the extra day and was settled into a room near Koko's with two hours to spare before her meeting with Archer. She had called Lee again and had received instructions to walk out if Archer was abusive or difficult. "Neither of us thinks anybody's going to go near what Lee's offering."

At ten o'clock Erin and Koko sat playing cards at a table in Koko's room while the rain drummed against the window. I was watching the TV in a stupefied state with the sound turned down. A preacher with larceny in his eyes and lust in his heart was on Channel Five, and on Channel Two I got some kind of political discourse, with the eyes of the senator just like the eyes of the preacher. I could tell from their faces the attitude and vacuous nature of what was being said, and none of it tempted me to turn up the volume. This country is doomed, I thought, not for the first time, and I closed my eyes and sank into boredom.

At ten-thirty I got up and moved to the door. "I'm going out for a little while."

Erin was immediately suspicious. "Where to?"

"There's a movie I want to see. *Debbie Does the Old Duffers*."

"I heard that doesn't have much of a plot. Where are you really going?"

"To the store for some male needs."

They looked at each other and tried not to laugh.

"Hey, I don't ask about your female needs."

"Just don't try anything foolish, like ditching us and going after people on your own."

"I'll bet he's going to buy a gun," Koko said. "He couldn't bring the one we had on the airplane, so he's going to buy another one."

"Is that where you're going?"

"Jesus, lighten up. You can't get a gun on Sunday. I need some razor blades."

"I only ask because as your lawyer I'm the one who's got to worry if there are laws here against carrying concealed weapons. Just in case I need to defend you or bail you out."

"It's Sunday, Mama," I said again. "You guys play cards and I'll be back in a while."

I walked up Meeting Street in the rain, looking at people on both sides of the street. The gun felt snug against my back.

John Wayne's ass. These women had no clue.

Erin had left to meet Archer when I got back and Koko was gazing at the same stupid TV fare with the volume off. "So what caliber razor blades did you get?"

"Big enough to fit a size thirty-two razor."

"Even on Sunday."

"Rexall's always open."

She smiled foxily. "I saw that man again. Same one who followed me up the street."

"Where?"

"Out on the street. I had to go to the store for some female needs."

"You're becoming a real wit, Koko. So tell me about him."

"Nothing to tell. He was just going into a store up the street when I saw him."

"I guess it's possible he's just some guy who lives around here."

"What else is possible?"

"Maybe he's the mayor of Charleston, scouting for people to welcome to his fair city."

Her face was pensive. "I don't know how Erin will feel about this. Me, I'm glad you got those razor blades."

She roused herself from the bed. "I'm going to the library. I don't expect to find anything, but I've got to do something or go mad in this room."

"Library's closed today. It's Sunday."

"We could go to a movie."

"I'm for that. Point out this dude if you see him on the street again."

I had already made up my mind that Erin's date with Archer was the last thing she would do solo. I wasn't leaving Koko alone anymore, either. I left a note under Erin's door telling her to stay put and we drove out to a suburban mall theater. Three hours later we came out frustrated: the film had been like the weather, lousy. "At least it got us through the afternoon," Koko said. "Just one more day of this. I'll kill that woman at Fort Sumter if she plays around with us."

Erin was there when we got to the motel.

"I hope your lunch was charming," I said.

"Lunch was fine. I waited two hours and ate alone. Archer never showed up."

In the morning we learned why.

34

The story was on the front page of the second section in the *News and Courier*. The headline said AUTHOR BEATEN, HOSPITALIZED. Hal Archer, a Pulitzer prize–winning historian now living on Sullivan's Island, had been brutally attacked and was in fair condition at Roper Hospital. Police had no motive and the victim had refused to talk to the press.

"I'm going to see him," Erin said.

"We'll all go."

"I don't think that's wise."

"Maybe not but we're going with you anyway. We'll try not to get in your way."

Roper Hospital was on Calhoun Street near the Ashley River. Erin inquired about Archer at the desk and was given his room number. His condition had been upgraded to good. Koko and I sat in the lobby, where we could watch the flow of people coming and going, and Erin went up in the elevator alone.

We had only been there a few minutes when Dean Treadwell appeared. "Here we go," I said softly. I got up, motioned Koko to come with me, and we followed him across the lobby to the elevators. We stood waiting in a small crowd, and when an elevator arrived we all got in the same car. Up we went, picking up doctors and nurses until we were all packed tightly together. Dean stared at the floor. The door opened and he got out. We were a few steps behind him as he moved down the hall. I didn't know till that moment what I would do, but suddenly the sound of Erin's voice moved me to his side.

"Hey, Dean."

He stopped and looked at me but I didn't seem to register. "How'd you know me?"

"I'm a psychic. I looked at your face and you looked like a Dean."

"That's interesting," he said, but the flat tone of voice said it really wasn't. "'Scuse me now, I've got to go see somebody."

I put a hand on his arm. "Uh-uh."

His eyes opened wider.

"He's got company," I said. "One visitor at a time."

He coughed that raspy smoker's cough I had first heard on the telephone. "Who the hell are you?" he said, coughing into his fist. "You don't look like any doctor."

"That's misleading. I took my Ph.D. in mayhem and hell-raising."

"So you're a wise guy." His eyes narrowed. "Haven't I seen you before?" He looked at Koko, searching for help.

"This is Ma Barker," I said. "Ma, this is Dean Treadwell."

"Hi, Dean," Koko said with a perfect edge of joyous malice. That was too good to have been intentional, but I winked at her.

Dean patted his shirt pocket for a smoke, then seemed to remember he was in a hospital. "You talk like crazy people," he said.

"I am a little crazy, Dean. I really get crazy when things don't go my way. Right now, for instance, I'd like you to go quietly downstairs with us. When my friend comes down, we can all walk quietly up the street till we find a nice, quiet coffee shop. Then we can sit down and have us a quiet talk. I like things quiet. You got any problem with any of that?"

"I don't guess so," he said. "I don't know what the hell you want with me."

"That's what we'll find out, Dean," I said, and we all went downstairs and waited quietly.

Erin came down almost on our heels. "Who's your friend?"

"This is Dean, he owns that bookstore in Baltimore. Dean, this is Lizzie Borden."

"Lizzie Borden my ass. Who the hell do you think you're fooling?"

"Nobody, but let's leave it at that. And watch your language, there are ladies here."

"I know who you are. I don't know these two but I know you. I've been trying to remember your voice and it just came to me."

"Come on, let's walk up the street."

He started to balk. I stepped on his foot and frosted him with a look. He said, "I don't have to go anywhere with you," but I pinched his arm hard enough to hurt and he went. We found a drugstore on Rutledge Avenue and I ordered coffees except for Koko, who had some awful-looking carrot juice concoction.

"It's good your memory's working, Dean," I said. "I need to ask you some things."

Again we had to go through a certain dance but I expected that. The conversation went like this.

"Tell me about Archer."

"Archer who?"

"You know Archer who."

"I have no idea what you're talking about."

"He's the schmuck you were going to see in the hospital, so knock off the stupid routine."

"I don't know what you're talking about."

"How are your kidneys, Dean?"

"What does that mean?"

"You look like a guy who needs to go to the bathroom. C'mon, I'll go with you."

"If you think I'm going in any back room with you, you're nuts."

"Then tell me about Archer, and remember I haven't got all day."

"Archer's a customer."

"I see. Do you always travel all around the country with your customers?"

"If they pay my freight I do."

"So Archer's paying you. What's he paying you for?"

"You're a bookseller, you know I can't answer that. That violates all kinds of ethics."

"Dean's going ethical on us," I said to the ladies.

"Would you answer that question?" Dean said.

"No, but I might kick your ass right here in this drugstore if you don't."

Erin cleared her throat loudly. I looked in her eyes and said, "Why don't you ladies meet me back at the hotel. Take the car, I'll walk."

Koko said, "Did you ever get one of them two-by-fours, Lizzie?"

"What's that supposed to mean?" Dean said.

I said, "It means that unless you give us some information, you could be in real trouble. Liz can tell you about it."

I threw it to her without warning and instantly she began shooting from the hip, part bluff, making it up as she went along. "You've been conspiring with a book thief, Dean. We're not talking about nickels and dimes, this is a work of major historical importance, worth at least way up in five figures. You know what it is. This can bring you serious grief in Maryland, Colorado, or South Carolina. It's known as grand theft pretty much everywhere, but it does have a bright side: they'll come feed you three times a day and you won't have to worry about making a living for a long time."

"I don't know what in the hell you're talking about."

She made a "too bad" motion with her eyes. "Then I guess we've got nothing more to say to each other."

He fished for his cigarettes but I pointed to a NO SMOKING sign just above his head. "That stuff'll kill you, Dean. Stinks up your books too. I had a guy bring in Hemingway's signed limited one time and I couldn't even buy it. He was a chain-smoker and you could smell his book clear across the room."

"Yeah, yeah, spare me the fucking lecture. And you." He nodded at Erin. "Why don't you try saying what you've got to say in plain English?"

"Your friend Archer has a hot book. We have good reason to believe you're mixed up in it. Is that plain enough for you?"

"I had nothing to do with that."

"With what? I thought you didn't know what we were talking about."

"I had nothing to do with any theft that either did occur or might have occurred."

"I've had enough of this bird," I said. "Let's stick a fork in him."

"Just calm down," Erin said. "Give the man a chance. If I can't persuade him to be reasonable, we'll see him in court."

"What court?" Dean said.

"That's a question of jurisdiction, isn't it? Depends on where a theft occurred and where the hot goods are disposed. Doesn't matter to me, I'll go after you wherever I can."

"Let's get one thing straight. I never did anything illegal."

"You don't get anything straight just by saying it. You can tell it to a judge, but I doubt if your word will meet any rules of evidence. No offense, Dean, I know you mean well."

They all sat quietly. I commented on the rain, the heat, the touristy things: the houses along Rainbow Row, the fact that we had missed Charleston's fabled azaleas at the peak of their glory. Erin finished her coffee and Koko drank her carrot stuff.

"We're leaving," Erin said. "This was your chance and it's slipping away."

"I'm not worried," Dean said. "Archer says the book is his."

"Archer lies."

"Well, I believe him. I was never told anything about any theft."

"That could be a mitigating factor. If you cooperate."

"Cooperate in what? You're no goddamn prosecutor; who the hell are you?"

"This is who I am. I represent the injured party. My recommendation in any proceeding will carry some weight, maybe a lot. Are you going to help us or not?"

"Depends on what you want."

She took out a notebook and a ballpoint pen. "Answer my questions. Then read what I've written and sign it; we'll get a copy made and you get to keep that."

He didn't like it. He shook his head and sat coughing.

"Dean?"

"I'll tell you right now, you won't like what I've got to say. I've got nothing that puts Archer in any kind of bad light."

"Just tell the truth. That's all I want."

"Yeah, right. You're like everybody else. You can't get along with him so you want to sandbag him."

A moment later he said, "You've got to understand something. Archer's special. He's not like you and me. There's no use talking if you don't understand that."

"I do understand it," Erin said. "I've read his books."

He looked at her for most of a minute. Then he began to talk.

Long before he had moved to South Carolina, Hal Archer had discovered Treadwell's. As a teenager in the late forties, he had spent time at his parents' summer home in Baltimore and had bought books from Dean's father.

Carl and Dean were kids then, working in the store, stocking the shelves, moving stuff, whatever needed doing. One day Archer said something to Dean and that's how it started. They were about the same age, and whenever he came in they'd pass the time of day. Sometimes Archer would sit on one of the chairs upstairs and tell young Dean Treadwell what a great writer he was going to be.

"Nobody believed in him then, nobody but me. And I had no doubt at all."

Dean was Archer's first cold audience. By then Archer had begun to drift away from his few boyhood friends, even the one who later became a judge: "I think he became afraid of Huxley's judgment; they had been too close, they went back too far, and Huxley was always too kind. What Archer hated most was being patronized, damned by faint praise. Me, I had no reason to care whether his stuff was any good or not. I was the unwashed reader he craved, and right from the start I knew he was a good one."

Archer began coming to the store with pages of manuscript. He didn't want any so-called constructive criticism; what he was dying for was hero worship, adulation: he wanted to be someone's idol, and Dean was simply in awe of his talent.

"I gave him something he needed and he gave me something I loved. He never doubted my sincerity; he had no reason to because it was real. You couldn't fool him, I knew he would sense any lie right away, but I never had to lie. He had an ability to create a world, he was like God, I never got tired of hearing him read. I loved seeing him come into the store. I loved every line he wrote. Still do.

"We had to hide from my old man. He was a mean son of a bitch about slackers; if he caught me dreaming or slacking off, he'd whip my ass good. So we went way upstairs, Archer and me, where the old man couldn't go. He had asthma, he couldn't climb those stairs, and sometimes on Saturdays when the store got busy the old bastard just forgot I was alive.

"I could kill the whole afternoon, dreaming with Archer."

As time went on, Archer found it difficult and finally intolerable to be with Lee. It wasn't that Lee ever did anything to make him feel that way. "It's just that the judge had done everything right in his life and it seemed like Hal had fucked up his own six ways from Sunday."

He raised an eyebrow at Erin and she smiled, waving off the language.

"Hal needed me. I think he still does. He never got a break from anybody."

"And by the time he did get a real break . . ."

"He was full of anger. He even wanted to tell the Pulitzer committee to keep their fuckin' prize, shove it up their pretentious asses." He coughed. "I talked him out of that."

"Best thing you ever did for him."

"The best thing I ever did was just believe in him. He sure hasn't had a happy life. He thinks everybody who came along after the prize was a fair-weather friend."

"He had Lee. He always had Lee. Lee always wanted the best for him, even if Archer didn't know or believe it. Now look what's happening to them."

"I think there's some old bitterness there. The judge never took a wrong step. While Archer was scratching to keep body and soul together, Huxley's legal career was upwardly mobile all the way, always on the fast track."

"That wasn't Lee's fault."

"Did I say it was? But it does get old if you're on the opposite end of the stick."

Erin paused, then said, "Tell me about the book."

"Nothin' to tell. Hal says it's his and I believe him."

"Did he ever tell you where he got it?"

"No, and I wouldn't ask. Tell you this much: I don't think he stole it."

"Deny it if you want to, but don't take that too far, it might come back and bite you."

"I don't know anything about it and I don't want to hear it. Put that down on your paper: Dean Treadwell's heard every story ever floated about what a bastard Hal Archer is—I don't need yours too. Look, can we get out of this goddamn place? If I don't get me a smoke I'm gonna start punching something."

Out on the street, Dean lit up and we watched him smoke his weed in three mighty drags. "That's all I got for you, lady," he said. "If you don't like it, go ahead and sue me."

"Thank you. I think I'm done for now."

"I've got a couple of questions," I said. "Tell me about your brother."

"Carl's a flaming asshole but that's got nothing to do with me. We each inherited fifty percent of the store, but in real life we don't have much to do with each other."

"He's got some bad friends. One of them burned this lady's house down. You know anything about that?"

"Hell no, but it doesn't surprise me. That's why I stay away from him. Ten years ago he started gambling and going around with those hoods. He won big one year but he squandered that trying to impress a pack of thugs. Now he's got no money left and that gunsel is calling the shots. Frankly, I don't give a damn what they do to him, the little bastard deserves everything he gets. I'd get out of the store and let him have it, if I just knew what else to do."

He lit a new smoke from the old and threw the butt into the gutter. "I've been in the book business since I was twelve years old. I'm fifty-five now and I'm tired of bullshit. This used to be a great way to make a living. Now it's like everything else, polluted with bullshit and fast-buck artists. You're a bookman, Janeway, but you're fairly young yet. What'll you do when the life goes sour?"

He took another massive drag and two contrails of smoke poured out of his nose, obliterating his face. "Your silence says it all, pal. For a bookman there isn't anything else."

At the car, Erin said, "That wasn't exactly what we expected, was it?"

"I don't know. What did you expect?"

"Almost anything but for Archer to turn into some deity."

"What about Archer? You didn't have time for much of an audience with him."

"They broke his jaw. His face was all wired up and he couldn't talk. Looks like they broke some of his fingers and his collarbone. He's in a lot of pain. He got pretty agitated when he saw me, and the nurse asked me to leave."

"I wonder what the motive was."

"With Archer, who needs a motive?"

"Yeah, but he's been a jerk for a long time, why beat him up now? I'm wondering if they just found out about his book. And if they did, whether they took it from him."

"I don't know. That was on my list of things to ask."

We sat at the curb for a while and I watched the traffic fore and aft. A cooling breeze blew through the open car and there was no real incentive to move, no rush to get anywhere. It was just noon and I was trying to figure out what we'd do and how. For some reason Dean's words kept playing in my head, interrupting my thought pattern. I began playing the What-If Game, something I had done many times as a cop. The game had only one rule: you throw stuff at a mental wall and nothing is sacred; no crazy notion is too crazy to consider.

"Looks like another great day of solitaire coming up," Koko said. "Whoop-de-do."

I heard her words but I was only listening with half a brain. She and Erin began talking about tomorrow and Fort Sumter. "We've still got sleeping bags to buy," Koko said. "We'll need three now." Absently I nodded yes, we would need three, but I couldn't stop thinking about Dean Treadwell and his strange lifelong friendship with the man everybody loved to hate.

Only later did I begin pondering our escape from Charleston. That afternoon we drove in an apparently aimless circle around greater Charleston till I spotted what I wanted—a sporting goods store in the north area, with parking lots on both sides of the building. I didn't stop but I noted the landmarks as I drove past. I made a slow loop and headed back downtown.

35

How do you give people the slip when you don't know where they are, when you're not even sure they're really there and you have no idea how many they might be or what they look like? Sitting in Erin's room that night, we considered and rejected everything three times over. Go to the police? "With what?" I asked. "Some cock-and-bull story about a Baltimore gangster who we think might have followed us here?" Tell the cops about Archer? "Tell them what?" I said. "That these thugs who beat Archer half to death, we think, are coming after us next?" This might not be half-bad if Archer would corroborate our story; maybe then we could get some police protection long enough to blend into the Southern landscape and give them the slip. Maybe we could get on that boat for Fort Sumter without being seen, return the next day and get out of town. Once we were on the road, we could disappear upstate.

We settled on this: Tomorrow afternoon we would drive to that sporting goods store, leave the rental in the east parking lot, go in and buy three sleeping bags, then exit the opposite door, where a cab would be waiting to take us to the marina. There we would buy our tickets and after that it was a crapshoot. We'd have to wait in the open line, where anybody could see us, until we were inside the boat and under way. As a plan this did not rank with the wooden horse that defeated the Trojans, but it was what we had, what we would do.

We had Pizza Hut send in supper for two. I paid at the door and scanned the lot and what I could see of the street. Nothing. Erin and I ate the pizza while Koko feasted on nuts and seeds and scoops of yummy-looking gray stuff from a plastic bag. We watched the depressing TV fare and later the ladies played more cards. They both left at nine, and for a long time I stood at the window of my room watching the courtyard and saw nothing suspicious.

None of us slept well. When I saw them in the morning they looked haggard and weary.

Another long morning waiting. Gradually we took our suitcases out to the car, watching everything around us. At noon I called a cab company and left an order for a taxi in the south parking lot of the sporting goods place for exactly one-fifteen. I gave them a credit card number and told the dispatcher that the cabbie must be on time and I would pay him double, including time spent waiting, with an extra fifty bucks when we were delivered to the marina at two o'clock.

We didn't bother to check out: the motel had my credit card number and I'd call them later and have them bill me. We were out of the room and in the car in ten seconds flat. I eased into Meeting Street and turned right toward North Charleston.

It all went like clockwork. I kept an eye peeled, watching my mirrors constantly, and nowhere behind me did I see anything that even hinted of a watcher, a tailgater, or a spook. If Dante or any of his elves were back there, they were mighty good at this.

At the store I watched the crowd while Erin bought the three bags; at the last minute I bought a flashlight and some batteries, and we hustled out the opposite door. The cab was there with its meter running. Koko and Erin got in the back and I rode up front. We drove into town the way we had come up, and the cabbie deposited us at the FORT SUMTER TOURS sign with time to spare. "Just wait with us," I told him, and we all sat there for fifteen minutes. I paid him, gave him the half-C, and told him he was a gentleman and a scholar. We scrambled up the dock with only a few minutes to spare.

The boat eased away and the pilot began telling us about the sights we were seeing. Erin came close and took my hand. "Looks like we beat him," she said. But as I watched the receding buildings, one man in the crowd caught my eye. I saw him for just a second before he disappeared beyond the ticket shack. From that distance I couldn't quite make him out. But he did remind me of someone, and I wasn't so sure we beat him after all.

This time Libby was waiting on the dock to greet us. A brilliant smile lit up her face, as if she'd been waiting there for three days doubting our return. Now we had come as budding friends. The ice had been broken and it didn't seem to matter that we had known each other less than half an hour; we had a common cause. Libby made light of Erin's unexpected arrival. They were roughly the same age and they chatted easily as we walked up the long pier and turned into the fort. "Luke's giving the tour again," she said. "We usually alternate. I do it every other day when time permits, but he's catching double-duty now that my studies are piling up. Let's stash your bags and I'll show you around."

She gave us a private mini-tour in a low voice as we walked into the shadows under the wall. "This is the sally port. For you laymen, that means the passage in and out. The name comes from the military term *sally*, to attack and repel invaders. The old sally port was over there." She pointed to a low place in the wall to our right. "That's the gorge wall. This is the left flank we just came through. Straight across the fort, on the other side of the battery, is the right flank. The other two walls are the right face and the left face. I will quiz you later, so take notes. You don't get any supper unless you get a passing grade."

"In case the enemy attacks us tonight," Erin said.

"Exactly," she said, deadpan. "It wouldn't do if I yelled, 'Reinforcements to the left flank!' and all of you fell into the harbor looking for it."

Erin laughed. "I can see we're going to get along fine."

"Speaking of supper," Libby said. "I hope you're not finicky eaters. The menu here is not our strong point."

We stared at each other, somewhat shamefaced. None of us had given food a thought.

"Don't worry about it. All I'm hoping is that you're not too put off by TV dinners."

"We can eat anything," I said. "Right, Koko?"

"Absolutely," said Koko. "I'm ready to tear into a raw shark."

"Can't help you there," Libby said. "Maybe I can scare up some canned squid."

She made a *shhh* motion as we went past Luke, who stood above a crowd giving the same speech we had heard on Saturday. She moved us down under the left flank wall and continued her lecture in a low monotone.

"Imagine this whole structure two and three levels high. Above us was another tier of casemates—gun rooms—and the enlisted men's barracks were three stories high on both flanks, with guns on top of each wall."

We skirted the left face. "This was a formidable fort then," she said. "That's all gone, pounded to smithereens in the Union siege. After they shelled that little band of Yankees out, the Confederates held this rock for almost four years, living in rubble much of that time. For two years they were battered by gunboats and by big guns from Morris Island, which we'll see in a minute. Historians say seven million pounds of iron were fired in here. The Yanks thought they could take anything if they shelled the bejesus out of it long enough. But this old baby was tough, and the more they reduced it, the tougher it became. In the end there was nothing here but piles of bricks and whatever was buried under them—these walls you see and those ruins over there, the remains of a proud old fort. By then the Confederates had replaced their artillery forces with infantry, and the Union still couldn't take it."

She gestured at the guns as we walked past. "Some of these cannons were used against the fort by Union forces on Morris Island—moved over here years later."

We went up to her little apartment in the battery. "Just throw your stuff down anywhere," she said, and we went out again. She led us along the right flank and we stood facing the sea. "So anyway," she said, "this is what I call home."

Koko asked how long they had been here.

"A year. They'll rotate us; they say it keeps us from going stir crazy, but I'm going to miss this terribly when I leave. I think about it even now, how quickly we move past things, sometimes without ever seeing them. There's so much here that's of the past, and soon it will all be part of my own past. Maybe Luke and I will come back years from now as tourists and I'll think of these days. But I'll never again be part of it, so I make the most of every day I do have."

She pointed to a long, sandy beach across the channel, facing the sea to our right. "That's Morris Island. Fort Wagner sat near the end, just where it hooks in toward the city. Union forces tried their best to take it in the summer of 1863. Get Wagner, get Sumter—that's how they figured it; get Sumter, get Charleston. Get Charleston and they could close down the whole Southern seaboard. But they never did any of that, not till the Confederates pulled out and left it to them in 1865."

We stood on the point, the right gorge angle she called it, and looked where she looked. "That narrow beach on Morris Island is where the Fifty-fourth Massachusetts Colored Infantry was butchered trying to dislodge the Confederates. Not to take anything away from those black warriors, you've got to admire the Southern fighting man. You don't have to like his cause to know he and his pals were a tough, valiant bunch."

We stood there for a while. The day was almost perfect, the sun warm, the harbor full of sailboats. Closer in, smaller, power-driven craft skimmed across the water. Libby walked to the right gorge and shaded her eyes, peering out toward the long, flat island. "Lots of ghosts out there," she said. "Over here too. I just felt a breath tickling my cheek."

"My gosh, I felt it too," Koko said. "That wasn't the breeze I felt."

Libby put a hand on her arm. "Don't worry, they won't bother you. They are ghosts of a time when women were put on pedestals and cherished. You must be sensitive to spirits."

"I've always thought so."

"That doesn't happen to everybody but I feel it all the time. I'll be out here on the wall and suddenly I'll get a feeling someone's here with me . . . as if he's just touched me or tried to whisper some mysterious thing in my ear. What about you two? You feel anything just then?"

Erin shook her head and Libby gave me a penetrating look. "I never feel anything," I said. "I never think, I barely believe in people, and I let ghosts alone."

"Shame on you. If there are spirits anywhere, how could they not be here? I feel a constant connection with the men who died here. . . . Here comes Luke, you're saved by the bell. I was about to break into lecturitis profundis of a kind that's not covered on the tour."

He came toward us from the left face, walking briskly along the edge of the wall. All his reticence from Saturday seemed gone and he greeted us warmly. "Good to see you," he said, shaking hands. "Libby's been awaiting your arrival nervously, to say the least."

"Oh, stop. That's not nerves, I'm just overworked. Too much to do, too little time."

I introduced Erin and Luke shook her hand. "Glad you're here. The more the merrier."

"I've got to go down for a while," Libby said. "Got a little housekeeping to do and a few last *t*'s to cross before I turn in my paper tomorrow. Luke will show you around, give you the lay of the land. Pay attention, people, it gets dark here when the sun goes down."

"It gets very dark, even on a clear night," Luke said. "I've got a hunch tonight'll be cloudy again. In any case, watch where you step. We don't want any broken legs."

He walked us around the ruin as the afternoon waned. We went through dark catacombs under the walls, and he told us what each

of them had been. When we climbed back to the top, the tour boat
was well out in the harbor.

"There she goes," he said. "You're officially stuck here till
tomorrow."

Luke suggested a look through the museum while he did a few
chores. "That's probably where you'll throw down your bags
tonight. Last summer we had a fellow who was writing a book and
that's where he slept, on the ramp in front of the original battle
flag."

We spent the next two hours playing tourist, looking at old uni-
forms and muskets, minié bullets and bayonets, reading exhibit
plaques. When we emerged the sky was dark gray in the east, with a
thin streak of purple just above the western horizon. The setting sun
broke over James Island, casting the harbor in a kind of eerie velvet
light. Most of the boats had gone in now, and far away the church
spires of the city were barely visible. I figured we still had some twilight time, and while I could see I walked off and made my own tour
of the walls and the ruins around them. I walked along the gorge
wall and stood where the original sally port had been. The wall
dropped to a height of a dozen feet; below was a tiny beachhead,
and straight ahead water flowed through the channel to the sea as
the tide went out. A lone boat was still out on the water, cutting
across the harbor in a slow arc maybe half a mile away: a skiff under
power, with a canopy covering and three or four shadowy people on
board. The sun cast its last orange rays across the water and I saw a
glint from something—maybe a smoke being lit, maybe a light being
tested or a tool being used on some sudden trouble. Maybe binocu-
lars. I didn't know what it was, but I stood still and just watched it.

After a while Koko came up beside me and we tried to find the
city, all but invisible in the deepening dusk. "So," she said. "What
are we going to do and how are we going to do it?"

I watched the boat turn in toward the city and I made a few

gruntlike thinking noises. At last I said, "My hunch is we'll have to level with them. Mrs. R. may have some information but she's like you, she's cautious about who gets it."

"I can't speak for her, but for once I shall try to behave myself."

"That would be good. I don't want you clobbering me before we get on an even keel with her. We've got a few things on our side if we play it right."

"Give me a *for instance* and maybe I'll feel better."

"She knows that we know about Charlie but she may not know much more than his name," I said. "She was fishing pretty hard. She wants what we've got."

"Whatever that is. But you're still just guessing, and if she doesn't know anything more than that, what good will she do us?"

"It may help a lot if she'll tell us where she got that name. Maybe what she knows makes sense only when you put it with what we know. I think she's got a hunch, just like me. That's why she saved the Charlie card till the very end on Saturday, and that's why she was standing on the pier waiting for us. She acts self-confident but I think she'd have been heartbroken if we hadn't been there."

"You're reading way more into her than I would. I still don't know how much we need to tell her."

"You get what you give, Koko. I think we should level with her— tell her who Charlie was and where he came from, how Josephine turned up in your life and later in mine. If she asks us a question, answer it. Don't dangle carrots in front of her, let's just tell her what we know and try to establish some camaraderie."

"That's giving away a lot on a wing and a prayer."

"But she can't do anything with it without us, and without her we're back on first base. She strikes me as a straight shooter."

"All right, I'll shut up and follow your lead. Your track record with her so far has been a lot better than mine."

The boat in the harbor had come to a dead stop, drifting now with no obvious destination. "What're you looking at so hard?" Koko said, and I told her I was just wondering if those people were in any kind of trouble. Impulsively I put an arm over her shoulder and hugged her hard, as if I could squeeze all the pain out of her unhappy life. I felt her tremble and she looked away, shunning any kind of sentiment as always. I said, "How ya doin' these days, Koke?" and I squeezed her hand. She said, "I'm fine, you fool, why wouldn't I be?" I hugged her again and she laughed up at me. "I'm fine, dammit, go away, leave me alone." I followed her around the point, pestering. "Talk to me," I said, and she gave in with a sigh. "What do you want me to say, how glad I am to know you? I'm glad I know both of you, okay? Does that make you happy? No matter how it all turns out, I'm not sorry it happened. Is that good enough?" I hugged her again and said, "Yeah, Koko, that's good enough for today."

She walked away and I lingered for a moment, watching the boat in the harbor. There was no real need to worry about those guys, whoever they were, but I worried anyway, in a distant, passive kind of way.

Now in the last moments of daylight Luke and Libby came out to take down the flags. We all gathered on the right flank, where the string of flags represented Union and Confederate forces of the 1860s and the state of South Carolina, with the big modern U.S. flag in the center. Luke lowered the American flag and Libby snapped to attention with a crisp salute. Erin, Koko, and I watched from one side. Carefully they folded the flags, Libby draped them over her arms, and we started back toward their tiny apartment as the last of the sun vanished in the west.

"Time to eat," Libby said gaily. "Who wants the great white shark fin?"

Their room looked smaller than ever with all of us crowded inside. In fact, it wasn't much bigger than the utility room of a modern house, and we scattered our sleeping bags, still rolled and tied, and made good use of the floor. We lounged wherever there was a vacant

spot while Libby cut greens and made a salad. Erin said, "I won't
even offer to help, I'd just get in your way," and Libby smiled her
appreciation. The time for niceties was at hand. Erin said how awful
she felt that we hadn't brought anything but Libby dismissed that
with a wave. "Totally understandable. You didn't think you were
coming to dinner, you came to visit a national monument. Who
brings food to something like that?" Luke said, "We'll come to Denver sometime and you can treat us like royalty," and Erin said, "I'll
stop feeling bad if you'll make me a solemn promise to do that." We
were in the first stages of feeling one another out, strangers trying to
find a comfortable meeting ground.

"Take off your jacket and get comfortable," Luke said. "It gets
warm in here."

But I kept the jacket, preferring the heat to the necessity of trying
to explain the gun I wore under it. We broke some ice, literally and
conversationally. Nothing was said in these early moments about
Burton or the quest that had brought us there. Once Libby caught
my eye and held it for a moment, as if she knew that whatever was
coming would be largely between her and me. I sensed it on her
mind, but the moment passed in a lighthearted comment from Luke,
leaving the Burton topic to find itself as the night deepened. First
came the matter of getting acquainted. We four laughed as if we
were old college classmates, and Koko watched us like a dorm
mom, quietly amused from a chair by the door.

Luke was from Minnesota; Libby had been an army brat who
happened to finish high school in St. Paul. They had defied her
father's attempt to rule her life, had married six years ago and joined
the National Park Service as a pair. In their Charleston assignment
they had found themselves liberals in a land of hot-blooded segre-
gationists, John Birchers, crackers, and rednecks. "That's how
Libby sees 'em," Luke said.

"Not true," she said. "I'm the first to tell you there are lovely
people here."

"As long as nobody talks race, religion, politics, or anything real.

People here think Libby's a communist. She meets the conservatives coming around the other side. They only avoid bloodletting because, one hundred thirty years after the Civil War, they still think of them-selves as knights with pretty young women."

"This man is a sexist pig," she said behind her hand. "That remark does nothing but reduce me to some sexual airhead."

"I'm only talking about what they think, sweetheart. These old birds like nothing better than reforming a young liberal woman. The better-looking she is, the more they enjoy straightening her out."

"How do I stand him?" she said to the wall.

We commiserated with serious looks, there was more light ban-ter, and in a while the food was ready. We ate with the door pushed open, watching the interior of the fort go from gray to black to really black. Still nothing had been said about Burton, but the night was young, our cautious probing seemed reasonable and our reti-cence proper. Libby smiled at me fleetingly, again her eyes said it would come when it came, and I hoped my own attitude conveyed no need for hurry. I strived for nonchalance: we were in Charleston, after all, where civilized society always came before business.

It was Luke who brought up the topic almost an hour later. "Lib's an honor student," he said. "She's writing a paper on Fort Wagner. She wanted to do Burton, except—"

"Except there's no Burton to be done," Libby said. "I wouldn't want to turn in a paper full of hot air, would I? I could kiss my hon-ors good-bye then."

"Maybe it isn't just hot air," I said.

"Yeah, but *maybe* won't cut it. Look, I know Burton was here. I've got no tangible proof of that, but I know it in my heart. Even if he was here, I don't know if he did anything but drink, chase women, and watch boats on the harbor. It's all speculation, and aca-demics tend to depreciate that. For me to make any use of it I've got to know where he was and when, most of all why. They'll want to see footnotes and references, some proof that I haven't been stealing my stuff from all their favorite old historians. If I could pin Burton down with new data, they'd sit up and take notice, but it looks like I'll have to rehash those gallant black soldiers of the Fifty-fourth. I won't get extra credit for a single original thought, but I do have a few new diaries, a few sources that haven't been quoted to death. And that's a story that never loses its appeal."

She looked at me suddenly and said, "So what've you got for me that I can use in this academic quagmire?"

"We know who Charlie was."

"That's a good start," she said brightly.

"Proving he was here with Burton is the tough part."

"This will amaze you but I'm in exactly the opposite place. I don't know who he was, but I know he was here, and Burton was here with him."

"Still, there's no proof."

"Nothing that would change history. But I didn't just pull the name Charlie out of thin air, either." She stared me into the woodwork, all kidding aside. "You show me yours and I'll show you mine."

"That seems fair enough."

Behind me I heard Koko cough. I said, "First maybe we should try to figure out what the whole story might be and who gets to write it."

"That's a novel approach." Libby glanced at Koko. "You're writing a book, I take it."

"I've compiled some data," Koko said. "Any book that comes out of it would be based on the memoir of an old woman who died recently. It's actually her book."

"Do I get to know who this woman was?"

"Charlie's granddaughter."

"Oh, wow." A smile lit up her face. "Sounds like you've actually done a lot of work on it. The last thing you'll want is to get scooped by a college student. And to be asked to contribute to the scooping, what an indignity that would be."

"At the same time," I said, "you'll need it—"

"—nailed down tight. So where does that leave us?"

"Maybe we could give you enough for your paper," Koko said. "And still leave me what I need for Josephine's book."

"Thank you but I doubt it. My paper is of the moment and it sounds like your book will be on the fire for some time to come. If I write a word of this, people will be all over it. And they'll demand to know where to look for corroboration before they give me any credit at all."

"Wouldn't do 'em much good. They're not gonna find this in any archive."

"Meaning what?"

"I've got possession of the tapes and transcripts. And there are no other copies."

"But if you can't make your sources public, what good is it?"

"It'll all come out in due time."

"Way too late for me, it sounds like. How do you know this is real?"

"Good Lord, hon, that's what we're chasing all over creation trying to do."

"How close are you to verifying it?"

"Pretty close," I said. "Close and yet so far."

"Well, at some point we'll have to trust each other," Libby said. "We are honorable people, you know. If we give you our word, we'll live up to it."

"At least that's what my uncle Dick Nixon always said," said Luke.

"But I'll have to know it all," Libby said. "Everything you've got."

This was met by silence as we considered what she was saying.

"I can't write anything unless I know everything," she said.

We ate quietly for a few minutes. I could almost hear the wheels turning in her head.

"Surely you understand that," she said.

"Of course," Erin said unexpectedly. "For your paper to be valid,

it's got to be based on source material that's open to public exami-
nation. Or at least available long enough for somebody with impec-
cable credentials to verify that it's real."

"I don't know any other way. They'd certainly demand to see
what it comes from."

"There might be another source—a more conclusive one—at
some point."

Libby just looked and waited. Cautiously, Erin said, "There's a
journal."

"As in a journal kept by Richard Burton? In the master's own
hand, do I dare hope?"

Erin said yes with her eyes.

Libby took a deep breath. "What might the master have said in
such a thing?"

"We hope it would confirm what Koko has on tape. We don't
have possession yet."

"Sounds like you intend to get it, though."

Erin shrugged. "Even if we do, it belongs to another party. It
would be up to him what and if anything gets released. It's totally
his call."

"This gets better and better, doesn't it?"

"He's a decent guy, I can vouch for that. My guess is . . ."

"Yes?"

She shook her head. "That's crazy. I can't go there, not till I speak
with him. I've already said more than I should."

"Well then," Libby said. "How about some ice cream?"

We ate our ice cream and thought some more. Finally Erin said,
"Look, if anything's going to get done here tonight, you'll have to
trust each other at least this far. Agree that nothing coming from the
other party, either directly or as follow-up, gets used without that
party's permission. And go from there."

"You talk like a lawyer."

"Oh, please, don't hold that against me."

"What do we do, sign our names in blood?"

"I'd suggest shaking hands and taking each other at our word."

"That's not very lawyerly advice." Libby paused, then said, "I'm okay with it."

"Koko?"

"Sure," she said in an unsure voice.

I said, "As a demonstration of good faith, we'll go first," and I launched into the tale before anyone could have second thoughts. I told them how Josephine had come into my bookstore, how I had met Erin at the home of a Denver judge, and how Koko had been involved in Baltimore long before any of us. I told her how the old lady had died and of the deathbed promise I had given her. I left out the death of Denise, the Baltimore mob connection, and the facts of Archer's beating.

"Oh wow," Libby said again. "You've done a lot more on it than I have."

I shrugged, and the moment stretched.

Suddenly she said what I hoped she'd say. "I'll give you my part, for whatever it's worth. Use it if you can. If you can find a way to share it, that would be lovely."

She poured coffee. "I told you how I heard about the Burton club when I first came here, and about Rulon Whaley, the old man I met who thought Burton was a spy. Rulon was a true Charleston eccentric, but he had a forceful way of making me believe him. He told me about a photographer on East Bay Street who had taken a picture of two men in May 1860."

"Burton and Charlie," Koko said excitedly. "How'd he know it was them?"

"Long ago—forty years at least—he bought a bunch of papers at an estate liquidation. Ledgers, records, mostly junk. There was also some personal correspondence, but no one had ever attached any importance to it. Just old letters between obscure, forgotten people, that's what anyone would think, looking at it. Rulon was then in his late twenties, just starting his law practice, but he had already read everything on Burton, and there was one letter that haunted him all his life. It had been written at the beginning of the Civil War by a young man to a former classmate. Apparently they had been best pals in school, and the fellow who wrote the letter was trying desperately to be a photographer.

"He was having a hard time of it. He was poor and the equipment was expensive. He was young, no one took him seriously, and photography itself was suspicious to a lot of people then. He had borrowed money from his friend to buy a camera and he was trying his best to get established, making portraits when he could get people to sit for him, shooting street scenes, whatever he could do to improve himself.

"One day the two men appeared. One was dapper-looking, the other . . . well, you could tell he had been around in the world. They had their picture made on East Bay Street. He remembered it because the worldly one had terrible scars on his cheeks. I've done a little photography, enough to know that's the kind of thing you look for, something that sets off a face and makes it unforgettable. I don't remember the exact date but I've got it written down, even to the time of day when the picture was made."

"It was noon," I said. "The sun was too bright and the photographer fussed over it. And Burton got impatient and almost walked away."

"Yes! How did you know that?"

"It's on my tapes," Koko said. "Jo's family had a copy of that picture but it got lost. We tried but we couldn't find any evidence of a photographer on that stretch of street."

"That's because he never had a real place of business. He was living with his sister and her husband, people named Kelleher, and even that was just for a short time. I think he was only there for a month. I doubt if he ever had more than a hand-printed sign stuck in the window. By June, Kelleher had thrown him out."

"Kelleher was the dentist," Koko said.

"He was a dentist, and his wife was named Stuyvessant," Libby said. "The photographer was nicknamed Barney—Barney Stuyvessant. He was just a kid on fire with the artistic possibilities of the camera. Rulon gave me the letter when he knew he was dying."

Erin said, "And just from that your friend was convinced Burton had been here."

"Sure. How many men have scars like that? Rulon had already read everything about Burton, so yes, that's the first thing he thought when he read Barney's letter. He knew Burton was in the country then. He knew about the blank period that Burton's biographers had never been able to pin down. He knew Burton had come through the South. And over time his belief grew stronger, even when there was nothing to back it up. That's how he was."

"So this is where we are," I said. "Koko has a lot of anecdotal material on tape, which no academic or publisher would accept on its face value. You have a photographer's letter, which seems to back us up, but it's still not enough. And Erin has a lead on a journal that might solve everybody's problem."

"There's one other thing," Libby said. "I've seen the picture."

This was a stunning announcement, which she had saved for the last, but she gave it to us with a dismissive wave of her hand. "Poor Barney Stuyvesant had a miserable jerk for a brother-in-law and then had his life cut short to boot. He might have been an important early photographer, but he went into the Confederate Army in 1861 and was killed at Bull Run in July that year. His sister apparently had possession of his records, papers, letters, and books as well as his original glass plates. She had believed in him all her life, but she died in childbirth in 1862, and Kelleher got rid of all that stuff.

"I don't know what happened to it in the years after the war. Sometime in the 1960s it surfaced in a North Charleston junkshop. Rulon heard about it and went to see it. The man only wanted five hundred for everything: my God, those glass plates alone were a steal at that price, but Rulon was one of those maddening people who never paid the asking price for anything. He certainly could afford it, but he just had to dicker and the fellow got offended. What happened next depends on what you want to believe. Rulon either walked or was thrown out and had second thoughts almost at once. But he had a huge ego, he hated to admit he'd been wrong, and by the time he got back there two weeks later, the junkman had sold it to someone else. And was just delighted to tell him about it."

"Who bought it?"

"A fellow named Orrin Wilcox, who was traveling through town. He was a . . ." She looked at Luke. "What was it he called himself? A booksmith, a booksomething, I can't remember."

"A bookscout," I said.

"That's it. A junkman by another name: someone who deals primarily in books but knows about letters and photographs as well. An eccentric man."

"Many of them are."

"By then I was determined to follow it to the end. I tracked him to Charlotte, where he has the most incredibly cluttered bookstore I have ever seen. It wasn't even a bookstore in the normal sense of the word: it was like a cave of books that went back and back through I don't know how many rooms, all so crowded with stuff that you could barely move. You got the feeling if you pulled one book out the whole building would tumble down. No place for a claustrophobic. But I went up there and saw this stuff. I had some notion that I was on the verge of a major discovery. Maybe I was, but we'll never know that now, will we?"

"What happened?"

"I scraped together some money and I left Luke here to mind the store, then I caught a bus for North Carolina. I found Mr. Wilcox with no trouble at all. He was a gnarled little man, very old, very crotchety, so cantankerous I didn't know what might set him off. But he let me in and for a while we got on reasonably well. I thought I was playing it so cool, but when we got down to brass tacks I got a bit spooked. I asked if he still had the Barney Stuyvessant archive and he said, 'Whaddaya think I did with it, dearie, threw it out with the blinkin' trash?' I told him I was looking for a picture I had heard might be in there, just a street scene with two men in it, and right away he said, 'Charlie 'n' Dick.'

"I couldn't believe it. I felt my heart turn over. I said, 'Oh yes!' and he got this evil grin on his face and said I should follow him. Back we went into the cave, all the way into a far back room. It was just like the rest of the place—oh, Janeway, you have no idea."

"Actually, I do."

"Well, there the stuff was—boxes and boxes of glass plates. I guess he'd long ago sold off the books but the plates were all there, piled in wooden boxes, one on top of another. He found the one I wanted right away. The original label was still on it—Barney had marked each one with a piece of adhesive or some kind of old tape and it was identified in his own hand. The writing said, *Charlie and Dick on East Bay.* He had taken down only their first names and that's the title he had given it. The date on it was still legible, May something, 1860. Old Wilcox held it up to the lightbulb and said, 'That look like what you want?' And I came a hell of a lot closer than I wanted to come, we stood side by side with our arms almost touching, and I looked up at the image and there they were, in negative, Charlie and Dick, and even on the negative I could make out those shadows on Burton's cheeks, and behind them was the Exchange Building. I'd know that anywhere, in positive, negative, or CinemaScope. And I said, 'Yeah, that's it,' and I tried to keep my heartbeat from knocking us both down, but when I looked in his face he had a grin that was almost cadaverous. I could see his skull right through the skin, and he grinned and said, 'Bet you'd like a picture of that, wouldn't you, honey?' I said, 'I'd be happy to pay you for one,' and he said, 'Only a thousand dollars to you, sweetie.'"

She looked a little sick now, recalling it. "I know that doesn't sound like much, but it was out of the question. There's just no way we could have done that."

She shrugged. "Maybe you can."

We talked some more and retired just before eleven o'clock. By then
we all had a good sense of each other and they made a serious
pledge to visit us in Colorado. "Maybe we'll even get lucky and be
assigned there," Luke said. "I always wanted to work in the mountains, at Mesa Verde or Rocky Mountain National Park." I told
them my house would always be their house, and I promised Libby
I would keep her informed as the Burton story developed. We called
it a night and walked the few feet to the museum, where the three of
us would bed down on the floor. Outside, the night was oppressively
murky: inky, bleak, black-hole dark, with a stout wind that came at
us in gusts off the sea. The sky was cloudy: only a small streak of
stars could be seen through a seam across the top of the world, but
that did nothing to relieve the blackness of the harbor. Charleston
was nowhere to be seen, lost in some distant fog.

I stood at the door and heard Erin say my name.

"Hey, you coming?"

"Yeah, I'll be along. You two go ahead."

They went inside and I got out my flashlight and climbed along
the edge of the battery toward the gorge wall. I thought I'd heard
the sound of a boat again, and I wanted to give things a last look
before turning in. I had no real reason to be uneasy or suspicious:
Dante would have to be crazy to mount an assault on Fort Sumter
with rangers on duty, and guys like Dante don't stay alive by being
fools. But that's what old Judge Petigru said about the secessionists
of olden days, that South Carolina was too small for a republic and
too large for a lunatic asylum, and look what happened anyway. My

uneasiness persisted and grew as I moved around the battery above the black ruins.

Whatever I had heard, it was gone now: nothing but the wind assaulted my ears, that and the sea washing against this ghostly black shoal. I still wasn't satisfied. I wanted to stand at the edge of the fort and behold the nothingness, and that meant I had to go down through the old parade ground and pick my way back up to the right flank where the high ground was. From there I had a sweeping view: more pitch-blackness than I could ever remember in my life. I circled the old wall, keeping my light pointed down in front of me, and at last I came to the point where I turned off the light and just stood there. Nothing . . .

Nothing.

Except for the wind, this must be what death is like.

I walked along the gorge and down the left flank. From there I could see into the tiny room where Libby and Luke were talking, washing dishes, putting things away. It floated in space and a few minutes later she drew a curtain across the front window. Almost at once their light went out.

I turned back toward the channel, feeling rather than seeing it. Morris Island, I thought: Fort Wagner. In that void it was hard to imagine what had happened over there: one of the great epics of warfare, overshadowed by Vicksburg only because that involved greater numbers and grander strategy and bigger names, and because it was coming to its climax at the same time. I stared at the nothing and closed my eyes, which made no difference at all, and when I opened them I seemed to see the flash of a very old rocket against the eastern sky. Just for a moment I imagined that battle and all those black warriors charging up the beach to certain death.

I thought of death . . .

Thought of Denise . . .

And strangest of all in that time and place, I thought of Dean Treadwell and his unshakable faith in everybody's bastard, Hal Archer.

Dean and Hal . . .

I thought the unthinkable and I shivered in the wind.

I picked my way back across the ruins to the battery. Erin stood at the museum door, waiting.

"What are you doing? I was just about to come looking for you."

"Without a light? You're smarter than that."

"Never mind the light. What's going on out there?"

"Nothing. Go to bed."

She bristled at my abruptness. "Is this how it's going to be, being your special friend?"

"I don't know. We've got forty days and forty nights to resolve stuff like that."

"Thirty-eight as of this morning. This doesn't bode well for us to make it to thirty-seven."

I felt her come close in the half-light. I saw her in shadow.

"I want to get this thing resolved," she said. "It's not in my nature to live like this, worrying about a madman every waking moment."

"I intend to resolve it."

"How?"

"How I should've done in the first place. A little grit, a little steel, a little help from an old friend."

"Okay," she said calmly. "Whatever that means, I want to be in on it all the way."

"I don't need an attorney for this kind of work."

That was a stupid thing to say, I knew it almost before the words were out, and she reacted as if she'd been slapped. She slammed me back against the wall and whirled away down the ramp. "Well, fuck you, Mr. Janeway."

"Hey, Erin, wait a minute."

She stopped and looked back.

"That didn't come out right."

"It sure didn't, you barbarian son of a bitch."

"I'm sorry." I reached out to her.

She gestured wildly with her hands. "Jesus Christ, you are such an idiot sometimes."

"I am, I am." I made a helpless shrugging dipshit motion. "I know I am."

"Goddamn male chauvinist turkey-farmer dickhead. What am I going to do with you?"

"Whatever you want. As long as you don't—"

"If I don't what?"

"Leave."

She seemed to melt and flow back up the ramp. She wrapped her arms around me and I buried my fingers in her thick hair.

"Are we okay now?" I dared ask.

"I don't like being brushed off. Chisel that on your brain if you can find a tool hard enough. Write *Erin hates being patronized, Erin won't sit still for the little girl treatment.*"

"I'm sorry. I'm beginning to sound like a broken record but I really, really am sorry."

"Okay, where were we?" she said cheerfully.

"I was about to say something practical. How this is a man's job and a woman never does anything but screw up a mission."

"And I said something uncalled for. 'Fuck you, Janeway,' or something like that."

"You've really got a nasty streak that I never saw before. Your vocabulary is amazing."

"Actually, I never swear in real life. Bad language is just bad manners, it's a symptom of a bankrupt mind. Lee taught me that when I was a kid and I still believe it. But you, you pigheaded medieval-godfather cocksman, you bring out the absolute worst in me."

"Am I not getting through here? I thought I groveled, whined, and said I was sorry. 'Medieval-godfather cocksman!' 'Turkey-farmer dickhead!' I thought Koko was tough, but I never got past 'poopy old picklepuss' with her."

"Koko is a lady. I, unfortunately, am not. So who is this hit man we're going to hire?"

I told her in general terms who, what I wanted him to do, and why he'd do it—not for money but to clear a debt that was decades old. "He's just gonna be my insurance policy," I said. "If there is such a thing for this kind of stuff."

Suddenly she realized I was serious. "Does this guy have a name?"

I almost said I'd take care of it but I thought much better of that and I gave her his name.

"Oh God," she said. "Oh my dear. You do have some bad friends."

"Yeah. He was like my brother long ago. People were sure I'd end up just like him."

"No way could you have been like that."

"You might sing a different tune if you had known me when I was fifteen. It was amazing, really, that I lived all that down. Became a cop."

"And you literally saved his life?"

"As literal as it gets."

"Tell me again what we're going to have him do."

"He's gonna help us teach a certain bad-ass some manners, like Lee taught you but with different powers of persuasion. And I hope with better results."

"Generally speaking, I like the sound of that," she said without much enthusiasm.

"You'll like this even better. I've been thinking about it for a while now and I've finally come to a couple of ugly conclusions. We've gone too far to slip into some live-and-let-live detente, like two bully nations in a cold war, even if that option suddenly became possible. Maybe I'd be okay with a standoff if he hadn't torched Koko's house, but that's not an option anymore. Now there's got to be an evening-up of the score. I can't just walk away from here and make like none of this ever happened. I've thought about it; can't do it."

"What would satisfy you, she asked in fear and trembling."

"If Dante were to build Koko a new house, that might square it. I don't know, I'd have to think about it."

When she spoke again it seemed like a long time had passed. "You must be mad."

"I'm damned mad."

"I meant mad as in crazy."

"That too."

"He'll never do that."

"He might." I put an arm over her shoulder. "A guy like Dante only understands one thing. But he really understands that."

"He didn't understand it the first time."

"He understood it, he just didn't quite believe it. My fault; something about my performance must've been lacking. Maybe because, no matter how big a bad-ass I tried to be, at the bottom line it was still just a performance. Those guys have a way of knowing."

"It's got to be real."

"Oh yeah."

"So now it's real. You would kill him."

"In a Hungarian heartbeat. But don't tell Koko yet; I don't want her to get her hopes up in case it doesn't work out that way."

Suddenly she seemed to change the subject. "Do you remember the night we met?"

"Are you kidding? That was one of my all-time high spots."

"Do you remember what I said?"

"How could I forget? Among other things, you called me a wimp."

"I never said that. I only wondered innocently how you'd have done in Burton's shoes."

"I tried to tell you. All I got for my trouble was ridicule and the rolling-eyes routine."

"Tell me now."

"I'd have leaped up from my stretcher and shaken off the fever, found the big lake, made a map that even the Royal Geographic Society couldn't challenge, left Speke dead in the hot sun, raced home and claimed the glory I should have had all along. So what's your point?"

"There is no point. Except maybe I love you." She rose on her toes and kissed me fiercely. "I guess that's my point."

"It's a good one. Maybe now it won't hurt so much . . . you know, when we all die together."

37

Inside, we planned our next move. Erin and Koko had put their bags near the bottom of the museum ramp. Koko had hung her clothes over the rail and crawled into her bag, and she watched us sleepily from the floor, occasionally piping in with an opinion while the two of us stood there and talked. We all hated to quit Charleston with Burton's journal still in limbo. Erin wanted another try at Archer on her way out of town, but that struck me as risky with little to be gained. "Something might well be gained," she said, "if Archer told us what happened to the journal." At this point I had to doubt if Archer had ever planned to produce Burton's journal, no matter how much money Lee was able to throw at him—he had come up empty, with new conditions or half-baked reasons to stall, every time. Erin couldn't believe that. "Lee has done nothing but defend Archer and praise him to the rooftops. What would Archer gain by taunting his oldest friend? What would be the point if he's not going to sell us the book anyway? Now he's alienated Lee, they can't even speak to each other, and what good does that do him?"

Well, Archer was a prick: at least we could all agree on that. "Maybe he's secretly hated Lee all these years for being born with a silver spoon in his mouth," I said. There were plenty of precedents both in history and literature for such unholy relationships. One party is undercut and sabotaged for years without ever dreaming that his so-called friend is behind it all. If that were true, the only mystery, aside from the enigmas of a black heart, was why Archer would let his secret out now instead of any other time. Koko said, "Maybe Lee found out what Archer really thinks and Archer no longer had any reason to hide it." Erin shook her head. "No, I'm sure Lee would've told me that." Since we were into wild ideas, it was also possible that Archer had never had the book at all, or maybe Dante had taken it from him if he had. But if Dante now had it, he'd probably have been on the first flight back to Baltimore. He'd want to dispose of the goods first, get what money there was to get, and settle old scores later. So I thought, with no facts to go on, but at that point I wasn't sure enough to bet on anything.

Erin hated to give up on Archer. "I'll do it your way but I don't want to forget why I was sent here. I would still feel better if I could see him once more, even if he doesn't do anything but have me thrown out again." What worried me about this was that the hospital was such an obvious place for someone to set up a watch and catch us coming or going. I had plans for Dante, but I wanted them to unfold on my timetable, not his: I needed to live long enough to put them in motion and see how they went. In the end we were all just talking. Always in the back of my mind was the possibility that Dante knew exactly where we were, and whatever was going to happen would be on his schedule after all.

Our only hard decision was that we were done with Charleston: there was nothing more for us to find here. If things went well and we could get away in the morning without being seen, I had at least some reason for optimism. We'd retrieve my rental car and head north to Florence; from there to Charlotte, and on to Denver. Koko didn't see why she needed to go to Denver. "We've got to stick together for now," I said, and Denver was my home base. "You can stay with me," Erin said, "as long as you need to." "Good," I said. If we made it that far, I had to feel good about our prospects. Then I could go on offense. We left it at that and I went back up to the entryway where I had stashed my sleeping bag.

The sight of it gave me no craving for sleep. I was in one of those dark moods, bone-tired but still wide awake, and for a long time I sat outside on the edge of the battery with my legs dangling, watching the sky and listening to the air. I thought of Libby and I under-

stood how she could come to love this place. Ultimately it would
get on my nerves—I am too much a product of my time and this is
undoubtedly one of my failings, among many. I can go like Erin on
long sabbaticals in the mountains, but at some point cabin fever
sets in and I need to hunker down in civilization's dirty places, go
book hunting around the fringes of Denver, talk to someone, mix
it up with crazies, go to a party of book lovers at Miranda's, or just
sit in a bar with an old pal. My life went from the nearest pockets
of the sublime to the most distant reaches of the ridiculous, and I
didn't know if that was my ideal or if I could even guess what an
ideal was. But in any other time, in limited doses, I would love it
here.

A rumble of thunder sounded far away in the east, but soon it got
quiet again, with only the wind and the sea in my ears. I closed my
eyes and at some point I found myself thinking of Vince Marranzino. Vinnie: that told me how long ago our mutual history had
been. He didn't seem like a Vinnie to me. That sounded too much
like a gangster's nickname, and no matter how much I had learned
about him via newspapers and our own departmental intelligence, I
still thought of him as a kid named Vince, not a Vinnie-hood. I
heard his voice out there with the ghosts of Battery Wagner: *How do
ya really like this book racket of yours, Cliffie?* Just a wisp of him
there in the harbor, then he was gone. A whisper to the wisp: that's
all it would take and a man would die in Baltimore.

I took out my notebook and wrote a short message: *Hey Vince.
Go see a man named Dante in Baltimore and we are all squared up
in the hereafter.* Vince would understand, and I could die knowing
that if I had to.

I folded the sheet and wrote his name on the outside. I put in his
Osage Street address and put the paper in my shoe. Once the probes
and the postmortems were over, the cops would see that he got the
message.

If Dante got to me, he'd be killing himself.

"Now it's real," I said to nobody.

* * *

I lay in my sleeping bag outside the museum door and stared at that crack in the sky. It was beginning to fuzz over now as the cloud cover fattened and spread. I felt a drop of rain, thought I should move inside, but I only moved deeper into my bag. Sleep was impossible but that didn't matter. Once we were in the car heading north, Erin could drive and I'd catch up then.

I thought these things and the time was heavy. At some point I fell asleep, but not for long. I am good with time and I opened my eyes knowing it was somewhere near three o'clock. I wiggled out of my bag and sat up straight. Some noise, some fleeting thing out there where the wind blew, had wafted around my head. It had shifted from an easterly blow to southwesterly, and suddenly I felt an alarm go off under my heart. I told myself it was nothing but that hunch; not even the sound I thought I had heard had any true substance or source in this black world. My practical nature said I had been dreaming, that's all it was, I had come out of the dream thinking of Dante and those guys in the boat, there was no reason to make that connection, it was just a case of nerves. But it wouldn't go away, and now I got completely out of the bag and stood on my tiptoes looking out toward Morris Island.

Dante. I saw his face swirling through the dark in various shades of clarity. He was certainly insane, and that, combined with his other charms, made him far more dangerous than any thug I had ever faced as a cop. I had humiliated him in front of his men—that was another part of the case against me—and I had done a lot of damage to his face. His bruises would look worse day by day until they began to get better, and by then it wouldn't matter anymore. After a week of staring at his own black-and-blue face in the mirror, who could tell how crazy he'd be? He would have a score to settle and in his mind there could be none bigger, ever, and the longer it went unresolved the angrier and more dangerous he would be. This was strictly a guess: How reckless could he be? What was he going to do, scale the wall and kill everyone on this island just to get me? That would be the act of a real madman, but it wouldn't be the first time such a thing had happened. It depended on the depth of his hate versus the degree of his own survival instinct. I fiddled with a mathematical formula—Dead Janeway equals Perp's Survival over Perp's Hate squared. Maybe by now his hate would be at the fourth or fifth power, or the fiftieth power, all but obliterating even his instinct for self-preservation. In that case, anything could happen. Madmen have been known to walk into certain death to get at the object of their loathing. Dante would have covered himself as well as possible, and maybe that would be enough. Who else knew of his connection to us? There would be half a dozen cronies back in Baltimore who'd line up and swear that he had never left town, he had been there among them, having dinner in full view of a dozen witnesses, at the very moment when this strange carnage began, six or seven hundred miles away. *I had nothing to do with it,* he would say, and the cops would have the job of proving that he had. But they wouldn't have to prove it to Vinnie Marranzino, and in death I'd have my victory. A damned hollow one, but I was glad, on this side of death, that I had it.

I thought of Luke and Libby. It had never occurred to any of us that we might be putting them in danger. This is how different things can be at three o'clock in the morning.

None of this was at all likely. To be out there in a boat now would mean he had known or anticipated our every move: that he had gotten the boat and made his plans, and all this had been done from the time the Fort Sumter tour boat had arrived back at the marina in the late afternoon without us on it. Not likely, but not impossible either. Thugs like Dante know people like themselves in many towns. He may have lined up some local pal two days ago, and in this town a boat was easy to get.

I looked at the sky and saw nothing. If he was coming at all, it would be now.

I felt the uneasiness filling up my soul. I began to pace along the front of the battery, looking for something I couldn't see and listening for a sound that wasn't there.

I stood at the top of the stairs and waited.

At some point I started down. I followed my light around the battery and up to the old wall. There was a wooden barrier at the lowest point; they would have to scale it at the higher wall and come into the fort from there. I was beginning to know the way now, and I moved easily out toward the edge, keeping my light down at my feet and shaded by my hand, so it couldn't be seen from the water. Fifty yards from the gorge, I stopped and turned off the light.

I saw a soft glow out there, at the base of the wall.

Something moved. Some bump in the night. The squeak of an oar, maybe . . .

Then I heard a voice. They were out there. They had defied the odds.

I shucked my way out of my coat and got out my gun. Got down on my knees and crawled along a rough surface to the edge.

The rain began. I barely felt it.

I peeped over the edge. They were there on the little beachhead below. Four of them, and Dante had been the first to step out on land. There was no mistaking that overgrown palooka: I had his number even in the dark. He stood outlined against a dim light, then he spoke. "Come on, let's get that ladder out here, we ain't got all fuckin' day." No mistaking that nasty baritone: it was packed with authority and gave orders like other men breathe. I heard a brief metallic sound, and by the same dim light I saw an aluminum ladder being slipped hand to hand over the bow of the boat.

I could've killed them all then; they were like four fat fish in a barrel just waiting to be shot. I had the gun in my hand, why didn't I just do it? I could still get all four before any of them could clear their own guns; I had been that fast and my gut told me I still was. I could get them now. I could get them all. Their asses were mine. But at the last second, God knows why, I stayed my hand.

I knew why. I had never shot a man that way. I could kill him, but not that way.

I shrank back from the edge as the ladder bumped against the wall. Who would come over the top first? If Dante came up, my job would be easier. But my hunch told me it would be someone local, a pathfinder who could lead them across the treacherous parade ground to the place where, they thought, we'd all be happily asleep. I heard the ladder shake, saw it move in the dim glow from the boat far below. I slid back on my belly with the gun in my hand, getting very still as a head came over the edge. I had been right, it wasn't Dante. But I was sure he'd be the next one: it wasn't in his nature to take up the rear. The pathfinder came head and shoulders over the wall, a little penlight in his teeth, and in that moment I knew how it was going to go. If I was lucky, it would be a replay of Baltimore.

He turned his head and his light went right over my back. He looked down and nodded, then he came over the wall and stood up, waiting.

Again he nodded his head. *Coast is clear, boys.*

My heart was pumping like a war drum, I could feel my gun hand trembling, I could hear the blood pounding in my ears. The ladder moved: Dante was on the way up. I felt cold one second, giddy the next. I almost laughed out loud, these guys were such schmucks, in their own dumb way as stupid as those kids I had faced down on the street so long ago. I knew what was going to happen ten seconds before each move. The pathfinder would reach down and give the man a respectful hand, leaving them both vulnerable for that moment. I could push them both off the wall: I could easily get close enough to kick them out into space. It probably wouldn't be a lethal fall unless Dante landed on his ass, but it was high enough to do some real damage and at least they'd be stunned for a moment. Then perhaps they'd come up shooting, and that was my kind of action; I could kill them all then and sleep just fine tomorrow. And in the heat of that moment, I found myself actually craving it, savoring what might come.

I saw Dante clear the wall. A Confederate defender with a Whitworth rifle could've popped his thick head from a bunker a mile away on Morris Island, that's what a target he made. There was a moment: I hung back, waiting for some defining motion to egg me on. The ladder bumped again. I knew it was the third man, on his way up, and that was something I couldn't wait around for.

I stepped up beside them, still a foot back in the shadow. Both were looking over the edge: neither had a gun out and that gave me a huge advantage. I cocked my gun and even in the wind it sounded like the clap of doom. I saw them stiffen. "Don't move," I said. "I will kill you both right where you stand."

In almost the same breath the third guy began to clear the wall. He still didn't know anything had happened and his moment of clarity came slowly. He said, "Hey," and that was it, his sudden awareness in a nutshell as I kicked him in the head. He tumbled into space, clawing wildly for something to grab. I heard him hit the sand and the ladder crash over on top of him. All this time I kept my light in Dante's eyes. "You don't learn very good, do you, stupid?"

The pathfinder started to back up, away from the edge. "Wrong way, fuck-knuckle," I said, and I lifted my foot and shoved him off. He screamed, going down like I'd just pushed him off a thousand-foot cliff.

Dante and I stared at each other, primal, mortal enemies. He looked at my gun, then at me. I taunted him. I wanted him to try something.

"Come on, fatso, you're such a tough guy, come take my gun away from me."

"You'd like that. You need that excuse. You haven't got the balls to just do it."

That was his only try at bravado. I leaned into the light and said, "Is that what you think?" and in that moment I became one with the killer: whatever difference I thought had existed between us was gone now. I was going to kill him, there wasn't a shadow of doubt in my mind, and in that second he knew it too. I saw it in his face: the born intimidator who had spent his life watching people cringe had never once faced the possibility of his own death. He saw it now.

The flesh began to sag around his mouth, under his eyes. He tried to recoil but I grabbed him by the shirt and heaved him around. "You lose, asshole," I said, and I banged him in the mouth with the barrel of the gun. He let out a little cry and tried to back away, he stumbled and fell. Again I shoved the gun into that gaping mouth, bloody now where two teeth had broken off. My hand trembled: any little movement might've set it off and I didn't care.

"Wait," he said.

I rammed the gun down to his tonsils. "Wait for what?"

He gurgled out something that sounded like, "Just wait."

I leaned down close to his face. "Wait for what, asshole? Wait for what? You got something to say, say it now." I jerked the gun out of his face. "Say it now. Say it. What've you possibly got to say that I would care about?"

"We could make a deal."

"Don't make me laugh. What've you got that I want? I've got your nuts in my pocket, Dante, what can you give me for that? Give me Burton's notebook for starters. Maybe then I'll let you live another five minutes."

Suddenly he looked like a gored weasel, a rat trapped in a flooding sewer. His eyes had the same dead look as Little Caesar, who couldn't believe he was dying even in death. Mother of mercy, is this the end of Rico? Same dead eyes. Same incredulous face. I put the gun to his eyes and he shivered in what he must have expected to be his last minute on this earth.

"Are you scared, Dante?"

Even then he couldn't say it.

"Are you scared?"

His lower lip trembled. His head scrunched down between his shoulders and he closed his eyes.

"What's going on in that pea brain of yours? Is it fear? Are you scared?"

Go on, stop talking, I thought. Kill him.

For Christ's sake, stop playing around and just do it. The hell with history and notebooks, just do it. I took a deep breath. "So long, stupid . . ."

Then he cracked. It came out of him as a pathetic, whimpering sound. "Please . . . don't do this . . ."

"Please? Did you say *please?*"

I put the gun to his ear, he groaned out a "No . . . please . . ." and for the second time I backed away.

I stuck the gun in my belt. He could've made a grab for it: he didn't dare. He had never made a move for his own gun, which I now frisked away from him and threw into the sea.

I gripped his shirt and balled it up in my fist, drawing him close. "You got one last chance to live, Dante. Here's what's gonna happen. Later this morning you will get your fat ass on a plane back to Baltimore. There you will wait for further instructions. It might take a week or a month, but at some point a friend of mine will come visit. He will make damn sure you understand me this time. You are going to hurt for a long time after he sees you, but if you resist, or if you surround yourself with bodyguards and armor, it will be much, much worse. You had better listen to what he says because there won't be any more chances. I'm telling you the truth now and you'd better believe it. He will tell you what to do and he'll tell you in a way you'll never forget. You'll be told what you must do to stay alive. That's your choice, asshole. Agree or die right now."

I took out the gun and cocked it and he whimpered out a watery "Okay."

"Okay what?"

". . . Whatever . . . whatever you say."

"You got that right, Dante. Now get the hell off my fort."

I rolled him to the edge and pushed him off. He flailed away at the air and I heard him hit the ground with a mighty grunt. He rolled over desperately sucking air, all the wind knocked out of him, maybe some bones broken; I didn't know and I didn't care. I sat in the dark, cross-legged and invisible, and after a while I did peer over and I saw them loading Dante onto the boat. He looked hurt bad. They pushed away, the oar squeaking, the boat fading slowly in the early morning. They slipped out into the water and disappeared. A few minutes later I heard the motor start as they turned back toward Charleston.

38

I was still sitting there when the sun cracked over the sea. The harbor was empty at dawn, a couple of sailboats just heading out from the marina. Erin came out. I was facing the wrong way to see her, but I heard her climbing up to the wall and I knew who it was. She picked up my balled-up coat and sat beside me.

"What happened?"

"Nothing," I said. But I looked in her face and I knew I couldn't sell that and I'd better not try. "They came for us during the night. Three of them got thrown off the wall. Dante might be hurt pretty bad."

She sat down beside me. "Well," she said, and that was all for a moment.

"If this didn't discourage him . . ." I shrugged.

"Wish I could've helped you." She put an arm over my shoulder. "I slept like a baby."

"That's good."

"Cliff?"

"Yeah?"

"About us . . ."

"What about us?"

"I don't know."

We sat watching the sun, listening to the waves lap against the fort.

"What now?" she said.

"Now we go into Charleston and get our car."

"Are we still looking over our shoulders?"

"In the long run, who knows? You can never know with a guy like that." I shrugged. "I think we're safe for today at least."

"What about Archer?"

"Whatever you want. If you want to go by the hospital, fine."

She leaned against me. "That must've been some fight."

"It could've been better. I had the terrain on my side."

"Like the Confederates."

"Yeah. This old fort is still a tough place to take."

Luke came out and put up the flags. Libby watched pensively from the window.

We ate a simple breakfast with the Robinsons. I left my coat off now and I rolled up my sleeves and put the gun in my bedroll. The three of us made a final tour of Sumter, I promised Libby we'd keep in touch, and we took the morning boat back to the city.

We had the cab drop us at Roper Hospital. All of us went up together. I wasn't surprised to find Dean Treadwell sitting in the visitor's chair.

"If you've come to see Archer, he still can't talk. He's doped up and hurting pretty bad."

"I just came by to say we're leaving," Erin said. "See if anything's changed."

"As a matter of fact, yeah. He's gonna give you the book."

Her first reaction was no reaction at all. As the moment stretched, she finally said, "Really?" but she was unflappable even when news was sensational.

"Some things just ain't worth the grief, no matter how much money's involved," Dean said. "Naturally, we're hoping the judge's offer is still on the table."

"I'm sure it is. I'll call him and give you something in writing if you want."

"He doesn't think that'll be necessary."

"Tell him not to worry, then. Lee will do the right thing."

"Let's just go get it," Dean said. "We want to be rid of it."

It was like Poe's gold bug, buried in the sand on Sullivan's Island.

Archer had triple-wrapped it in plastic, put it in a metal box, stuffed the box with plastic bags, and buried it in the dry sand under his back steps.

"He had a hunch," Dean said. "Sooner or later that bozo would come after us."

I wondered why now.

"It wasn't the book. They were lookin' for you. Archer made a mistake, said the wrong thing. You know how he can be, sometimes he pops off. This time he never got a chance to say I'm sorry. They never even asked about the book."

"What if they'd killed him? Nobody'd ever know where it was."

"At that point, what did he care?"

We looked at each other in the hot noonday sun, two bookmen from different worlds, pulled together briefly by the same quest. Dean lit a smoke and I found a clumsy way of apologizing for the razzing I had given him back in town. "I've been thinking about what you said."

"I said a lot. Sometimes I say too much."

"I've been thinking about one particular thing."

I didn't have to tell him, he knew what it was. "Hal Archer's never told me a lie of any kind, not that I'm aware of. How many friends have you had that you can say that about?"

Not many, I thought. Maybe none.

He shuffled uneasily. "If that's all, let's get out of here."

Fifteen minutes later we were across the Cooper River, heading for North Charleston. None of us said a word the whole way across.

My rental was still where I'd parked it. Dean didn't offer to shake hands and neither did I. He drove out of the lot and turned back toward Charleston and a moment later we went the other way, north to Florence.

39

There were towns along every road now. There was sprawl that had never been part of any town at all. There were long fingers of commerce and drugstores and housing developments where only forests and swamps and farmlands had been in that earlier time. Then there had been occasional outposts to comfort a traveler in the wilderness; now there were motels and gas stations, Dairy Queens and Burger Kings, Piggly Wiggly and Winn-Dixie super-markets and antiques malls. There were X-rated magazine stands and gunsmiths and temples of any god a man wanted to pray to. There were places to stop and get quietly drunk or get a car fixed after a sudden breakdown. No one would ever go hungry or thirsty, get horny or spiritually deprived for more than a few minutes in any direction. What had then been a two-day trek in 1860 was two hours now in air-conditioned ease. But there were still stretches of wilderness where the pines grew thick and the way resembled noth-ing more than a tunnel with sky. Imagine this on a dirt road at night, I thought: imagine 120 miles of it. As we traveled upcountry I followed the odyssey of Richard Francis Burton and Charles Edward Warren in my head. As I slumped in the backseat reading Burton's words, I could almost see them coming down from the north, and I could still get some faint, faraway sense of what it had been.

We reached Florence in the early afternoon. From then on our journey was charmed. If anything, it was too easy.

A librarian knew right away what we were looking for. That junction where the roads had intersected was still called Wheeler's

Crossing. It was out of town a stretch and there was nothing there now. A roadside sign would show us where it had been.

The library had a number of Wheeler papers: letters, some of the old man's ledgers, even a few menus in Marion's hand. The Wheelers had all been buried in an old graveyard near the crossroad. Marion Wheeler's mother had been put there before her; her father, who had outlived them both, died in 1881. "Look at this," Koko said. "She died in childbirth, just like her mother . . . exactly nine months after Burton and Charlie would've been there. Her father made no attempt to cover it up."

Her son had lived. Her father had honored her deathbed wish, named him Richard, and raised him as his own.

Richard Wheeler. One sketchy account existed of his youth: no more than a few lines in a letter written near the end of the old man's life. His schooling, three years in a classroom, was probably average for the time. He was fair with numbers but brilliant with language. He had learned Latin on his own, becoming fluent in six months, and had been studying Spanish. He was a good and energetic dancer and girls loved him. In that passage he was described as tall and dark with a keen sense of honor.

A lady killer.

He went to sea at sixteen and that was all that was known of him.

We arrived at the site of Wheeler's inn late that afternoon. It was a bend in the road now, marked by a simple state highway sign that said WHEELER'S CROSSING. The graveyard was on a dirt road not far away. It was dusk when we found the Wheeler plots: the father and mother side by side, Marion a few feet away. The simple stone said, HERE LIES MARION WHEELER, BELOVED DAUGHTER, WHO DEPARTED THIS EARTH JANUARY 30, 1861, AGED TWENTY-FOUR YEARS, ELEVEN MONTHS, FOURTEEN DAYS. Koko took notes and in the waning light tried desperately to take pictures.

I had to pry her away.

Now for the first time she asked my opinion of Burton's journal. It looked real, I said. By then I didn't need to add the line about my own lack of expertise. Most impressive were the scores of Negro spirituals and slave songs that Burton had written down, word for word, in dialect, as he and Charlie had traveled through the South. He had filled page after page with them, adding extensive notes on where he had heard them and what he suspected their African roots might be.

There was a full account of Burton's first meeting with Charlie. It jibed with what we knew and added color to Charlie's tale. There was a detailed description of the day they went walking in Charleston. Burton had made a sketch of Fort Sumter from the Battery, and had written with fond amusement of Charlie's outrage at the slave auction. Best of all, he told of having their picture taken outside a dentist's office on East Bay Street.

We headed west into the night.

At Camden we turned north, picking up Interstate 77. From there it was a straight shot into Charlotte, but we stopped in Rock Hill, taking two rooms in a motel overlooking a river. Erin called Lee in Denver and told him the news. She called my room and suggested that we meet downstairs for a drink.

"Lee is ecstatic," she said.

"That's good," I said flatly.

"What's wrong with you? In case you hadn't noticed, we won."

I made the obvious excuse: I was tired after last night. But there was something else and she sensed it.

"It's Denise, isn't it? She's been forgotten in all this fuss."

"Not by me."

"What are you going to do about it?"

"I don't know yet. Something."

"You had your chance at Dante and let him go. Is that what's bothering you?"

"No. I told you, I'm just tired."

But it was more than that.

We turned in but I still couldn't sleep. At midnight I thought of Dean Treadwell, and for the hundredth time about his strange friendship with Archer. Again I thought the unthinkable, pushing it away at once, but it was there now and it kept me awake. I must've slept at least a few hours because I opened my eyes suddenly and knew I had been dreaming. I had dreamed of Archer and his mother Betts, and it took me a while to remember that Betts hadn't been Archer's mother at all.

In the morning we had a quiet breakfast in the café. Lee had already called Erin and they had discussed air passage. "We can get a flight to Atlanta at seven o'clock tonight. It'll be tight, but we should just make the connecting flight to Denver. Lee wants me to put all three fares on my credit card and he'll reimburse me."

"No," I said. "You cover your own, I'll take care of Koko and me."

She insisted. "Cliff, he wants to do this."

"Well, he can't."

We went into Charlotte and found Orrin Wilcox. Libby had been painfully accurate in her description of the ghoulish old bookscout and the incredible clutter of his store. He gave the impression of a guy who didn't give much of a damn about anything, but he responded eagerly enough to the sight of my money.

"I believe you quoted Mrs. Robinson a thousand dollars," I said.

"She should've taken it then. It's fifteen hundred now. I got overhead, y'know."

"Two prints," I said.

"Two-fifty for the second print. Plus lab expenses."

We went to a studio not far from his store. I wanted my continuity unbroken; I needed to keep that glass plate in my sight and see the prints being made. The photographer liked the color of my money and I stood at his side in the darkroom and watched Burton and Charlie come to life in the soup. Slowly Burton materialized . . . first the vague shape of him, then the street and a tree and some kids beyond them. Burton's scars appeared suddenly like two cuts slashed on the paper. Then came the hat, then the eyes . . . and there was Charlie beside him, the man I had never seen but had always imagined looking just about like that. The contrasts were stark, the clarity superb. They stood on the street enjoying a day long vanished but now immortalized, the affection between them almost palpable. Burton had a look of amused tolerance, Charlie one of happy friendship. Two black children stood near the palmetto tree on the walk, gawking at the photographer and his strange apparatus, and half a block away a dog was crossing the street. In the distance a horse was pulling a wagon toward us, and people were coming and going, in and out of the Exchange Building. I saw all this but my eyes kept coming back to Burton. His face was as clear as if it had been photographed only yesterday. And in his hand, draped over Charlie's shoulder, was the notebook I had just been reading.

I put one of the prints in an envelope and addressed it to Libby Robinson at Fort Sumter. A few hours later we dropped off our rental car, I paid the extra tariff, and we caught a plane for Atlanta, hoping to get on a 9:38 flight to Denver.

DENVER

The plane was crowded and we felt lucky to squeeze in from standby. Our seating was scattered: I sat three rows behind Erin, mashed against the window by a bad-tempered fat woman who sprawled across all three seats, and Koko was out of sight, somewhere near the front. Once we were in the air Erin spent ten minutes on the airline telephone, talking to Lee again, I learned later. "He wants to see us all tonight if you're up to it," she said as we worked our way through the crowded Denver terminal. "It's nothing urgent, so please don't think of it as a command performance. He just wants to say thanks and offer us a drink. And maybe convince you to let him pay for the trip."

"A drink would be good," I said.

A bumpy three-hour flight had put us into Stapleton Airport at half-past eleven, Mountain Time. We caught a cab and arrived in Park Hill just after midnight. I looked at familiar houses drifting past and at shady familiar streets, and somehow they all seemed different. I rolled down the window and tasted the dry air. Home: it felt like a long time since I'd been here.

I paid the cabbie over Erin's objections and we walked up the path to the judge's front door. I could see his silhouette in the doorway. He opened the door as the night-light came on, illuminating the front yard, and he met us at the top step of his porch.

"God, it's good to see you people." He hugged Erin and gripped my hand fiercely. I introduced him to Koko and we were shuffled into his library, taking soft chairs in the friendly environment of great books. He moved to the bar and asked our pleasure. Erin took something sweet, Koko asked for water, and I had bourbon on the rocks.

"Miranda's sorry she had to miss you," Lee said. "We had an old friend here late last night and she was dead tired. Our timing was lousy but it had been planned for weeks. No rest for me these days: I'm still mired in a case that's testing all my patience, and I think—I hope—she'll be happy to have me back again when it's over. Then we can all get together."

Erin took Burton's journal out of her bag and gave it to him.

"Well, you did it," he said. "I can't imagine how you persuaded him."

"It wasn't us," I said. "Dante beat him up pretty badly. Didn't Erin tell you?"

"Yes, of course. I still find it all hard to believe."

We socialized for a while. Lee and I talked books, while Erin showed Koko the library.

"You're a good detective, Cliff. I always knew that."

"I was pretty good," I said with my usual modesty. "I had good juice, a good feel for the work. Maybe I still have. Maybe I haven't left it all between the bookshelves."

"I'm not sure what that means exactly, but if it's a requirement for—"

"It means you get a hunch. You keep after it even when the facts you've gathered won't quite support your hunch. Even when you don't like what you're finding."

I almost let it go then. I wanted to let it go, but Lee asked one more question and the unthinkable wafted up between us.

"What do you do when that happens?" he said. "How do you just 'keep after it' when it doesn't want to fit?"

"It always fits, Lee. Usually when it doesn't seem to it's only because you're missing something. So you keep asking questions, you become a pain in everybody's ass. Most of all you think about it, day and night. You keep asking questions till the fat lady screams."

"That almost sounds like you're still at it."

"I am. I can't help myself. I want to let it go. I want to be done with it. It would be so easy to let it go, but I can't."

He looked away.

"Lee?"

"I'm sorry, I just lost my concentration. It's this case, it's got me punch-drunk."

"I wonder if I could ask you a few questions."

"You mean now? Tonight?"

"This shouldn't take long. Otherwise, you see, I won't be able to sleep, and if there's one guy in Denver who's as tired as you, that's probably me."

Suddenly the air in the room changed and was charged with conflict. Lee said, "Then by all means go ahead," but his back had stiffened and the skin around his mouth tightened. I had seen that look many times, when a man says something and means exactly the opposite.

"Archer says the book was his all along," I said. "He made a pretty convincing case for that to a Baltimore bookseller we met. But the way Erin was negotiating, it's almost like you all knew he had stolen it."

"Did Erin tell you that?"

"Erin told me as little as possible."

"What exactly did she say?"

I found myself losing patience. It was late, I was tired, I was in no mood to be stonewalled. "Are you and Archer somehow related?"

His eyes opened wide. "What on earth does that have to—"

"Just something that occurred to me in the last twenty-four hours. Archer had a grandmother named Betsy Ross. At some point something was mentioned about your own grandma Betts. That would be fairly unusual, two grandmas with such similar names."

"We're cousins. This is not exactly a big dark secret."

"But it's not something either of you go out of your way to promote."

"Why should we? What difference does it make?"

"Maybe none at all." But I pushed ahead. "Betsy Ross married old Archer, but it was her second marriage, is that right? Her first was your grandfather."

He didn't confirm or deny: he just looked at me.

"And when the Archer men died young, Grandma Betts got control of the estate. Which included the books."

Erin had caught the drift of the conversation and now she moved in close. "Is this going somewhere?"

I smiled at her. "That sounds very lawyerly, Counselor. Just calm down. Lee and I are only trying to put this thing to bed."

"I thought it was to bed."

"Not as long as there's an unanswered question."

"Which would be what?"

"Who killed Denise, and why."

Lee turned away and went to the bar. "Well, Cliff," he said, refilling his glass. "I don't know what more I can tell you. I don't even know what you're looking for."

"I'm looking for a killer, Lee."

"This is a strange place to be looking for him," Erin said.

I bypassed her and looked at Lee. "I woke up this morning thinking about Archer and his grandma Betts. Then I remembered that Grandma Betts was actually your grandmother. It took a while but I finally remembered—that first night we met him, Archer told us how you had inherited the books from your grandma Betts. What a dear old gal she was. But the way he said that was anything but dear. He was bitter, almost like he couldn't stand the thought of her."

"Hal's bitter about everything. Nothing new there."

"Then in South Carolina I found out about his grandmother, Betsy Ross, through a routine check on his background. That was new."

"So they were cousins," Erin said. "What are you trying to make of this?"

"Did you know they were cousins?"

She said nothing but I sensed an answer and the answer was no.

"That might put a new light on these books."

"I don't see how."

"I've been wondering, Lee: What kind of woman was Betsy Ross?"

"She was . . ." He gave a little laugh. "Oh God, she was a pow-erhouse. Nobody pushed Betts around, not the Archers or anybody. And she really loved her daughter."

"From the first marriage. And I imagine she loved her daughter's son as well."

"Yes, she did." He smiled. "They all said I was the apple of her eye."

"And your mother?"

"The world's sweetest woman. There was nobody who didn't love her. All she lacked was Betsy's strength."

"What did Grandma think of her grandson on the other side?"

"Hal was always the odd man out with all of them—most of all with her. It's not that Betts didn't love him in her own way, she just couldn't show it. In her eyes, he never made a right decision. He was shiftless, lazy. She had no idea how hard he really worked at what he wanted to do."

"Cliff, you must have a point here somewhere," Erin said. "Can we please get back to here and now?"

"Yeah, let's do that. Only five of us knew Denise had that book. You said you went up to the mountain the next day and never told anyone. But that's not true, is it?"

"She discussed it briefly with me," Lee said.

"So what difference does that make?" Erin said. "I told him in confidence—what are you trying to make of it?"

"Yes, what's your question?" Lee said.

"Did old Archer hire Treadwell to rook Josephine's mother out of those Burton books? What happened to all those letters and papers?"

"How would I know that?"

"How would you not know it?"

"That's a very ugly question," Erin said.

"Yes, it is. It breaks my heart to ask it."

A streak of impatience flashed across Lee's face. "This almost sounds like you're accusing me of something."

We were all quiet now: even Koko had come over to listen, and the only sound in the room for half a minute was the ticking of the clock.

"Good God," Lee said. "Do you think I killed that woman?"

I said nothing.

"Cliff!" he cried. "My God, Cliff! Listen to yourself!"

The moment thickened. I desperately wanted to hear something that would make the question go away. Our eyes met but he turned his head to one side.

"Lee," I said softly.

He forced himself to look at me.

"When Grandma Betts died, the books were left to you. You alone. The old Archer men were dead: she had outlived them all, she had complete control of the estate. Young Archer was an outcast and she left everything to you: money, books, a yellow brick road to a glorious legal career. But you were always a decent guy, Lee, and I mean that. So you shared those books with Archer, gave him the two best of the lot, all under the table so the family wouldn't hear. The problem always was, you both knew where they'd come from. It was the big dark family secret that all of you knew and no one ever discussed. You all had this common knowledge that old Archer the first had heard about the books and hired the Treadwells to buy them for next to nothing. You knew there was at least one Warren heir and when they came to you, that could have been your chance to make it right. But you let it pass and kept the books. That's where it all started."

I looked at Erin, expecting an objection.

"You and Archer had this conspiracy of silence. You had these wonderful books, but you couldn't do anything with them—not as long as anyone was alive who might have even a remotely rightful claim to them. The trouble began when Archer ran dry—his bank account and his creativity, all at once. So he sent one of those Burtons to auction, hoping he could sell it and still keep the secret."

Suddenly the room felt hot. "Now I've got to ask you something," I said. "I want to be very careful here but I can't. There's no way I can do this with any tact."

I felt Erin's eyes burning into my face but I stared at Lee. He looked away, ostensibly to refill his glass, but I knew that look, I had seen it on too many people too many times. It pushed me to the bottom line, to give voice at last to the unthinkable and cut through all the bullshit.

"You tell me, Lee. Did you kill Denise?"

I heard Erin cry out in protest but my eyes never left Lee's face, and he couldn't look at me, and suddenly there was no need to answer the question.

"Oh, Lee," I said, and my voice broke.

He tried to recover. "I didn't kill anyone, Cliff. How could you even think that?"

"It's a question I've got to ask. I'd sooner cut out my tongue."

Lee made a great effort and forced himself to look in my eyes. "Then tell me why in God's name you'd even think such a thing."

"Somewhere along the way I began to believe Archer's story. It's as simple as that. His story and yours can't exist side by side. They just can't work."

"What is his story, exactly? Help me understand it."

"Nothing very complicated. He says Burton's journal is his. He told that to a bookseller he's known almost forty years. A guy who may be his only friend."

"You show me the thief who doesn't believe he owns what he steals. There's got to be more than that."

"There is now. Now there's you. There's the look on your face and the way you can't look me in the eye and deny it."

He did look at me at last. It took a vast effort, but his eyes met mine and he said, "I don't need to justify myself to you. Goddamn it, do you know who you're talking to?"

He looked at Erin and said, "For God's sake, you don't believe this?"

"Of course not." But her voice lacked the certainty that should have been there. She was rattled: for the first time that calm, professional demeanor had deserted her.

"Just tell him what he wants to know," she said. "Tell him and let's all go to bed and be done with this." She looked at me coldly and her look said, *And I'll be done with you.*

Instead Lee said, "I'd like to ask you something, Cliff, then I'd like you to please get out of my house. Do you really think I would kill someone over a book? Do you think I'm that stupid, that desperate to own any book, when I could just buy the damned thing anyway? Or is it the money that drove me crazy? You tell me, then we'll both know."

"I'll give you my guess. Long ago you and Archer should have been joint heirs to this marvelous library of Burton material. You got it all, but you shared it with Hal on the q.t. You made that unholy alliance with Archer that you would give him a couple of the books, including Richard's journal, which you knew even then was worth more money than most of the others combined. You and Archer made a pact that they could never be sold until the last real heir was dead, because you both knew where they had come from, and the fraud your family had worked to get them away from the Warren family for nothing.

"The easy thing to do, the right thing, would have been to seek out Mrs. Gallant and pay her. Just a good wholesale price might have made all the difference in her life. But you didn't do that; you were afraid to admit you had those books because that would put them all at risk. For once in your life you went against your own sense of decency and what's right. You and Archer decided not to tell anyone. The books were legally yours, you didn't have to pay the old woman or anyone else. But if you had, if you'd just been as fair to the old woman as you were with Archer, maybe none of this would've happened. Instead you decided to keep quiet, take no chances. Just keep quiet and she'd go away, fade into the woodwork, die or whatever.

"You should've paid that old woman, Lee. I know that's what

your instinct would have been, pay her and get this blot out of your life. But then time passed and that window of opportunity closed. You became a judge, then a prominent judge. The real point of no return was your interview with Reagan. By then you'd have been glad to get rid of all the books, just give them away. They were like a millstone around your neck when the president began considering you for the Supreme Court. That's your motive, Lee. You'd do anything for a chance at that appointment, and even a small scandal, even something like this where you were legally right, would be enough to kill that possibility dead in the water."

I finished off my drink.

"Lee?" It was Erin, and her tone begged him to deny it. "Tell him he's crazy."

"He can't," I said.

"I didn't kill her," Lee said. "I didn't kill her."

Then he said, "She just . . . died."

"Oh my God." Erin sank to the sofa. "Oh my God."

"Erin, Cliff, listen to me," Lee said. "I didn't kill anybody. I went over to see her. I shouldn't have, I know that. But I was so certain I could get the book away from her. I knew they were poor, you told me that, and people will sell out anyone if you pay them enough. I thought if I paid her enough she could tell you she lost it. My God, I don't know what I was thinking. I was only there a few minutes. But something went wrong . . . she felt threatened by something I said . . . Jesus, it was nothing, just a veiled threat, what might happen if she told anybody I had been there. I had no intention to hurt her or her husband, but she got frightened. I tried to hush her— Please, I said, PLEASE! She started to scream and then everything unraveled. I picked up the pillow—not to smother her, for Christ's sake, just to shut her up till I could talk sense to her. Christ knows I had no reason to kill her. All I wanted then was to get her quiet and get out of there. You've got to believe that!"

"I do believe it, Lee," I said. "I just wish it had turned out that way."

"I tried to reason with her. I told her just to forget I was there— she could keep the book, keep the book and the money, she could keep all the money, I didn't care about it then. I tried to shove money at her . . ."

"And left some of it tangled in her bedclothes. The cops have those bills, Lee."

"I wanted to do what was right. That's all I ever wanted. I argued with Hal from the start. We needed to find that old woman and pay her something, a substantial amount that would erase that blot from our lives. Ask Hal, he'll tell you what I tried to do."

I put down my empty glass and went to the door. Somewhere behind me I heard Lee saying, "This was no crime, Cliff. This was an accident. It was an accident, I swear. There was no evil intent. You know I couldn't do that. I could never kill anyone."

I touched the door.

"Cliff, please . . . I'll make her husband a wealthy man."

I turned and said, "You took away all he ever wanted."

"I'll make it right, I swear."

"You can't."

"I can! No one needs to know about this."

"Yeah, they do. I'm sorry, Lee. You'll never know how sorry I am."

"Erin. You talk to him. Talk to him! This doesn't have to go anywhere."

I looked at Erin, who sat numbly with streams of tears on her cheeks.

"Good-bye, Lee," I said.

I walked out. A moment later I heard Koko running along the sidewalk behind me.

"Under the circumstances, I'd rather stay with you tonight. If you've got room for me."

I put an arm over her shoulder. "I'll always have room for you, Koke."

Sometime before dawn that same morning, Lee Huxley locked himself in the garage and sat with his motor running until he died. That's how it ended.

For two days he was front-page news and a hot topic for talk radio. All the yakkers sounded off, speculation ran wild: Denver was treated to the usual tasteless nonsense from vacuous morons with too much time on their hands. Give an idiot a microphone and he's just a louder version of the same old idiot.

There were a few high spots. To his colleagues Lee was the best and the brightest, a man who weighed every judgment and always strove mightily to do the right thing. Judge Arlene Weston was interviewed and said good things. He was such a fine man, so cultured and well liked. No one could have imagined that he'd do this to himself. It only proved that even a great poet like John Donne could be wrong. Every man is indeed an island, and deep personal torments can coexist with all the ingredients of a happy life.

A rumor leaked out that the president had been interested in Lee as a possible Supreme Court Justice, and the yakkers ran with disappointment as a possible motive. The White House had no comment. Press Secretary Marlin Fitzwater confirmed that Lee had had two meetings with Mr. Reagan, but nothing was revealed of what might have been said or how serious Reagan's interest might have been.

His service was mobbed. The entire legal community turned out: the church overflowed, people stood in the street and then swarmed across the graveyard, and the procession from one to the other tied up traffic for twenty blocks.

I watched it on television with Koko. Lee was buried in Crown Hill Cemetery and instantly became a fading memory.

How quickly even a prominent man is forgotten.

On Saturday after the funeral a car stopped in front of my store. I cringed when Miranda leaped out. Twenty people were in the store but she saw only me. She flung open the door, screaming, "You BAS-TARD! You fucking bastard, I hate you, I wish I'd never set eyes on you, I hope you die!" She charged across the room and beat at me with her fists until she collapsed.

Apparently Lee had left her a note. I can only imagine what was in it.

A week later I got a vicious letter. If she could kill me she would happily do it. At the end she said, "You will never see that book again. I burned it."

Who knows if she actually did that? Miranda always had a deep interest in money, she must have had at least some idea of the book's value, but I have a dark, hollow feeling about it. I think of those books and all that handwritten correspondence, and sometimes I wonder where Lee kept those signed copies and if Miranda might be angry enough to destroy them all. The irony that she may have burned Richard's journal a hundred years after Isabel burned his papers gives me a headache.

The real story still hasn't come out. Maybe in his despair that's what Lee was hoping: that at least I would leave him his good name. From what I could tell, Whiteside wasn't going anywhere with Denise's death: it had slipped off his front burner as new murders occurred. I knew Lee must have left some evidence in that room—after all, what did he know about covering up a crime, especially in the heat of the moment?—but a cop doesn't just ask for random hair samples or fingerprints from a prominent jurist who has no obvious connection to the deceased. If Whiteside had a name, a reason to be suspicious, he could close this case in a few hours. If Denise had been one of Denver's so-called important people, he might be forced to consider the unthinkable, but that's not likely to happen now. It remains one of those cases without a probable perp, and Ralston is still the only suspect.

Who knows where a chain of events begins? Some would say that the tragedy of Lee Huxley was set in motion long before he was born, when Richard Burton came to America and met Charlie Warren. Me, I can't quite make that reach, I'm not that kind of cosmic thinker. To me it began when Lee and Archer made their unholy pact. Everything unfolded from that.

Wherever it began, it ended in Lee's garage.

There is a postscript. Reagan nominated Anthony M. Kennedy from the Ninth Circuit Court of Appeals, and Kennedy joined the Court in February 1988.

In the weeks after Lee's death most of the related events worked themselves out. I got a call from Vinnie Marranzino. He didn't even say hello, just, "Hey, Cliff, everything's fine. Let me know if you have any more trouble in that neck of the woods."

I tried to thank him but he brushed it off. "You don't thank an old pal, Cliff. We should get together sometime. Break some bread for old times' sake."

But he knows we won't.

Workmen arrived to begin clearing the site of Koko's house in Ellicott City. Mysteriously the house began to rise from the ashes, and her friend Janet gave her reports on its progress almost every day. The money from the insurance payout may be hers to keep, give back, or throw in the Potomac River: I don't know what the rules say about that. No bills have yet been submitted to anyone, and I'm betting they won't be. "Maybe I'll give some of it to a library, if they let me keep it," Koko said. "They can have a Charles Warren Room, even if they don't have his books or know who he was."

She stayed with me for a month.

I didn't know where Erin went.

I did drive out to Vegas and found Ralston dealing cards in a

*casino. I had covered Denise's funeral and there wasn't much money
to give him, but I fudged it a little on his side of the ledger. "There's
ten grand in the bank, any time you want it, but you've gotta come
back to Denver to get it. I won't send it, and I'll need your word that
you won't piss it away in a gambling house, or on booze."*

"You don't want much, do you?"

"Only what Denise would want, Mike."

*I told him what had happened, the whole sad story of Judge Lee
Huxley. He hasn't come yet, but he's young and he still has time to
find himself.*

*Life does go on. I went back to work, schlepping books on East
Colfax Avenue.*

*I thought of Lee almost constantly on those warm days and
nights. Sometimes I thought of the deathbed promise I had given
Josephine Gallant and I knew it would always leave me with a hollow, unfulfilled feeling.*

*On a night in early autumn I sat in my store watching the lights
go on along the street. If there's a winner in this whole sorry business, I thought, it's probably me. I had two of Burton's greatest
works in flawless inscribed first editions, books that few other bookmen can imagine owning or handling, but I didn't seem to care
much. Too much of the joy had gone out of having them; maybe I'd
sell them after all. I would give them away in a heartbeat if none of
this had happened, and I knew Lee would have done that at any of
half a dozen places along the way. I still believed in him: at heart he
was a decent man, done in not so much by his own hand as by the
sins of his grandfather. Once in his life he went against his own good
instincts and he paid a terrible price.*

*I looked out at the street. Tonight was going to be a long one, full
of ghosts.*

*I knew I had to shape up. I had not run in weeks and I had begun
drinking much too much. I was avoiding people, I wasn't eating well,
and my outlook was poor. I saw myself in a distant future, a crazy old
man like the bookscout in Charlotte, burrowed into my own nutty*

world, snapping at people, gouging for every dime. Was this a fantasy or prophesy? I didn't know but it cast a deeper pall on the night.

Outside, the night people came out and walked along the street. Time to call it a day. Then the phone rang, and something about the day made me answer it.

"Hi."

I knew her voice at once and I told her how sorry I was.

"I know you are," she said gently. "I'm sorry too."

"So what are you doing these days?"

"Trying to finish my book. It's not very good but I guess I'll finish it anyway."

"You're probably not the best judge of that."

"I'm the only judge."

There was a long pause at the word judge.

"Even if that's true," I finally said, "you're not exactly finishing it under ideal circumstances."

"I'm tired of fooling myself. I'm not even going to send it out."

"Give it time, Erin. Just give it time."

"Sure."

Then she said, "A wise man once told me, some of us are not meant to be writers."

"Even a wise man can't know everything."

"Same old Janeway. You've got an answer for everything."

"Here's another one. Maybe you were meant to be a bookseller."

"I've thought of that."

"You can always write when the muse comes back."

"If it does."

This felt depressingly like the end of the conversation. But after some dead phone time, she said, "Do you happen to know what day this is?"

Of course I knew, that's why I'd answered the phone. I'd been thinking about it all day long. It was the fortieth day.

I listened to the phone noise for a moment. Then she said, "Stay there, I'm coming over."

Readers wishing to learn more about Richard Burton are referred to three excellent biographies. Fawn Brodie's *The Devil Drives* (Norton, 1967) was the first major "life" to separate Burton from his blackguard reputation, and remains a highly readable account. *Captain Sir Richard Francis Burton,* by Edward Rice (Scribner, 1990), admirably captures the details and mysteries of Burton's life. *A Rage to Live* (London: Little, Brown, 1998) by Mary S. Lovell is a massive, well-researched dual biography of Richard and Isabel.

A biographical novel by William Harrison, *Burton and Speke,* was filmed as *Mountains of the Moon,* 1990, and is recommended viewing.

Norman Penzer's *Annotated Bibliography of Sir Richard Francis Burton* (London: 1923) is still the best source of information on Burton's vast literary output.

ABOUT THE AUTHOR

John Dunning is the Nero Wolfe Award–winning author of two pre-vious Cliff Janeway novels, *Booked to Die* and *The Bookman's Wake*, a *New York Times* Notable Book of 1995. An expert on rare and collectible books, he owned the Old Algonquin bookstore in Denver for many years. His most recent novel was *Two O'Clock, Eastern Wartime,* which focused on old-time radio. John Dunning lives in Denver, Colorado, with his wife, Helen. His website is www.oldalgonquin.com.